PRAISE FOR
ALI HAZELW

"A literary breakthrough. . . . *The Love Hypothesis* is a self-assured debut, and we hypothesize it's just the first bit of greatness we'll see from an author who somehow has the audacity to be both an academic powerhouse and divinely talented novelist."

—*Entertainment Weekly*

"Contemporary romance's unicorn: the elusive marriage of deeply brainy and delightfully escapist. . . . *The Love Hypothesis* has wild commercial appeal, but the quieter secret is that there is a specific audience, made up of all of the Olives in the world, who have deeply, ardently waited for this exact book."

—Christina Lauren, *New York Times* bestselling author

"With her sophomore novel, Ali Hazelwood proves that she is the perfect writer to show that science is sexy as hell, and that love can 'STEM' from the most unlikely places. She's my newest must-buy author."

—Jodi Picoult, #1 *New York Times* bestselling author of
Wish You Were Here

"Funny, sexy, and smart, Ali Hazelwood did a terrific job with *The Love Hypothesis.*"

—Mariana Zapata, *New York Times* bestselling author

"Gloriously nerdy and sexy, with on-point commentary about women in STEM."

—Helen Hoang, *New York Times* bestselling author, on
Love on the Brain

"STEMinists, assemble. Your world is about to be rocked."

—Elena Armas, *New York Times* bestselling author, on
Love on the Brain

"This tackles one of my favorite tropes—Grumpy meets Sunshine—in a fun and utterly endearing way. . . . I loved the nods towards fandom and romance novels, and I couldn't put it down. Highly recommended!"

—Jessica Clare, *New York Times* bestselling author, on
The Love Hypothesis

"Pure slow-burning gold with lots of chemistry."   —PopSugar

"A beautifully written romantic comedy with a heroine you will instantly fall in love with, *The Love Hypothesis* is destined to earn a place on your keeper shelf."

—Elizabeth Everett, author of *A Lady's Formula for Love*

"Smart, witty dialog and a diverse cast of likable secondary characters. . . . A realistic, amusing novel that readers won't be able to put down."   —*Library Journal* (starred review)

"Hilarious and heartwarming, *The Love Hypothesis* is romantic comedy at its best. . . . A perfect amalgamation of sex and science, sure to appeal to readers of Christina Lauren or Abby Jimenez."

—Shelf Awareness

"With whip-smart and endearing characters, snappy prose, and a quirky take on a favorite trope, Hazelwood convincingly navigates the fraught shoals of academia."   —*Publishers Weekly*

Also by Ali Hazelwood

ADULT NOVELS

The Love Hypothesis

Love on the Brain

Love, Theoretically

ADULT ANTHOLOGY

Loathe to Love You

Check & Mate

ALI HAZELWOOD

putnam

G. P. PUTNAM'S SONS

G. P. PUTNAM'S SONS
An imprint of Penguin Random House LLC, New York

First published in the United States of America by G. P. Putnam's Sons,
an imprint of Penguin Random House LLC, 2023

G. P. Putnam's Sons is a registered trademark of Penguin Random House LLC.
The Penguin colophon is a registered trademark of Penguin Books Limited.

Visit us online at PenguinRandomHouse.com.

Library of Congress Cataloging-in-Publication Data

Names: Hazelwood, Ali, author.
Title: Check & mate / Ali Hazelwood.
Other titles: Check and mate
Description: New York: G.P. Putnam's Sons, 2023. |
Audience: Ages 14 years and up. | Summary: When eighteen-year-old
Mallory begrudgingly agrees to return to chess in one last charity
tournament, her surprise upset against Nolan Sawyer, the reigning
world champ and bad boy of the chess world, sets her on a whirlwind
adventure as she rediscovers her passion for the game.
Identifiers: LCCN 2023017578 (print) | LCCN 2023017579 (ebook) |
ISBN 9780593698440 (library binding) | ISBN 9780593619919 (trade paperback) |
ISBN 9780593619926 (epub)
Subjects: CYAC: Chess—Fiction. | Interpersonal relations—Fiction. |
Family problems—Fiction. | LCGFT: Novels.
Classification: LCC PZ7.1.H39724 Ch 2023 (print) | LCC PZ7.1.H39724 (ebook) |
DDC [Fic]—dc23
LC record available at https://lccn.loc.gov/2023017578
LC ebook record available at https://lccn.loc.gov/2023017579

Printed in the United States of America
1st Printing

LSCH

Book design by Kristin del Rosario
Interior art: Chess art © JuliPaper/Shutterstock.com
Text set in Chaparral Pro Regular

To Sarah A. and Helen,
who'll always be my faves.

Check & Mate

Prologue

"I am reliably informed that you're a Gen Z sex symbol."

I nearly drop my phone.

Okay: I do drop my phone, but I save it before it splashes into a beaker full of ammonia. Then I glance around the chemistry classroom, wondering if anyone else heard.

The other students are either texting or puttering around with their equipment. Mrs. Agarwal is at her desk, pretending to grade papers but probably reading Bill Nye erotic fanfiction. A hopefully-not-lethal smell of ethanoic acid wafts up from my bench, but my AirPods are still in my ears.

No one is paying attention to me or the video on my phone, so I press Play to resume it.

"It was on Time *magazine two weeks ago. On the cover. A picture of your face, and then 'A Gen Z sex symbol.' How does that feel?"*

I am expecting to see Zendaya. Harry Styles. Billie Eilish. The entirety of BTS, crammed on the couch of whatever late-night show the YouTube autoplay algorithm decided to feed me after the pH experiment tutorial ended. But it's just some dude. A boy, even? He looks out of place in the red velvet chair, with his dark shirt, dark slacks, dark hair, dark expression. Intensely unreadable as he says in a deep, serious voice, *"It feels wrong."*

"It does?" the host—Jim or James or Jimmy—asks.

"The Gen Z part is correct," the guest says. *"Not so much the sex symbol."*

The audience eats it up, clapping and hooting, and that's when I decide to read the caption. *Nolan Sawyer,* it says. There's a description explaining who he is, but I don't need it. I might not recognize the face, but I can't remember a moment in my life when I didn't know the name.

Meet the Kingkiller: The No. 1 chess player in the world.

"Let me tell you something, Nolan: smart is the new sexy."

"Still not sure I qualify." His tone is so dry, it has me wondering how his publicist talked him into this interview. But the audience laughs, and the host does, too. He leans forward, obviously charmed by this young man who's built like an athlete, thinks like a theoretical physicist, and has the net worth of a Silicon Valley entrepreneur. An unusual, handsome prodigy who won't admit to being special.

I wonder if Jim-Jimmy-James has heard what *I've* heard. The gossip. The whispered stories. The dark rumors about the golden boy of chess.

"Let's just agree that chess is the new sexy. And you're the one who made it so—there has been a chess renaissance since you started playing. Someone was running commentaries of your games, and they went viral on TikTok—ChessTok, my writers tell me it's called—and now more people than ever are learning how to play. But first things first: you are a Grandmaster, which is the highest title a chess player can achieve, and just won your second World Championship, against"—the host has to look down at his card, because

normal Grandmasters are not as famous as Sawyer—*"Andreas Antonov. Congratulations."*

Sawyer nods, once.

"And you just turned eighteen. When, again?"

"Three days ago."

Three days ago, *I* turned sixteen.

Ten years and three days ago, I received my first chess set—plastic pieces, pink and purple—and cried with joy. I'd use it all day long, carry it everywhere with me, then snuggle it in my sleep.

Now I can't even remember the feel of a pawn in my hand.

"You started playing very young. Did your parents teach you?"

"My grandfather," Sawyer says. The host looks taken aback, like he didn't think Sawyer would go *there*, but recovers quickly.

"When did you realize that you were good enough to be a pro?"

"Am I good enough?"

More audience laughter. I roll my eyes. *"Did you know you wanted to be a pro chess player from the start?"*

"Yes. I knew all along that there was nothing that I liked as much as winning a chess match."

The host's eyebrow lifts. *"Nothing?"*

Sawyer doesn't hesitate. *"Nothing."*

"And—"

"Mallory?" A hand settles on my shoulder. I jump and tear out one pod. "Did you need any help?"

"Nope!" I smile at Mrs. Agarwal, sliding the phone into my back pocket. "Just finished the instruction video."

"Oh, perfect. Make sure you put on gloves before you add the acidic solution."

"I will."

The rest of the class is almost done with the experiment. I furrow my brow, hurry to catch up, and a few minutes later, when I can't find my funnel and spill my baking soda, I stop thinking about Sawyer, or about the way his voice sounded when he said that he never wanted anything as much as chess. And I don't think of him again for a little over two years. That is, until the day we play for the first time.

And I wipe the floor with him.

PART ONE

Openings

Chapter One

Two years later

Easton is smart, because she lures me out with the promise of free boba. But she's also dumb, because she doesn't wait till I'm sipping my chocolate cream cheese foam bubble tea before saying, "I need a favor."

"Nope." I grin at her. Pluck two straws from the bin. Offer her one, which she ignores.

"Mal. You haven't even heard what—"

"No."

"It's about chess."

"Well, in that case . . ." I smile my thanks to the girl holding out my order. We went out twice, maybe three times last summer, and I have vague, pleasant memories of her. Raspberry ChapStick lips; Bon Iver purring in her Hyundai Elantra; a soft hand, cool under my tank top. Sadly, none of said memories include her name. But she wrote *Melanie* across my boba, so that's okay.

We share a brief, secret smile, and I turn to Easton. "In that case, double no."

"I'm short a player. For a team tournament."

"I don't play anymore." I check my phone. It's 12:09—twenty-one more minutes before I need to be back at the garage. Bob, my boss, is not exactly a kind, forgiving human being. Sometimes I doubt he's even human. "Let's drink this outside, before I spend the afternoon under a Chevy Silverado."

"Come on, Mal." She glowers at me. "It's chess. You still play."

When my sister Darcy's sixth-grade teacher announced that she was going to send the class guinea pig to a "farm upstate," Darcy, unable to ascertain whether the farm really existed, decided to kidnap him. The piggie, not the teacher. I've been co-habitating with Goliath the Abducted for the past year—a year spent denying him scraps of our dinners ever since the vet we cannot afford begged us on his knees to put him on a diet. Unfortunately, Goliath has the uncanny ability to stare me into submission every single time.

Just like Easton does. Their expressions exude the same pure, unyielding stubbornness.

"Nuh-uh." I suck on my tea. Divine. "I've forgotten the rules. What does the little horsie do, again?"

"Very funny."

"No, really, which one is chess? The queen conquers Catan without passing Go—"

"I'm not asking you to do what you used to do."

"What *did* I use to do?"

"You know when you were thirteen and you'd beaten all the other kids at the Paterson Chess Club, then the teenagers, then the adults? And they brought in people from New York for you to humiliate? I don't need *that*."

I was actually twelve when that happened. I remember it

well, because Dad stood next to me, hand warm on my bony shoulder, proclaiming proudly, *I haven't won a game against Mallory since she turned eleven a year ago. Extraordinary, isn't she?* But I don't point it out, and instead plop down in a patch of grass, next to a flower bed full of zinnias barely hanging on to life. August in New Jersey is no one's favorite place.

"Remember halfway through my exhibition matches? When I was about to pass out and you told everyone to step back—"

"—and I handed you my juice." She sits next to me. I glance at her perfect eyeliner wing, then at my oil-stained coveralls, and it's nice, how some things never change. Perfectionist Easton Peña, always with a plan, and her messy sidekick Mallory Greenleaf. We've been in the same class since first grade but didn't really interact until she joined the Paterson Chess Club at ten. She was, in a way, already fully formed. Already the amazing, stubborn person she is today.

You really enjoy playing this crap? she asked me when we got paired for a match.

You don't? I asked back, appalled.

Of course not. I just need a wide range of extracurriculars. College scholarships don't win themselves. I checkmated her in four and have adored her ever since.

Funny, that Easton never cared for chess like I did but stuck with it much longer. What an odd love triangle the three of us make.

"You owe me for the juice box, then—come to the tournament," she orders. "I need a team of four. Everyone's either on vacation or can't tell the difference between chess and checkers. You don't even have to win—and it's for charity."

"What charity?"

"Does it matter?"

"Of course. Is it for a right-wing think tank? The next Woody Allen movie? A made-up disease, like hysteria or gluten sensitivity?"

"Gluten sensitivity is *not* made-up."

"Really?"

"Yes. And the tournament is for—" She taps furiously on her phone. "I can't find it, but can we cut this short? We both know you're going to say yes."

I scowl. "We know no such thing."

"Maybe *you* don't."

"I have a spine, Easton."

"Sure." She chews on her tapioca balls, aggressive, daring, suddenly more grizzly bear than guinea pig.

She remembers ninth grade, when she talked me into being her VP as she ran for class president. (We lost. Overwhelmingly.) And tenth grade, when Missy Collins was spreading gossip and she recruited me to hack her Twitter. Eleventh grade, too, when I starred as Mrs. Bennett in the *Pride and Prejudice* musical she wrote and directed—despite my better judgment and my half-an-octave vocal range. I probably would have agreed to something moronic during senior year, too, if things at home hadn't been . . . well, from a financial standpoint, less than good. And I hadn't spent every spare second working at the garage.

"We all know you're unable to say no," Easton points out. "So just say yes."

I check my phone—twelve more minutes in my break. Today's hot as soup, I'm done scarfing down boba, and I eye her cup with interest. Honeydew melon: my second-favorite flavor. "I'm busy."

"Busy how?"

"Date."

"Who? Carnivorous plants guy? Or the Paris Hilton look-alike?"

"Neither. But I'll find someone."

"Come on. It's a way to spend time together before college."

I sit up, knocking my elbow against hers. "When are you leaving?"

"In less than two weeks."

"*What? We just* graduated, like—"

"Like three months ago? I have to be in Colorado by mid-August for orientation."

"Oh." It's like waking up from an early afternoon nap and finding out that it's already dark. "Oh," I repeat, a little shocked. I *knew* this was coming, but somewhere between my sister's bout of mono, my mom's week at the hospital, my *other* sister's bout of mono, and all the extra shifts I picked up, I must have lost track of time. This is terrifying: I've never *not* lived in the same city as Easton. I've never *not* seen her once a week to play *Dragon Age*, or talk about *Dragon Age*, or watch *Dragon Age* playthroughs.

Maybe we need new hobbies.

I try for a smile. "I guess time flies when you're having fun."

"*Are* you, Mal? Having fun?" Her eyes narrow on me, and I laugh.

"Don't *laugh*. You're always working. When you aren't, you're chauffeuring your sisters around or taking your mom to doctor's appointments, and—" She runs a hand through her dark curls and leaves them mussed—a good indicator of her exasperation. Seven out of ten, I'd estimate. "You were number one in our class. You're a math whiz and can memorize *anything*. You had *three* scholarship offers—one to come to Boulder, with me. But you've decided not to go, and now you seem *stuck* here, with no end in sight and . . . you know what? It's your choice, and I respect you for it, but at least you could let yourself do *one* fun thing. One thing that you enjoy."

I stare at her flushed cheeks for one, two, three seconds, and almost open my mouth to tell her that scholarships pay for you to go to college, but not for the house's mortgage, or your sister's roller derby camp, or your other sister's kidnapped pet's vitamin-C-reinforced pellets, or whatever it takes to melt the guilt that sticks to the bottom of your stomach. Almost. At the last minute I just look away, and "away" happens to be toward my phone.

It's 12:24. Shit. "I gotta go."

"What? Mal, are you mad? I didn't mean to—"

"Nope." I flash her a grin. "But my break is over."

"You *just* got here."

"Yeah. Bob's not a fan of humane schedules and work-life balance. Any chance you're *not* planning on finishing that bubble tea?"

She rolls her eyes hard enough to pull a muscle, but holds out her cup to me. I fist-pump as I walk away.

"Let me know about the tournament," Easton yells after me.

"I already have."

A groan. And then a serious, pointed "Mallory," which has me turning around despite the threat of Bob's smelly breath yelling that I'm late. "Listen, I don't want to force you to do anything. But chess used to be your entire life. And now you don't even want to play it for a good cause."

"Like gluten sensitivity?"

She rolls her eyes again, and I jog back to work laughing. I barely make it on time. I'm gathering my tools before disappearing under the Silverado when my phone buzzes. It's a screenshot of a flier. It says: *Clubs Olympic team tournament. NYC area. In affiliation with Doctors Without Borders.*

I smile.

> **MALLORY:** okay that is a good charity

> **BRET EASTON ELLIS:** Told you so. Also:

She sends me a link to the WebMD page on gluten sensitivity, which apparently does exist.

> **MALLORY:** okay, so it IS a real thing

> **BRET EASTON ELLIS:** Told you so.

> **MALLORY:** you know that's your catchphrase
> right

> **BRET EASTON ELLIS:** That would be "I was
> right." So you'll do the tournament?

I snort and almost type *no*. I almost remind her *why*, exactly, I never play chess anymore.

But then I picture her gone to college for months—and me here, alone, trying to have a conversation about the latest *Dragon Age* playthrough with some date who just wants to make out. I think about her coming home for Thanksgiving: maybe she will have an undercut, become a vegan, get into cow print. Maybe she'll be a new person. We'll meet up at our regular places, watch our regular show, gossip about our regular people, but it won't be the same, because she'll have met new friends, seen new things, made new memories.

Fear stabs into my chest. Fear that she'll change, and bloom, and won't ever be the same. But I will be. Here in Paterson, stagnating. We won't say it, but we'll know it.

So I type:

> **MALLORY:** k. last hurrah

> **BRET EASTON ELLIS:** See? I was right.

> **MALLORY:** 🖕

> **MALLORY:** you'll pay me back by driving my sisters to camp next week so i can pick up more shifts

> **BRET EASTON ELLIS:** Mal, no.

> **BRET EASTON ELLIS:** Mal, please.
> Anything else.

> **BRET EASTON ELLIS:** Mal, they're TERRIFYING.

> **MALLORY:** 😈

"Hey, Greenleaf! I don't pay you to browse Instagram or buy avocado sandwiches. Get to work."

I roll my eyes. Internally. "Wrong generation, Bob."

"Whatever. Get. To. Work."

I slide my phone into my coveralls, sigh, and do just that.

"MAL, SABRINA JUST PINCHED MY ARM AND CALLED ME A DICK-breath!"

"Mal, Darcy just yawned in my face with her gross, smelly *dickbreath*!"

I sigh, continuing to prepare my sisters' oatmeals. Cinnamon, skim milk, no sugar or "I'll stab you, Mal. Ever heard of something called *health*?" (Sabrina); peanut butter, store-brand Nutella, banana, and "Could you add a bit more Nutella, please? I'm trying to grow a foot before eighth grade!" (Darcy).

"Mallory, Darcy just *farted* on me!"

"No—*Sabrina* is a douchewad who put herself in ass range!"

I absentmindedly lick discount Nutella off the spoon, fantasizing about pouring nail polish remover in the oatmeal. Just a dollop. Maybe two.

There would be some cons, such as the untimely demise of the two people I love most in the world. But the pros? Unbeatable. No more middle-of-the-night, likely-rabid bites on the toes from Goliath. No more vicious verbal abuse for washing Sabrina's pink bra, for misplacing Sabrina's pink bra, for allegedly stealing Sabrina's pink bra, for not keeping abreast of the whereabouts of Sabrina's pink bra. No more Timothée Chalamet posters staring creepily at me from the walls.

Just me, sharpening my shiv in the peaceful silence of a New Jersey prison cell.

"Mallory, Darcy is being a total poopstain—"

I drop the spoon and stalk to the bathroom. It takes about three steps—the Greenleaf estate is small and not quite solvent.

"If you two don't shut up," I say with my most hard-ass 8:00 a.m. voice, "I'm going to take you to the farmers market and trade you for cotton candy grapes."

Something weird happened last year: almost overnight, my two sweet little dumplings, who used to be the best of friends, became rival swamp hags. Sabrina turned fourteen, and began acting as though she was too cool to be genetically related to us; Darcy turned twelve, and . . . well. Darcy stayed the same. Always reading, always precocious, always too observant for her own good. Which, I believe, is the reason Sabrina used her allowance to buy a new lock and kick her out of the room they shared. (I took Darcy in—hence Timothée Chalamet's Mona-Lisa-effect eyes and the forthcoming rabies.)

"Oh my God." Darcy rolls her eyes. "Relax, Mallory."

"Yes, Mallory. Unclench your butthole."

Oh, yeah: the only time these ingrates manage to get along? When they're ganging up against me. Mom says it's puberty. I lean toward demonic possession, but who knows? What I do know for sure is that imploring, tearing up, or even trying to reason with them are not effective techniques. Any display of weakness is seized, exploited, and always ends with me being blackmailed into buying them ridiculous things, like Ed Sheeran body pillows or graduation hats for guinea pigs. My motto is *rule through fear*. Never negotiate with those hormonal, anarchic, bloodthirsty sharks.

God, I love them so much I could cry.

"Mom's asleep," I hiss. "I swear, if you're not quiet I'm going to write *dickbreath* and *douchewad* on your foreheads in permanent marker and send you out into the world like that."

"Might want to rethink that," Darcy points out, wagging her toothbrush at me, "or we'll sic Child Protective Services on you."

Sabrina nods. "Possibly even the police."

"Can she afford the legal fees?"

"No way. Good luck with your overworked, underpaid, court-appointed defense attorney, Mal."

I lean against the doorframe. "*Now* you two agree on something."

"We always agreed that Darcy's a dickbreath."

"I am *not—you* are a ho-bag."

"If you wake Mom up," I threaten, "I'm going to flush you both down the toilet—"

"I'm awake! No need to clog the plumbing, sweetheart." I turn around. Mom ambles down the hallway, shaky on her feet, and the bottom of my stomach twists. Mornings have been tough for the past month. For the entire summer, really. I glance back at Darcy and Sabrina, who at least have the decency to look contrite. "Now that I'm up with the chickens, can I have hugs from my favorite Russian dolls?"

Mom likes to joke that my sisters and I, with our white-blond hair, dark blue eyes, and rosy oval faces, are slightly smaller versions of each other. Maybe Darcy got all the freckles, and Sabrina has fully embraced the VSCO aesthetic, and I . . . If there weren't so many five-dollar boho chic outfits at Goodwill, I wouldn't look like an Alexis Rose cosplayer. But there's no doubt that the three Greenleaf girls were made with a cookie cutter—and not Mom's, given her once-dark, now-graying hair and tanned skin. If she minds that we take so much after Dad, she's never mentioned it.

"Why are you guys up?" she asks against Darcy's forehead before moving on to Sabrina. "Do you have practice?"

Sabrina stiffens. "I don't start until next week. Actually, I'm *never* going to start if someone doesn't sign me up for the Junior Roller Derby Association, which is due *next Friday*—"

"I'll pay the dues by Friday," I reassure her.

She gives me a skeptical, distrustful look. Like I've broken her heart one too many times with my paltry auto-mechanic's salary. "Why can't you pay right now?"

"Because I enjoy toying with you, like a spider with her prey." And because I'll need to pick up extra shifts at the garage to afford them.

Her eyes narrow. "You don't have the money, do you?"

My heart skips a beat. "Of course I do."

"Because I'm *basically* an adult. And McKenzie has been working at that froyo place, so I could ask her to—"

"You're *not* an adult." The idea of Sabrina worrying about money is physically painful. "In fact, rumor has it that you're a douchewad."

"Since we're requesting and obtaining things," Darcy interjects, mouth full of toothpaste, "Goliath is still lonely and depressed and in need of a girlfriend."

"Mmm." I briefly contemplate the number of turds two Goliaths could produce. Yikes. "Anyway, Easton kindly offered to drive you guys to camp next week. And I'm not going to ask you to be good, or normal, or even decent for her, because I enjoy toying with her, too. You're welcome."

I step out of the bathroom and close the door behind me, but not before noticing the wide-eyed look my sisters exchange. Their love for Easton is historied and intense.

"You look cute today," Mom tells me in the kitchen.

"Thanks." I show her my teeth. "I flossed."

"Fancy. Did you also shower?"

"Whoa, calm down. I'm not a fashion influencer."

She chuckles. "You're not wearing your jumpsuit."

"They're called coveralls—but thank you for the make-believe." I look down at the white T-shirt I tucked into a bright yellow embroidered skirt. "I'm not going to the garage."

"Date? It's been a while."

"No date. I promised Easton I'll . . . " I stop myself.

Mom's fantastic. The kindest, most patient person I know. She probably wouldn't mind it if I told her that I'm going to a chess tournament. But she's using a cane this morning. Her joints look swollen and inflamed. And I haven't used the c-word in three years. Why break my streak?

"She's leaving for Boulder in a couple of weeks, so we're hanging out in New York."

Her expression darkens. "I just wish you'd reconsider continuing with your schooling—"

"Mom," I whine, tone as hurt as I can make it.

After several trials and many errors, I finally discovered the best way to get Mom off my back: to imply that I want to go to college so little that every time she brings up the topic, I'm tragically wounded by her lack of respect for my life choices. It might not be the truth, and I'm not a fan of lying to her, but it's for her own good. I don't want anyone in my family to think that they owe me anything, or to feel guilty about my decisions. They shouldn't feel guilty, because none of this is *their* fault.

It's exclusively mine.

"Right. Yes, sorry. Well, it's exciting that you're hanging out with Easton."

"Is it?"

"Of course. You're being youthful. Doing eighteen-year-old stuff." She gives me a wistful look. "I'm just happy you took a day off—YALO and all that."

"That's YOLO, Mom."

"You sure?"

I laugh as I pick up my purse and kiss her on the cheek. "I'll be back tonight. You're okay alone with the ingrates? I left three meal options in the fridge. Also, Sabrina was a total pain last week, so if McKenzie or another friend invites her, *don't* let her go to their place."

Mom sighs. "You know you're my child, too, right? And you shouldn't be stuck co-parenting with me?"

"Hey." I mock-frown. "Am I not doing a good job? Should I crush more prescription-strength Benadryl into the harpies' breakfasts?"

I want Mom to chuckle again, but she just shakes her head. "I don't like it that I'm surprised that you're taking a day for yourself. Or that Sabrina looks at you when she needs money. This doesn't—"

"Mom. *Mom.*" I smile as earnestly as I can. "I promise you, it's fine."

It's probably not. Fine, I mean.

There's something supremely un-fine about the fact that my family has the Wikipedia entry on rheumatoid arthritis memorized. That we can tell whether it'll be a bad day by the lines around Mom's mouth. That last year I had to explain to Darcy that *chronic* means forever. Incurable. It won't ever go away.

Mom has a master's degree in biology and is a medical writer—a damn good one. She has written health education materials, FDA documents, fancy grant proposals that have won her clients millions of dollars. But she's a freelancer. When Dad was around, and when she was able to work regularly, it wasn't much of an issue. Unfortunately, that's not an option anymore. Some days the pain is so bad that she can barely get out of bed, let alone take over projects, and her impossibly convoluted Social Security disability application has now been denied four times. But at least I'm here. At least I can make things easier for her.

So maybe, just maybe, it will be. Fine, I mean.

"Rest, okay?" I cup her face. There are about seven gray circles under her eyes. "Go back to bed. The creatures will entertain themselves."

When I let myself out. I can hear Sabrina and Darcy kvetching about their oatmeals in the kitchen. I make a mental note to stock up on nail polish remover, and when I spot Easton's car rounding the corner, I wave at her and jog up to the street.

And that, I guess, is the beginning of the rest of my life.

Chapter Two

"It's a Swiss-system tournament. Kind of. Not really, though."

Easton gathers our team around her, like she's Tony Stark briefing the Avengers, but instead of quippy one-liners she hands out Paterson Chess Club pins. There must be three hundred people on the second floor of the Fulton Stall Market, and I am the only one who didn't get the business casual memo.

Oops.

"Each one of us is going to play four matches," she continues. "Because it's for charity, and because the tournament is open to amateurs, instead of using FIDE ratings, players are going to be matched according to self-reported ability."

FIDE, the World Chess Federation (Why isn't the acronym WCF? Not sure, but I suspect the French language is involved) has a complicated system to determine players' skill levels and rank them accordingly. I knew all about it when I was seven, chess obsessed, and wanted to grow up to be a mermaid Grandmaster. By now, though, I've forgotten most bureaucratic stuff, probably to make room for more useful information—like the best way to crimp a wire terminal, or the plot of the first three seasons of *How to Get Away with Murder*. All I remember is that to get a rating one needs to sign up for FIDE-sponsored tournaments. Which, of course, I haven't done in ages—because I haven't played in ages.

Four years, five months, and two weeks, and no, I will not stoop to counting the days.

"So we have to self-report our level of skill?" Zach asks. He's a Montclair freshman who joined the Paterson Chess Club after I left and has some ambitions of going pro. I've met him once at Oscar's place and I'm not a fan, for reasons that include his penchant for derailing conversations with unrelated mentions of his FIDE rating (2,546), his ability to carry out hour-long monologues on his FIDE rating (2,546), and his lack of understanding that I'm not interested in going out with him, no matter his FIDE rating (2,546).

But he's still better than our fourth member, Josh, whose claim to fame is repeatedly implying that Easton would be a little less gay if only she made out with him at least once.

"Since I'm the team leader, I went ahead and declared your skill levels," Easton tells us. "I put—"

"Why are you the leader?" Zach asks. "I don't remember having an election."

"Then I'm the team dictator," she hisses. I fix my pin to my tee to hide a smile. "I put Mallory in the highest bracket."

I drop my arms. "Easton. I've *barely* played in—"

"Zach's in the highest, too. Third highest for myself," she continues, ignoring me. Then she looks at Josh and pauses for effect. "The lowest for you."

Josh bursts into his wholesome, golden boy laughter. "Joking aside, what bracket did you . . ." Easton keeps staring, serious as death and taxes, and he lowers his eyes to the floor.

"Does the PCC have your browser history?" I ask Easton once it's just the two of us, heading toward the hall.

"Why?"

"There's no way you're here of your own free will, not with those two. So either they found out about the tentacle porn, or—"

"There's *no* tentacle porn." She gives me a scathing look. "The manager of the club asked me to put together a team. I couldn't say no, since he wrote me a rec letter for college. He was just exploiting the fact that I owe him a favor." She shoulders past two older men in suits to get to the tournament area. "Like you did when you sicced your sisters on me."

"It's what you deserve for bringing Zach and the rook he shoved up his ass."

"Ah, Zach. If only we could know what his FIDE rating is."

I laugh. "Maybe we should ask him and . . ."

We walk through the doors, and my voice trails off.

The noise in the bustling room dims, then quiets.

People walk around me, past me, into me, but I stand still, frozen, unable to step out of the way.

There are tables. Many tables pushed together to form long, parallel rows—rows and rows, covered in white-and-blue cloth with plastic, foldable chairs tucked into each side, and between each pair of chairs—

Chessboards.

Dozens of them. Hundreds. Not good ones: I can tell even from the entrance that they're old and cheap, the pieces chipped and poorly cut, the squares dirty and discolored. Ugly, mismatched sets all around me. The smell in the room is like a childhood memory, made of familiar, simple notes: wood and felt and sweat and stale coffee, the bergamot note of Dad's aftershave, home, belonging, betrayal, happiness, and—

"Mal? You okay?" Easton tugs at my arm with a frown. I don't think it's the first time she's asked.

"Yeah. Yeah, I . . ." I swallow, and it helps. The moment breaks, my heart slows, and I'm just a girl—perhaps a slightly fawn-kneed one. It's just a room that I'm standing in. The chess pieces— they're just stuff. Things. Some white, some black. Some can move in any number of unoccupied squares, others not so much. Who cares? "I need a drink."

"I have Crystal Light. Strawberry." She hands me her CamelBak. "It's disgusting."

"Guys." Zach comes up to us from behind. "Don't freak out, but I've spotted some preeetty big names walking around. I'm talking international."

Easton lets out an exaggerated gasp. "Harry Styles?"

"What? No."

"Malala?"

"No."

"Oh my God, Michelle Obama? Do you think she'll sign my pocket constitution?"

"No—Rudra Lal. Maxim Alexeyev. Andreas Antonov. Yang Zhang. Famous chess people."

"Ah." She nods. "So regular, not-at-all-famous people?"

I do love watching Easton mess with Zach, but I *have* heard these names. I wouldn't be able to pick them out of a lineup, but at my most fervent, chess-obsessive stage I've studied their games on books, simulation software, YouTube tutorials. Old impressions surface quickly in my brain, like long-unused synapses sputtering awake.

Lal: versatile openings, positional

Antonov: tricky, but technical

Zhang: calculating, slow

Alexeyev: still young, uneven

I shrug the memories away and ask, "What are they doing at an amateur tournament?"

"The director's well connected in the chess world—she's the owner of a respected New York chess club. Plus, the winning team gets twenty thousand for a charity of their choice." He rubs his hands together like a cartoon villain. "I hope I get to go against the big guns."

"You think you can beat them?" Easton's eyebrow lifts, skeptical. "Aren't they pros?"

"Well, I've been training." Zach brushes nonexistent crumbs off his blazer. "My rating's 2,546"—we all roll our eyes—"and Lal's not exactly at the top of his game. Did you see him lose to Sawyer at Ubud International two weeks ago? It was embarrassing."

"Everyone's embarrassing against Sawyer," Josh points out.

"Well, plenty of people are embarrassing against *me*."

Easton's eye twitches. "Are you comparing yourself to Sawyer?"

"People say we have similar playing styles . . ."

I cough to hide a snort. "Do we know who we've been paired with yet?"

"Sort of." Easton unlocks her phone and texts everyone a screenshot of the organizers' email. "We don't know *who* we're going up against, because it's a team tournament. But Mal, you're PCC Player One, and you've been paired with the Marshall Chess Club Player One. Row five, board thirty-four. Good news: you're White. Round one starts in five. The time limit is ninety minutes, then round two starts. So we should get going." Easton tugs at my hand. "Wouldn't want to make Lal wait for the thorough ass-kicking he's about to get, right, Zach?"

I can't tell whether Zach recognizes the shade. He puffs up and struts to his board, and I'm left wondering how soon the black hole of antimatter that is his ego will swallow the solar system.

"Listen," Easton whispers before we go separate ways, "I put myself in a too-high bracket. I'll probably be destroyed in about five moves, but it's okay. All the PCC wanted was for us to have a presence here, and I delivered. That's to say, if you let whoever you're playing destroy you quickly, we can pop by Dylan's Candy Bar and be back before round two."

"Are you buying?"

"Fine."

"One of those macarons stuffed inside a cookie?"

"Sure."

"Deal."

It won't be hard, getting checkmated like a total loser, not with how rusty I am. I take a seat at board thirty-four, White side, and watch the chairs around me fill up, people shaking hands, the introduction and chitchatting as everyone waits for the start announcement. No one is paying attention to me, and . . . I just do it.

I reach for my king. Pick it up. Feel its slight, perfect weight in my hand and smile softly as I trace the corners of the crown.

The stupid, useless, good-for-nothing king. Can barely move one square, scurries into hiding behind the rook, and he's so, so easy to corner. A fraction of the queen's power, that's what he has. He is nothing, absolutely *nothing*, without his kingdom.

My heart squeezes. At least he's relatable.

I put the king back on his square and stare at the skyline made up by the pieces—the trivial and yet monumental landscape of chess. It's more familiar than the view from my childhood bedroom (unspectacular: a busted trampoline, lots of ornery squirrels, an apricot tree that never learned how to bear fruit). It's more familiar than my own face in the mirror, and I can't tear my gaze away, not even when the chair in front of mine drags across the floor, not even when one of the tournament directors calls for round one to begin.

The table shifts as my opponent takes a seat. A large hand stretches into my line of sight. And just as I'm about to force myself out of my reverie to shake it, I hear a deep voice say,

"Marshall Chess Club Player One. Nolan Sawyer."

Chapter Three

He's not looking at me.

He's holding out his hand, but his eyes are on the board, and for a split second I can't figure out what is happening, where I am, or what I came here to do. I can't figure out what my name is.

No. Wait. I do know *that*.

"Mallory Greenleaf," I stammer, taking his hand. It completely engulfs mine. His shake is brief, warm, and very, very firm. "PCC. That is, Paterson. Club. Uh, chess club." I clear my throat. Wow. So eloquent. Much articulate. "Nice to meet you," I lie.

He lies right back at me with a "Likewise," and still doesn't look up. Just sets his elbows on the table, keeping his gaze fixed on the pieces, as though my person, my face, my identity, are utterly irrelevant. As though I am but an extension of the white side of the board.

It cannot be. This guy cannot be Nolan Sawyer. Or, not *the* Nolan Sawyer. The famous one. The sex symbol—whatever that even means. The guy who a couple of years ago was number one in the world and now . . .

I have no clue what Nolan Sawyer's up to now, but he *can't* be sitting across from me. The people on our left and right seem to be not-so-subtly eyeing him, and I want to yell at them that this is just a doppelgänger. Plenty of those going around. Doppelgänger-palooza, these days.

It would explain why he's sitting there, doing nothing. Clearly, bizarro Nolan Sawyer doesn't know how to play and thought this would be a mah-jongg tournament and is wondering where the tiles are and—

Someone clears their throat. It's the player sitting next to me: a middle-aged man who's neglecting his own match to gawk at mine, pointedly staring between me and my pieces.

Which are white.

Shit—I have the first move. What do I do? Where do I start? Which piece do I use?

Pawn to e4. There. Done. The most common, boring—

"My clock," Sawyer murmurs distractedly. His eyes are on my pawn.

"What?"

"I need you to start my clock, or I won't be able to respond." He sounds bored, with a dash of annoyed.

I flush scarlet, utterly mortified, and look around. I can't find the stupid clock until someone—Sawyer—pushes it an inch toward me. It was right by my left hand.

Perfect. Lovely. Now would be an excellent time for the floor to morph into quicksand. Swallow me alive, too.

"I'm sorry. Um—I *knew* about the clock. But I forgot, and—" *And I'm thinking of stabbing myself in the eyeball with that pencil over there. Is it yours? Can I borrow it?*

"It's fine." He makes his move—pawn in e5. Starts my clock.

Then it's my turn again, and—shit, I'm gonna have to move more than once. Against Nolan Sawyer. This is unjust. A travesty.

Pawn in d4, maybe? And then, after he takes my pawn, I move another to c3. Wait, what am I doing? Am I . . . I'm not trying a Danish Gambit with Nolan Sawyer, am I?

The Danish Gambit is one of the most aggressive openings in chess. Dad's voice rings in my ears. *You sacrifice two pieces in the first few moves—then shift quickly into attack. Most good players will have learned how to defend themselves. If you really must use it, make sure you have a solid follow-up plan.*

I briefly consider my glaring lack of follow-up plans. Well, then. I could *really* use a puke bucket, but instead I just sigh and resignedly push my bishop into the midst, because the more the merrier.

This is a disaster. Send help.

I make five moves after that. Then two more—at which point Sawyer starts pressing me, dogging me insistently with his queen and knight, and I feel like one of the bugs that sometimes wander into Goliath's cage. Pinned. Squashed. Done for. My stomach tightens, gelid, slimy, and I spend futile minutes staring at the board, scouring for a way out of this mess that's just *not there.*

Until it is.

It takes three moves and I lose my poor, battered bishop, but I disentangle myself from the pin. The dread of the opening is slowly melting into an old, familiar feeling: *I am playing chess and I know what I'm doing.* After each move I punch Sawyer's clock and glance up at him, curious, though he never does the same.

He's always unreadable. Opaque. I have no doubt that he's taking the game seriously, but he's distant, as though playing from far away, locked in a cell on the top level of one of his rooks. Here, but not really *here*. His movements, when he touches the pieces, are precise, economical, strong. I hate myself for noticing that. He's taller than the men sitting at his sides, and I hate myself for noticing that, too. His shoulders and biceps fill his black shirt just right, and when he rolls back his sleeves, I notice his forearms and am suddenly grateful that we're playing chess and not arm-wrestling; I hate myself for that the most.

The Mallory-hate party is clearly in full swing—and then Sawyer moves his knight. After that, I'm too busy trying to remember how to breathe to berate myself.

It's not that it's the wrong move. Not at all. It is, in fact, a flawless move. I can see what he's planning to do with it—move it again, open me up, force me to castle. Check in four, or five. Knife to my throat, and I'd be toast. But.

But, I think it's possible that elsewhere on the board . . .

If I forced him into . . .

And he didn't retreat his . . .

My heart flutters. And I don't defend. Instead I advance my own knight, a little light-headed, and for the first time in—oh my God, have we been at this for fifty-five minutes? How is that possible?

Why does chess always *feel like this*?

For the very first time since we started, when I look up at Sawyer, I notice a trace of something. In the shifting line of his shoulders, the way he presses his fingers against his full lips, there's a hint that maybe he really *is* here, after all. Playing this game. With me.

Well. *Against* me.

A blink and it goes away. He moves his queen. Takes my bishop. Stops the clock.

I move my knight. Capture his pawn. Stop the clock.

Queen. Clock.

Knight, again. My mouth is dry. Clock.

Rook. Clock.

Pawn. I swallow, twice. Clock.

Rook takes pawn. Clock.

King.

It takes Sawyer a couple of seconds to realize what has happened. A few beats to map all the possible scenarios in his head, all the possible roads this game could take. I know it, because I see him lift his hand to move his own queen, as though it could possibly make a difference, as though he could wiggle his way out of my attack. And I know it, because I have to clear my throat before I say,

"I . . . Checkmate."

That's when he lifts his eyes to mine for the first time. They are dark, and clear, and serious. And they remind me of a few important, long-forgotten things.

When Nolan Sawyer was twelve, he placed third at a tournament because of an arguably unfair arbitral decision on castling short, and in response he wiped the chess pieces off the board with his arm. When he was thirteen, he placed second at the very same tournament—this time, he flipped an entire table. When he was fourteen, he got into a screaming match with Antonov over either a girl or a denied draw (rumors disagree), and I can't recall how old he was when he called a former world champion a fuckwhit for trying to pull an illegal move during a warm-up game.

I do recall, however, hearing the story and having no idea what a fuckwhit might be.

Each time, Sawyer was fined. Reprimanded. The object of scathing op-eds on chess media. And each time, he was welcomed back to the chess community with open arms, because here's the deal: for over a decade Nolan Sawyer has been rewriting chess history, redefining standards, bringing attention to the sport. Where's the fun in playing, if the best is left out? And if the best sometimes acts like a douchebag . . . well. It's all forgiven.

But not forgotten. Everyone in the community knows that Nolan Sawyer is a terrible, moody, ill-tempered ball of toxic masculinity. That he's the poorest loser in the history of chess. In the history of any sport. In the history of *history*.

Which, because he just lost against me, is possibly going to develop into a problem.

For the first time since the match started, I realize that a dozen people are standing around us, whispering to each other. I want to ask them what they're looking at, if I have a nosebleed, a wardrobe malfunction, a tarantula on my ear, but I'm too busy staring at Sawyer. Tracking his movements. Making sure he won't hurl the chess clock at me. I'm not one to be easily intimidated, but I'd rather avoid a checkmate-induced traumatic brain injury if he decides to smash a foldable chair on my head.

Though, surprisingly, he seems content to just study me. Lips slightly parted and eyes bright, like I'm simultaneously something odd and familiar and puzzling and larger than life and—

He looks. After ignoring me for twenty-five moves, he just *looks*. Calm. Inquisitive. Upsettingly *not* angry. Something funny occurs to me: top players are always given cutesy nicknames by the press. The Artist. The Picasso of Chess. The Gambit Mozart. Nolan's nickname?

The Kingkiller.

The Kingkiller leans forward, ever so slightly, and his intense, awestruck expression feels much more threatening than a folding chair to my head.

"Who—" he starts, and I cannot bear it.

"Thank you for the game," I blurt out, and then, even though I should shake his hand, sign the scorecard, play three more games—despite all of that, I leap to my feet.

No shame in retreating your pieces if you're being pinned and can get out, Dad used to say. *No shame in knowing the limits of your game.*

My chair falls to the ground as I run away. I hear the grating sound, and still don't stop to pick it up.

Chapter Four

"Mal?"

"*Mal.*"

"Maaaaaal!"

I blink awake. Darcy's nose is pressed up against mine, eyes Galápagos-blue in the morning light.

I yawn. "What's going on?"

"*Ew*, Mal." She recoils. "Why does your breath smell like a skunk during mating season?"

"I . . . is everything okay?"

"Yes. I made my own oatmeal this morning. We're out of Nutella."

I sit up, or some approximation of it. Rub sleep out of my eyes. "Yesterday we had more than half a jar left—"

"And today we're out. The circle of life, Mal."

"Are Mom and Sabrina okay?"

"Yup. McKenzie and her dad picked up Sabrina. Mom's fine. She got up, then went back to bed because she was having a rough morning. But there's someone at the door for you."

"Someone at the—?"

Memories of yesterday slowly begin to surface.

Sawyer's king, held in check by my queen. Tripping on the sidewalk as I ran to the train. Texting Easton about a made-up emergency, then turning off my phone. The dull urban landscape outside the train's windows, ever morphing into a chessboard. Then the rest of the night—a *Veronica Mars* marathon with my sister, my head emptied out of everything else.

Not to brag, but I'm good at compartmentalizing. Together with always picking the best item on the menu, it's my greatest talent. That's how I made myself get over chess years ago. And that's how I manage to survive day by day without hyperventilating about all sorts of stuff. It's either compartmentalizing or going broke buying inhalers.

"Tell Easton that—"

"Not Easton." Darcy flushes. "Though you could invite her over. Maybe this afternoon—"

Not Easton? "Who, then?"

"A random person."

I groan. "Darcy, I told you: when people from millenarian restorationist Christian denominations come knocking—"

"—we politely inform them that eternal salvation is beyond us, I know, but it's someone else. They asked for you by name, not for the head of the household."

"Okay." I scratch my forehead. "Okay—tell them I'll be there in a minute."

"Cool. Oh, and also, this arrived yesterday. Addressed to Mom, but . . ." She holds out an envelope. My eyes are still blurry. I have to blink to read, but when I do, my stomach twists.

"Thank you."

"It's a reminder, right?"

"No."

"That we have to pay the mortgage?"

"No. Darcy—"

"Do you have the money?"

I force myself to smile. "Don't worry about it."

She nods, but before stepping out she says, "I pocketed it when the mailman brought it. Mom and Sabrina haven't seen it." The freckles on her nose are shaped like a cloudy heart, and with the single neuron currently working in my brain I contemplate how unfair it is that she needs to worry about this stuff. She's twelve. When *I* was twelve, my life was boba and refreshing chess.com.

I slip on dirty shorts and yesterday's tee. Given Darcy's gentle feedback, I decide to gargle with mouthwash while I turn on my phone. I discover that it's 9:13, and that I have a million notifications. I swipe away dating app matches, Instagram and TikTok alerts, News highlights. I scroll through my texts from Easton (a panicked string, followed by Essay question: what does Nolan Sawyer smell like? Two paragraphs or longer and a picture of her vengefully biting into a cookie-macaron), then head outside.

I'm not sure who I expect to find. Definitely not a tall woman with a pixie haircut, a full sleeve of tattoos, and more piercings than I can count. She turns around with a grin, and her lips are a bold, perfect red. She must be in her late twenties, if not older.

"Sorry," she says, pointing at her cigarette. Her voice is low and amused. "Your sister said you were sleeping and I thought you'd take longer. You're not going to start smoking because you saw me smoke, right?"

I feel myself smile back. "Doubtful."

"Good. You never know, the impressionability of the youths."

She puts out the butt, wraps it in a napkin, and pockets it, either to avoid polluting or to conceal her DNA.

Okay, no more *Veronica Mars* for me.

"You're Mallory, right?"

I cock my head. "Have we met?"

"Nope. I'm Defne. Defne Bubikoğlu—but unless you speak Turkish, I wouldn't try to pronounce it. It's nice to meet you. I'm a fan."

I let out a laugh. Then realize she's serious. "Excuse me?"

"Anyone who trounces Nolan Sawyer like you did gets a lifetime supply of admiration from me." She points to herself with a flourish. "Free home delivery, too."

I stiffen. Oh, no. No, no. What *is* this? "I'm sorry. You have the wrong person."

She frowns. "You're not Mallory Greenleaf?"

I take a step back. "Yes. But it's a common name—"

"Mallory Virginia Greenleaf, who played yesterday?" She takes out her phone, taps at it, then holds it out with a smile. "If this is not you, you have some serious identity theft issues."

She has pulled up a video. A TikTok of a young woman checkmating Nolan Sawyer with her queen. There are wisps of white-blond hair falling across the side of her face, and her eyeliner is smudged.

I can't believe Easton didn't tell me that my eyeliner looked like shit.

Also, I can't believe that this stupid video was taken and it has over *twenty thousand likes*. Are there even twenty thousand people who play chess?

"What was up with the dramatic exit, by the way?" she asks. "Did you double-park?"

"No. I—okay, that *is* me." I run a hand down my face. I need coffee. And a time machine, to go back to when I agreed to help Easton. Maybe I could go back even further, just murder our entire friendship. "The game . . . It was a fluke."

Defne's brow furrows. "A fluke?"

"Yeah. I know that it looks like I'm some kind of . . . chess talent, but I don't play. Sawyer must be in some kind of funk, and—" I stop. Defne is laughing and laughing. Apparently, I'm hilarious.

"You mean, the current world chess champion? Who also happens to be the current rapid *and* blitz champion? In a funk?"

I press my lips together. "He can be the current champion and still be having a bad month."

"Unlikely, since he won Sweden Chess last week."

"Well," I scramble, "he's tired because of all the winning, and—"

"Dude, stop." She takes one step closer, and I smell something pleasantly citrusy mixed with the tobacco. "You won against the best player in the world. You completely blindsided him in a damn good game—the way you feinted a feint? How you got yourself out of that pin? Your queen? Stop putting yourself down and take credit for it—you think Nolan would be half as reticent? You think *any* guy would be?"

Defne is yelling. With the corner of my eye I see Mrs. Abebe, my neighbor, stare at us from her yard, a clear *Do you need saving?* in her eyes. I subtly shake my head. Defne just seems like a very passionate, very loud cheerleader. I think I might even like her. *Despite* the fact that she's here to talk about chess.

"I can't be the first person to win against Sawyer," I say. As a matter of fact, I know I'm not. I studied his play, back when I still . . . studied plays. Antonov-Sawyer, 2013, Rome. Sawyer-Shankar, 2016, Seattle. Antoni-Sawyer, 2012—

"No, but it's been a while. And when people win against him, it's because he makes dumb mistakes—which he didn't, not that I could see. It's just that you were . . . better."

"I'm not—"

"And it's not like this is your first feat when it comes to chess." I shake my head, confused. "What do you mean?"

"Well, I looked you up, and . . ." She glances at her phone. Her case says, *Check, mate!* on a galaxy background. "There are articles of you winning tournaments in the area, and pics of you doing blindfolded simultaneous exhibitions—you were an *adorable* kid, by the way. I'm surprised you didn't play in rated tournaments, 'cause you'd have *killed* it."

I might be flushing. "My mother didn't want me to," I say, without quite knowing why.

Defne's eyes widen. "Your mother doesn't support you playing chess?"

"No, nothing like that. She just . . ."

Mom loved that I played. She even learned the rules to be able to follow my never-ending chess-related chatter. However, she also didn't shy away from pushing back against Dad. For most of my childhood, the greatest hit in the Greenleaf household was Dad insisting that someone as good as I was at manipulating numbers and pattern recognitions should be cultivated into a pro; Mom replying that she didn't want me dealing with the hyper-competitive, hyper-individualistic environment of rated chess from a young age; Sabrina emerging from her room to ask flatly, *When you're done arguing about your favorite daughter, can we maybe have dinner?* In the end, they agreed that I'd start competing in the rated divisions of tournaments when I was fourteen.

Then I turned fourteen, and everything changed.

"I wasn't interested."

"I see. You're Archie Greenleaf's daughter, aren't you? I think I met him—"

"I'm sorry," I interrupt her sharply. Sharper than I mean to, because of the sour taste in my throat. The things she's saying, it's like unearthing a corpse. "I'm sorry," I repeat, gentler. "Was there . . . Is there a reason you're here?"

"Right, yes." If she's offended by my bluntness, she doesn't let it show. Instead she surprises me by saying, "I'm here to offer you a job."

I blink. "A job?"

"Yup. Wait—are you a minor? Because if so, one of your parents should probably—"

"I'm eighteen."

"Eighteen! Are you heading off to college?"

"No." I swallow. "I'm done with school."

"Perfect, then." She smiles like she's giving me a gift. Like I'm about to be happy. Like the idea of making *me* happy makes *her* happy. "Here's the deal: I run a chess club. Zugzwang, in Brooklyn, over by—"

"I've heard of it." Marshall might be the oldest, most renowned club in New York, but in the last few years Zugzwang has become known for attracting a less traditional crowd. It has a TikTok account that sometimes goes viral, community engagement, strip-chess tournaments. I vaguely remember hearing about a more-or-less acerbic rivalry between Marshall and Zugzwang—which would explain her glee at my beating Sawyer, a Marshall member.

"Here's the deal: some of our members decide to use their

overgrown chess brains for something that isn't chess, and—well, they go out in the world, get jobs in finance and other lucrative, amoral fields, make tons of money, and *looove* tax write-offs. Long story short, we have a bunch of donors. And this year we instituted a fellowship."

"A fellowship?" Does she want to hire me to keep track of donors? Does she think I'm an accountant?

"It's a one-year salary for a player who has the potential to go pro. You'd be mentored and sent to tournaments on our tab. The primary goal is to give a head start to promising young chess players. The *secondary* goal is for me to eat popcorn while you hand Nolan his ass, *again*. But that's not, like, a must."

I scratch my nose. "I don't understand."

"Mallory, I'd love for you to be this year's Zugzwang fellow."

I don't immediately parse her words. Then I do, and I still have to turn them around in my head over and over, because I'm not sure I heard them correctly.

Did she just offer to pay me to play chess?

This is wild. Incredible. This fellowship—it's like the stuff of dreams. Life changing. Everything fourteen-year-old Mallory Greenleaf would have wished for.

Too bad fourteen-year-old Mallory Greenleaf is nowhere in sight.

"I'm sorry," I tell Defne. She's still looking at me with a bright, happy expression. "I told you, I don't play anymore."

The bright, happy expression darkens a little. "Why?"

I like her. I *really* like her, and for a moment I almost consider explaining things to her. Stuff. Life. My sisters, and Mom, and roller derby fees. Bob, and changing windshield wipers, and the fact that I don't need a one-year fellowship but a job that will be there next year, and the year after, and the one after that. Dad, and the memories, and the night I swore to myself that I was done with chess. Forever.

It seems like too much for a first meeting, so I condense the truth. "I'm just not interested."

She's instantly subdued. Her brow furrows in a slight frown and she studies me for a long while, as though realizing that there might be something she doesn't know about me. Ha. "Tell you what," she says eventually. "I'm going to get going—Sunday's peak day at Zugzwang. Lots of prep. But I'll give you a few days to think about it—"

"I'm not going to change my mind—"

"—and in the meantime, I'll email you the contract." She pats my shoulder, and I'm enveloped by her lemony scent once again. One of her tattoos, I notice, is a chessboard, with pieces developed on it. A famous game, perhaps, but I don't recognize it.

"I— You don't have my email," I tell her. She's already at her car—2019 Volkswagen Beetle.

"Oh, I do. From the tournament database."

"Which tournament?"

"Yesterday's." She waves goodbye as she gets into the driver's seat. "I organized it."

I don't wait for her to drive off. I turn around, walk back inside the house, and pretend not to notice Mom looking at me from the window.

Chapter Five

I am surrounded. Under siege. Relentlessly attacked from all sides.

Honda Civic leaking coolant? On top of me.

Mortgage letter from the credit union? In my backpack.

Sabrina's text reminding me that her derby fees are due on Friday and if I don't pay them, her life will be in shambles? On my phone.

Bob's supervillain presence, raging because I refused to push an early brake job on a high school junior? Hovering all over the garage.

Easton, whining at me nonstop like I'm her local congressman? Somewhere next to the Civic.

I successfully avoided her for three days. Now it's Wednesday, she's shown up to the garage, and I have nowhere to retreat. Except under a steady stream of coolant.

"You're acting like a total weirdo," she says for the twentieth time. "Winning against Sawyer and then *running away*? Refusing *money* to play chess?"

"Listen," I say, and then stop. Partly because the leaking has intensified. Partly because I exhausted my explanations ten minutes ago. *"I need a stable, long-term job that allows me to pick up extra shifts when money gets tight. I need it to be here in Paterson in case something happens to Mom and my sisters need me. I have no interest in getting sucked back into chess."* There's a limited number of ways I can paraphrase these three simple concepts. "You're leaving next Wednesday, right?"

She ignores me. "People are *talking* about your game. They're analyzing it on ChessWorld.com. They're using words like *masterpiece*, Mal. Zach keeps sending me links!"

I patch the radiator and roll from under the Civic, take in Easton's University of Colorado crop top, and scrunch my nose. Seems a bit premature. "Did Zach ever end up playing against Lal?"

"*Now* you're interested in the tournament?" She rolls her eyes. "No. But that's probably for the best, since he lost every single game." I smile my schadenfreude, but she wags her finger at me. "Hey—at least Zach didn't leave me without a player because he freaked out when Nolan Sawyer winked at him."

I huff. "First of all, I seriously doubt Nolan Sawyer has ever winked, will ever wink, or even knows the meaning of the word *wink*." I stand, wiping my hands on the butt of my coveralls. Sawyer's serious, intense expression is not something I've been letting myself think about. Okay, *maybe* I dreamed of him staring at me from across a chessboard that spontaneously burst into flames. Of him pushing the chess clock at me, smiling faintly, and saying with his deep voice, "Did you know that I'm a Gen Z sex symbol?" Of him tipping me over like people do with their kings when they resign, and then stubbornly holding out a hand for me, eager to help me up. Okay, *maybe* in the past week I've had three separate Nolan Sawyer dreams. So what? Sue me. Send the sleep police. "Secondly, I had an emergency."

"Forgot to turn on the Crock-Pot, did you?"

"Something like that. Hey, I want to come to the airport when you—" Bob's voice rises in the main garage, and I frown. "Wait here a sec," I say, running to check on the too-familiar noise.

My uncle used to co-own the garage with Bob, and I was working here during summers since well before he should have agreed to have me underfoot. I've always been intuitive about fixing stuff—figuring out how the different pieces are connected in a larger system, visualizing how they work together as building blocks of a whole, calculating how changing one could affect the others. *So much like chess*, Dad used to say, and I don't know if he was right, but Uncle Jack was happy to have me around. Until *he* wasn't around anymore: the week after I graduated and began working for him full-time, he made the unfortunate decision to sell his share to Bob and move to the Pacific Northwest "for the Dungeness crab." As a consequence, I now have the pleasure of answering only to Bob.

Lucky me.

I find him standing in front of a woman I don't recognize, flanked by his other two mechanics, hands on his hips. They all look angry.

Pissed, even.

"—for an oil change, and I was told that it would cost around fifty bucks, not two hundred—"

"That's because of the engine flush."

"What's an engine flush?"

"Something cars need, lady. Maybe we forgot to tell you when you brought yours over. Who did you talk to?"

"A girl. Blond, a little taller than me—"

"I did the intake." I smile at the client and step inside, ignoring Bob's glare. "Is there a problem?"

She scowls. "You didn't mention that my car would need an engine . . . whatever. I-I can't afford this."

I glance at the cars around the shop, trying to place her. "It's a 2019 Jetta sedan, right?"

"Yeah."

"You won't need an engine flush." I smile reassuringly. She looks distraught and rattled over money—something I can relate to. "The car's well under fifty thousand miles."

"So the engine flush was *not* necessary."

"Not at all. I'm sure it's a mistake, and . . ." I trail off as I realize what she said. *Was.* "Excuse me, do you mean that the engine flush has *already* been done?"

She turns to Bob, steely. "I'm not paying for a job that even *your own mechanic* says wasn't needed. And I won't be using this garage again. But nice try."

It takes her less than a minute to settle the fifty-dollar bill. The tension in the garage is thick and ugly, and I stand by the counter, feeling painfully awkward, until the Jetta has driven off. Then I turn to Bob.

Surprise surprise, he's fuming.

"I'm sorry," I say, a mix of contrite, defensive, and gloating. Working with Bob clearly arouses complex, multilayered emotions within me. "I didn't know you'd already done the flush or I wouldn't have told her it wasn't necessary. She seemed like she didn't have the money for—"

"You're fired," he says without looking at me, still fiddling with the credit card transaction.

I'm not sure I heard him right. "What?"

"You're fired. I'll pay you what I owe you, but I don't want you back."

I blink at him. "What are you—"

"I am *sick of you*," he yells, turning to me and coming forward. I take two steps back. Bob's not tall and he's not large, but he's *mean*. "You *always* do this."

I shake my head, glancing at the other mechanics, hoping they'll intervene. They just look at us stone-faced, and I—

I can't lose this job. I *can't*. I have a letter in my purse and a text in my phone, and apparently guinea pigs get depressed if they're not living in damn pairs. "Listen, I'm sorry. But I've been working here for over a year, and my uncle wouldn't—"

"Your uncle ain't here anymore, and I'm done with you. Not only do you never upsell, but you also don't let *me* do it? Get your stuff."

"But that's not my job! My job is to fix people's cars, not sell them stuff they don't need."

"Ain't your job anymore."

"She's right, you can't fire her like that." I turn around. Easton is standing behind me with her best *I will now correct your grammar* face. "There are regulations in place that protect employees from unjust termination—"

"Luckily, Blondie here was never on the books to begin with."

That shuts Easton up. And the realization that Bob can do anything he wants with me—that shuts *me* up, too.

"Get your stuff and leave," he says one last time, rude and obnoxious and cruel as always. I can't do anything about it. I'm completely, utterly powerless, and I have to clench my fists to stop myself from clawing his face. I have to force myself to walk away, or I'll tear him apart.

"And Mallory?"

I stop, but don't turn around.

"I'll be deducting the cost of the engine flush from what I owe you."

STRICTLY SPEAKING, I HAVE NEVER BEEN ENGULFED BY A MUD-slide and had my seizing body dragged down the jagged, rocky face of a mountain to be summarily deposited at its foothills and fed to the wild boars. However, I can imagine that if I were to find myself in a similar scenario, it would be no more painful than the week that comes after I get fired.

There are several reasons. For one, I don't want to worry Mom or my sisters, which means not telling them that Bob fired me, which means finding a place to hide during the day while I search for another job. Not easy, considering that it's still August in New Jersey, and that free places with AC and Wi-Fi are not common enough in the year of our Lord 2023. I find myself rediscovering the Paterson Public Library: it's changed very little since I was seven, and welcomes me and my battered laptop to its underfunded bosom.

God bless libraries.

"Upon exhaustive investigation," I tell Easton on the phone on Thursday night, after a day of less-than-fruitful research, "I discovered that you *cannot* pay bills with Candy Crush gold bars. A travesty. Also, to be hired as an auto mechanic by someone who's not your crab-enthusiast uncle, you need fancy things like certifications and references."

"And you don't have them?"

"No. Though I do have that *Mallory the Car Mechaness* comic Darcy drew me when she was eight. Think that might count?"

She sighs. "You know you have another option, right?"

I ignore her, and spend the following day looking for something else—*anything* else. Paterson is the third-biggest city in New Jersey, dammit. There has got to be a job, *any* job for me, dammit. Though it also happens to have the third-highest density in the United States, meaning lots of competition. Dammit.

Also, dammit: the red numbers that blink at me later that night when I peek at the online bank account Mom gave me access to once Dad wasn't in the picture anymore. My belly knots over.

"Hey," I tell Sabrina when I find her alone in the living room. I shove my hands down into my pockets to avoid wringing them. "About those derby fees."

She looks up from her phone, eyes scared wide open, and blurts out, "You're going to pay them, right?"

My eyes are scratchy from staring at a screen all day, and for a moment—a horrible, terrifying, disorienting moment—I am angry with her. With my beautiful, intelligent, talented fourteen-year-old sister who doesn't know, doesn't understand how hard I'm trying. When *I* turned fourteen—on the very stupid day of my stupid birthday—everything changed, and I lost Dad, I lost chess, I lost the very *me* I'd been, and since then all I've done is try to—

"Mal, can you please not screw *this one thing* up for me?"

The "unlike everything else" is unsaid, and the swelling bubble of anger bursts into guilt. Guilt that Sabrina has to ask for what is due to her. If it hadn't been for my stupid decisions, we'd have had no problem affording her fees.

I clear my throat. "There's been a mix-up at the credit union. I'll go check tomorrow, but could you ask for an extension? Just a couple of days."

She gives me a level stare. "Mal."

"I'm sorry. I'll pay as soon as I can."

"It's okay." She rolls her eyes. "Deadline's next Wednesday."

"What?"

"I just told you a few days earlier because I *know* you."

"You little—" I gasp, relieved, and flop on the couch to tickle her. In thirty seconds I have maneuvered her into a hug, and she laughs while saying *yikes* and *gross* and *Seriously, Mal, you're embarrassing yourself.*

"Why do you smell like old books and apple juice?" she asks. "Do we have apple juice?" I nod silently and go to the kitchen to pour her a glass, choked in my throat because of how much I love my sisters, and how little I can give them.

That night, my Gmail snoozes an unanswered message from defne@zugzwang.com. *Received 5 days ago. Reply?* I stare at it for a long time, but don't open it.

On Saturday and Sunday I get a lucky break: a couple gigs— yard work for a neighbor I sometimes babysit for; dog walking— and it's nice to have some cash, but it's not sustainable, not long term and not with a mortgage.

"It just needs to be paid," the credit union teller says on Monday morning, when I show her the *reminder, urgent, you are behind and failing at taking care of your family, you useless member of society* letter. "Preferably, all three overdue months." She gives me an assessing look. "How old are you?" I don't think I look younger than my age, but it doesn't matter, because eighteen's plenty young, even when it feels anything but. Maybe I'm just a child playing at grown-up. If that's the case, I'm losing. "You should probably let your mom handle this," the teller says, not unkindly. But Mom's having a terrible week, one of the worst since the nightmare of her diagnosis started, and we probably need to change her meds again, but that's expensive. I told her to rest, that I had everything under control, that I was picking up extra shifts.

You know, like a liar.

"You look tired," Gianna tells me when I show up at her place later that night, in desperate need of a distraction from thinking about money. She and I used to take calculus together. We'd have study sessions in this very house that's probably a McMansion, and would spend approximately one minute working on functions and two hours having lots of fun in her room. Her parents are out of town on a sailing trip, and she's leaving for some small liberal arts college in less than a week. Hasan, my other *good* friend, the week after.

"Tired is my default state," I tell her with a forced smile.

When I get home, not nearly as relaxed as I'd hoped, I find Easton's text (Just take the fellowship, Mal) and force myself to look at the sample contract.

It's good money. Good hours. The commute wouldn't be ideal, but not impossible once my sisters' school starts. Defne might allow for a flexible schedule, too.

Still, there's lots to consider. My feelings about chess, for one, which I cannot disentangle from my feelings for Dad. They are twisted, knotted together. There's pain. Regret. Nostalgia. Guilt. Hate. Above all, there's anger. So much anger inside me.

Mountains of it, entire blazing landscapes without a single fury-less corner in them.

I'm angry with Dad, angry with chess, and therefore I cannot play it. Pretty straightforward.

And setting that aside, am I even good enough? I know I'm talented—I've been told too many times, and by too many people not to. But I haven't trained in years, and I honestly believe that beating Nolan Sawyer (who in my latest dream broke off a piece of his queen and offered it to me like a KitKat) was nothing more than a stroke of luck.

On the twin bed next to mine, Darcy snores like a middle-aged man with sleep apnea. Goliath is in his cage, wandering aimlessly. The fact is, competitive chess is a sport, and like other sports, there's little room at the top. Everyone knows who Usain Bolt is, but no one gives a shiitake mushroom about the fifteenth-fastest person in the world—even though they're still pretty damn fast.

The diner where I used to wait tables has a full roster, and the local grocery store *might* be looking for help, but starting positions are minimum wage. Not enough. I contemplate the news on Tuesday and whine about it on the phone.

"Listen, you stubborn bitch: just take the fellowship and fake your way through it," Easton says, exasperated, affectionate, and suddenly I'm afraid again. That she'll forget all about me, that I'll never measure up to Colorado and the people she'll meet there. I'm about to lose her, I know I am. It seems such an inevitable, predestined conclusion, I don't even bother voicing my fears.

Instead I ask, "How do you mean?"

"You can take the money for a year and play your best, but also *not care* about chess. Don't think about it after hours. It doesn't have to be obsessive or consuming like it used to be before your dad . . . Just clock in, clock out. In the meantime, you can get those mechanic certifications."

"Ha," I say, impressed by her more-or-less devious plan. "Ha."

"You're welcome. Can you do that?"

"Do what?"

"Not be a total lunatic weirdo about something?"

I smile. "Unclear."

She leaves on Wednesday, after stopping by my place to say goodbye. I just figured it'd be different. I expected a TSA farewell and to stare at her plane as it flew off, but it doesn't make sense: we're eighteen. She has parents—a non-bedridden, still-together set that takes care of her, and drives her to the airport, and pays for a nice dorm room with the 529 that did not need to be cashed out when the old water boiler sputtered to its timely but heart-wrenching demise.

"You have to come visit," Easton says.

"Yeah," I say, knowing that I won't.

"When I'm back, we're going to New York. Get that macaron you don't deserve."

"I can't wait," I say, knowing that we won't.

She just sighs, like she knows exactly what I'm thinking, and hugs me, and orders me to text her every day and watch out for STDs. Darcy, who's been hovering around us with heart-shaped eyes, asks her what that stands for.

I watch the street long after the car has disappeared. I take a deep breath and empty my mind of everything, allowing myself a rare, beautiful, luxurious moment of peace. I think about a deserted chessboard. Only the white king on it, standing on the home square. Alone, untethered, safe from threats.

Free to roam, at least.

Then I go back inside, open my laptop, and write the message I knew I'd write ever since this mudslide of a week started.

Hey Defne,

Is that fellowship still on the table?

PART TWO

Middle Game

Chapter Six

8:55 am—Arrive at Zugzwang! There's coffee & bagels in the
lounge room—help yourself! (Do not eat the rainbow bagel:
it's Delroy's, one of our resident GMs. He gets cranky when
his food has less than five colors.)

9–10 am—Memorize assigned list of opening variations

10–11 am—Memorize assigned list of end-game positions

11 am–noon—Go over assigned list of old games/tactics

noon–1 pm—Break. I've included a list of nearby food places
you might like. (Gambit, the club's cat, will meow at you like
he hasn't been fed since the Weichselian glaciation; it is but
a well-practiced, devious act. Do not feel obliged to share
your meat lunches with him.)

1–2 pm—Analyze assigned opponents' games

2–3 pm—Logical thinking and positional chess review

3–4 pm—Training with software/databases

4–5 pm—W–F Meet with GM trainer to go over weaknesses

Make sure to take a short break as needed to keep your focus.
Workout schedule: 4, 5 days/w, ~30 mins. Keep hydrated
and wear sunscreen, at least 30 SPF (even if it's cloudy—
that's not how sunrays work).

I glance over the schedule Defne just handed me to make sure that I really read what I just read. Then I look up and say,

"Um."

She smiles wide. Today her lipstick is pink, her shirt Spice Girls themed, and her pixie haircut has me wanting to grab the closest utility knife and hack my own hair off. She looks cool in a vintage, effortless way. "Um?"

"Just, this is an awful lot of . . ." I clear my throat. Bite my lip. Scratch my nose. "Chess?"

"I know." Her smile widens. "Great, right?"

My stomach knots. *Why don't you just fake it?* Easton said, and this morning on the New Jersey Transit, during my brand-new one-and-a-half-hour commute, I repeated it to myself like a mantra: This is a job. Just a job. I won't think about chess one second past 5:00 p.m. Chess and I broke up years ago, and I'm not some simpering girl who'll take back her cheating ex after being dumped during the slow dance at prom. I'm only going to do the necessary amount of it.

I just didn't expect the necessary amount of it to equal a ba-jillion craploads.

"Yeah." I force out a smile. I may not be thrilled to be here, but Defne is saving me and my family from the underpass. And I'm not an ungrateful little shit—I hope. "There's a . . . workout schedule?"

"You don't work out?"

I haven't voluntarily broken a sweat since my last PE requirement—junior high, I believe. But she looks surprised to find out that I'm a sloth, so I massage the truth. "Not quite *that* often."

"You'll want to up that. Most chess players work out every

day to build stamina. Believe me, you'll need it when you're in the middle of a seven-hour game."

"A seven-hour game?" I've never done anything for seven hours straight. Not even sleeping.

"Players burn, like, six thousand calories a day while playing a tournament. It's ridiculous." She gestures for me to follow her. "I'll show you your office. You don't mind sharing, do you?"

"No." This morning my roommate repeatedly farted on my pillow because I dared to ask her not to practice her xylophone at 5:30 a.m. "I'm used to it."

The Paterson Chess Club is a room in the rec center, made up of painfully fluorescent light bulbs, vinyl planks sticking out of the floor, and enough asbestos to fry the brains of three generations. I expected Zugzwang to be more of the same, but every corner is sun-dappled hardwood floors, expensive furniture, and sleek, state-of-the-art monitors. Tradition and technology, new and old. Either I underestimated the kind of money one can make from chess, or the place is just a mob front.

I nearly gasp when Defne shows me the library, something straight out of Oxford—if on a smaller scale. There are rows and rows of high shelves, fancy ladders, something that, from watching *Selling Sunset* with Mom exactly twice, I believe is called a mezzanine, and—

Books.

So. Many. Books.

So many books that I recognize from the living room shelves stocked by Dad, then hastily packed away in old Amazon boxes once the silent decision to erase his presence was made.

"You're welcome to use the library whenever you want,"

Defne says. "Several volumes in here are on your reading list. *And* it's right by your office."

That's correct: my office is across the hall, and this time I do gasp, shamelessly. It has three windows, the largest desk I've ever seen, various chess sets that probably cost more than a gall-bladder on the black market, and—

"Quiet, please."

I turn around. On the desk opposite to mine sits a scowling man. He must be in his twenties, but his blond hairline is already receding into deep hills. There's a developed chess game in front of him, and three open books.

"Hey, Oz." Either Defne doesn't notice his frown or she doesn't care. "This is Mallory. She'll take the empty desk."

For a few seconds, Oz stares like he's fantasizing about dis-emboweling me and using my large intestine to crochet himself a scarf. Then he sighs, rolls his eyes, and says, "Your phone is on mute at all times—no buzzer. Computer on mute, too. Use a silent mouse. If you see me thinking and you interrupt me, I *will* stuff my chess pieces into your nostrils. Yes, all of them. No pacing around while you're thinking through games. No per-fume, hot foods, or wrappers. No sniffling, sneezing, heavy breathing, humming, burping, flatulating, or fidgeting. No talk-ing to me unless you're having a stroke and need me to call 911." A thoughtful pause. "Even then, if you can manage to alert me, you can probably dial on your own. Understood?"

I open my mouth to say yes. Then remember the no-talking rule and nod, slowly.

"Excellent." He grimaces at me. Oh God, is that *a smile*? "Wel-come to Zugzwang. We'll get on great, I'm sure."

"Oz is one of our resident GMs," Defne whispers in my ear,

like it explains his behavior. "Have a good first day!" Her hand-wave is a little too chipper, considering that she's leaving me alone with someone who'll flog me if I get the hiccups, but when I glance at Oz, he's back to staring at his game. Phew?

I grab the many lists Defne has given me, retrieve books from the library, boot up the computer, sit in the nice ergonomic chair as quietly as possible (the semi-leather creaks, which I'm sure has Oz on the verge of freeing me from the mortal coil), find the chapter I need to memorize from the fifteenth edition of *Modern Chess Openings*, and then . . .

Well. I read.

It's not a new book to me. Dad would recite passages about initial gambits and positional play in his soothing, low baritone, ignoring Darcy and Sabrina screaming in the background, Mom puttering around the kitchen and warning about dinner getting cold. But that was centuries ago. That Mallory didn't know any-thing about anything, and she had nothing in common with *today* Mallory. And anyway, do I really need to *study* all this stuff? Am I not supposed to *reason* my way through a game?

It seems like a ridiculous amount of work, and over the day it doesn't get any better. At ten, I switch to reading Dvoretsky's *Endgame Manual*. At eleven it's *The Life and Games of Mikhail Tal*. Interesting stuff, but just *reading* about it seems like studying a manual on how to knit without ever touching needles. Utterly pointless. Every once in a while, I remember that Oz exists and look up to find him immobile, reading the same stuff I am—except he doesn't seem to be wondering about the meaning of it all. His hands are a visor on his forehead, and he looks so deep in concentration, I'm almost tempted to say, "Rooks, amirite?"

But he's clearly not here to make friends. When I leave for

lunch (PB&J; yes, Defne's list of nearby eateries looks amazing; no, I don't have the money to eat out), he's at his desk. Just like when I return—same exact position. Should I poke him? Check whether rigor mortis has set in?

The afternoon is more of the same. Reading. Setting up chess engines on the computer. Taking occasional long breaks to rake the Zen garden my desk's previous inhabitant left behind.

On the train back home, I think about Easton's *fake your way* advice. It won't be hard. I'm not going to fall in love with chess again—not if I'm not playing and just reading about distant, abstract scenarios.

"How did the new job go, honey?" Mom asks when I let myself into the house. It's past six and the family's having dinner.

"Great." I steal a pea from Sabrina's plate, and she tries to stab me with her fork.

"I don't get why you needed to change jobs," Darcy says sullenly. "Who would rather organize bocce tournaments for old people than tinker with *cars*?"

There is a specific reason I'm lying to my family about my new job, and that reason is:

I don't know.

Obviously, chess is tied to painful memories of Dad. But I'm not sure that justifies making up an entire new workplace—a senior rec center in NYC I've been hired to manage because a former hookup recommended me. And yet, when I told Mom I'd left the garage, the lie just rolled off my tongue.

I figure it won't make a difference. A job's a job. And this one's temporary, to be left at the door when I come home.

"Old people are nice," I tell Darcy. Unlike Sabrina, who's currently ignoring me and texting thumb-sprainingly hard, she's thrilled to let me steal her peas.

"Old people smell weird."

"Define *old*."

"I dunno. Twenty-three?"

Mom and I exchange a glance. "Soon you'll be old, too, Darcy," she says.

"Yes, but I'll be living with the monkeys like Jane Goodall. And I won't be hiring young people to come to the park to help me feed the pigeons." She perks up. "Did you see any cute squirrels?"

I slip out silently around nine, when the entire house is asleep. Hasan's car is parked at the end of my driveway, the internal light soft on his handsome features. We've been doing this all summer, and when he leans in for a casual peck, as though we have a routine, as though this is a date, I think that maybe it's good he's leaving soon.

I don't really have room for that. Not with everything else going on.

"How are you?"

"Good. You?"

"Great. Taking some really cool courses this semester. I'm thinking of declaring my major—medical anthropology." I listen and nod and laugh in the right places as he tells me about a professor who once said *prostituted* instead of *prosecuted*, but the second the car is parked, I hand him a condom, and then it's hushed words, hurried movements, muscles clenching and releasing.

Easton, who's surprisingly romantic and painfully monogamous, once asked: *Do you feel close to them?*

To whom?

The people you hook up with. Do you feel close to them?

Not particularly. I shrugged. *I like them as people. We're friendly. I wish them the best.*

Why, then? Wouldn't you rather be in a relationship?

Truth is, it seems safer not to. In my experience, commitment leads to expectations, and expectations lead to lies, and hurt, and disappointment—stuff I'd rather not experience, or force others to experience. But I still like sex as a recreational activity, and I'm grateful that I was raised by a very open-minded family. No your-body-is-a-temple, it's-time-to-have-the-talk crap in the Greenleaf household. Mom and Dad discussed sex in almost embarrassingly honest terms, like they would opening a credit card: You'll probably want to try it, there'll be pros and cons, do it responsibly. Here's birth control. We're here if you have any questions. Need a diagram? You sure?

Dad had been gone for almost two years when Alesha Conner smiled at me shyly from across the homeroom, then brushed her hand against mine during a lacrosse game, then giggled while pulling me inside the second stall from the left in the restroom next to the chem lab. It was clumsy, and new, and good. Because it *felt* good, and because for a moment I was just . . . me. Not Mallory the daughter, the sister, the maker of mistakes, but Mallory the breathless, pulling up her panties and sucking one last bruise into Alesha's skin.

I don't have room to care about anything that's not family. I don't have room to care about myself—not that I deserve it. But it's nice to steal brief, harmless, contained moments of fun. To wave Hasan goodbye less than thirty minutes after he's picked me up, slide into bed relaxed and with no intention of thinking about him for months.

After last week's scare, everything's fine. The mortgage is paid (well, the most overdue month, anyway), so are the roller derby fees, and everything is fine. At night I dream of Mikhail Tal telling me with a heavy Russian accent that I should go into the hallway to dial 911, and everything is fine.

DAY TWO IS MORE OF THE SAME. LONG COMMUTE, READING, memorizing. Pondering the hows and whys of this weird schedule Defne put me on. I consider texting Easton and asking her opinion, but we haven't talked since she left last week, and I'm afraid to disturb her while she's . . . I don't know. Beer-ponging, or discovering Leninist Marxism, or having a foursome with her dorm RA who happens to be a sapiosexual furry. *She* knows what she left behind, but *I* have no clue what she's doing, what I'm competing with, whether she's already forgotten about me. Is this FOMO? Yikes. Either way, I'd rather not reach out and avoid being sad because she didn't answer. Plus, the sound of me texting might give Oz a seizure.

I replay Bobby Fischer's games, trudge through a dissertation on the pros and cons of Alekhine's Defense, learn about the Lucena position in the rook and pawn versus rook end game. It feels like a diluted version of chess, with everything exciting sucked out of it. Like taking the tapioca balls out of bubble tea: what's left is okay, but just tea.

I don't care, though, because this is just a job. And it's still just a job on Wednesday morning, when I step into my office and

Oz is already there, in the same position as yesterday. I want to ask if he went home to sleep, but I won't, because I also want to have my eyes *not* gouged out of my skull, so I just spend four hours reading about king safety. At lunch I go to the park and read my commute book (*Love in the Time of Cholera*—kinda sad). When I come back, I'm supposed to learn about pawn structure, but instead I glance furtively up at Oz—still in the same position; does he need to be watered daily?—and hide my book inside a larger one to keep on reading about Fermina's questionable romantic choices. At four I almost pick up my bag and head to Penn Station, then remember:

W–F: Meet with GM trainer to go over weaknesses

The schedule doesn't say where. "Oz? If you had to meet with a GM, where would you go?"

He looks up for the first time in three days—eyes blazing, nostrils flaring. He's going to unhinge his jaw, eat me, and then dissolve me in his gastric acids. "*Library*," he barks. I hurry across the hallway before I become a statistic, expecting to find the rainbow-loving Delroy. The only person inside the room is Defne, sitting at a massive wooden table.

"Hi. Maybe I'm in the wrong place. Oz said—"

"Oz *spoke*?"

"Under duress."

She nods knowingly.

"I'm supposed to meet with one of the GMs, and—"

"That's me."

"Oh." I flush. "I—I'm so sorry. I didn't think you were—" A GM. I flush some more. Why did I not think that? Because she looks cool? Plenty of cool people play chess—I'm not a jock from a nineties teen comedy. Because she runs the place? You need a chess player to run a chess club. Because I'd never heard about her? It's not like we keep a copy of *Chess Monthly Digest* in the bathroom at home. Because she's a woman? There are *tons* of women GMs.

God, is this what Easton means when she talks about internalized misogyny?

"Are you okay?" Defne asks.

"Ah. Yes."

"You look like you're having a pretty intense internal monologue over there. Wouldn't want to interrupt."

"I . . ." I scratch my forehead and take a seat across from her. "I'm always having intense internal monologues. I've learned to tune myself out."

"Good! How were your first few days?"

"Great."

She studies me for a few moments. Today she's wearing cat-eye eyeliner and an upper-arm bracelet shaped like a scorpion. "Let's try again. How were your first days?"

"Great!" She keeps staring. "No, really. Great, I swear."

"You have a bad poker face. We'll have to work on it before tournaments."

I frown. "Why would you think that—"

"If something isn't working about your training program, you should let me know."

"Everything's fine. I've been reading a lot—going through the list you gave me, searching the chess engines. It's fun."

"But?"

I huff out a laugh. "There's no *but*."

"But?"

I shake my head. "Nothing, I promise." But Defne is still staring, like I'm unsuccessfully hiding a shady murderous past from her, and I hear myself add, "Just . . ."

"Just?"

"It's . . ." Something screams at me not to tell her. *If you tell her, it means that you care. Which you don't. You can half-ass this, Mal. You can do it.* "It's just . . . If reading all this stuff is supposed to help me improve my game, I'm not sure that's the case." Defne's expression is not quite as open as usual, and I don't know whether it's because I want her approval or just her money, but I find myself backtracking, panicky. "I'm sure you know what you're doing! Studying's important—reading old games, going through openings. But if one never actually *plays* chess . . ."

I wring my hands under the table. Defne gives me a long, level look before smiling and shrugging. "Okay," she says.

"Okay?"

"Let's play!"

She drags a set between us, white on my side, and adjusts the pieces. Then gestures at me to start. "No clock today, okay?"

"Ah . . . okay."

At the start, I'm almost pumped. Reading about chess without playing has been some serious edging, a little like having a carrot dangled in front of me. Now I get to eat, and it's going to be *so damn good*. Right?

Wrong. Because I realize soon enough that this is nothing like my game against Sawyer. I can't immediately tell the difference, but after thirty minutes or so, when the pieces are developed and the play's underway, I know what's missing.

There was specific tension with Sawyer. A tight, heart-stopping dance made of aggressive attacks, slithering ambushes, obsessive outthinking. This . . . It's nothing like that. I try to make things more exciting by showing initiative, making threats Defne cannot ignore, but . . . well. She does ignore me. Defends her pieces, guards her king, makes some silent filler moves, and that's about it.

We've been playing for forty-five minutes when I try for a breakthrough. I want to penetrate her defenses so bad, I get a little reckless and lose my bishop. My stomach knots in a mix of boredom and dread, and I go back to playing it safe for a while, but—no. Something needs to happen. Her knight, for instance. It's overloaded. It has to defend too many other pieces. If I take it with my rook—

Crap. Defne takes my pawn. Now I'm down two pieces and—

"Draw?"

I look up. She's offering me a draw? *No way.* I frown, don't bother replying, and try for another attack. It's getting late. If I don't make the next train, I'll be home later than usual and Darcy and Mom will be disappointed. Sabrina won't care much, but—

"Check."

Defne's queen comes for my king. Shit. I was so busy mounting an attack that I missed it. But I can still—

"I think we can stop now," she says, smiling at me like she usually does—genuinely kind, amused, without a trace of smugness, even though we both know that she has the upper hand. "You got the idea."

I blink, confused. "The idea?"

"What just happened, Mallory?"

"I—I don't know. We were playing. But you . . . well, no offense, but you weren't really doing much. You were playing . . ."

"Conservatively."

"What?"

"I was playing safe. Cautious. Even when I was in the position to push for an advantage, I didn't. I was defensive. Which confused you, then frustrated you, then had you making basic mistakes because you were bored." She points at the positions. "This is easy for me, because I grew up with a formal chess education. Now, you're a much better player than I am—"

I scoff. "Clearly I'm not."

"Let me rephrase, then: you have more talent. I've seen videos of your plays—your instinct when it comes to attack is fantastic. It reminds me so much of . . . well." She shakes her head with a wistful smile. "An old friend. But there are some basics that all top players know. And if *you* don't know them, any opponent with a solid technical foundation will easily exploit them against you. And you won't even get to use your talent."

I digest what she said. Then nod, slowly. Suddenly, I feel as though I'm running behind. As though I've wasted the past four years. Which . . .

No. It was a decision I made. The *best* decision. Running behind on my way to *where*, anyway?

"It doesn't help that you're ancient," Defne adds.

I frown. "I'm eighteen and six months."

"Most pros start much younger."

"I've been playing since I was eight."

"Yeah, but the break you took? Not good. I mean, this"—she gestures to the board—"was embarrassingly easy for me."

My cheeks redden. I swallow something bitter and rusty, suddenly remembering how much I hate losing.

So. Much.

"What do I do, then?"

"I thought you'd never ask. You do . . ." She grins, pulling a piece of paper out of her back pocket and holding it out to me. I tear it open. "This."

"This is the schedule you handed me on Monday."

"Yeah. I printed two by mistake. So glad it came in handy—I hate wasting paper. Anyway, we'll have you in shape in no time. That is, if you do every single thing on this list. And we'll review everything you learn during our meetings to make sure you're on track."

Fantastic. I'm going to be tested.

I look at the list again—all the things I'm supposed to do every single day for the entire year. I think about my plan to phone it in. About Fermina's questionable romantic choices. About Defne's expectant, encouraging smile.

I want to head-desk. But I just sigh, and nod at her.

Chapter Seven

Oz doesn't talk to me for two weeks—then he does, and I want to kill him.

It's a Thursday morning. I'm at my desk, staring at the Zen garden, replaying a Fischer–Spassky 1972 game in my head, when he says, "So you're coming to the Philly Open."

I startle. Then hiss: "What?"

I'm supremely, virulently, irrationally annoyed that he's interrupting me this close to a breakthrough. Earlier today, while making Darcy's oatmeal (*Call it what it is: Nutella with oats sprinkled on top,* Sabrina muttered while biting into a Granny Smith) I realized that Fischer made a mistake, one that Spassky could have exploited. I've been thinking about it ever since, sure that if Black used the knight to—

"I'll drive," Oz says. "We leave at six."

Why is he talking? I am *so* irritated. "Drive where?"

"To Philly. What's wrong with you?"

I ignore him, go back to focusing on my replay until my afternoon session with Defne. I've started looking forward to my meetings with her—partly because she's the only human adult I interact with aside from Mom, but also because I genuinely need her to parse chess stuff with me. The more effort I put into learning technical stuff, the harder it hits me how little I know, and how much I need a sounding board. I guess that's why GMs have coaches and trainers and whatnot.

"Can we go over a play?" I start the second I step into the library, sliding my notebook in her direction. "I've been stuck on—"

"Let's first talk about Philly Open."

I stop. "Philly what?"

"Philly Open. The tournament. Your first tournament—this weekend."

I blink. "I . . ."

She cocks her head. "You?"

Oh. *Oh?* "I doubt . . . There's no way . . ." I swallow. "Do you think I'm ready?"

She smiles cheerfully. "Honestly, not at all."

Lovely.

"*But*, it's too good an opportunity. Philly's close by, and this is a very reputable open tournament." I only have a vague idea of what that means, which must be why Defne continues. "It attracts elite players, the top ten in the world, but also allows unrated players like you in the rated section. And it's a knockout tournament—the loser of each match is eliminated, the winner moves forward. So you won't be stuck with mediocre players just because you're currently unrated. Provided that you keep winning." She shrugs. The single feathered earring she's wearing tinkles happily. "I'll come with. Worse comes to worst, you just make a fool of yourself."

Super-duper lovely.

And that's how I find myself in the passenger seat of Oz's red

Mini Hatch on a Saturday morning. In the back seat, Defne lists tournament rules as they come to mind, her voice too loud for 7:00 a.m. "Touch-move and touch-take, of course—if you touch a piece during your turn, you'll have to move it. You must record all your moves on the score sheet, in algebraic notations. No talking to your opponent unless it's your turn and you're offering a draw. When castling, use only one hand and touch the king first. If there's a conflict or a disagreement, call one of the tournament directors to solve it for you, don't *ever* fight with—"

"What do you think you're doing?" Oz barks. I follow his eyes to the foil-wrapped PB&J I just took out of my bag.

"Um—want a piece?"

"Eat that—or anything else—in my car, and I will chop your hands off and boil them in my urine."

"I'm hungry."

"Then starve."

I bite the inside of my cheek. Honestly, I think I'm growing on him. "But this is my emotional support sandwich."

"Then have a mental breakdown." He turn-signals and swerves to the right so hard, I almost hit my head against the window.

Philly Open is nothing like the NYC charity tournament, and my first clue is that there's press. Not a ridiculous amount, like the paparazzi on Taylor Swift ca. 2016. But a sizable gaggle of journalists with camerapeople and photographers in tow crowds the hall of the Penn State engineering building, where the tournament will take place. It's vaguely surreal.

"Was there a homicide or something?" I ask.

Oz gives me his usual *you're too dim to live* glance. "They're covering the tournament."

"Are they under the misconception that this is the NBA?"

"Mallory, at least *pretend* to have some respect for the sport that is your livelihood."

He's not wrong. "The tournament won't start for another hour, though."

"They're probably just hoping to get a glimpse of—"

Someone enters the lobby and Oz turns that way—together with everyone else. There's some commotion as the journalists spring into action. I can't see much: a tall head of dark hair, then *another* tall head of dark hair, both peeking through the cameras and the boom mics and heading straight for the elevator. I can't quite make out what the press is asking, only vague words that make little sense together—*in shape, prize, Baudelaire, win, breakup, candidates, World Championship.* By the time I've pushed to my toes, the elevator doors have swished closed. Journalists murmur their disappointment, then slowly scatter about.

Part of me wonders who that was. Another part, the one that's been having odd, invasive dreams of dark eyes and large hands wrapped around my queen, is almost certain that—

"Your registration's all set, guys." Defne appears to hand us lanyards with name tags. "Let's go to the hotel, leave our stuff, then come back for the opening ceremony."

I nod, hoping to sneak in a micronap, when an older man with a mic takes a few steps toward us. "GM Oz Nothomb?" he asks. "I'm Joe Alinsky, from ChessWorld.com. Do you have time for a short interview?"

"Oz is currently number twenty," Defne whispers in my ear while Oz affably answers questions about his shape, training, hopes, favorite pregame snacks (surprisingly: gummy bears).

"Twenty?"

"Twenty in the world."

"Twenty in the world of . . . ?"

"Chess."

"Ah, right."

Defne smiles encouragingly. Considering that I lived and breathed chess for nearly a decade, and how much I still remember about the game itself, I know surprisingly little about the nitty-gritty of professional chess, probably because of Mom's moratorium on rated play. But Defne never makes me feel like I'm a total idiot, even when I ask totally idiotic questions. "The top twenty in the world is important. They're the ones who manage to make the shift from competitive chess to pros."

"Are those not the same?"

"Oh, no. Anyone can be a competitive player, but pros make a living from chess. They support themselves through cash prizes, sponsorships, endorsements from companies."

I picture a Mountain Dew Super Bowl ad featuring a chess player. *Mtn Dew: The Drink of Grandmasters.* "Is Oz also a fellow?"

"The opposite. He *pays* some of the GMs at Zugzwang to train him."

"Oh." I mull it. "Does he have a side job?" Maybe he does Instacart deliveries from 2:00 to 5:00 a.m.? It would explain the perennial bad mood.

"Nope, but he does have a dad who's an exec at Goldman Sachs."

"Ah." I notice that the ChessWorld.com journalist is taking a picture of Oz and quickly step out of frame.

It's stupid. Sabrina and Darcy are with friends till tomorrow; Mom has been better and is working on a few technical writing pieces, which should bring in some needed cash; I told them that I'd spend the day in Coney Island with friends, then stay at Gianna's place for the night. So I *am* lying to them about what I'm doing, but there's no way they'll find out where I really went from the background of Oz's picture on ChessWorld.com.

I'm being paranoid. Because I'm tired and hungry. Because Oz didn't let me eat my PB&J. Monster.

"Hey," Joe Alinsky says, suddenly ignoring Oz, eyes narrow on me, "aren't you the girl who—"

"Sorry, Joe, we gotta go freshen up before the tournament." Defne grabs my sleeve and pulls me outside of the building. The morning air is already too hot.

"Was he talking to me?"

"I feel like Starbucks," she says, walking away. "Do you want Starbucks? It's on me."

I want to ask Defne what's going on. But I want an iced kiwi starfruit lemonade harder, so I jog after her and drop the subject altogether.

WHEN I SIT DOWN FOR MY FIRST MATCH, IN FRONT OF A MAN who could be my grandfather, my heart pounds, my palms sweat, and I cannot stop nibbling at the inside of my lip.

I'm not sure when it happened. I was fine till ten minutes ago, looking around the crowded room, staring down at my lilac sundress, wondering if it's proper chess attire or whether I care. Then the tournament directors announced the start, and here I am. Afraid of disappointing Defne. Afraid of the sour flavor in my throat whenever I lose.

I don't remember the last time I was this nervous, but it's okay, because I still win in twelve moves. The man sighs, shakes my hand, and I'm left with forty-five minutes to kill. I walk around, studying interesting positions. Then I snap a picture of the room and text it to Easton.

MALLORY: i blame you for this

BOULDER EASTON ELLIS: Where are you?

MALLORY: some tournament in philly.

BOULDER EASTON ELLIS: Dude, are you at Philly Open???

MALLORY: maybe. how's higher ed treating you?

BOULDER EASTON ELLIS: I've been sleeping three hours per night and joined an improv group. Put me out of my misery.

MALLORY: LMAO tell me about the improv

The little dots of Easton's reply bounce on the bottom of the screen, then disappear and never come back. Not in five minutes, or ten. I picture a new friend walking up to Easton, her forgetting about me. She's already posted a handful of selfies with her roommates on Instagram.

I slide my phone into my pocket and move to the next round, which I also win easily, just like the third and the fourth.

"Fantastic!" Defne tells me while we share a Costco bag of Twizzlers on the campus quad. She's surreptitiously smoking a cigarette, which she lit saying, *FYI, I am* not *modeling good behavior.* "But it *is* an elimination tournament. The more you win, the better your opponents, the harder it'll get." She notices my frown and bumps her shoulder against mine. "This is chess, Mallory. Painstakingly engineered to make us miserable."

She's right. I get a taste on my last match of the day when I find myself dropping a rook, then a bishop against a woman who looks eerily like my middle school's librarian. Not-Mrs.-Larsen is a fidgety, anxious player who takes ages to make a move and whimpers whenever I advance on her. I alternate between doodling on my score sheet and feeling like I'm at the zoo, staring at the sloth's cage and waiting for it to move. The game drags until the end of the round, when we're both out of time.

"It's a draw," the tournament director says dispassionately, surveying our board. "Black advances."

That's me. I'm moving to the next round because I was at a disadvantage. I know draws are exceedingly common in chess, but I am distressed. Frustrated. No—I'm *furious.* With myself.

"I made tons of mistakes." I tear angrily into the dried apricots Defne handed me. I want to kick the wall. "I should have played rook c6. She could have had me three times—did you see how close she came to my king with her bishop? It was such a *shitshow.* I cannot believe I am even allowed within ten feet of a chessboard."

"You won, Mallory."

"It was a *disaster.* It qualifies for federal relief—I didn't deserve to win."

"Lucky for you, in chess deserving and undeserving wins count the same."

"You don't understand. I messed up so many—"

Defne puts a hand on my shoulder. I quiet. "*This.* This feeling you have right now? Remember it. Bottle it. Feed it."

"What?"

"This is why chess players study, Mallory. Why we're so obsessed with replaying games and memorizing openings."

"Because we hate to draw?"

"Because we hate feeling like we did anything less than our absolute best."

The hotel is a five-minute walk from campus. My room is nothing to write home about, except that it is because: privacy. I cannot remember the last time I had access to a bed without the audience of a twelve-year-old goblin and the three-thousand-year-old demon who possesses her guinea pig. I should take advantage of it. I consider watching a movie. Then I consider whipping out my phone, pulling up dating apps, looking for matches in the Philly area. Perfect no-strings-attached opportunity. Plus, orgasms do improve my mood.

Instead I stare out the window, replaying my last game as the sun sets slowly.

It's like that time I accidentally sexted Mom. Like that day the entire cheering team walked in on me while I pretended to open the automatic sliding doors with the Force. Like in middle school, when I walked into the teachers' restroom to wash my hands and found Mr. Carter sitting on the toilet doing a sudoku. Whenever I do something really embarrassing, for days after the incident I live in a state of utter mortification. At night I close my eyes and my brain will yank me back to the deep well of my shame, projecting cringeworthy scenes in excruciating detail against my eyelids.

(Overdramatic? Perhaps. But I sexted my mother. I am *allowed*.)

My neurons cling to every splinter of embarrassment, won't let go of the mistakes I made during my matches. I won, fine, but in my second game I left my knight open like *that*. Gross. Disgusting. Appal—

Someone knocks.

"Defne asked me to take you to the social and introduce you around," Oz says when I open the door. He's staring at his phone.

"The social?"

"There's a reception downstairs, for players who moved to day two. Defne can't go, since it's only for players. There's free food and booze." He glances up, assessing. "How old are you?"

"Eighteen."

He mutters something about babysitting toddlers and not being Mary Fucking Poppins. "They probably have Sierra Mist somewhere in a cooler. Come."

I'm not sure what I expected from a chess party. Easton aside, I never hung out with the PCC people, but they always struck me as quiet and escapism-driven. The players here, though, look more like businessmen, wearing tailored suits and laughing over champagne glasses. There are no sweater vests in sight, and no one is bemoaning the untimely end of *Battlestar Galactica*. They all seem boisterous and confident. Young. Wealthy. Sure of their place in the world.

One of them notices Oz and leaves his group to approach us. "Congrats on breaking the top twenty." He glances at me—first distracted, then appraising, then lingering. An unpleasant shiver travels up my spine. "I didn't know we could bring a plus-one."

Oh, yeah—the people in this room? They're 98 percent male.

"Is this your sister?" He must be around my age, and theoretically he should be handsome in a classic, wholesome way, but there's something waxy about him, something unsettling in his blue gaze that lifts my hairs.

"Why the hell would she be my sister?" Oz asks.

"I dunno, man." He shrugs. "She's blond. You're blond. And she's way too hot to be your girlfriend."

I stiffen. Surely I misheard.

"Mallory is a chess player, *man*." Oz's tone drips disdain. Whatever antipathy he may harbor toward me, the Office Intruder, it's nothing compared with what he feels for this guy.

He doesn't hate me, after all. I might even be his best friend. How heartwarming.

"If you say so." His English is perfect, if slightly accented. Vaguely Northern European. "Well, honey, this party is for people who won all their matches, so . . . wait." He leans back, making a show of studying me. "Are you the girl who trashed Sawyer at the charity tournament?"

"I—"

"Yes, you are. Guys, this is the chick who humiliated Sawyer!"

I'm not sure what's happening, or why, but the group of people (men, all men) Northern Europe was chatting with give us interested glances, then make their way to us.

"What did you do before the game?" a tall man in his thirties asks. His accent is so thick, I can barely make out the words. "I need that kind of luck."

"Was Sawyer having a really bad day?"

"Were you wearing something low-cut? Is that the trick?"

"Does he know she's here?"

"Well, she's still alive. So, clearly no."

Everyone laughs, and I am . . . paralyzed. Mortified. They're staring like I'm a barely sentient slab of meat, and I feel like a daft child, on display, out of place in my flowy lace sundress. I'm no withering flower, and over my years with Bob I've had my fair share of sparring with older, sexist men, but these people are just so—so blatantly, *openly* rude, I'm not even sure how I should be responding to—

"Excuse us"—Oz grabs my elbow and tugs me away—"we're going to go find some food and maybe people who aren't *total* assholes."

"Oh, come on, Nothomb!"

"Learn to take a joke."

"Let her stay—bet she wants to get to know us!"

I stumble after Oz, mouth dry, hands shaking. He drags me all the way to the other side of the room, to a table laden with hors d'oeuvres. I think I'm shell-shocked. "Who *were* they?"

"Malte Koch and his minions."

I shake my head. Rack my brain. His name sounds familiar, but I can't quite point—

"He's been world number two for the last couple of years. And an asshole since birth, one can only assume. The slightly older guy who asked if Sawyer knows you're here is Cormenzana, number seven, the tall Serbian is Dordevic, somewhere around thirty, but the others are about as consequential as a block of concrete with googly eyes. Little shits whose claim to fame is licking Koch's anus." He rolls his eyes and reaches blindly for a bacon-stuffed mushroom. Oz Nothomb: unexpectedly, an emotional eater. "I had no intention of introducing you. *No one* should ever talk to them. Their place is on a top-secret mining colony on Mars, if you ask me. Sadly, no one ever asks." He chews on his mushroom for a moment and then mumbles a stilted "Sorry about that."

I wonder if it's the first apology of his life. It sure sounds like it. "It's not your fault. But that was . . . I think I hate them?"

"Yeah, I'll get you the club's laminated badge." He studies me. "Are you going to cry?"

"No."

"Are you going to pass eye water?"

"*No*. I'm fine. I just . . ." I lean against the wall behind me. "Are they like that with all women?"

Oz snorts. "Look around. How many women do you see?" I don't need to look around. Instead I reach out for a piece of Brie melted on a crust of bread. "Most women in chess decide to skip these events and compete in women-only tournaments. I bet you're wondering why."

"Total mystery." I put my cheese on a napkin. I have no appetite. "What did it mean, that thing about me being alive?"

He sighs. "Koch and his gang *love* it that you made a fool out of Sawyer, because they hate him. But they also hate that you beat him in one go, because Koch fancies himself to be Sawyer's lifelong rival."

"But he isn't?"

"He cannot compete. No one can compete with Sawyer, really. He's been dominating for nearly a decade. I mean"—he pops half a deviled egg in his mouth—"Koch's an excellent player, if inconsistent. He has moments of brilliance. He's forced Sawyer into draws, and once even came close to beating him. But ultimately they're not comparable."

Must be miserable, losing game after game. "Koch's not aware?"

"I'm sure he's plenty aware, but you've seen the kind of people he holds court with. Their narrative is that Sawyer is some super-evil villain who made chess predictable by being unbeatable—as though he isn't the reason chess got so big among younger people in the last few years. They make it sound like Sawyer's Thanos and

Koch's Tony Stark." He rolls his eyes. "Obviously, they're *both* Thanos."

Oz Nothomb: unexpectedly, a Marvel guy. "Are we . . . in middle school again?"

Oz shrugs. "Close enough. Koch *is* just a child, salty because he always ends up dead in FMK. Meanwhile Sawyer gets all the attention, makes serious bank, ends up on *Time*'s Most Influential, and sleeps with Baudelaires or whatnot—"

"Baudelaires?"

"Yeah. It's this experimental rock band—"

"I know who the Baudelaire sisters are." Sabrina is obsessed. I like their music, too. "Sawyer *sleeps* with them?"

"Yes. And Koch wants that for himself. As if."

My head is exploding. "Did he— Which Baudelaire did Sawyer . . . ?"

"I don't know, Mallory. I do *not* watch reality television."

"Right." I look away, chastised. I'm going to have to google this. I'm *dying* to whip out my phone right now. "Well, the top ten sounds pretty crowded with assholes."

"Mostly just Koch and Cormenzana. And Sawyer, but he's a better brand. I'm not gonna make a friendship bracelet for him, but I'll take a sphincter-clenchingly scary asshole like Sawyer over a slug-slurping-moisture-after-a-rainstorm slimy asshole like Koch any day."

They both sound uniquely horrible, I think as a man plucks custard-filled beignets off the table and quickly scurries away, unimpressed with the anus talk.

"Anyway," Oz concludes, "everyone else in the top ten is less punchable."

I smile faintly. "Is 'less punchable' Oz-speak for 'nice'?"

He arches one eyebrow. "And what does *that* mean?"

"Well, you're not the nicest guy I've ever met."

"I am a motherfucking *delight*, Greenleaf. And for the record, you and I are *equally* hot."

I only stay at the reception for about thirty minutes. Oz is right, and not everyone in chess is a dick: he introduces me to several people who do not insult me, sexually harass me, or act with a messianic-grade superiority complex. But his group of friends is a few years older than me, and I drift out of conversation when it falls on their wives and graduate education. I feel the occasional side glances from Koch's gang on me, and cannot quite relax, so I wave goodnight and head back to my room, ready to spend the rest of the evening berating myself over my mistakes.

Until I see the sign in the elevator. Three little words next to the fifth floor:

Indoor Pool & Gym.

I head there without thinking it through. The entrance for the pool slides open under my keycard. When I peek inside, I'm instantly enveloped by heat, chlorine, and silence.

I love swimming. Or whatever that thing I do that passes as swimming is—float for hours, occasionally move about like a drowning puppy. And here's this amazing, deserted pool.

Problem: I don't have a swimsuit. The tattered bikini that barely fit me a cup size ago is somewhere in my dresser at home, and Goliath is probably using it at this very moment to wipe his butt. What I do have, however, is underwear that's *basically* a bikini. And a strong yearning for a swim.

So I don't think about it too much: I pull my dress over my head, shrug off my sandals, and toss them on the nearest bench. Then I jump in with a loud, messy splash.

I need to minimize my blunders, I tell myself fifteen minutes later, drifting over the water and staring at the ceiling. The reflection of the waves on the ceiling is a mangled, distorted chessboard. *I should aim for breadth of knowledge, since I'm unlikely to achieve much depth in one year. I should play more offbeat lines.*

By the time I lift myself out, I'm in better spirits. I screwed up today, but I'll focus on improving. If I know my weaknesses, I can tailor my training. I train a ridiculous amount anyway.

You are faking your way through this fellowship, a voice reminds me. It's either mine or Easton's.

Well, yes, I reply defensively, grabbing my dress and shoes, rubbing chlorine off my eyes. *But I've signed a one-year contract, so I might as well—*

I stop dead in my tracks.

I'm not alone anymore. Someone is standing right in front of me. Someone barefooted, who's wearing swim trunks. I look up, and up, and up, and up *even more,* and—

My stomach drops. Nolan Sawyer is staring down at me, a faint scowl between his eyes. I'm dumbfounded by the fact that he's . . . fit. His chest. His shoulders. His biceps. No one who spends hours a day moving one-ounce pieces around a chessboard has any business looking like that.

"I— Hi," I stammer. Because he's standing right *there,* and I don't know what else to say.

But he doesn't answer. Just stares down, taking in my now-see-through bra, my panties with little rainbows all over them. The temperature in the pool increases. The gravity, too. I'm concerned that my legs won't hold me.

Then I remember what Koch's friends said: *Does he know she's here?*

Well, she's still alive, so clearly no. Fear pops into me.

Nolan Sawyer despises me. Nolan Sawyer wants to murder me. Nolan Sawyer is staring down at me with the sheer soul-cutting intensity one reserves for those he hates with the strength of a million bloodthirsty bears.

Didn't he once break another player's nasal septum? I remember hearing some stories. Something had happened *after* a tournament, and . . .

Is he going to tear me to pieces? Will the local morgue not know how to put me together? Will they have to call in a professional makeup artist, one of those YouTube beauty gurus who are always making callout videos about each other—

"Cooooooming throuuuuuuuugh!!!!"

Someone runs past us, a blur of dark skin and red trunks, and cannonballs into the pool with a tsunami-like splash. Sawyer mutters something like "Shit, Emil," and it's the escape chance I was waiting for. I scamper away, feet slapping against the wet floor. I'm at the door when I make the mistake of looking behind me: Sawyer is staring at me, lips parted, eyes darker than dark.

So I do the only sensible thing: I slam the door in his face, and don't stop running until I'm in my room, dripping on my bed.

It's the second time I've met Sawyer. And the second time I've retreated like a pinned knight.

Chapter Eight

I sleep poorly, stuck in dreams of chess blunders surveyed by dark, judgmental eyes, and wake up too early with a cramp in my left leg.

"I hate my life," I mutter as I limp into the bathroom, contemplating chopping off my foot with a meat cleaver. Then I find out that my period just started.

I glare down at my ill-timed, uncooperative, treacherous body, and vow to never feed it leafy vegetables again in revenge. *Take that, you little bitch.*

I packed another sundress for today, blue with a lace hem and flouncy sleeves, but the second I slide it on, I remember Malte Koch's leering.

Were you wearing something low-cut?

During sophomore year, Caden Sanfilippo, a junior whom I'd known since grade school and whose mission statement was being a dick, started making fun of me for the way I dressed. My theory is that he had a crush on Easton and was trying to get her attention by annoying her best friend, because the harassment stopped the very day she came out. Either way, whenever I'd walk into physics class, Caden would say creative stuff like *Hey, granola,* or *Good morning, discount hippie,* or *This is not a Whole*

Foods. He did it for months and months. And yet I never once considered altering my fashion choices.

Today, though, I look in the mirror and instantly take off my dress. "Because they'll be blasting the AC," I tell myself, adjusting my jeans and flannel shirt, but I don't quite meet my own eyes before going downstairs.

I win my first match easily, even feeling like a waterlogged corpse. After the abashing performance I gave last night, I'm very careful about each move. It eats up some of my time, but being less reckless pays off.

"Merde," my opponent murmurs before thrusting his hand at me, presumably to concede defeat. I take it with a shrug.

My second opponent is late. One minute. Two. Five. I'm playing White, and the tournament director encourages me to make the first move and start the clock, but it seems dickish.

As eliminations happen, the number of games per turn is dwindling. I can spot only a handful, all at distant tables, and notice that most of the remaining players seem to be around my age or just a little older. I remember something Defne said the other day, when she checked on whether I had upped my workout schedule (I had not): chess is a young person's game, so physically, mentally, cognitively taxing, most of the top GMs start declining in their early thirties. The more I train, the more I believe it.

To pass the time, I doodle flowers on the scorecard, thinking about the email Darcy's school sent: there are two kids with nut allergies in her class, and PB&Js won't be allowed. They suggested sunflower seed butter, but I have a nonzero number of reasons to believe that if Darcy doesn't like it, she'll email CPS that I'm poisoning her—

"I am *so* sorry," a British accent says. A tall guy folds into the chair across from mine. "There was a line for the bathroom, and I had *three* cups of coffee. *The Hunger Games* have nothing on the men's restroom at a chess tournament. I'm Emil Kareem, nice to meet you."

I straighten. "Mallory Greenleaf."

"I know." His smile is open and warm, teeth ivory-white against clean-shaven dark skin. He's movie-star handsome— and he's aware.

"Have we met before?" I ask.

"We have not." He grins again, and the dimple on his left cheek deepens. There's something familiar about him, and it doesn't occur to me what it is until three moves in.

He's the guy from the pool. Running. Wearing red trunks. Splashing water all over me and Nolan Sawyer, giving me a way out. I should probably weigh the ramifications of this information, but Emil is too good a player for me to let my mind drift. His style is careful, positional with bursts of aggressive advances. It takes me several moves to get used to him, and even longer to mount a sensible counterattack.

"Greenleaf," he says with a self-deprecating smile when I take his queen, "show some mercy, will you?" He's the first player to talk to me during a match, and I have no idea how to reply. Clearly chess is destroying my social skills.

"Well, well, well." I have him cornered, and he almost sounds pleased. "I see why he's been going on about you now," he murmurs. Or maybe he doesn't, I can't quite make out the words. He's smiling at me again, pleasant and welcoming.

I want to be his friend.

"Are you a pro?" I ask.

"Nah. *I* have a life."

I laugh. "What do you do?"

"I'm a senior at NYU. Economics." I tilt my head to study him. I thought he'd be closer to my age. "I'm nineteen, but I skipped a few grades," he says, reading my mind.

"Are you a Grandmaster?"

"At this stage of the tournament, every player is. Except for you," he says, with no malice and a lot of relish. "You're going to send several of them weeping into the men's restroom."

"They seem to be more likely to key my car."

"Just the wankers. Let me guess—you met Koch?"

I nod.

"Ignore him. He's a pitiful little slug, forever bitter because he once popped a boner on national television."

"No way."

"Oh, yeah. Prize-giving ceremony at Montreal Chess. Puberty's a bitch, and so's the internet. They meme'd it into eternity. Just like that time he played an entire match against Kasparov with a ginormous booger dangling from his nose. That shit scars you."

I cover my mouth. "It's his supervillain origin story."

"It's not easy growing up as a prodigy in front of the cameras— journalists are *merciless*. When Koch was sixteen and decided to grow a goatee? Everyone took pictures. No one told him that he looked like his own malnourished evil twin with an iron deficiency."

I let out a laugh—a real one, my first since the tournament started, maybe even since Easton left. Emil stares with a kind, curious expression.

"He has no chance," he says cryptically.

I clear my throat. "Have you been playing for long?"

"Since forever. My family moved to the United States when I was little so I'd have the best training available. But unlike all these people"—he gestures around the room—"I only love chess a *reasonable* amount. I'd rather work in finance and play the occasional tournament for fun. It also doesn't help when your closest friend is the best player the sport has seen in a couple hundred years. You keep losing your Spider-Man action figures to him. Makes you rethink your priorities."

I frown. "What do you—"

"White moves forward," the tournament director says, interrupting us. "Next round's in ten minutes."

I hate cutting my chat with Emil short, even more so when I find Defne outside, sitting next to a sullen, gloomy, seething Oz.

"What happened?" I ask.

"My wedding planner is out of peonies. What do you *think* happened? I lost." He glares. "This entire tournament could have been an email."

I scratch my head. I want to ask Defne if she has any Costco Twizzlers left, but it seems like a bad moment. "I bet it was a really tough game."

"Do *not* patronize me."

I snap my mouth shut and retreat one step.

"I saw you were matched with Kareem," Defne says. "He's an excellent player."

"He is."

"How did it go?"

I glance around, uneasy, considering the chances that Oz will attack me. I can probably take him, but what if he whips a sickle out of his pocket? He's *definitely* the portable-sickle type. "I got really lucky. He wasn't in great shape, so—"

"Oh my God." She leaps to her feet. "You *won*?"

"I'm sure it was just—"

She hugs me around the neck. "This is *fantastic*, Mal! Why are you idling here?"

"It was just a game. I didn't—"

"You advanced to *quarterfinals*!"

Wait. "Wait." What? "What? There is no way we're already at quarterfinals."

"Did you even *glance* at the tournament board?" Oz asks acerbically.

"I'm . . . not sure where it is. I was kind of taking it game by game—"

"Pearls before swine," Oz mutters.

I frown. "Did you just call me a pig—"

Defne pulls me back inside the building, excitedly blubbering about my FIDE rating. I expect her to lead me back to the large tournament room, but she takes a sharp turn left.

"Where are we—"

"The quarters are in here." She gives me a long, appraising glance. "Did you want to put on makeup?"

"Why would I want to put on makeup?"

"Oh, you don't have to. I didn't mean to imply that you should." She gives me an apologetic glance. "You look fantastic. You *always* do. Plus, bodies are but the meaty shells we dwell inside as we move about the mortal plane. No need to doll them up for the cameras—"

"The *cameras*?"

"Yeah. Lots of close-ups, too. Come on, we're late."

The new location is smaller, glitzier, and more crowded. There are dozens of chairs rapidly filling up, and people whisper excitedly, like the next *Fast & Furious* movie is about to be screened. All the seats are facing a dais with a row of four boards. The chess sets are fancy. The clocks are fancy. Even the water bottles are fancy—Fiji? At three bucks a pop? *Really?*

"The cameras film each set of players and their board, and the matches are live streamed on those large screens behind the dais. And"—she points to the side—"the commentators are over there."

"Commentators?"

"Don't worry. They work for various streaming services and TV channels. You won't have to listen to them narrate your every blunder." Jesus. "The tournament director will call you onstage, but—"

"Here we are," an announcer starts. "Board one, Malte Koch and Ilya Miroslav. Board two, Mallory Greenleaf and Benul Jackson. Board three, Li Wei and Nolan Sawyer. Board four—"

Anxiety knots inside me. I turn to Defne. "What happens if I win?"

Defne gives me a confused look. "You move to semifinals."

"Against who?"

"Against whoever won their match. Why? What's the problem?"

What's the problem? What's the *problem*? "Defne, I don't want to go against—"

"Please, players, come to the stage and stand next to each other for a few pictures."

My knees buckle. Defne gives me an encouraging nod. Then an encouraging smile. Then, when it's clear that my legs are made of concrete and have no intention of moving, an encouraging push. I trudge through my own dread up the dais, fully expecting to trip on the steps. It is I, Jennifer Lawrence at the Oscars. The temple priestess of public mishaps. Maybe I'll puke all over myself, too, just for fun.

I take myself to the end of the row of finalists, next to Koch (who gives me a *they really let anyone in here nowadays* glance) and two heads down from the other player, the one taller than the others, the one with the deep scowl and the temper.

I refuse to think of his name.

"Greenleaf, right?" the tournament director asks me. I'm tempted to deny it, but I nod. It's not hard to guess: I'm the only player unfamiliar to him, since I'm no one from Noonetown. Not to mention, the only girl. I am careful not to look toward the audience. The sounds of flashes and whispers are bad enough. "Board two. On the right."

I shuffle there, keeping my head down. There are dark, broody eyes I wouldn't want to risk meeting.

Benul Jackson is at least three years younger than me, and pulls out of me some of the best chess I've ever played. There is an elegance to his moves, a beauty to his attacks, a class to his defense, that have me nearly forgetting that I'm in the most public moment of my life. Dad once told me, *There are two types of players: the warriors and the artists*. Jackson is the latter.

He's also painfully slow.

During my other matches, whenever my opponent would take too long to decide on a move, I'd stand and stroll around, stretch a bit, maybe even take a peek at interesting positions on the nearby boards. On the dais, though, I do not dare. What if I slip? What if I stand up too quickly and faint? What if my tampon leaks through my jeans? Malte Koch and his untimely boner should be a cautionary tale for us all. So I just look around—the commentator table, the vertical line on Jackson's forehead, my annotation score sheet. I record my moves and scribble in the margins. Flowers. Hearts.

Deep-set, dark, intense eyes.

I stop myself, flushing. Thankfully, Jackson chooses that

moment to take my rook and fall into my trap. *Too much of an artist, not enough of a warrior.* I win in four moves, and he shakes my hand with a confused, befuddled smile.

"Impressive," he says. "Remarkable. Your style reminds me of . . ." His gaze drifts somewhere past my shoulder. He trails off with a head shake before leaving the dais. When I look around in search of Defne, several journalists eye me curiously. I close my eyes and whisper a silent prayer to the pantheon of chess demigods: *Don't let my next match be against Sawyer. Please. I will gut an abducted guinea pig with depression at your altar.*

It's not until the tables are set up for semifinals that I realize the error of my ways. Someone announces that Sawyer's next game will be against Etienne Poisy. I inspect my brain to make sure that it's not my name—phew—and merrily head to my board, hoping Darcy won't be too mad when I slaughter her pet.

That's when I see Malte Koch, sitting on the White side.

I halt abruptly.

No. Nope. Nope-ity nope. I'm not playing against some dick whose understanding of gender can be dated somewhere in the 1930s. No way I—

"Everything okay?" the tournament director asks, noticing my hesitation.

I'd rather drink a can of Axe body spray while feral raccoons feast on my exposed bone marrow than sit across from this twat. "Yeah." I swallow.

Koch's smirk is quite possibly the most slappable thing I've ever seen, but the way he handles his pieces on the board gives it a run for its money. Whenever he moves them to a new square, he adds a little flourish, like he's putting off a cigarette butt. It makes me want to skin him and use his hide to reupholster Mom's couch.

Then he starts talking. "So you got to semifinals."

"Clearly."

"Are you here through the Make-A-Wish program? Was there a memo about letting you win that I never got?"

I move my pawn in response to the variation of the Ruy Lopez that he opened with, which I happen to have been reading about ad nauseam for the past two weeks. I'm pretty sure it's against the rules for him to talk to me during my turn. Pretty sure, but unfortunately not certain.

"Did you know that single-elimination tournaments are also called sudden death? As in, when you lose, you're as good as dead."

I clench my jaw. "Is the conversation necessary?"

"Why? Are you annoyed?"

"Yep."

Another smirk. "Then yes, it is."

I want to cut his brake lines. Just a little bit.

"You know," he continues casually, "I like it better when women stick to their own tournaments. I find that there's a natural order to things."

I look up and smile sweetly. "I like it better when men shut their mouths and stuff their rooks up their asses, but clearly we can't always get what we want."

Koch's smile widens. He lifts his hand to signal to the tournament director to come closer. "Excuse me, could you ask Ms. Greenleaf to avoid using profane language?"

The director gives me a withering look. "Ms. Greenleaf. You're new here, but you must follow the rules. Like everybody else."

"But—" I snap my mouth shut, cheeks heating.

I'm going to kill him. I am going to murder Malte Koch. Or I'll do the next best thing: annihilate his damn king.

Probably.

Maybe.

If I manage to.

The worst part is—I'm not surprised to hear that he's number two in the world. He's an *excellent* player. I try to pin his queen, but he weasels out. I try to take control of the center, but he pushes me back. I try to wreck his defense line, but not only does he field my attempts, but he also mounts an attack of his own that almost has my king in check.

This is a very dangerous player, I tell myself.

On top of being the worst sack of shit you've ever met, a voice inside me adds. I let out a silent huff of a laugh, and play even more aggressively.

Our game lasts long past the other. Seventy minutes in, and we're still battling. I have his queen, but he got my rook and my knight, and a dense, concrete-like dread starts churning at the bottom of my stomach. I break a sweat. The back of my neck is hot, hair sticky against my skin.

"What are you doing here? Came to see how it's done?" Koch's tone is low enough that the mics won't pick it up. He's not talking to me.

"She'll have you in less than five moves," a deep, assured voice says from behind me. I recognize it but don't turn around, not even when I hear footsteps fading away.

Sawyer's in the midst of some delusion. I'm nowhere near winning. There's next to nothing I can do with this position. Then again, Koch's pretty much at the same . . .

Oh.

Oh.

It suddenly makes sense. *In less than five moves.* Yes. Yes, I only have to—

I move my pawn. A silent, safe move, but Koch's eyes narrow. He has no idea what I'm doing, and I've trained him to expect backdoor attacks. He studies the board like it's a WW2 cypher, and I sit back and relax. I take my pen, annotate my move, attempt a portrait of Goliath on the scorecard to kill time. That stupid beast has truly infiltrated my heart—

Koch moves his knight. I immediately respond with my bishop, confusing him even more. Repeat that, with minimal variations, again, and again, until . . .

"Time's up," the director says. Koch looks up, wide eyed, thin lipped. My intentions dawn on him. "It's a draw. Black moves forward."

Koch's jaw clenches. His nostrils flare. He's staring at me like I just stole his lunch money and bought myself a feather boa with it. Which, let's be real, I kind of did.

Sudden death, I mouth at him.

"You tricked me," he spits out.

"Why? Are you annoyed by it?"

"Yes!"

I smile. "Then yes. I tricked you."

There's a forty-five-minute break before the final, which I spend with Defne and Oz on a patch of grass shaded by the hibiscus bushes. The high of owning Koch fades fast, and another kind of dread rises.

My next match is against Sawyer. And because my brain is made of applesauce, I can't stop thinking about his stern expression. The chlorine-thick air curling the hair on his neck. His full lips almost moving, as though he was ready to say something—

"First tournament, and you get to the final," Oz mumbles, angrily splitting a twig in a million pieces. "Damn child prodigies."

"I'm eighteen," I point out.

"You are a chess *child*. An infant. I could shove my nipple in your mouth and you wouldn't be able to latch on to it."

Defne's eyebrow lifts. "I didn't know you lactated, Oz."

"All I'm saying, she's *unjustly* brilliant. Wunderkinds are so déclassé. You know what's in? Hard work. Tribulations. People like you and Sawyer, with your gifted brains and boundless talent are the real plebs."

I exchange an amused look with Defne. Maybe I'm *not* growing on Oz, but he's sure growing on me.

"Have you ever played against Sawyer?" I ask him.

"Of course. Since he was a brat."

"Ever won?"

He looks away cagily, chin high. "Not as such. But once I offered him a draw and he considered accepting."

"What about you?" I ask Defne.

I'm almost positive her "Yeah. I have" is a bit tense.

"Any tips on how to avoid making a fool of myself?"

"Open with the Ruy Lopez or the Caro-Kann. Castle early." She seems uncharacteristically un-chatty. Reticent. "You'll be fine. You know what to do with Nolan." I wonder why she calls Sawyer by his first name, when last names seem to be the norm in the chess world.

"Assuming that you even *want* to win," Oz points out. "Since he's pants-crappingly terrifying, rudely storms out of press conferences, punches walls, and once called an arbiter a shitstain. Plus, we all know the kind of genes that run in that family, so—"

"Oz." Defne's tone is sharper than I've ever heard it.

"What? It's true. About Sawyer's grandfather *and* about Sawyer being a hotheaded asshole."

"He was a *child*. He was only ever violent with Koch, which he can hardly be blamed for, and hasn't done any of that in *years*," Defne retorts. "When he lost to Mallory, he just sat there and stared after her and . . ." Defne shrugs and holds my eyes. "No need to hold back, Mal. He's a big boy. Whatever you'll dish out, Nolan can take it." Her smile is faint. "He probably *wants* it."

I doubt Nolan No Emotional Regulation Skills Sawyer wants anything from me. I'm probably working myself up for nothing, and he barely knows that I exist, doesn't remember we ever played, and stared at me last night only because I was bathing half-naked in the pool, like some nutty girl who talks with lampposts.

The match will be fine. Uneventful. Not a big deal. A micro deal. Nano deal. I'm probably going to lose, because Nolan Sawyer is Nolan Sawyer, and although the competitive part of my brain (i.e., all of it) hates the idea, it doesn't matter. I am *faking my way* through this fellowship—

"Mallory, do you have a moment?"

Someone pushes a mic into my face the second I'm back in the tournament room. The press seems to have tripled—or maybe it feels like it, because the journalists from earlier are crowding around me, asking what my background is, if I'm training at Zugzwang, what my strategy for the final match is, and my personal favorite: "How does it feel to be a woman in chess?"

"Excuse us," Defne says, smiling politely, then slides between me and the cameras, and weaves us through the crowd. Photos are taken, requests for comments are made, and there's only one escape route.

Up the stage.

Sawyer is already there. Waiting. Sitting on Black, tracking all my movements. His eyes on me are unsettling. There's something too sharp, too ravenous, almost acquisitive about them. Like the match is an afterthought, and *I* am what he came here for.

The only possible explanation is that he does hate me. He's thrilled to have me where he can easily rip me to shreds— revenge for that time I defeated him. He's going to chop me into pieces, smear me with balsamic vinegar, and relish every bite.

Calm down. It's your overactive imagination. Like when you see birds in the sky and can't help but wonder if they're a family of vultures circling above your head. Thick, warm tension coils inside me. Sawyer is an intense guy. He probably does dislike me, but just a little. Leisurely. As a side gig.

I force myself to go to him, step after step after step. Flashes click and the crowd buzzes and I finally get to the White side of the table.

Sawyer stands.

I extend my hand.

He takes it immediately, almost eagerly. Holds it for a touch too long. His palms are warm, unexpectedly calloused.

"Mallory," he murmurs. His voice is deep, somber against the shuttering of the cameras, and I shiver. Something hot and electric licks down my spine.

"Hi," I say. I can't tear my gaze from his. Am I out of breath?

"Hi." Is *he* out of breath?

"Hi," I repeat, like a total idiot. I should just sit down, I really should—

"Excuse me." An unfamiliar voice. I'm focused on Sawyer,

and it takes a while to penetrate. "Ms. Greenleaf, I'm sorry. We need to talk."

I turn. The tournament director is watching our handshake with an apologetic, harried expression.

"There has been an error, Ms. Greenleaf." He clears his throat. "You will not be playing this match."

Chapter Nine

In the Fyre Festival reenactment that is my life, I should probably not find any of this surprising. But even *I* cannot believe—simply *cannot* believe, that I began playing chess three weeks ago, and I'm already involved in drama.

Honestly: what the hell?

People are tweeting about you, Defne whispered a few minutes ago. *This is a sham. Everyone's on your side.*

I nodded blindly, nauseously grateful that neither my mom (too sensible), nor Darcy (too young), nor Sabrina (too TikTok) are on Twitter. I should have gotten myself a chess nom de plume. Quinn Von Rook. Horsie McCastle. Knighterella Black.

"She won." Defne, who introduced herself as my trainer to the tournament director, has been championing me for the past ten minutes. I stand by her side, barely following the conversation.

"She did, yes," the director says, looking *May I have some fentanyl?* levels of pained. He moved the conversation off the stage, ostensibly to be away from the cameras, but the press circles around us like piranhas.

This chess drama I'm involved in? It's apparently *televised*.

"But there *are* rules," the director continues, "and one of these rules is that nothing but the moves should be annotated on the scorecard. And Ms. Greenleaf wrote and, um, drew several things on hers, and—"

"Come on, Russel." Clearly, he and Defne go way back. "It's her first tournament—she had no idea."

"Nevertheless, her opponent has complained. As is his right."

Ten pairs of eyes turn to Koch, who surveys us placidly from the height of his Smirking Personality Disorder. He has the upper hand, and I want to parboil him and feed him to the New Jersey tree frogs.

"What even is the purpose of the no-doodling rule?" I ask Defne under my breath.

"To prevent players smuggling in notes that might help against their opponent. But"—she raises her voice—"it's a rule that hasn't been enforced in ages. It's like those *No eating fried chicken with a fork* laws!"

"What *was* she drawing?" Sawyer asks, deep voice almost lazy.

Because to make things cherry-on-top unpleasant, Nolan Sawyer and his manager—a sharp-looking redhead in her thirties—are part of this conversation. He stands tall, arms crossed on his chest, black blazer over a white button-down open at the collar. *Stupidly attractive*, an unwelcome, inopportune voice inside me blathers.

I quash it silent.

At least seeing Sawyer interact with Koch is tangible proof that he absolutely abhors him. I'm still not sure how he feels about me, but even if he hates me, I'm a distant number two in his disaffections.

"Here." Defne holds my scorecard to him, and I flush.

"I fail to see how doodling a"—he looks at the margin of my sheet; his eyebrow arches—"cat helped her win the match."

"It's a guinea pig," I mutter, and get a dozen dirty looks for my effort.

"Unfortunately, the rule is phrased broadly," Russel explains. "I wouldn't enforce it if it were up to me, but if Ms. Greenleaf's opponent—Mr. Koch—asks us to do so . . ."

"This is bullshit." Sawyer returns the sheet, unimpressed.

"What, Sawyer?" Koch says. The smirking intensifies. "You scared I'm going to beat you?"

Is this the reason Sawyer is siding with me on this? Because he considers me the least dangerous opponent? Tendrils of disappointment curl in my belly, but I remind myself that I don't care—about chess, or about the man-boys who play it. *Faking. I'm faking this.*

"Just shut the fuck up, Koch," Sawyers drawls, more annoyed than angry, like Koch is a mosquito he's swatting away. "If you eliminate Mallory," he says, like he has a right to my name, like he can say a word and make me blush, "I won't play."

Russel pales. Having the best player step away from your tournament is probably not a good look. "If you forfeit, Mr. Koch will automatically win first prize."

"Sounds good to me," Koch says.

Sawyer is silent for a moment. Then he shakes his head bitterly. His jaw clenches, and I expect him to do what he's known for: Yell. Make a scene. Break some stuff.

He doesn't, though. He turns to me with a long, unreadable look. Then mutters, "I hate this shit," and starts up the stage, taking his place once more.

Russel deflates with relief. I barely resist the temptation to trip Koch as he follows Sawyer up the stage.

"Gross," Defne tells me. Her eyes are on the live-feed monitors as the match commences. "What a douchebag."

"Yeah. Honestly, we should leave. I don't want to watch Koch play . . . Wait. What's Sawyer doing?"

He moves his queen knight in a weird pattern. Forward and back, and then again. A bunch of useless, silent moves—while Koch mounts an attack in earnest. With White.

"He's . . ." Defne's grin unfurls slowly. "Oh, Nolan. You little shit."

"What's he doing?"

"Giving Koch a two-moves odds."

"What's that?"

She covers her laugh with one hand. The room is a mess of whispers. "He's telling Koch that he can beat him, even with a handicap."

"That's . . ."

"Some serious shade."

"And reckless. I mean . . . what if he loses?"

He doesn't. Lose, that is. He wins in a number of moves that can only be described as embarrassing—mostly for Koch, who's still flushed with rage during the awards ceremony, when Russel the Tournament Director Who's About to Develop a Drinking Problem hands Sawyer a fifty-thousand-dollar check.

My eyes bulge out so hard, I'll probably need surgery. "Fifty *thousand* dollars?"

"Well, it's just an open tournament," Defne explains. "I know it's small, but—"

"It's a bucketload of money!" I nearly choke on my saliva. I hadn't expected the prizes to be this high. What *is* this, OnlyFans?

I can't help following Sawyer's movements as he nips off the stage. The press immediately crowds him, starts asking questions, but a raised hand from him has them instantly backing off, like they're alarmed by this historically mercurial, unpredictable twenty-year-old. And then . . .

Then, a beautiful girl with long black hair runs toward him, and he's hugging her. I see her laugh, I see him half smile, I see him drape an arm over her shoulder and head for the exit. I look away, because . . . wouldn't want to meet his eyes and end up with my soul devoured. I'm musing over how miserable his girlfriend must be, what with the temper and Baudelaire rumors, when a dark-haired young woman in a BBC badge approaches me. I open my mouth to say *No*, please *no, don't make me do this, don't make me give an interview*, but she talks first. "Mallory? I'm Eleni Gataki. It's so nice to meet you."

"I don't really . . ."

She follows my gaze to her badge. "I'm not here for—I'm just an intern."

"Oh." I relax.

"Well, for now. I hope one day I'll get to cover chess for the BBC. Anyway, I just wanted to let you know, your play at this tournament was *amazing*. I'm already a fan! Between us, the BBC's current chess correspondent is a boring old-school guy who only writes about the same three dudes, but I'm going to try to pitch my first article about you. Well, not *you* you, but your chess style. It's so engaging and entertaining!"

I'm bewildered by her enthusiasm. With no clue how to reply, I'm almost relieved when Russel interrupts us and asks for a moment alone. "So sorry about earlier." He hands me an envelope. "Here is the semifinalist prize."

I open it, expecting . . . I'm not sure. A brochure on how to effectively use the Sicilian Defense. A coupon for two hours of counseling with a sports psychologist. *Lilo & Stitch* stickers.

Not a check. For ten thousand dollars.

It's clearly a mistake. And yet my first greedy, ugly instinct is to pocket it. Conceal it. Abscond with it.

I want this money. Oh, the things I could do with it. I could be zero months behind with our mortgage. Set up a savings account. Pay for my auto-mechanic certifications. Say yes to Darcy and Sabrina next time they ask for whatever trivial crap they've fallen in covet with. Roller skates. Slime. Piano lessons. A cotton-top tamarin plushie.

God, *how* I want this money. So much so, I need to get rid of it. Immediately.

"I have to tell you something," I say to Defne. She's washing her hands in the unsurprisingly deserted ladies' restroom. "I— They gave me a check. By mistake, I think. Ten thousand."

"It's the semifinalist prize." She briefly struggles with the soap dispenser. "Didn't you see the info on the tournament website?"

There is a tournament website? "I . . ." I blink. *Ten. Thousand. Dollars.* Oh God. But—I can't. It should go to her. "Here." I hold the check out. "You sponsored me. You have it."

"Nuh-uh. You *earned* it. Though you might have to pay taxes on it. Check with your accountant."

My accountant. Right. The one currently on vacation in Seychelles with my hedge fund manager.

"I'll go get the car so we can head home, but Mal." She gives me a loaded look. "The prize for the World Championship is two million dollars. The Challengers, a hundred thousand. Just making sure you know, since you hate tournament websites." She leaves with a wink, and I stare down at my check for a long time.

Plan Fake Your Way Through Chess is going to need some serious reworking.

Chapter Ten

Defne orders me to stay home on Monday, to sleep off my "chess hangover" and the "tournament crud." It's a rare free day without my sisters underfoot, and when I go to bed on Sunday night, I'm fully committed to drooling on my pillow till midmorning, then going to the Krispy Kreme drive-through in my PJs to purchase my weight in donuts, then eating 90 percent of them with Mom while we watch *Hoarders* on YouTube.

I fail miserably.

For reasons that may have to do with the check hidden in the inside pocket of my hobo bag, I'm up at six thirty, scrolling down ChessWorld.com, browsing through every game Malte Koch has ever played.

There are a lot, and he's a damn good player.

But, also: he's not without exploitable weaknesses. I'm half comatose, eyes full of sleep boogers, and yet I'm finding blunders in his games.

Also, also: I have a new archenemy. *I like it better when women stick to their own tournaments.* My life mission is to repeat the words back to him while I checkmate his useless, bloated king.

"Pleeeease, drive us to school!" Darcy asks after giving me her back to fart in my direction—her new favorite morning ritual. In the car she talks my ear off: male seahorses carry the offspring, jellyfish are immortal, pigs' orgasms last thirty minutes (mental note: install parental control software). Sabrina sits quietly, headphones in her ears, head bent to her phone. I try to remember whether she has said anything this morning. Then I try to remember the last time I've had a conversation with her.

Mmm.

"Hey," I tell her at drop-off, "you get out an hour before Darcy, right?"

"Yeah." She sounds defensive.

"I'll come get you early, then."

"Why?" Now she sounds defensive *and* dubious.

"We can do something together."

"Like what?" The defensiveness is still there, but laced with something else. Hope, and maybe a bit of excitement. "We could get coffee at that place on the corner."

"Okay. Decaf, though," I add.

She frowns. "Why?"

"You're too young for caffeine." The frown deepens. I'm losing her. "I can help you with your homework," I offer, trying to revive her enthusiasm.

"I drink coffee all the time. And I've been doing my homework alone for years. If you haven't noticed, I'm not nine anymore, Mal." She rolls her eyes, and I know I've lost her. "I'll just hang out outside school with the other derby girls so you don't have to do two trips." She slips out of the car without saying goodbye, and I seethe about the youths till I get to the credit union.

I'd love to deposit the check to the family account, but I can't think of a believable excuse that won't involve me mentioning chess. *Mom, I won the Powerball. I microwaved Darcy's oatmeal for too long and it turned into a diamond. I have a secret writing career in furry erotica.* Yeah. No.

I pay outstanding bills, deposit what's left in my account, and run errands that would usually fall on Mom. And if in the grocery line, at the recycling center, by the library's return desk, while I wait for Mom to finish working to have lunch with her— if whenever I have ten minutes to myself I spend them analyzing Koch's games on my phone, well . . .

I shouldn't. Boundaries and all that. Chess is just a job, and today I'm off. I made a promise to myself.

But it's okay, a voice rebuts. *You're thinking of prize money. You're* not *falling in love with chess again. You're firmly out of love.*

Yeah. Exactly. Precisely. That.

I pick up my sisters midafternoon and I'm aggressively thrown into the Grade 7 Cinematic Universe, which is more riveting than a Brazilian soap opera.

". . . so Jimmy was like, 'Pepto pink makes me throw up,' and Tina was like, 'My shirt is Pepto pink,' and Jimmy was like, 'No, your shirt's a *good* pink,' and Tina googled Pepto pink and it was the same color as her shirt, and Jimmy was like, 'What do you want me to say?' and Tina was like, 'Admit that you hate my shirt.'"

"And what did Jimmy say?" I ask, pulling up our driveway, genuinely entertained.

"He was all, like—"

"There's a guy on the porch," Sabrina interrupts us.

"Probably the mailman," I say distractedly. "What did Jimmy do?"

"That's *not* the mailman," Sabrina says. "I mean, I *wish*."

I look at where she's pointing. Then immediately flatten myself as deep into the driver's seat as I can go. "Shit."

"Should you be saying *shit* in front of us?" Darcy asks.

"Yeah—what happened to the pedagogical modeling of appropriate behaviors?"

Impossible. He's *not* here. He can't be. I'm hallucinating. Paranoid delusions. Yes. From the chemicals in the Twizzlers. All that dye.

"Mal. Mal?"

"What's wrong with her?"

"A stroke, maybe? She's starting to be of a certain age."

"Call nine-one-one!"

"On it."

"No—Sabrina, *don't* call nine-one-one. I'm fine. I just thought I saw . . ." I glance to the porch again. He is still there.

Nolan.

Sawyer.

Is.

On.

My.

Porch.

Well. It's either Sawyer or an alien wearing his skin. I'm kind of rooting for option two.

"Do you know him?" Sabrina asks.

"She sure looks like she does," Darcy says. "Is he another one of your sex friends?"

"Maybe he's her stalker," Sabrina offers.

"Mal, you have a stalker?"

Sabrina snorts. "You didn't let me watch *You* because I'm fourteen, and now I find out that you have *your own stalker*?"

"Should we run him over? Does blood stain wood?"

"No!" I raise my hands. "He's *not* my stalker, he's just, um, a . . . friend." *Who might hate me. If I am found strangled, look into his credit card purchases. You'll find rope. Or lots of floss.* "A colleague, actually."

Darcy and Sabrina exchange a long, dangerous look. Then they jump out of the car with an overeager "Let's go *meet* him!" I hurry after them, hoping this is a lucid dream.

Well. Nightmare.

Sawyer is leaning against the porch, arms crossed on his chest, eyes traveling between the three of us as if to soak up the resemblance that always leaves people befuddled, and I have to stop myself from blurting out, *They're my sisters, not my daughters—* yes, people do assume. He's wearing jeans and a dark shirt, and maybe it's because there are no chessboards, no arbiters, no press in sight, but he almost doesn't look like himself. He could be an athlete. A college student on a football scholarship. A stern, handsome young man who has not (allegedly) dated a Baudelaire, who has not (confirmedly) called an interviewer a dickhead for implying that his game looked tired.

"Are you Mal's friend?" Darcy asks him.

He cocks his head. Studies her. Doesn't smile. "Are *you* Mal's friend?"

If the world were fair, Darcy and Sabrina would roast him and heckle him off our property. And yet, they giggle like they usually do in Easton's presence. What the—

"What's your name?"

"Nolan."

"I'm Darcy. Like Mr. Darcy. And this is Sabrina. Like Sabrina Fair. Mal didn't get a literary name because . . . we're not sure, but I suspect that our parents took a look at her and decided to temper their expectations. She said you work together?"

He nods. "We do."

"At the senior center?"

Nolan hesitates, puzzled. Looks at me for the first time. Finds me on the verge of a panic attack. Then says, "Where else?"

"Do you ever feed the squirrels?"

"Guys," I interrupt, "go tell Mom we're home, okay?"

"But Mal—"

"Now."

They drag their feet and slam the screen door, like I'm depriving them of a fantastic afternoon staring at Sawyer. It's not until they're out of earshot that I let myself focus on him again.

There is, I believe, a bit of a standoff. Where I look at him, he looks at me, and we're both fairly still. Assessing. Feeling each other out. In my case, monitoring escape routes. Then he asks:

"Are you going to run away?"

I frown. "What?"

"You usually run away from me. Are you going to?"

He's right. He's also *rude*. "You usually lose your king to me. Are *you* going to?"

I was aiming for a sharp, jugular-cutting jab. But Sawyer does something I did not expect: he *smiles*.

Why is he *smiling*?

"Where did you get my address?"

"It wasn't difficult."

"Yeah, that's not a real answer."

"No. It isn't." He turns around, taking in my yard: the rusty trampoline I can't be bothered to throw away, the apricot tree too dumb to yield fruit, the minivan I patch up once a month. I feel vaguely embarrassed, and hate myself for it.

"Could I have a real answer, then?"

"I'm good with computers," he says cryptically.

"Did you hack Homeland Security?"

His eyebrow lifts. "You think Homeland Security stores home addresses?"

I don't *know*. "Is there a reason you're here?"

"Do you really work at a senior center?" He faces me again. "On top of chess?"

I sigh. "Not that it's any of your business, but no."

"Lying to your sisters, huh?"

"It's not a good idea, mentioning chess around my family." And I'm telling him this . . . why?

"I see." He leans his forearm against the rail, drumming his fingers unhurriedly. "You know, I played against your father once."

I freeze. Force myself to relax. "I hope you won." *I hope you humiliated him. I hope he cried. I hope it hurt him. I miss him.*

"I did." He hesitates. "I'm sorry that he—"

"Mallory?" Mom leans out from the doorframe. While we're talking about Dad. Shit, *shit*— "Who's your friend?"

"This is . . ." I close my eyes. She probably didn't hear. It's fine. "This is my colleague Nolan. We work together, and we . . . made plans to go get a bite, but I forgot about it, so he'll just . . . he'll leave now."

Nolan smiles at her, looking not at all like the sullen man-child I know him to be. "Nice to meet you, Mrs. Greenleaf."

"Oh, that's too bad. Nolan, would you like to stay for dinner? We have plenty of food."

I know what Nolan sees: Mom's in her late forties, but looks older than that. Tired. Fragile. And I know what Mom sees: a young man who's taller than tall and handsome to go with that. Polite, too. He showed up to visit the daughter who dates a lot but never brings anyone home. Ripe for misunderstanding, this situation. It needs to end ASAP.

That's what I'm thinking when I open my mouth to tell Mom that Nolan really can't stay. What I'm thinking when Nolan is just a fraction of a second quicker and says, "Thank you, Mrs. Greenleaf. I would love to."

HE SITS WHERE DAD USED TO.

Which doesn't mean much, since our dinner table is round. And it makes sense: he's left-handed, so am I. We should cluster—avoid elbowing the righties. Still, there's something beyond weird in Nolan Sawyer taking jaw-unhinging bites of Mom's meat loaf, wolfing down a portion, two, helping himself to more green beans, nodding gravely when Darcy asks, enthralled by his appetite, "Do you happen to have a tapeworm?" He obviously enjoys Mom's cooking. He made a deep, guttural sound after the first bite, something that reminded me of . . .

I flushed. No one else paid attention.

"Have you been working at the senior center long, Nolan?" Mom asks.

I stiffen, spearing a single green bean. I press my knee

against Nolan's under the table, to signal him to be quiet. "We don't have to talk about—"

"A while," he says smoothly.

"Do you like it?"

"It has its ups and downs. I used to love it, but a little . . . sameness set in, and I actually thought about quitting. Then Mallory arrived." His knee suddenly pushes back against mine. "Now I love it again."

Mom cocks her head. "You two must work very closely together."

"Not nearly as much as I'd like."

Oh my God. Oh. My. God.

"How's Mallory at work?" Darcy asks. "Do the old people like her?"

"She has a reputation for pocketing puddings." Everyone stares at me like I'm that Pharma bro who hiked basic meds' prices. "And for public near-nudity."

Mom's eyes widen. "Mallory, this is concerning—"

"He's kidding." I kick Nolan's calf, hard. He doesn't seem to care, but he *does* trap my foot between his own. "He's known for his *terrible* sense of humor." My leg is now twined with his. Cool. Cool.

"Okay." Sabrina sets her glass down. "I'll go ahead and ask it, since we all want to know: Are you guys having sex?"

"Oh my God." I cover my eyes. "Oh my *God*."

"Sabrina," Mom chides, "that is *really* inappropriate." She turns to me. "But yes, are you?"

"*Oh my God*," I moan.

"We aren't," Nolan says between bites of meat loaf. Third helping.

Oh.

My.

God.

"Maybe you'll have sex tonight?" Darcy asks. "Is that why you came over?"

My twelve-year-old sister, who sleeps with a stuffed fox, just asked the world's number one chess player if he came over to bang me. And he just replies, matter-of-fact, "It seems unlikely. And no, it's not why I came."

"Did you know Mal has sex with boys *and* girls?" Darcy adds. "I'm not outing her—she told me I could tell anyone."

Nolan glances at me. Lightning-quick. "I did not."

"He doesn't care, Darcy. And FYI, that didn't mean '*please* go tell everyone.'"

"Would you like more meat loaf, Nolan?" Mom interjects, and leaves for the kitchen when Nolan nods gratefully.

"So, Nolan," Sabrina continues, "do you *also* have sex with boys and girls?"

"Jesus." An image of the entire Baudelaire family flashes in my head. "Okay, I'm going to nuke this conversation and remind you that you cannot ask people you barely know about their sexual orientation during dinner. Or *at all*."

"Maybe he doesn't mind," Sabrina says. "Do you mind, Nolan?"

"I don't," he says, remarkably unperturbed.

Sabrina shoots me a triumphant smile. Sistercide. Sistercide is the only option. I'll make Darcy help me hide the body. Or Mom. Or Goliath. "So, boys *and* girls?"

Nolan shakes his head. "Nope."

"Mostly girls?"

"No."

"Mostly boys?"

"No."

Sabrina looks briefly confused, then delighted. "You don't want to exclude nonbinary people!"

"So," Darcy interjects, "*when* are you guys going to have sex?"

Nolan's "Hard to tell" overlaps with my "Never!" and completely swallows it.

I face-palm.

"I bet Mallory's really good at it. She sure practices a lot."

Nolan gives me a long, assessing look that's mercifully interrupted by Mom arriving with more meat loaf. "Do you have any siblings, Nolan?" she asks. I've never been more grateful for a change of topic.

"Two half brothers. On my father's side."

"How old are they?"

He squints, as if trying to remember a remote piece of information. "Somewhere in their early teens. Maybe younger."

"You're not sure?"

He shrugs. "I never see them."

Mom's brow furrows. "You must spend most holidays with your mother."

He lets out a hushed laugh. Or maybe it's a scoff. "I haven't seen either of my parents in years. Usually a friend invites me over."

"Why don't you see your parents?" Darcy asks.

"A . . . difference of opinions. Over my career."

"They don't like the senior center?"

Nolan bites back a smile and nods solemnly.

"That's kinda sad," Darcy says. "I see my family every day of every week of every year."

"That's *also* kinda sad," Sabrina mumbles. "Wouldn't mind some space."

Darcy shrugs. "I like it, that we're always together. And we tell each other everything."

The pointed look Nolan gives me makes me want to kick him in the gonads, but my leg is still stuck between his, so I consider drowning myself in the gravy. A slow, nutritious, tasty death.

I'm not sure how it happens, or what atrocious deeds I committed in past lives to deserve this indignity, but after dinner Nolan gets talked into staying "just a little bit longer! Pleeeeease!" and watching TV with my sisters.

"Do you like *Riverdale*?" Sabrina asks eagerly. She and Darcy flank him on the couch, and Goliath is in his lap. ("What a strangely familiar beast," Nolan said when she deposited him in his hands. "I wonder if I've recently seen a portrait of him." I nearly forked him in the eye.) Mom leans against the doorframe, taking in the scene with a level of enjoyment that I vastly resent. I've been sent to fetch ice cream sandwiches, then sent back when I brought the chocolate kind instead of strawberry.

"I've never seen *Riverdale*."

"Oh my God. Okay, so, that's Archie and he's, like, the main character, but everyone likes Jughead better because hello, *Cole Sprouse*, and there's this murder that . . ."

"He's cute," Mom whispers while I'm loading the dishwasher.

"Cole Sprouse?"

"Nolan."

I huff. It doesn't come out as indignant as I'd like. "No, he's not."

"And he seems to have great taste."

"Because he ate a stomach-pumping amount of your meat loaf?"

"Mostly that. Only secondarily because he doesn't seem to be able to look away from my most oblivious daughter."

I'm 93 percent sure that he's about to place a napalm bomb in our basement, I don't tell her. *Or maybe he wants to rob us. He'll abscond with the family nickel jar the second we're distracted. And with what's left of the meat loaf.*

I still have no idea why he's here. He's asking my sisters "Which one of the characters is *Riverdale*?" with his soothing NPR voice, making them giggle and slap his forearms, and I want him gone from my house. Stat.

And yet it's over one hour before Mom reminds Darcy that she needs to finish her English homework, and Sabrina locks herself in her room to video-chat with derby friends about how Emmalee should be jammer and what's wrong with Coach these days, anyway?

"I'm going to bed," Mom says, a tad too pointedly. I look outside the window: the sun's not done setting.

"Nolan's leaving, too."

"He doesn't have to." She gives him a brilliant smile and walks away, leaning on her cane.

"Yes, he does," I yell after her.

Eavesdropping is not something I'd put past my family, so when Nolan follows me outside, I walk all the way to the apricot tree. This time of the year, it's little more than a handful of leaves on scrawny branches—as any other time.

Hands on my hips, I turn around to face him. At dusk he's even more imposing than usual, the angles and curves of his face clashing dramatically against each other.

Honestly, it doesn't make sense. I shouldn't find him this handsome, because he simply isn't. His nose is too large. His jaw too defined. Lips too full, eyes set too deep, those cheekbones too . . . too *something*. I shouldn't even be *thinking* about this.

"Now that you've eaten approximately twelve pigs with my

mom's meat loaf as a vehicle, do you mind telling me why you're here?"

"Pretty sure it was ground beef." He reaches for one of the tallest branches. Easily. "Does your family think we're dating?" He doesn't look upset. More in the ballpark of proud.

"Who knows." *Probably.* "Is it a problem?"

I want him to say yes, and then throw in his face that it's his fault for showing up unannounced. He thwarts my move. "Who doesn't love a good fake dating scheme."

I arch my eyebrow. "I'm surprised you're familiar with the concept."

"A friend is a huge Lara Jean fan. I sat through, like, six of her movies."

He means his girlfriend. "There are only three."

"Felt like more."

He's so assured. So effortlessly at ease. You'd expect a known sore loser with temper problems who spends 90 percent of his time studying opposite-colored bishop end games not to excel in social situations. And yet.

I think about the mountains of self-confidence he must have within himself. Wherever they might come from. *Look at him,* the voice in my head supplies. *You know where they're from.*

Oh, shut up.

"Why are you here, Nolan?"

He lets go of the branch. Watches it bounce a few times, then settle against the darkening sky. When he reaches out for me, I'm ready to roundhouse kick him in the chin, but he pushes a loose strand of hair away from my face. I'm still dizzy from the brief contact when he says, "I want to play chess."

"You couldn't find someone in New York? You had to drive all the way to New Jersey?" I'm assuming he owns the Lucid Air parked in front of the Abebes' place. Because of course he'd own my dream car.

"I don't think you understand." He holds my eyes. I think his throat moves. "I want to play chess with *you*, Mallory."

Oh.

Oh? "Why?"

"It should have been you, yesterday. It was . . . I had you there. In front of me, across the board." His lips press together. "It should have been you."

"Yeah, well." *It would have been fun if it had been me.* A knot of regret squeezes inside me, and I have the sneaking suspicion that it has nothing to do with the prize money, and everything to do with the fact that my match against this guy—this sullen, handsome, odd guy—was the most fun chess I've ever played. "Malte Koch had other ideas."

"Koch is a nonentity."

"He's the second-best player in the world."

"He has the second-highest *rating* in the world," he corrects me.

I remember the way Nolan humiliated him yesterday, and say, "Have you considered that Koch might be less of an all-around jerk to all of us if you spent a couple of minutes per week pretending to indulge his delusions of archrivalry?"

"No."

"Right." I start to turn around. "Well, this was fun, but—"

His hand wraps around my forearm. "I want to play."

"Well, I don't play."

His eyebrow lifts. "Could have fooled me."

I flush. "I don't play unless I'm at work."

"You don't play unless you're at Zugzwang?" He's clearly skeptical. And still holding my wrist.

"Or at a tournament. Never in my free time. I try not to think of chess at all in my free time, actually, and you're kind of making it impossible, so—"

He scoffs. "You think about chess all the time, Mallory, and we both know it."

I would laugh him off, but I've been going over Koch's games all day in my head, and the jab hits close. I pull free, ignoring the lingering warmth of his skin, and square my shoulders. "Maybe *you* do. Maybe *you* are thoroughly addicted. Maybe you wrap chess sets in plastic bags and hide them in your toilet tank because you have nothing else to think about." I remember the Baudelaire rumor, and it hits me that out of the two of us, the one without a life is certainly *not* Nolan. Still, I've come too far to stop. "But some of us see chess as a game, and enjoy work-life balance."

He leans in. His face is just a few inches from mine.

"I want to play chess with you," he repeats. His voice is lower. Closer. Deeper. "Please, Mallory."

There's an openness to him. A vulnerability. He suddenly looks younger than I know him to be, a boy asking someone to do something very, very important for him. It's hard to say no.

But not impossible.

"I'm sorry, Nolan. I'm not going to play against you unless it happens in a tournament."

"No." He shakes his head. "I can't wait that long."

"Excuse me?"

"You barely have a rating. You're not going to be allowed into invitationals or super-tournaments for years, the next open isn't until late spring—"

"That's not true," I protest, even though I have no idea. His stubborn, displeased, near-worried expression lets me know that it likely is.

Something twists in my stomach.

"Why?" he asks. "Why this bullshit no-play-outside-work rule?"

"I don't owe you an explanation." *Then why are you giving him one?* "But . . . I don't like chess. Not like you do. It's just a job, something I fell into backward, and . . ." I shrug. It feels tense, unnatural. "It's just the way I want it."

He studies me, silent. Then: "Is this because your father—"

"*No.*" I close my eyes. There's a loud roar in my ears, drums pounding at my temples. Slow, deep breaths make it recede. A little. "No." I hold his gaze. "And please, don't *ever* bring up my dad again."

He briefly looks like he won't let it go. Then nods. "I'll give you the money."

"What?"

"I'll give you the tournament prize. The one you should have been competing for."

"Are you for real?"

"Yes."

"If I beat you, you'll give me fifty thousand dollars."

"I'll give it to you even if I win."

I laugh. "Bullshit."

"I'm not lying. Fifty thousand dollars is nothing for me."

"Yeah, well." Having him say so in front of my lower-middle-class house-and-apricot-tree combo stings. "Screw you."

I walk away again, and this time he doesn't grab my wrist. He doesn't need to: with two steps he's in front of me, between me and the house. The sun has set again, and the garden is pitch black. "I meant that I'm good for the money. I'll pay you to play with me."

"Why? Is it because you can't stand to have someone best you? Are you like Koch, unable to accept that you once lost to a woman?"

"What?" He looks genuinely appalled. "No. I am *nothing* like him."

"Then *why*?"

"Because," he near-growls. "Because I—because *you*—" He stops abruptly and takes a few steps away. He makes a frustrated, abortive gesture with his arm, something I recognize from his rare losses at chess.

I guess I won, then.

"Listen, Nolan. I'm sorry. I . . . I'm not going to play with you." I expect the disappointed expression on his face. The mirror feeling in my chest, not so much. "It's not personal. But I promised myself that I'd keep chess at a distance."

I turn without saying goodbye and walk back inside the house, hating myself all the way to my room for the odd feeling of loss in the pit of my stomach.

I'm stupid. He just hates the idea that we played once and he lost. I'm not special. This is not about me—it's about him. His status. His insecurities. His need to dominate.

I let myself into my room. My head throbs, and I cannot wait to go to bed. I cannot wait for this day to be over.

"Did Nolan leave?"

Darcy's voice startles me. I'd forgotten she'd be in here, doing homework at her desk.

"Yes. He had to go home."

"Well, that's understandable."

I nod, looking for my pajamas.

"He must be very busy. He's the number one chess player in the world, after all."

Chapter Eleven

I blink.

I blink again.

I blink once more and make a split-second decision: lie. "You have him confused with someone else, honey." I cough. "Did you need help with your homework?"

"Nolan Sawyer, right?"

"It's just two people with the same name." I wave my hand airily. "Like when you were in kindergarten and there were, like, four Madison Smiths in . . ."

She turns her tablet around. It's on Nolan's Wikipedia page, which includes a high-res candid of him scowling down at a chessboard. As much as I'd love to deny it, he is *undeniably* the same guy who just raided our meat loaf stash.

I blink.

I blink again.

I blink once more and make another split-second decision: lie again. Darcy's twelve. I can talk myself out of this.

I gasp dramatically. "No *way*! Are you serious?" I am a terrible actress. I'm talking elementary school play level. "He never mentioned. I'll have to ask him next time we . . ."

I fall quiet, because Darcy has navigated to a new page. It has a picture of two people: Nolan, looming darkly on one side of the board, shakes the hand of a blond girl wearing a flannel top that looks just like mine. Neither smiles or speaks, but they're holding each other's eyes in a way that seems almost intimate, and—

My eyes fall on the title of the page: *Who is Mallory Greenleaf, chess's new breakout player?*

"Fuck."

"There's a whole article about you."

"Fuck."

"And pictures."

"Fuck."

"And even a video, though I can't make it work. I think pop-ups are blocked?"

"Fuck fuck *fuck*." Of course this shit's online. The press was everywhere—what did I think they were going to do with the footage, scrapbook it? "Fuck."

"You should stop swearing in front of twelve-year-olds. Mrs. Vitelli says that my brain's still all squishy. I'll probably end up in juvie if you swear just once more."

"*Fuck.*"

"Here goes another promising young woman."

I pluck the tablet from Darcy's hands. The article is on ChessWorld.com. The header boasts *Largest chess website, over 100 million unique visits per month.*

I groan.

    . . . *entered the tournament as an unrated player, but surprised everyone by not losing any match. Greenleaf, who currently trains at Zugzwang with GM Defne*

Bubikoğlu, is the daughter of the late GM Archie Green-
leaf (peak FIDE ranking: 97), who passed away a year
ago. Last month, at the NYC Charity Tournament, she
defeated World's No. 1 Nolan Sawyer. Sawyer had a
chance for a rematch at Philly Open, but—

I toss the tablet onto the bed. My hands are shaking. "How did you find this?"

Darcy shrugs. "I was doing homework."

"Homework."

"It's genealogy week. I'm supposed to write about my paternal great-grandparents, and it's not like I can ask you or Mom, since you both go in to covert operation mode whenever I mention Dad, so I googled Archie Greenleaf, and I'm sorry if I—" Darcy's voice is high pitched, and she looks about to cry. My heart twists.

"Okay—it's okay! You didn't do anything wrong, honey. I swear I'm not mad. And . . ." She's right that we don't really discuss Dad, or what happened to him. Maybe we should? Maybe *I* should be talking about Dad to her? Not Mom—it would be painful for her. It would be my responsibility.

It's only fair, considering that it's my fault in the first place he's not around anymore.

I kneel in front of her and take her hand in mine. "Do you want to talk about Dad?"

"Not now." The relief that sweeps over me is embarrassing. "I'd like to know what a Zugzwang fellow is, though."

Walked right into that one. "It's a . . . a job. I am being paid to learn about chess. For one year."

"And the senior center?" Her eyes widen. "And the *pigeons*?"

"There are no—well, there *are* pigeons, plenty, more than we need. But no senior center."

"Do Mom and Sabrina know? Did you lie just to me?"

"No." I shake my head energetically. "No one knows."

She seems relieved. For a split second. "So you're playing chess for money?"

"Yes."

"Isn't that like gambling?"

"What?"

"And isn't gambling illegal?"

"I—"

"Is that why you're lying? Because you're working for the gambling mob?"

"It's *not* gambling, Darcy. It's a sport." I notice her raised eyebrow. She knows my athletic prowess. "Kind of."

"Why don't you want us to know, then?"

"There are . . . things you might not remember, because you were very young when they happened, but—"

"Because Dad used to play chess."

I sigh. "Yes. Partially. I just want to protect you guys from something that could hurt you."

"I'm not fragile or—"

"But I am. And so is Sabrina—even though she's in her rebellious phase and would deny it. And Mom . . . Many painful things happened, Darcy. But we're happy now."

"Sabrina's mostly just sullen."

I chuckle. "True. I just want to take care of all of you."

"And yet, you brought the Kingkiller into our house."

"How do you even know about—"

"The Wikipedia entry was very thorough. Did you know that

he once played Jeff Bezos for charity? He beat him in twenty seconds, then asked if the water bottle next to the chessboard was for peeing."

"A true hero of the working class. Darcy—"

"Also, there's tons of fanfiction on AO3, mostly of him making out with some Emil Kareem guy, but—"

"What? How do you know what fanfiction is?"

"I read it all the time."

"Excuse me?"

"Chill. The PG-13 stuff."

"PG means parental guidance, which means that a parent—me—should be there with you."

She cocks her head. "You are aware that you're not my parent, right?"

I take a deep breath. "Listen, Darcy, the reason I was keeping a secret—"

"Oh my God. Mal, now it's *our* secret!" All of a sudden, she looks seriously pumped up.

"No. No, I don't want you keeping secrets from Mom—"

"I don't mind," she says quickly. "I want to!"

"Darcy, you were all about us telling each other everything at dinner. I'll explain to Mom—"

"*You* said it might be painful to her. And I want to have a secret with you. Something just *ours!*"

I study her hopeful, shining eyes, wondering if she's been feeling isolated. I'm in NYC a lot, after all. It's not like Sabrina can be coaxed away from her phone, and Mom is too low-energy to spend much time with her. Plus, telling the truth would open a whole silo of worms. And I'm reasonably confident that neither Mom nor Sabrina will be looking me up on the internet.

"Okay," I say. It's a terrible idea, but Darcy fist-pumps. Then her face takes on a calculated expression.

"But it'll cost you."

My eyes narrow. "Really? Are you going to blackmail me?"

"I just think that my morning oatmeal could use one more tablespoon of Nutella. Half? A teaspoon? *Please?*"

I shake my head and go in for a hug.

I DON'T SEE NOLAN AGAIN.

Not like, ever. But not for weeks, and I don't hear about him, either, with the exception of a Tuesday afternoon when he trends on chess Twitter, after forgetting about a virtual tournament and showing up on camera five minutes late while still pulling a Henley over his chest (#KingkillerSoHot). The fact that I notice his absence from my life has me slightly rattled. I might be even *more* rattled, but it's the busiest I've ever been.

After Philly Open, Defne changes my routine. She schedules more time for me with the GMs (including Oz, who *loves* it) to focus on specific weaknesses in my play. She also has me play online chess to increase my rating, and daily matches with Zugzwang's patrons. "It suits you better—learning by doing," she tells me.

She's right. My game improves quickly, positions and strategies easy at my fingertips. "Who'd have guessed that deliberately cultivating a natural talent would lead to the betterment of said talent," Oz says tartly. In retaliation, I chew an entire bag of kettle chips at my desk.

A huge chunk of my time is spent replaying old games. "Thanks for *not* buying the creamer I asked for," Sabrina huffs after I spend a hazy hour drifting through the grocery store aisles, wondering if Salov could have unpinned his knight in '95. I'm training so much, I can't seem to turn it off, not even in my sleep. Chess positions are taking over the back of my head, and after nights spent tossing and turning to Karpov's end games, I almost welcome fleeting dreams of dark, deep-set eyes glaring at me in frustration.

In the last week of September the morning air gets chilly, and I break out my favorite blue scarf, the one Easton made for me during her short-lived knitting phase. (*"Some stitches are missing. Poetic license and that."*) I snap a selfie and send it to her, scowling when her only response is a lazy heart emoji. I realize that we haven't talked in over a week, and I scowl harder when she doesn't reply to my How have things been? When my phone pings an hour later, I feel a burst of hope, but it's just Hasan, asking if I'd like to meet up over the weekend.

I'm not sure why, but I leave him on read.

For the first time, when I walk into the office, Oz is not at his desk.

"He's at a tournament," Defne explains.

I nearly pout. "Why didn't *I* get to go?"

"Because your rating is at the core of the earth. Most tournaments are either invitation-only or have strict access criteria."

I *fully* pout.

"You're in an unprecedented situation, Mal. Most players grow in the game, and their ratings grow with them. But even if you do nothing but win at chess and eat tuna straight from the can, it will still take you a couple of years to get to a point when your rating represents your actual skills." She pats my shoulders. "I did sign you up for the Nashville Open in mid-October. Prize is five thousand, but you're going to win—top players don't show up for that." She bites her lower lip, hesitating. "I've been approached with another opportunity, but . . ."

"What opportunity?"

She chews on her lip. "You know the Chess Olympics?"

I blink. "That's not really a thing, is it?"

"Of course it is."

"Let's say that I believe you. What is it?"

"Just a team tournament. Not *real* Olympics, but a similar format: one team per nation, four players per team. Five days. This year it's in Toronto, the first week of November—do you have a passport?" I nod. "Emil called and asked if—"

"Emil? Kareem?"

"Yup. The problem is, the Pasternak Invitational is right after, in Moscow, and that's a way more prestigious tournament."

"More prestigious than the Olympics." Seems fake.

"Well, you know how pro chess is." Defne must remember that I do not, in fact, know, because she continues, "In the end, it's all about the money. The Pasternak has ridiculous prizes, unlike the Olympics, and most pros and Super GMs don't want to tire themselves for nothing. Well, not *nothing*. There *is* a trophy. It looks nice, kind of like a cup. I guess you could eat cereal in it? Soup? Salads, if you don't mind your fork clinking against the metal—"

"Who's on the US team besides Emil?"

"Not sure." She sounds a little cagey. "Maybe Tanu Goel?"

"Do you want me to go?"

"I . . ." She scratches the back of her head, and her sleeve slides backward, revealing her chessboard tattoo. I study the positions while she seems to reach a decision. White is attacking with the rook, and Black is two pawns down. "It would be a great opportunity for you to raise your rating, gain expertise, network." She smiles. For the first time in this conversation. "I'd love to send you, if you can swing it time-wise."

A few hours later I sit at the dinner table with my family, munching on the tail of a tyrannosaurus chicken nugget and mentioning as casually as I can muster, "The senior center asked me to accompany the residents on a trip."

"Oh." Mom looks up from her plate. "Where to?"

"Toronto. Five days, in November." I can feel Darcy's eyes burning through me. Having a crucial secret with a naturally chatty twelve-year-old is not all it's cracked up to be. "They'd pay me time and a half. And it'd be cool to see Canada. I need to let them know by tomorrow—"

"Wait." Sabrina sets her phone on the table. Forcefully. "You're going to party in Toronto and leave us on our own? For real?"

I blink, taken aback by the mix of panic and anger in her voice. "I was just—"

"What if Goliath has a vet emergency? What if Darcy sticks a Monopoly token up her nose and needs to be taken to urgent care? What if I need a ride to a derby meet—am I supposed to hitchhike?"

"I'd arrange everything beforehand," I start just as Darcy says, "I haven't stuck anything up my nose since I was five!" and Mom points out, "*I* will still be around, Sabrina."

"Darcy's an idiot, and idiots are unpredictable, Mal. And that's the point of emergencies—you *cannot* prepare for them. What if Mom has a flare-up? Who's going to take care of her? How *egotistical* can you—"

"Sabrina." Mom's voice, usually gentle, cuts like a whip. "Apologize to your sisters."

"I didn't say anything that's not true—"

"*Sabrina.*"

She's gone in a flurry of screeching chairs and stomping feet. The room falls silent, and seconds later a door down the hallway slams into its frame.

Mom closes her eyes for exactly three breaths. Then says, "Mallory, of course you should go. We'll be fine."

I shake my head. Deep down, I know Sabrina is right. After all, I'm the one who keeps reminding her how fragile Mom's health is. I shouldn't be surprised if she's freaking out at the idea of me leaving. "No. Honestly—"

"Mallory." Mom covers my hand with hers. It's still clutching the fork, the half-eaten nugget speared at its end. "I am asking you to please tell your boss that you're going, okay?"

I nod. Then churn it over the entire night, sleepless, bitter, Sabrina's words a hateful ring in my ears. I am angry. Guilty. Furious. Sad.

Egotistical. Does she not understand the sacrifices I've made for the family? Does she think that I *wanted* to stop going to school? Does she think that I *enjoy* it, knowing that in four years Easton will have a degree and a career and I'll be stuck in some minimum-wage dead-end job? That we'll grow further and further apart as time goes on, as I fall behind, forgotten? Screw Sabrina, honestly.

But it's your own fault if your family is in this situation, that obnoxious little voice reminds me. *She has every right to be mad at you. And weren't you only going to compete in tournaments with money prizes? Why do you even want to go to Toronto?*

To build rating! To access future tournaments!

Not because you enjoyed the thrill of competitive chess so much, you've been jonesing for it since Philly? Cool. Just making sure.

Oh, shut up.

You just said shut up to yourself, but go off, I guess.

I wake up in the morning eager to apologize to Sabrina for . . . I don't know. Ruining her life four years ago, maybe? Her room, though, is empty.

"McKenzie's mom's driving her to school," Darcy explains. "For someone whose biggest fear is not having a ride to the ER, Sabrina the Teenage Bitch is pretty crafty at finding one on short notice."

"First of all, we do *not* use that word." I smile and step closer, pushing her bangs back. It's like looking into a freckled, rejuvenating Snapchat filter. "Secondly, you know Sabrina loves you, right? She doesn't really think that you're an idiot."

"I believe that she loves me *and* thinks that I'm an idiot. Because *she* is an idiot." She gives me an appraising look. "By the way, I don't think you're egotistical, Mal. I mean, you skimp on the Nutella and don't show Timothée Chalamet the admiration that's due him, and you are, objectively, a liar. But I don't think you're egotistical." I feel a lump swell in my throat. Until Darcy frowns. "Though I'm not one hundred percent sure I have the correct definition of *egotistical*."

A couple of hours later I'm in Defne's office, which is a bit like its owner: colorful, happy, and full of knickknacks that should not go well together but somehow do.

"Good morning!" She grins from her desk. "Did you steal Delroy's rainbow bagel? He's *very* upset."

"Nope. Just got here."

"Oh. How can I help you then?"

I clear my throat. Well, here goes. "Could you tell Emil that I'd love to do the Olympics?"

Chapter Twelve

I feel Nolan before I see him.

One second I'm struggling to drag my duffel bag onto the LaGuardia suitcase conveyor and wondering why the Greenleaf clan never invested in something with wheels (or a set of dumbbells, for upper body strength); the next, someone takes it from me, lifts it effortlessly, and deposits it on the belt.

I turn around, but my body already *knows*, like my atoms vibrate differently when he's near. Which probably just means that his presence gives me radiation poisoning.

"Hi, Mallory," he says. He's wearing sunglasses and a dark shirt, but his voice is the same. He *looks* the same: Tall. Unsmiling. Good.

A few pimples, that's what he needs. A wart to break the perfect imperfection of his face.

"Hi," I scratch out.

It's been over two months since I was in his presence. Two months of chess, chess, chess. Wrangling my sisters, taking Mom to the doctor, then more chess. Being glared at by Oz, putting off checking Tinder, then chess. I won the Nashville Open and another online tournament. I haven't lost a match yet, but my rating's not even in the nineteen hundreds. There's a little engine in a corner of my skull, constantly working on positions, pawn structure, square theory.

"Are you . . . flying somewhere?" I ask once he's been silent a little too long. My voice sounds breathy. I hope I'm not getting sick right before the Olympics.

The corners of his lips twitch. "That's what airports are for."

I bristle out of my breathlessness. "You could be flying in. Or picking up someone. Or be like Tom Hanks in that movie, living in a terminal because of funky immigration paperwork." I clear my throat. "Where are you flying?"

He tilts his head. "For real?"

For real, what? "Are you going to that tournament in Russia?"

"You haven't figured it out?"

"What am I supposed to—"

"Greenleaf." Emil Kareem appears and hugs me like I'm his long-lost sister. There's a girl with him, a supermodel who just flew into LaGuardia for fashion week. Wait, she's familiar. From Philly Open—Nolan's girlfriend, the one he hugged? I don't know, but she is hugging *me* like I'm her long-lost sister.

"Mallory, I'm so happy you're on the team. I cannot *believe* I'm going to have a meaningful conversation that doesn't revolve around fantasy football. Wait—are you into fantasy football?"

She smells amazing. Lavender, I think. "I'm . . . not sure what that is."

"Phew."

"Greenleaf, this is Tanu Goel. She *also* has no idea what fantasy football is," Emil says. "And of course you know Nolan. From trashing him back in the summer."

I glance at Nolan. He doesn't seem to mind being reminded—the opposite, in fact. Which, in itself, is annoying. I want to be the thorn in his side that he is in mine. I want him to dream of *my* stupid eyes.

"You guys know each other?" I say, glancing between Nolan and Emil.

"Unfortunately," they say at the same time, before exchanging a long, brotherly look, and that's when it occurs to me.

Nolan is on the team.

Nolan is coming to Toronto.

With us.

To play chess.

At the Olympics.

Emil never told me. Because I never asked. We've been in touch to arrange flights and accommodations, but I always figured that whoever the fourth member turned out to be, I wouldn't have heard of them.

Because Defne told me that all Super Grandmasters would skip the Olympics and go to the Pasternak.

Because I'm an idiot.

A very rattled idiot, who has to deal with her rattledness through security and boarding. I'm not the self-conscious type, but I feel like the odd man out with these three. They're warm (except for Nolan, who's his usual inscrutable self) and try to involve me in conversation (except for Nolan, who's his usual quiet self), but it's clear that they've spent years memorizing each other. Their inside jokes are indecipherable, hidden behind a thick bramble of unparseable references. Their dynamics, too, seem to be a well-beaten path—*several* paths, made of shifting alliances and a healthy dose of roasting.

"Is she seriously buying that?" Emil asks when Tanu picks up a pack of Werther's Original. "How *old* are you?"

"Leave her alone," Nolan murmurs, paying for the Werther's and peanut M&M's with a black credit card. "They're out of Jell-O salad."

Not five minutes later two separate groups recognize Nolan as "that chess guy in all the TikToks." It leads to selfies, autographs, and two beautiful women hastily writing down their phone numbers on Sbarro napkins, like he's Justin Bieber or something. Tanu and Emil pretend to stand in line, audibly asking, "Sir, I'm your biggest fan. I love the way you always castle on your fourth move. Will you please sign my underwear?" (Nolan is surprisingly good-natured through all of this; he also immediately throws away the napkins.)

Then, while waiting for takeoff, Emil starts playing Candy Crush on his phone. "Are you for real?" Tanu asks. She's half leaning back against Nolan's chest, his arm casually wrapped around her waist. I've been avoiding looking at them, telling myself that I don't care what they've been murmuring about in hushed, intimate tones. "We are scholars of the most sophisticated game in the world and you play *Candy Crush*? Nolan, say something."

He shrugs. "Seems unfair to kick him when he's so clearly down."

"Candy Crush is actually a highly intelligent game," Emil insists. "There's *strategy* involved."

Tanu groans. "Oh my God. Excuse me, Mallory, can we switch seats? I need to tell Emil how wrong he is. I need it right now."

Which is how I find myself in the window seat next to Nolan,

Tanu and Emil arguing loudly over jelly bean colors on the other side of the aisle. I study his profile, suddenly intimidated. Then I remember that he once came over to shoot my mom's meat loaf up his veins and asked Sabrina whether Jughead was "a first or last name."

"So, what's the deal here?"

He turns to me, puzzled.

"Are the three of you in some polyamorous relationship?"

"Did you just ask if I'm sleeping with *both* our teammates?" He lifts one eyebrow. "I'm going to FIDE's HR."

"What? No—don't go to HR."

"You're overstepping, Mal."

"*You* came to my house and ate *many* of my ice cream sandwiches."

"Right." He clucks his tongue. "Unforgivable. Do report me."

I roll my eyes. "Whatever. So, who's dating whom?"

"No one's dating anyone. Not anymore, at least."

I glance at Tanu and Emil. She stole his phone and is scowling at it, tongue peeking out from between her teeth as she matches Swedish fish. Emil stares at her, surprisingly somber.

"Was it them?"

Nolan nods silently. "Then they went to different schools—Tanu's taking the week off, but she's at Stanford. Emil's at NYU."

"I see. Have you known them for long?"

"Forever. We trained together with . . ." He stops. "Until they decided pro chess wasn't for them."

"When was that?"

"Three years ago for Emil. Tanu, before that."

I wonder if they are his Easton. And because I've been hearing from Easton less and less, about stuff that seems more and more trivial, the question slips out:

"Does it feel weird? That they went to college, and you didn't?"

He looks thoughtful for a moment. "Sometimes. Sometimes it feels like they're on their way to have lives I can never understand. Sometimes I'm just glad I don't have to read *Great Expectations* or study for a trigonometry final."

I smile. "Pretty sure trig's in high school."

"It is?"

"Yup. You didn't take it?"

He opens his M&M's, offering them to me. "I was home-schooled."

"Because of chess?"

"For many reasons. And I have no idea what a cosine is." He pops a yellow M&M in his mouth. When he swallows, his throat bobs, a strong, mesmerizing movement that I notice because . . . I'm going bananapants?

"You'll live. So Emil and Tanu broke up because of distance, but they're still into each other?"

"And refuse to do anything about it."

"Lots of pining, I bet."

"I do get several angsty late-night phone calls asking why Tanu just liked the shirtless picture of some Stanford swimmer on Instagram, or who's the skank who keeps dueting Emil on TikTok."

"I bet you're great at talking people off the ledge."

"I'd be better at it if I knew what the hell a TikTok duet is."

I laugh. Emil and Tanu glance at me, then exchange a glance I cannot decipher. "Were you jealous when they first got together?"

"Jealous?" He seems to find the question surprising.

"Yeah. I mean, you guys seem close. And they're both really attractive . . ." My cheeks heat. I think he notices because the corner of his mouth twitches.

"I wasn't jealous. I couldn't understand how someone could be so enthralled by the idea of being alone in a room with another person without a chessboard."

"But now you can?"

He gives me a long look through his sunglasses. "Now I can." He turns away. "But if *you* are interested in either of them—"

"That's not why I asked," I blurt out. "Besides, I don't hook up with people I work with. It makes things messy." Actually, I don't hook up at all, lately. It's been a surprisingly dry couple of months. Maybe chess kills my libido?

"Messy?"

"Yeah."

"How's that?"

"Too much proximity. People get ideas. They think I'm interested in giving them my time. My mental energy."

He studies me. "And you're too busy taking care of your family for that."

"How do you know that?"

He doesn't reply, just studies me through those dark lenses for several seconds, until I can't stand the stretching silence anymore and ask, "Why are you here, anyway? Aren't you going to that invitational next week?"

"Curious about my plans?"

The obvious answer is: yes. "They didn't invite you, did they? They know you'll hurl a chessboard at an arbiter and no insurance agency would let them have you."

"I leave for Moscow from Toronto. On Friday."

"You're doing *both* tournaments?"

He gives me his best *What, like it's hard?* shrug.

"Defne said that doing two big tournaments so close together would make anyone brain dead. And that most big play-ers don't see the point in the Olympics . . ." A thought occurs to me. "You're not here because I . . . ?"

You're not here because I'm *here, are you?*

Come on, Mal. He's not here because he's still into that idea of playing against you. No way. He wants to hang out with his friends. Maybe he lied and he is into Tanu. Or Emil. Or both. Not my busi-ness. Who cares—

"Yes," he says.

My internal monologue halts. "What?"

"The reason you're thinking." His stupid, deep voice. Argh. "That's why I'm here."

"You don't know what I'm thinking."

He smiles. "True."

"No, really. You don't."

"Okay."

"Stop saying that. Stop pretending you can read my mind and—"

The flight attendant rolls her cart, asking us if we want a drink. After that we're quiet—Nolan staring ahead, and me sul-lenly nursing my Sunkist, thinking that no.

He *cannot* know.

Chapter Thirteen

There are two main distinctions between the Olympics and a regular tournament: we get doping-tested (yup: it involves peeing in a cup), and we compete as a team. We still play all our matches individually, but our points will be added together. As the strongest among us, Nolan is first board. But then *I*, the least experienced player, am chosen for second. (I ask Emil repeatedly if it's a good idea. He gives me a wide-eyed look and huffs, "Come on, Greenleaf.")

It feels different, knowing that whatever victory I manage to bring home will be for *us*—no matter how temporary and abstract this *us* might be. It's nice when Emil high-fives me after I win on time against the Estonian player, or Tanu kisses my forehead because I narrowly avoided a draw with Singapore. I don't even mind Nolan's long, thoughtful, lingering looks. He always defeats his opponent quickly. Then he finds something warm to drink for the rest of the team, sets it by our boards, and comes to stand somewhere behind my opponent. His eyes alternate between me and my game, dark and focused and greedy in a way I don't fully understand.

He doesn't fist-pump when I win. He doesn't even tell me

that I did good. He just nods once, like every single one of my victories is expected and his faith in me is as solid as a boulder. As though he couldn't marvel at me playing well any more than at the sun setting at night.

The pressure that comes with it should be irritating. But I find the unwavering confidence from a player of his caliber flattering, which irritates me even more. So I do what I'm best at: I avoid thinking about it.

And it's not hard. Toronto is beautiful, and the tournament atmosphere is fun: backpacks, players sitting on the floor and unwrapping homemade sandwiches, people who haven't seen each other in years hugging it out between rounds. It's youthful and low pressure, like a school trip with excellent chess instead of museums. I wear jeans and an oversized sweater without feeling underdressed.

"Don't get cocky, though. We've been lucky so far," Emil tells me while walking back to the hotel at the end of the first day. Nolan is giving Tanu a piggyback ride, because *I really want one, Nolan.* "We haven't met any of the strongest teams."

"Which are?"

"China, India, Russia. And, like, twelve more."

"Who's the current champion, by the way?"

"Germany. But they won't be strong this year, with Koch already in Moscow."

"*That's* why the North American continent felt so much more pleasant than usual," Nolan mutters.

"Is your manager still pissed about you coming to the Olympics?" Emil asks.

"Can't say, since I stopped taking her calls." He shrugs.

It has Tanu giggling on his shoulders and asking, "Remember

years ago, when you pushed Koch and manhandled him a bit and he started calling for his mom?"

"One of my most treasured memories."

"The tears. The panic. Totally worth that fine FIDE slapped you with."

"Why *did* you punch him?" I ask, though I can imagine a million reasons.

"Can't really recall," Nolan murmurs, almost too casually.

"He was talking about your grandfather," Tanu says. "As usual."

"Ah, yes." His jaw tightens. "He does enjoy running his mouth about shit he doesn't know."

We're staying in a hostel, four separate bedrooms that converge into a shared living space and bathroom. Last night I wondered how Nolan, Mr. Fifty Thousand Dollars Is Nothing to Me, felt about it, but if he finds the accommodation subpar, he hasn't mentioned it. I went to bed early, and then spent hours listening to the soft, intimate tones of the others chatting, feeling vaguely jealous. I texted Easton (How's life? Are you puking your heart out in a toilet bowl?) and scrolled through her TikTok waiting for a reply that never came.

She's busy. It's fine.

After the first day I conk out on the couch before dinner, before I can even call home. It's a dreamless, exhausted, happy kind of sleep, vague impressions of bishops and rooks gliding softly across a large board. I wake up tucked in my bed, still wearing yesterday's clothes. Someone took off my shoes, connected my phone to the charger, put a glass of water on my bedside. Someone took care of me.

I don't ask who.

Day two is more of the same. In the morning, we win all of our matches—with the exception of Emil, who loses against Sierra Leone.

"Way to kill our streak, asshole," Nolan tells him mildly over some lunch poutine, ducking to avoid the fry Emil throws at him.

Tanu nods. "Told you we should have brought along someone who knows how to castle." Unfortunately, *she* ducks too slowly.

Nolan gestures at me with his chin. "It's your turn, Mallory."

"My turn?"

"To tear into Emil. It's tradition."

"Right." I swallow a cheese curd. Scratch my nose. "Emil, that was, um . . . badly done?"

Nolan shakes his head. "Pitiful."

"Really, Mal?" Tanu chides. "Is this the best you can do?"

"Clearly Mal's as good at trash-talking as I was at playing against Sierra Leone."

"She has other talents," Nolan says, locking eyes with mine. "Like drawing guinea pigs."

I hide my smile in my hand, but I'm feeling more comfortable with these three. Nolan is more approachable when consumed through the Brita filter of his friends, even if there's still something intimidating about his unignorable, often quiet presence. Something that keeps me on edge.

As our opponents get stronger, we accumulate more losses and draws, mostly from Tanu and Emil. I like to win—I *love* to win—but my teammates' defeats don't bother me as much, and Nolan seems to be the same. On the second match of the third day, Jakub Szymański from Poland blunders ten moves in, and I pull off a victory in record time. I blink away the soupy feeling of emerging from a game, stretch a little, then come to stand right behind Nolan.

It's the first time I've finished before him—the first time I get to watch him play. It's his turn to move, and he sits back in the chair, neck slightly bent, arms on his chest. Then he moves his rook, large hands incongruously graceful, and presses the clock.

I have yet to study his games. Defne chooses what plays I analyze, and I've found none of Nolan's in my list. Still, it's impossible to know anything about chess without having some theoretical notions about him as a player: he is famously cunning, aggressive, versatile. Active. Always doing something risky to raise the pressure. His strategies might seem impulsive, spontaneous, but they are long-sighted and convoluted, nearly impossible to thwart. He relentlessly exploits every advantage, position, distraction. I remember reading about a quality of chess players called *nettlesomeness*: the ability to not just play well but also *trick* others into playing poorly. Nolan, by all accounts, has it in heaps. And when the adversary has blundered their way into the middle game, he sinks his teeth into them and draws blood.

The Kingkiller, indeed.

I watch him at work as he advances, surrounds the center, moves his knight and bishop in tandem, takes everything on his path, and . . .

I feel breathless. Light-headed. Confused. That's how beautiful his moves are. Cruel and unstoppable. I won against him once, but I also know I might not win again—he's *that* good. And there's more: I'm a practical player, always focused on finishing off my opponent as quickly as possible rather than on the art and elegance of the game. But Nolan's play is stunning. In five thousand years archaeologists will cry at its grace. Though if we don't stop carbon emissions, the world will just be a pile of ashes, so maybe we should put it in a time capsule. Send it into space on an alien probe. Share with the rest of the universe—

"You okay?" Tanu asks.

"I—yes." I hadn't noticed her. Even though she's right beside me.

"You looked . . . entranced."

"No. I was just . . ."

"Yeah, Nolan's play will do that. Nolan, in general." She laughs softly. "I used to be so in love with him, I'd thought I'd die if we didn't get married and have four chubby kids named after opening gambits no one uses anymore." My eyes widen. "Oh, don't worry. I was, like, twelve? And he couldn't have cared less about that stuff." She shrugs. "I thought he was incapable of caring at all before . . . well. On paper, he should have *tons* of game, but in reality he has very little." She smiles reassuringly. I want to ask her why she assumes that I'd worry, or what *before* means, but Nolan buries his fangs into the Polish king and Tanu is too busy cheering.

I'm in a good mood until the last match of the day—Serbia. Because some chess divinity hates me, their second board is someone I remember from Koch's crew back at Philly Open— Dordevic, the name tag informs me, and I suddenly recall what he asked me that night.

What did you do before the game? I need that kind of luck.

"Greenleaf," he says, his sneer a clear sign of Koch affiliation.

I vow to myself to destroy him. And I'm true to my word for the first forty minutes or so, easily blocking his attacks and gaining control of the center. Until he takes a page from Koch's Little Bitch Manual, and accuses me of making an illegal move.

"It's not," I tell him.

"If you previously moved the rook—"

"But I didn't."

"Arbiter!"

I roll my eyes but let him flag the closest official—a blond woman who nods and walks over to us.

I recognize her immediately. My stomach flips, then freezes into a block of concrete that should drag me through the floor. Instead, snippets of a four-year-old conversation swarm my head.

Who was she?

No one.

But you were—

No one, Mal.

"Yes?" she asks Dordevic, and there's a pounding roar in my ears. I know everything about her—name, age, even her address. Or at least, a few years ago's. It's possible that she moved. That she doesn't work at the bank anymore, that she doesn't exercise at Pure Barre, that—

"It's not illegal," she tells Dordevic, who starts gesticulating his disagreement. My entire body is shaking, and I can't tune in.

"Are you okay?" a voice asks in my ear. Nolan. He just finished his game. "Mal?"

I thrust a trembling hand out to Dordevic. "Draw?" I offer. It's the first time.

His expression shifts from confused, to distrustful, to relieved when he accepts. We both know that if we'd continued, I'd have won, but—I can't. Not now.

"Not such a good talent, after all?" He sniggers. I'm already running to the bathroom when I hear Nolan calling him a shithead.

I wash my face, shuddering. I remind myself that it's fine, because nothing happened. It was years ago. *Nothing happened. Nothing happened. Nothing—*

"What's wrong?" Nolan asks the second I step out of the bathroom. He's been waiting for me, and I nearly face-plant into his chest.

"I . . . Sorry about the draw."

"I don't care. Who was that arbiter?"

Shit. He noticed. "No one. I just . . ." I step around him, but one hand closes around my upper arm.

"Mallory. You're not okay. What just happened?" His tone is firm.

But so is mine. "I need a minute, Nolan. Can you please—"

"Mr. Sawyer?" A group of players approaches us. "We're huge fans. Any chance we could get an autograph—"

I seize the opportunity and slip away from Nolan, from Heather Turcotte, from chess. At the hostel, I lock myself into my room, lie down, take deep breaths to clear my mind.

Maybe, if you'd minded your own business, none of this would have—

No.

I empty my mind again, this time for good, and slowly fall into a dreamless, blessed sleep.

I wake up in the middle of the night, feeling more like myself. When I sneak out to use the bathroom, I find a brown bag outside my door. Inside are a sandwich, a Fanta, and a pack of Twizzlers.

Chapter Fourteen

The last day is the perfect combination of challenging chess, high stakes, and teamwork. We already know we don't have enough points for the gold, but if we play our cards right, we can still make the podium.

And we do. I make the executive decision to put the events of the previous day out of my mind and focus on the play. My opponent tries the Muzio Gambit. I'm briefly confused, then remember going over it with Defne and know exactly what to do. We don't quite kick Russia's ass, but we spank it a little bit. At the medal ceremony, we all squeeze onto the lowest step of the podium, the national anthem mixing with the camera clicks in my ears. Tanu pulls me to her, Emil shouts, "It's what *we do*!" and Nolan gives us a half-pleased, half-reproachful look. I feel part of something. Like I haven't in a long, long time.

It's a stupid chess tournament. I swore I wouldn't care, and yet I feel happy. In the crowd, I spot Eleni Gataki from the BBC giving me the thumbs-up, and wave back at her, bemused. I guess I'm starting to know people in the chess world.

"Come, Mal—the press wants to interview us," Tanu calls afterward.

"Oh . . . Actually, I'd rather not."

"Why? It's *CNN*! This is how Anderson Cooper becomes my bestie!"

"I think he already has Andy Cohen."

"You have to come," she insists. "You're the reason we won. Oh, lower that eyebrow, Emil, you know it's true!"

"Really, I'm fine."

"But—"

"She doesn't want to," Nolan says, tone calm but final. I send him a grateful look. He stares back like either he didn't notice or he doesn't care about my gratitude. I'm pondering my frustrating, utter inability to read him, when someone taps my shoulder.

"Ms. Greenleaf." It's an older man in a gray suit. His beard is garden-gnome-long, his accent from somewhere I cannot place. "May I congratulate you on your victory?"

"Oh . . . sure." I search for a non-rude way to ask him who he is and find none. "It was a team effort."

He nods. "But you were by far the most impressive player on the team."

"No more than Nolan."

The man laughs. His gaze, however, is sharp. "It's hard to be impressed by Sawyer these days. He has accustomed us to a certain level of performance. Some people even say that he has *ruined* chess."

I frown, thinking about the people who have recognized him in the last few days, telling him that they took up chess after seeing him play. "I don't think it's true." Am I feeling defensive on behalf of Nolan Sawyer? It'll start raining frogs any minute. "He's made chess visible and popular."

"Certainly. But he always wins. He hasn't had a rival in years, and people rarely get invested in a sport whose outcome is a foregone conclusion. I would know. I organize the Challengers tournament."

"Oh." It sounds familiar, but I don't know why and I don't care. This man, his hawkish gaze, and the odd things he says about Nolan are making me uncomfortable.

"I'm sorry." I gesture somewhere behind me. "I need to meet up with my teammates."

"I've been hearing lots about you, Ms. Greenleaf. I believed the rumors were exaggerated, and yet . . ." His look is long and assessing. I want to hug myself. "Run along. You friends will be waiting for you. Whoever they are."

Yikes.

I wander away, checking my phone to look busy. I find a text from Defne (You done good, kid.) and millions from Darcy— apparently, they both spent the past four days refreshing ChessWorld.com.

DARCYBUTT: BRONZE!!!!!!!!

DARCYBUTT: You and Nolan got the most points in the whole Olympics. You guys should get married and have a child. She'd be so good at chess.

DARCYBUTT: Or she'd suck. She'd trudge through life saddled by crushing disappointment. Resent you well into your old age. Take away your car keys and put

you in a home the second you let your
guard down. Okay, abort plan.

DARCYBUTT: You'll be home tomorrow night,
right? I miss you. Sabrina only talks to me
to say "Ew."

MALLORY: ofc. and when she says ew she
actually means i love you. or something.

MALLORY: what present do you want from
canada?

DARCYBUTT: A mate for Goliath.

I sigh. And then the air rushes out of my lungs, because Tanu
is hugging me again; a cloud of lavender surrounds me. "Last
night in Toronto! You know what that means, right?"

"I was thinking of maybe taking a walk downtown—"

"Oh, no. No way." She pulls back and takes my face between
her hands. Her eyes are night stars bursting with excitement.
"Tonight, Mallory, we play *Skittles*!"

SKITTLES IS LIKE CHESS.

Actually: skittles *is* chess—without a clock or scorecard, surrounded by half-empty beer cans and Salt-N-Pepa songs that are
older than us, under the light of a starry-sky LED projector that

some girl from Belgium brought as a "hotel room–warming present."

It's a multicultural frat party, with chess instead of spin the bottle. For reasons that I must attribute to Tanu and Emil's event-planning skills and Nolan's reputation, taking place right in *our* shared area. People have been coming and going in a steady stream for hours, bringing their sets and playing blitz, rapid, Fischer Random.

Strip chess.

"Drinking age's nineteen, Mal," Tanu says when I decline a fruity drink for the second time. She lost a bishop and her socks about ten minutes ago. "It's legal! Like en passant capture! Or queening! Or castling sho— Crap, I'm so *sorry*!" She spills her glass onto the Italian guy Nolan defeated yesterday and promptly moves to paint whiskers on a cute Japanese guy, forgetting all about eighteen-year-old me.

I go back to focusing on my rapid game against a Sri Lankan girl I bonded with after noticing her *Dragon Age* Solas pin. She's very pretty, and a great player to boot, and a-couple-of-months-ago-Mallory would be making a move on her. I swore to Saturn and back that I wouldn't play for fun. Yes, it's exactly what I'm doing. Nope, I would *not* like to talk about it.

"—that time Nolan stole a black knight from Kaporani's board at GE's tournament and all matches were delayed by twenty minutes because of the search?"

"That was after Gibraltar, when Kaporani switched my water with distilled vinegar."

"We'd already gotten revenge for that with the glitter bomb. He sparkled for *months*."

People laugh. Emil and Nolan are on the couch, playing tactical team, surrounded by a mix of old friends and fans. There's a girl, for instance, who's almost as blond as me, curled up next to Nolan. Hard to tell how he feels about it, since he's so focused on his game. He must have run a hand through his hair, because it's vaguely mussed, unbearably attractive.

Something else I'd rather not talk about.

"Must be cool to play with him," the Sri Lankan girl says, following my gaze.

I look away. "He can be kind of a dick," I say, though he hasn't really been one to me.

She chuckles, low and smoky. She's really my type. "All geniuses are. I heard he has an IQ of 190. Maybe higher, but tests cannot measure it."

"He doesn't eat meat loaf like someone with a 190 IQ," I mutter, resentful.

"Sorry?"

"Nothing. Um, checkmate, by the way." I stand, wiping my palms over my leggings and abandoning my half-hearted seduction plans. My heart's not really in it, or maybe I'm too tired to get laid. "It was great to meet you. I've got an early morning and—"

"Where are you going, Mal?" Tanu appears out of nowhere. "It's like, not even midnight!"

"Oh, you don't have to keep it down for me. I just need to buy presents for my sisters tomorrow morning, so—"

"But don't go now! Don't you want pizza?"

"Pizza?"

"Yes, let's go get pizza!"

"I'm kind of tired, and—"

"Then we're getting it and bringing it back!" She turns around and bellows drunkenly, "Who wants to come get midnight pizza?"

Might be because Tanu is the life of the party, or because pizza is hands down the best food in the world, but in half a minute the music is turned off and our shared area empties out of everyone but me.

Maybe I'm eighty years old inside, but: Blessed. Quiet.

"You're not coming?" the blond woman who was with Nolan earlier asks from the door. Her accent is very pretty. But we've never really talked, so I'm confused why she'd want to know whether I—

"No."

I startle and turn around. Nolan—she was talking to Nolan. Who's still on the couch.

"You sure?"

He barely spares her a glance. "Very." He probably hates pizza. Only eats authentic Sicilian calzone made with tomatoes grown around the mouth of Mount Etna.

Whatever. I'm going to bed. "Nolan, when Tanu comes back, will you tell her that I went to sleep?" I wave past the chairs, the chess sets, the couch. "Have a good—"

His hand snatches my wrist. I'm too surprised to wiggle out. "Let's play a bit, Mallory."

I freeze. I stiffen. And this time I do wiggle out. "I told you, I don't—"

"—play outside of training and tournaments. Yes. But you've been playing all night, outside of training and tournaments. With five different people."

I scoff. "Did you count?"

"Yes." He looks up at me. Stars dance occasionally across the line of his jaw, his cheekbones. "I was sure you'd end the night in Bandara's room."

"Bandara?"

"Ruhi Bandara. You two were just playing."

I take a step back and refuse to admit that I entertained the same thought. Instead I say, "I don't want to play against you."

"A problem, since I *really* want to play against you."

I shiver, because it feels like he's saying something else. Like . . .

I don't know.

"You already have."

"Once."

"Once was enough."

"Once was *nothing*. I need more."

"I'm sure there are plenty of people who'd love to play. Who'd probably *pay* just to sit across from you."

"But I want you, Mallory."

I swallow heavily, then look away. He's right—I already broke all my no-chess-outside-work rules. So why am I resisting this so hard?

Maybe it's because I've seen him play. I've seen him be brilliant, read positions with a glance, do things I can't even understand. If we played, I'd lose. And yes, I hate losing, but this is hardly a fair match. So the number one player in the world is better than this year's reluctant Zugzwang fellow. Big deal. As newsworthy as being slower than Michael Phelps in the 200m butterfly.

Maybe something else bothers me, then. Not that I'll lose, but that he'll *know* that I lost.

Yes. This . . . interest, obsession, fascination he seems to have with me came because I beat him. *Once*. I'm innately good at chess, but I'm not better than someone who's just as innately good *and* has had decades of professional training. We'd play, he'd win, and then I'd be just like everyone else: someone Nolan Sawyer defeated.

His captivation with me would instantly wane, and—

That would be a good thing, wouldn't it? I don't like Nolan Sawyer showing up to my house and talking *Riverdale* with my sisters, do I? I should agree to play, and end whatever *this* is.

And yet.

"No," I hear myself say.

His jaw works. "Right, then." He relaxes and reaches across the glass bottles, chess pieces, half-eaten bags of chips, grabbing a pencil and a German Chess Federation flier. "Sit down."

"I told you, I—"

"Please," he says, and something in his tone stops me. I try to remember the last time I heard him say it. A simple word, *please*. Isn't it?

"Fine." I sit—across from him, as distant as possible. This is what I get for refusing pizza. "But I'm not going to play, so—"

"Chess."

"What?"

"You said you wouldn't play chess. You didn't mention anything else, so . . ." He turns the flier to me. He has drawn a three-by-three grid, put an X through a space, and . . .

I laugh. "Tic-tac-toe? *Really?*"

"Unless you have Uno handy? Checkers? Operation?"

"This is worse than Candy Crush."

He smiles. Lopsided. "Don't tell Tanu or she'll put another pushpin under my pillow."

"Another?" I shake my head, amused. "You can't really want to play tic-tac-toe."

He shrugs and takes a long swig of his IPA. "We could raise the stakes. Make it fun."

"I'm not going to play for money."

"I don't want your money. What about questions?"

"Questions?"

"If I win, I get to ask you a question, *any* question, and you answer. And vice versa."

"What could you possibly want to ask me that—"

"Deal?"

It seems like a bad idea, but I can't pinpoint why, so I nod. "Deal. Five minutes. Then I'm turning in." I pluck the pencil from his fingers and write down my O.

The first three games are draws. The fourth goes to me, and I smile ferociously. I do love to win. "So I get a question?"

"If you want."

I'm not sure what to ask, but I don't want to forfeit my prize. I wrack my brain for a moment, then settle on, "What's the Challengers tournament?"

His arches an eyebrow. "Your question to me is something you could easily google?" I feel slightly embarrassed, but he continues. "It's the tournament that determines which player will face the current world chess champion."

"Which would be you?"

"At the moment."

I snort softly. "And for the past six years."

"And for the past six years." There is no boast in his voice. No pride. But it occurs to me for the first time that he became world champion at the same age I left chess for good. And that if I'd only stuck around a couple of years longer, we'd have met much earlier. In completely different circumstances. "The Challengers has ten players, who qualify by winning other super-tournaments or are selected because of their high FIDE ratings. They compete against each other. Then, a couple of months later, the winner competes for the World Championship title."

"The one whose prize is two million dollars?"

"Three, this year."

My heart skips a beat. I cannot even conceive what that money would do for my family. Not that I'd win against Nolan in a multiday match. Or that I'd end up at the Challengers, since I'm not invited to super-tournaments and my rating is currently hanging out with a piece of gum under the sole of my shoe.

I grip the pen a little too forcefully and draw another grid. My mind must still be on the money, because Nolan wins the following game.

I roll my eyes. "I was distracted. You don't really deserve—"

"Why did you quit chess?"

I tense. "Excuse me."

"In September, after Philly, you said your father's death wasn't the reason you quit chess. What is it, then?"

"We never agreed that questions would be about—"

"We agreed to *any* question." He holds my eyes, a hint of a challenge in his tone. "Of course, you can always back out of the game."

It's exactly what I should do. Get out and leave Nolan alone with his stupid, invasive question. But I can't make myself, and after a few seconds of lip biting and a burning desire to carve my next O into his skin, I say, "My dad and I became estranged a while"—*three years, one week, and two days*—"before he died. I stopped playing then."

"Why did you become estranged?"

"That's two questions. And if you win again, no follow-up questions are allowed."

He frowns. "Why wouldn't they be?"

"Because I *say so*," I bite out. He is quiet for a second, but he reads my tone well, because he nods.

After that, we draw a few games. As in: twenty-three games. It becomes clear that neither of us wants to be in the position of being asked the next question when I win the twenty-fourth game, and Nolan channels his most traditional self by slapping his palm on the table. Honestly, it feels nice.

I wasted my Challengers question, so I think hard about what I'd like to know about him. Something about his relationship with Koch, maybe? The Baudelaire story? His grandfather? There's something I've been wondering for weeks, but it seems like too much.

On the other hand, he *did* ask about Dad, and I *am* feeling vengeful. Maybe even vicious.

"At my house, when Sabrina asked you who you have sex with, you said . . . *conflicting* things, and . . ." I trail off.

"What's the question? Who do I have sex with?"

I nod quickly. My cheeks are on fire. I'm already regretting this.

"No one."

Uh? "Excuse me?"

"I don't have sex. Or at least, I never have."

It takes a few moments for the words to penetrate. For it to really sink in: Nolan Sawyer, the Kingkiller, blithely admitting that he's a virgin at the age of twenty. Not that there's anything wrong with that. But.

No. I misunderstood. What about the Baudelaire thing?

"You've never had sex," I repeat.

"Nope," he says, confident, calm, like he has nothing to prove to anyone, like he doesn't care to be anyone but himself, fully himself. At least here, tonight, with me.

"Oh." I feel like I should tread carefully. "So you . . . ? I mean, are you happy with that, or do you wish that . . . ?" I flush harder. He takes pity.

"Do I wish I were having sex?"

I nod again. Jesus, I *can* speak. I am *better* than this.

"No." He doesn't even think about it. "Not until recently."

"What . . . what changed recently?"

He stares for a long moment. "No follow-up questions, I was told." The corner of his lip twitches into a smile. "Besides, I hear you have enough sex for the both of us."

I groan. "I've barely been— You should never believe any-thing Darcy says."

"It's not like it's a bad thing." He draws another grid. I'm still flustered, and he wins immediately. "What are you going to do at the end of your fellowship?"

"What do you know about my fellowship?"

"No answering questions with other questions."

I roll my eyes. "I'm going to look for auto-mechanics jobs. Any leads?"

"What about chess? Are you going to just stop playing?"

"Yeah." I steal the pen from his hand. "There's no future for me in chess."

He snorts. "You can't just—"

"Question answered. Next round." He gives an annoyed, stubborn look, and immediately wins. How? He's drinking and

I'm not, but I'm the one slipping. "Whatever." I roll my eyes. "No follow-up questions."

He leans toward me over the table, dark eyes earnest, stars traveling on his skin. "Do you know how incredible you are?"

I cannot breathe. Temporarily. So I force myself to laugh. "Really? You're wasting your question on this?"

"I am serious. Do you realize how exceptional you are, Mallory?"

"What are you—"

"I have never seen anything like what you do with chess. *Never.*"

"I— You are ten times better than me. I beat you *once*, while playing White, and you were probably expecting an easy game."

"You haven't answered my question." He leans in even farther. He smells like soap and beer and something good and dark. "Do you know how fucking *good* you are?"

My eyes hold his. "Yes, I *know*." It almost hurts to admit to it. To this boundless talent I have, for something that I swore to myself I wouldn't pursue—a promise I fully intend to keep. "Does it bother you, that I'm that good?"

"No." He's not lying. Does he ever lie? "Maybe it should. But." He lets that *but* dangle mysteriously.

"Why?"

He clucks his tongue. "You haven't earned a question." New grid. New game. New victory for Nolan. It's my turn to slam my fist on the table. Nolan's bottle, now empty, clinks against the cheap plastic, and irritation bubbles up my throat. Screw this game.

"Are you cheating?" I ask, acid. Angry.

"No. But it's fascinating how your performance suffers when you lose your composure. You might want to work on that."

"I'm *not* losing my composure, and my tic-tac-toe performance is hardly—"

"Question," he interrupts, a new edge to his voice. "Why do you pretend you don't want this?"

"This?"

He gestures around himself. But then he says, "Chess. Why do you pretend you don't *want* to play it?"

"You don't *know* me," I bristle. "I just don't like chess that much."

He shakes his head with a small smile and draws another grid—then wins easily when I fumble. My hands are shaking, and I'm *so* done with—

"You feel it, too, don't you, Mallory?" His tone is pressing. Low. "When you play, you feel the same thing I feel."

I grit my teeth. "I have no idea what you feel. Chess is a stupid board game, and—"

"It *is* a stupid board game, but it's *yours*. I see the way you look at the pieces. It's your world, isn't it? The one you choose for yourself, well within your boundaries. You can be the queen in it. The king. The knight. Whatever you want. There are rules, and if you learn them well enough, then you'll be able to control it. You'll be able to rescue the pieces you care about. So unlike real life, huh?"

How dare he act like he *knows* me, like he—

I hate him.

I don't remember the last time I've been this angry. There's bile churning in my stomach. I tear the flier from his hand and make another grid, almost ripping the paper in the process. It takes seven tries, but I finally win.

"What the hell do you *want* from me?" I snap, leaning closer with a glare.

He lifts one eyebrow.

"Because I don't understand," I nearly yell. "*Why* are you here when you have a tournament next week? Why do you presume to know anything about me? Why do you even care about my thoughts on chess—" I end with an angry, beastly noise.

If Nolan is affected, he doesn't show it. "I thought you were starting to get an idea."

"I'm not. Just *tell* me what you want and—"

A loud sound.

I turn to the door. Tanu and the others are walking inside, holding a stack of take-out pizzas, yelling something about pepperoni and anchovy discounts. I realize how close I am to Nolan and pull back. He keeps staring at me, the ghost of a sad smile on his lips.

"I guess the game is over," he says, getting to his feet to help Tanu. "Goodnight, Mallory. And good luck."

Chapter Fifteen

Darcy loves the guinea pig hoodie I bought her ("though it's a cop-out, as Goliath will not want to copulate with a 2D piggy") and even Sabrina is impressed with her new maple leaf skates that I almost missed my plane to buy and nearly couldn't fit into my luggage.

But her love for me comes and goes. "You're the best!" she tells me on Wednesday, after I give her a ride to McKenzie's. But on Thursday, when I find her crying in the living room over something McKenzie posted on social media, it's "Why do you have to be so *nosy*? Why can't you *ever* mind your own business?"

"If they find my corpse in a ditch," I say to Mom, "tell the police not to look into her. She probably did it, but I don't want her to spend her life in prison."

"It's not just you. She's mad at the entire world."

"Was I this intense at fourteen?" It's such a ridiculous question. I'm still eighteen, but I feel as ancient as the lady from *Titanic*. Except when I compare myself with Easton and feel stuck in some pubescent stage.

"I once asked you to stop leaving the peanut butter jar open, and you called me a dictator."

I groan. "Will Darcy be like this, too?"

"Yup." She pats my shoulder. "Though she'll leave the Nutella open."

All in all, though, I come back from my trip to the puzzling revelation that no life-threatening emergencies occurred, and that without me, my family . . . did just fine. I'm half shocked, half relieved.

Oz and Defne are at the Pasternak, which means that I'm mostly unsupervised. I should use the extra time to catch up on the García Márquez readathon I signed up for on Goodreads, memorize the world capitals, dye my hair vomit green. Anything, really. Instead, I study Nolan's games.

The fury of our last night in Toronto has settled into cold resentment. Nolan said lots of things about me, some of which were correct—by pure coincidence. Broken clock, twice a day. Still, he had no right. His question game was stupid. I hope to never see him again. Probably won't.

But I do want to study the aggravating masterpieces that are his games, and my hands itch to pull them up on the chess engine. I revel in his delicious ability to wear down his opponents, deprive them of active play, and then strike like a tiger. I'm developing a more-than-mild obsession, and that's probably why I'm thinking of him when I match up with a guy named Alex on an app on Sunday night.

ALEX: Hey!

MAL: love the dog in your profile pic, is he a pitbull?

My phone immediately pings with a reply, but for several minutes I'm too distracted with lying back on the couch and analyzing the Sawyer variation for the Berlin Defense to check it.

ALEX: Yup. How have you been?

How have I *been*? That's kind of a weird question. I scroll back to his profile pic, thinking that he looks a bit familiar. He's cute. Dark hair. Dark eyes. Not that dark, though. Not as dark as . . .

MAL: have we met before?

ALEX: Are you kidding?

Nope. Not kidding. Thankfully, he reminds me before I have to admit it.

ALEX: We went to school together. I was a year ahead of you. I asked you to junior prom.

Oh. *That* Alex—except, now he has facial hair. I do remember. He'd been so . . . bland. Probably why I haven't really thought about him since.

MAL: sorry, i didn't recognize your pic. how've you been?

ALEX: Good! I'm at Rutgers. What about you?

MAL: i'm not in school

ALEX: Taking a year off? It suits you, from
your profile pic. You were always really
hot, but now . . .

The next text is three fire emojis. Given the reason I'm
on this app, I should probably find it flattering instead of . . .
blah.

Instead, I wonder how Nolan would do this. Be online. Hook
up. Poorly, probably. Isn't he a virgin? Useless in the sack.

But it's so hard to picture him doing anything poorly.
With his dark, attentive eyes; the precise, purposeful way his
large hands close around the chess pieces; his voice, always so
careful; his beautiful, brilliant strategies. He'd murmur indiscernible words under his breath at the Olympics, when he
made a mistake or regretted a move. Sometimes the hairs at the
nape of my neck would rise, and it shouldn't have been pleasant,
but I—

My phone pings again and I look at it, startled. I forgot it was
in my hand.

ALEX: Do you want to meet sometime soon,
catch up?

Hook up, he means. Though he's being appropriately subtle
about it. I bet Nolan wouldn't be nearly as low-key. I bet he'd say
something like "to have sexual intercourse" and—

Oh God.

Oh *God*.

MAL: actually, probably better not. i'm way
too busy with work, shouldn't even be
online. so sorry to waste your time.

I silence my phone, and when it vibrates with Alex's response, I don't bother checking it. Why the hell am I thinking about Nolan right now, while setting up a meeting with another person? Why is he in my head?

That's it. I'm done. This is upsetting. Confusing. Stupid. Unprecedented. No more Nolan games. No more Nolan. I need to— I can't keep thinking about him.

Starting tomorrow, I tell myself as I wait for the shower jet to warm up enough. *I won't look at his games anymore. I'll purge him. Starting tomorrow.*

I actually believe it. Until tomorrow happens.

THE PIECE IS IN *VANITY FAIR*.

Which is a problem in and of itself, as I'm out of free articles for the month. It means that when Easton texts it to me (Are you hooking up with him? Good to know I have to find out about my BFF's life from Vanity Fair!!!), I can see the title (Sawyer places second at Pasternak invitational, draws to Koch in volatile final match) and nothing else.

I just woke up after tossing and turning all night. Outside it's still dark, the glow from my phone pierces my bleary eyes, and Goliath is proudly licking his butthole somewhere by my left ear.

I really do hate my life.

MALLORY: don't have access to the article.
tl;dr?

MALLORY: how are you, by the way? did a
sasquatch capture you and make you her
bride?

BOULDER EASTON ELLIS: You WANT to read this.

MALLORY: im poor and i hate jeff bezos.

BOULDER EASTON ELLIS: That's the *Washington
Post* and USE INCOGNITO MODE jeez
what's wrong with you. Boomer.

Incognito mode works, and how did I not know about that?
I'm wondering how to exploit this newfound knowledge when
the first paragraph of the article catches my eyes.

> . . . *that Sawyer seemed uncharacteristically out of shape.
> Of course, out of shape for the world's No. 1 is still better
> than most Super GMs, but many were surprised when he
> placed second at one of the most important tournaments of
> the year—and did not attend the awards ceremony.*
>
> *"He seemed tired," Andreas Antonov, the Georgian
> GM, said in an interview. "Which isn't surprising, con-
> sidering that he came on a red-eye straight from Toronto
> and played his first match one hour after landing." Saw-
> yer's decision to participate in the Olympics was a topic*

of much discussion in the chess community. He was the only top-20 player who chose to do so.

"That's what happens when you put chess after your girlfriend," Koch, Pasternak's winner, said to ChessWorld.com. "The Sawyer era of chess is over. Next month I'll triumph at the Challengers, and then I'll take the World Championship."

Although Sawyer hasn't spoken publicly about his personal life, it seems likely that Koch was referring to Mallory Greenleaf, a talented player who has drawn some attention since the Philadelphia Open. Greenleaf is currently rated 1,892 but is rapidly climbing the rankings. At the Olympics, Greenleaf and Sawyer were part of the US team with Tanu Goel (ranking: #295) and Emil Kareem (ranking: #84) and placed third. They were also spotted together outside the tournament (see this picture) . . .

I click on the link, which brings me to Page Fucking Six. It's a photo of Nolan and me on our last night in Toronto, playing tic-tactoe in a semi-dark room. My head is bent, pencil in hand. He's staring at me, an oddly soft expression on his usually unreadable face.

Who took this? When? *Why?*

. . . Sawyer, who's a bona fide rock star, is rumored to be dating fellow chess player Mallory Greenleaf. The two were caught having an intimate moment late on . . .

Oh, fuck. No no *no*. Oh, fuckity fuck fuck.

I spring out of bed. This is bad. Badder than bad. *Baddest.*

What do I do? How do I ask for a retraction from *Vanity Fair*? Do they have a manager I can pull a Karen with?

Nolan. Nolan will know. He'll want to fix this, too. I need to get in touch with him, but how? I don't have his number. Do I summon him with a pentagram made of rooks, or—Emil!

I text him, then remember his schedule back in Toronto: *not a morning person*. Who knows when he'll wake up, and I can't wait that long when someone is wrong about me on the internet. So I run a hand through my hair and do what anyone else would: I google Nolan. I have to comb through more results than anyone who's barely twenty years old should have, including a Tumblr of him as a cat, and explicit erotic fanfiction of him and Percy Jackson sixty-nining on a hippocampus. Then find something useful: an article about Nolan emancipating himself from his family and moving into a Tribeca penthouse.

And because the internet is a scary place that doesn't believe in boundaries, there is an address.

Apparently I don't believe in boundaries, either: I'm going there to talk to Nolan. It'll take over an hour. By then Emil will have replied, and I'll text Nolan that I'm in the area. Let's get Starbucks to talk about chess and a possible defamation lawsuit to a major news outlet! Coffee's on me! Perfect plan.

Made only slightly less perfect by the fact that I find myself in the lobby of Nolan's building, and Emil still won't reply or take my calls. Because he's still asleep. The doorman takes a look at the oversized sweater I threw over my most boho dress and is ready to eject me from the building.

I smile shakily. "I'm here to see Mr. Sawyer."

The doorman's expression clearly says, *I know you chess group-*

ies, and I won't hesitate to bother the police with this. It makes me want to die a bit.

"Please?"

"I'm under instruction not to let up unexpected visitors."

"But I . . ." An idea occurs to me. It makes me want to die a lot. "He just came back from Russia and I wanted to surprise him, because I'm his . . ." *Don't gag. Show the good doorman the Page Six article.* "Girlfriend. See?" *See this pic that's on the internet and must therefore be true?*

Two minutes later I'm on the fourth floor, thinking Nolan needs way better security, when he opens the door.

I fully expected to word-vomit at him and demand that he ask his . . . publicist? Press team? Masseuse? That he ask *someone* to fix this shitshow. But when he's standing in front of me, hair wild, skin pasty white, white tee and plaid pajama pants rumpled from the mattress, I cannot help but say . . .

"You look like death."

"Mallory?" He rubs the heel of his palm in his eye. His voice is hoarse with sleep and something else. "Another dream, huh?"

"Nolan—are you okay?"

"You should come to bed. This is a stupid setup. I like it much better when we—"

"Nolan, are you *sick*?"

He blinks. His expression clears. "Are you *really* here?"

"*Yes.* What's wrong with you?"

He scratches his nape and sinks into the doorjamb, like orthostatic balance is not something he has fully mastered. "Not sure," he mumbles. "Either everything or nothing."

Nolan's apartment is a duplex three times larger than my house, a giant expanse of uncluttered spaces, wide windows, hardwood floors, and bookshelves. In the middle of the hallway there's an open suitcase, abandoned; on a nearby table, a stack of books that include Emily Dickinson, Donna Tartt, and a monograph on the Macedonian phalanx; all over, the deep, complex scent I've come to associate with Nolan—but better. Stronger. Deconstructed in its separate layers.

I follow him as he leads somewhere he forgot to say, trying not to be nosy about his space, not to stare at the cotton clinging to his wide shoulders. It's odd, being here. Like the peculiar atmosphere that every room exudes as soon as Nolan Sawyers enters it has been distilled, condensed, poured over the walls and the floors.

This impromptu trip might not have been a wise decision.

"Do you have a fever?" I ask in the kitchen.

"Impossible to tell."

I arch my eyebrow. "Let me tell you about thermometer technology."

"Ah, yeah. I forgot." Thing is, I don't even think he's being a smart-ass. I watch him grab two regular-sized mugs that look almost comically small in his hands (one says *Emil's #1 Little Bitch*), a box of Froot Loops, a half-drunk gallon of milk that's visibly curdled. He offers me the non-Emil mug like it's a whiskey shot.

"Nolan, you—" I push up my toes to reach his forehead. He's *burning*. This close, he smells like sleep and fresh sweat. Not unpleasant.

"Your hand is so cool," he says, closing his eyes in relief.

I make to take it away, but he traps it under his. "Stay." He leans into me, breath warm, chapped lips against my temple. "You never stay."

"Nolan, you're ill. We have to do something about it."

"Right. Yes." He straightens away from me. "Breakfast. Will be like new after."

"After *this*? You need nutrients, not food coloring in micro-donut shape."

"It's all I have."

"Seriously?"

He shrugs. "I was gone somewhere. Canada?"

"You were in Russia. Also, you have a stack of bowls in that credenza—who has cereal in a mug?"

"Oh." He nods. Then collapses slowly, until his forehead rests on the kitchen island. "Who's Credence?"

I pinch the bridge of my nose. I'm a good person. I pick up Mrs. Abebe's garbage can when the wind tips it over, smile at the dogs at the park, never make fun of people who say *irregardless*. I don't *deserve* this. And yet. "Listen, stay here. Don't eat that. I'll be right back."

I half carry him to the couch, his solid muscles heavy and scorching hot against me. In less than ten minutes, I run downstairs, spend a small European country's GDP at the corner bodega, and come back up to find him sleeping.

I'm Mother Teresa. Reincarnated. I need a halo for my trouble.

"Take this." Nolan's couch is a giant sectional but still too short for him. Ridiculous.

"Is it poison?"

"Rapid-release ibuprofen."

"What's that smell?"

"Your armpits."

"No, the good one."

"I'm cooking."

His eyes spring open. "You're making chicken soup."

"Which you do not deserve."

"From scratch?"

"It's really easy, and canned stuff tastes like lead poisoning and despair. By the way, you owe me forty-three dollars. Yes, I'm charging you for the emotional-support Snickers bar I bought for myself—you can Venmo, but please don't write *For Drugs* in the memo line. Just . . . take a nap. I'll be back."

He doesn't, though. Take a nap. He sits at the kitchen island and watches me in a glazed-over, pleased way as I move around quietly. It doesn't bother me, really. His eyes on me usually do strange, uncomfortable things, but today . . . maybe I just love this kitchen. It's large and cozy and modern, and I want to use it every day. I want to common-law marry it and adopt an entire pack of incontinent shar-peis with it.

"Why are you here?" he asks twenty minutes later. With the meds kicking in, he seems a little less out of it.

"There is this article in *Vanity Fair*," I explain absentmindedly while chopping carrots. Now that I'm here, taking care of Nolan in his warm apartment that smells like him and comfort food, it's hard to scrounge up the level of indignation I felt one hour ago. "About you losing to Koch."

"I *drew* with Koch. But I did lose to Liu, who in turn won to Oblonsky, and I tied with Antonov, so I placed second at the tournament—"

"Yes, I'm sure your dick is longer than Koch's, but let's focus on the matter at hand, which is that Koch told *Vanity Fair* that you and I are dating, and Page Six published pics of us in Toronto, and now whatever small nerdy percentage of the world cares about chess thinks that we have a thing."

"And we don't?"

I turn to glare at him. "You don't have *things*. You told me so."

"I also said 'until recently.'"

My heart skips a beat. "You should be way more upset about this. Since you're on your deathbed, I'll let that slide, but we'll have to set the record straight."

"Sure. Feel free."

"What does that mean? Together. We'll do it together. We can release a press statement. Invest in skywriting. *Something*."

"I won't. But you can."

I scowl. "What do you mean, you won't? My sister, my friends, they'll read the article and think it's true."

"I'm happy to text your friends, or FaceTime them, or skywrite at them to explain the situation. But I won't talk about my personal life to the press."

"Why?"

"Mal, I understand that this is upsetting, but it's not the first time this has happened to me. There's no way to fight the press when they're wrong. You can only ignore it. First rule of Chess Club: never google yourself."

I cover the soup with a lid and lean against the counter, arms crossed. "Pretty sure the first rule of Chess Club is White moves first. And I understand you were burned by the Baudelaire rumor, but—"

"I was referring to the shit they printed about my grandfather." He gives me a vacuous look. "What's the Baudelaire rumor?"

I look away. Embarrassing, that I know of it and he doesn't. Makes it sound like I care more about his love life than he does. "Just . . . people said you dated a Baudelaire?"

"Oh, yeah. The sisters, right? Emil told me about it."

"Is it true?"

His eyebrow lifts. "You know it isn't."

Right. I do. "How did the rumor start, then?"

"One of them was at some party my manager made me go to, back when I still listened to her. That was probably enough."

I lean my elbows on the island, hating how interested I am. "Which Baudelaire?"

"Name started with a *J*, I think?"

I sigh. They all have *J* names. "So, what happened? You were talking and you didn't want to . . . you know."

"Would you?"

"If it were me? Hell yeah."

He tilts his head. "Why would you?"

"What do you mean?"

"What would you get out of it?"

I shrug. "I like sex. It's fun. It feels good—*really* good, sometimes. Especially when you're in the mood and you do it with attractive or interesting people. I'm not ashamed of it."

"You shouldn't be," he says, but I can tell that he doesn't completely get it. That sex, desire, are something he's still wrapping his head around. "What about feeling closer to someone? Making a connection?"

"Maybe. I'm sure sex means different things to different people, and they're all valid." I swat the memory of last night and Alex away, like it's a fruit fly. "But the human connection part . . . that's not why *I* do it. It's risky."

"Risky? How?"

I shrug, not about to explain. "I don't need that stuff. I'm busy enough."

He nods like he knows. "Taking care of your family, right?"

I arch an eyebrow. "Weren't we talking about your Baudelaire affair?"

"I don't really remember what happened. We— Wait."

"What?" I lean closer, wide eyed.

"Kasparov was there."

"The former world champion?"

"Yes. He wanted to play with me."

"And?"

"What do you mean, and? I went to play."

"Let me get this straight. You chose playing chess with an old man over getting laid?"

He looks at me like he's a cloistered nun and I'm explaining Bitcoin to him. "Did you get that it was *Kasparov*?"

I laugh. Then I laugh again. Then I laugh some more, forehead against my palms, thinking that when he's not a total dick, Nolan is actually kind of cute. When I look up, he has taken a strand of my hair and is rubbing it between his fingertips like it's mulberry silk. His eyes are still a bit glassy, so I let him.

"Was it at least the best game of your life?" I ask.

He stares into my eyes. "No. It wasn't."

"Which one was, then?"

More staring. A stray shiver travels up my spine, coming from who knows where. Then the kitchen timer rings, and we both glance away.

I put the soup in his Emil's Little Bitch mug because it's a mental image I deserve to have.

"This is good," he says after the first spoonful, sounding offensively surprised. "Not as good as your mom's meat loaf, but—"

I pinch him on the biceps, where there's almost no yield because his muscles strain the sleeves of his T-shirt, and his lopsided smile appears. He has four helpings, which he eats boyishly while I munch on my Snickers and pretend not to be flattered. My adrenaline high is coming down, and my body is starting to remember that I have given it fewer than five hours of sleep and no caffeine.

"Do you cook?" I ask distractedly.

"Rarely. And mediocrely."

"And yet, you have the best kitchen I've ever seen." I shake my head. "The money one can earn from tournaments is a bit obscene."

"It is, but I was a trust-fund baby. I'll let you decide if that's more or less morally vile."

"Nice of your parents."

"My grandfather," he corrects. "He used to own this apartment."

"Oh." I bite my lip, thinking whether I want to ask. "Was that your grandfather who . . ."

"Yup. Who played chess and went crazy and almost got me killed when I was thirteen." His smile is small, not as bitter as I'd have expected. I wince anyway.

"Not the best way to talk about mental health," I say neutrally.

"Right. My grandfather, who was diagnosed with rapid-decline behavioral variant frontotemporal dementia. Does that sound better?" I don't reply. Then he adds, "There is a familial variant of frontotemporal dementia, did you know?"

I open my mouth, then I close it. There's a faraway feeling to him that seems to have little to do with his fever. I should tread carefully.

Nolan Sawyer, needing care. Sounds fake. But.

"Are you afraid it'll happen to you?"

He huffs out a humorless laugh. "You know what's funny? I used to be terrified of it, but I know it won't. Because I got genetic testing as soon as I emancipated. But my father, as far as I know, did not get tested, and until I stopped taking his calls, he told me every day, every *single* day, that if I kept playing chess, I'd end up like my grandfather. As though that's what his problem was: he played too much chess."

"That seems . . . foolish."

"Yeah, well. Foolish people will say foolish things."

He's not meeting my eyes. He stares down into his empty mug, elbows on the marble counter, and I feel myself leaning closer. Nolan seems raw, and I don't want to risk touching him, but I'd like to be *here*. With him.

It's something I do with Easton, when she's feeling down. Darcy. Sabrina, when she lets me. Get a little closer than is polite. Share the same air. Let our scents mix together. I do it for my sisters and my friend, and now for this stupid overgrown world chess champion that I'm apparently nursing back to health.

Weirdos, both of us.

"This apartment he left you . . . It's big for one person," I murmur.

"Want to move in?" His tone matches mine, intimate.

"Sure. I'll sell my pancreas. It should cover the first three months of rent."

"You don't have to pay rent. Just pick a room."

"And I'll pay you back in company? Save you from having dinner alone at your candelabra-lit fifty-foot cherrywood table, like Bruce Wayne?"

"I usually have dinner standing up in front of that chess-board over there."

"I'm surprised you have dinner at all. And don't just sustain yourself on the tears of your rivals."

He smiles again, and God.

He is offensively, uniquely, devastatingly handsome.

I take a step back, reaching for my purse, throwing away the Snickers wrapper. "Leftover soup's in the fridge. Take ibuprofen again in five hours. And have someone come over so if you pass out, they'll notice before the rats eat your intestines."

"You're here."

"I *was* here. I'm leaving now."

Nolan deflates visibly, and something like compassion bites into me.

"Where's Emil?" I ask.

"I'm not going to call Emil because I have the sniffles. He's busy with midterms and spending three hours a day pining after Tanu."

"Someone else, then."

He shakes his head. "I'll be fine."

"You won't. You were half dead when I got here."

"Then stay."

"I'm already late for Zugzwang. I . . ."

He's staring at me with those dark, clear eyes, and I just can't go. I can't leave him. What if he gets dehydrated and dies? Will that be on me, then? I'm not giving his ghost the satisfaction of haunting several generations of Greenleaf women. I'm keeping this jerk alive.

"Since both our jobs consist of playing chess, we should play a game," he says while I text Defne that something urgent has come up. "Just to be productive members of this capitalistic society."

"Nice try."

"Did it work?"

"No. Nolan, you still look like death. Just go nap while I waste my day watching *Dragon Age* playthroughs on your Wi-Fi."

"Dragon *what*?"

And that's how I find myself on Nolan's leather couch, telling him about elves and eggheads and the end of the world, soothed by the video and by Nolan's presence.

"I like this better than the Jughead show," he says ten minutes in. I yawn, quite pleased.

Then, another ten minutes later, I'm only fast asleep.

THE EARLY AFTERNOON SUNLIGHT IS BRIGHT, BUT I DON'T care. I get to ignore it because the most delicious blanket is wrapped around me. Flawless, A+, 12/10, five-star Amazon review. It keeps me toasty and presses me into the back of the couch, solid and heavy, the perfect mix of hard and soft. Mostly hard, but in a good way. It even slipped a leg right between mine, and its arms are looped around my rib cage. It makes it nearly impossible for me to move, but I don't mind, because I feel protected from attacks from all sides. Like the king during good chess.

I'm not leaving this place, ever. I live here now, in heaven. I open my eyes to survey my new kingdom and—

Nolan is right here. Looking at me. And something within me tells me I should panic, but all I can do is say:

"Hey."

"Hey," he says back, and I nearly feel the gravel of his voice against my lips. He smells of something ineffably rich and good.

"Hey," I say again, stupidly, and we're both smiling, and the air between us is sweet, and his eyes, his nose, his lips are suddenly closer, and—

Something buzzes and I splash back into reality. I wiggle inside of Nolan's grip, shooting up to a sitting position.

"Ignore it," he orders, but I ignore *him*.

What just happened? Oh God. I've never slept with someone else. *Never.* Not like this. Not . . . what's happening?

And the buzz, it's still going on. "I think—my phone—" Here it is. How do you pick up? Red? No, green. "Hello."

"Mal? You okay?" Defne.

"Yes. Sorry about not coming in, I—"

"Have you seen the paper?"

Oh, shit. The article. "I . . . Don't worry about it. It's a lie, I'm not sleeping with Nolan." Nolan's eyebrow lifts. His arms are still looped around my waist, and I die inside. "I meant, we're not—"

"This has nothing to do with Nolan."

"Oh." Phew. "What then?"

"It's the Challengers, Mal. They chose you as one of this year's participants."

Chapter Sixteen

"—*chess drama is usually boring, but this one might actually be juicy. Could you explain to our audience what's going on in the World Championship?*"

"*Here is the deal, Mark: out of the ten people who make it into the Challengers tournament, nine are selected because of ratings, or because they win qualification tournaments. The tenth—the wild card—is chosen by FIDE. It's usually a way to include a top-ten player who for some reason didn't make it in. This year, everyone thought that the wildcard would be Antonov. Or Zemaitis. Or Panya, though he's due to have a baby in February, when the championship will be on, and probably would have declined. Instead, last week the committee selected a low-rated, inexperienced player. Now, to be fair, Greenleaf is a talented player with great promise. But she's only played professionally for a couple of months, and is still unproven. Her performance at the Olympics was remarkable, but choosing her for the Challengers is akin to asking a third grader to play an NFL game. The tournament is happening the week after Thanksgiving in Las Vegas, and many doubt that she can hold her own against other stratospheric players.*"

"*Some say she was chosen because she's a woman?*"

"*There has been lots of conversation over the lack of female representation in professional chess, and Greenleaf's invitation could be a response to that. But there are many women with higher rankings and more experience who earned that spot. Which had some people speculating that it's not because she is a woman, but because she's the woman of a particular chess player.*"

"*Juicy!*"

"*Yup. Nolan Sawyer— You've heard of Sawyer, right?*"

"*Of course.*"

"*He's chess royalty, a bona fide rock star. So influential in the sport, he might have pressured FIDE into choosing a specific player for the Challengers. And he has been photographed with Greenleaf in positions that are . . .*"

"*I see what you mean.*"

"*I bet you do! So people are wondering if—*"

"You should stop torturing yourself, Mal."

I look up from my iMac to find Defne leaning against the doorframe, silver septum ring gleaming as she gives me a worried look.

"And if you decide to *continue* torturing yourself, could you use your headphones?" Oz glares at me from his desk. "Some of us are not unlearned prodigies mistakenly assumed to be Nolan Sawyer's new concubine. Some of us have to actually *practice* chess."

"I just . . ." I massage my temple. "Why's the *Today* show talking about chess? Shouldn't they cover important stuff? Fracking, or the sustainable terraforming of Mars, or Malala's book club?"

Oz blinks. "Have you literally *ever* watched cable television?"

I groan and head-desk.

I know I'm being Sabrina-level sullen, but I earned the right, because November has been *sucking*: everyone thinks I'm some Nolan groupie who slept her way into chess. Easton loves Colorado too much to come home for Thanksgiving—a scary ellipsis at the end of the dangling sentence that's our friendship. And someone I went to middle school with texted to ask if I'm "really a professional softball player now, pregnant with a Dutch underwear model's triplets?" A game of telephone, but still a clear sign that my name's going around too much, and that Mom or Sabrina might come across my secret career any day.

So, yeah. *Sullen* is now my defining personality trait. I'm more sulk than woman, ready to brood with reckless abandon at a moment's notice.

"I should have refused the invitation," I mumble against the polished wood.

"The prize is one hundred thousand dollars," Oz reminds me acidly. "We've been over the tax withholdings and the net earnings and the amounts of mortgage payments you'll be able to afford when you were moping all over yourself last week. I did *not* whip out the calculator app for you to step back now."

"It's just . . . mortifying. People are saying on national television that I'm too weak to survive the winter."

"People have said on the same national television that the California wildfires were started by space lasers." Oz rolls his eyes. "Listen, it's not that I don't want to provide scaffolding for your delicate nerves, but as I mentioned before, I'd rather die impaled by a harpoon while farming beets than engage with the fungus of human emotions—"

"Oz," Defne interrupts, "could you leave us for a few minutes?"

"What?"

"Mallory and I need some privacy. To talk about mushrooms and such."

"But all my stuff is here. What am I supposed to do?"

"I don't know. Go farm beets? Find a harpoon? Come back in half an hour. Chop chop."

Defne's my boss, but she's never *felt* like my boss so much as she does now, rounding my desk with a serious expression, sitting on it with an agile hop, a cloud of merrily jingling earrings and citrus and tobacco. She stares like we're about to have a solemn talk, and it occurs to me that the misery of the past few days could be exponentially more pukeworthy if I were to be fired.

Crap.

"I know I've been whining, but I promise—"

"They're right, Mal."

"Who is right?"

"FIDE *did* choose you because you are a woman." She pauses, letting her words land. "The Nolan thing is bullshit, of course. He doesn't have *nearly* as much sway on FIDE, and FIDE must have made the decision before those pics came out. I don't know what's happening between you two—"

"Nothing!"

It's true enough. I haven't seen Nolan since I ran out of his apartment three weeks ago in an internet-induced panic, though he did get my number (from Emil, I assume) because he's been texting me. Initially stuff like Ran away again, did you? and Mallory. Are you okay? and I just want to talk to you. Then, a few days later, while I was watering Darcy's chia porcupine, Cormenzana always opens with the Ruy Lopez. It was followed by many similar messages, with little advice (Kotov vs. Pachman, 1950) and big (Make sure you hydrate).

I don't reply. I never reply, because . . .

Because I don't want to.

Because we're not friends.

Because I woke up on his couch and my first instinct was to burrow into him. A horror story in fifteen words.

I don't reply, but I do read. And in between bouts of sulking, I do what he recommends, because it's irritatingly good advice. I tell myself that he's helping me only because he hates Koch, but I don't bother trying to believe it.

It's not like I'm going to win the Challengers anyway. After all, they only chose me because . . .

"Did you say FIDE *did* choose me because I'm a woman?"

Defne nods. Then amends, "Not only. But it played a big role."

"Why? Tons of women play."

"What do you know about women in chess?"

"Not much." I remember Koch's sneer in Philly. *I like it better when women stick to their own tournaments.* "Just that there are separate tournaments, only for women."

"Bigger than that—there are separate leagues, separate rankings. It's a controversial topic: some say these leagues shouldn't exist, because they hold women back and imply that they cannot hold their own against male players. Others disagree, and want to preserve a space in which we're not harassed or made to feel like we're less."

"What do you think?"

She sighs. "I think it's damned if you do, damned if you don't. There's no winning here, and that's part of why I stopped playing competitively and chose to focus on . . . still chess, but the part of it that doesn't make me want to stab a down pillow with a cutlery knife. That stuff's *expensive*."

I'm no stranger to overt and covert sexism—I used to work in a *garage*, for *Bob*—and dudes with moronic takes have been a constant in my life, so—

Except that, no. They *haven't*.

"I don't remember it being like that when I played as a kid," I tell Defne. "Maybe because I was unrated, or my dad shielded me from it, but chess wasn't *always* a male-dominated sport."

She nods. "When you were young, everyone was fascinated with chess and no one really commented on gender, right?"

"Yes."

"You probably narrowly missed the interesting part. When kids grow up, start looking up to the greats, and find out that Kasparov, their *fave*, once said that no woman could ever sustain a prolonged battle."

I stiffen. "Are you serious?"

"Once, after a tournament, I went to dinner with other players. Someone pulled up a YouTube video—an old interview of Fischer saying that women are stupid and bad at chess. Everyone thought it was hilarious." Defne looks down at her shoes, uncharacteristically subdued. "I was seventeen. And a GM. And the only woman at the table."

"I— Screw that, Defne." I stand, livid. She was younger than I am now. Alone with dickheads. "Fischer was a raging antisemite anyway. He doesn't get to—"

"The hurtful part wasn't Fischer, but the guys in my age group who thought that wearing a *Female chess player is an oxymoron* shirt might be a fun joke. The hurtful part was FIDE not doing anything about it. And I'm there, going to tournaments, losing more and more, often to these chess bros who joke about how female brains are too folded to really comprehend king safety, and I start wondering if they're right. Female GMs are what, one percent? That's nothing. Maybe we really *are* less. Maybe we do need our special league."

"Do you . . ." I blink at her, betrayed. "Do you really think that?"

"I did. For a while. And the more I did, the more I lost. I took a chess break, actually. Went to college, got my MBA—did you know I have an MBA? Now you do, please don't tell anyone, it's my most shameful secret. Anyway, I thought I was done with chess. Then, one day, I read about a study.

"Some scientist in Europe took a bunch of women and had them play online chess against male opponents in their same rating bracket. When the female players didn't know the gender of their opponent, they won fifty percent of the games. When the female players were led to believe that their opponent was a woman, they won fifty percent of the games. When they were *told* that they were playing against men, their performance dropped. But in truth, their opponents were always the same." She shrugs. Her earrings jingle again, despondent. "If you're a woman, this system tears you down. Makes you doubt yourself and drop out of the chess club to leave room for the ones who are actually talented. Oz, Emil, Nolan . . . even the good ones, they don't know how it feels. They don't know what it's like, being told that you're inherently destined to be second best." Suddenly, Defne's expression shifts into an impish smile. "But it's not true. And once we know it, they cannot take it away from us. The day after I read about the study, I went to get this." She slips her arm out of the sleeve of her cardigan. The chessboard tattoo curves against her biceps.

"What is it?"

"Moscow, 2002. The final position of the game Judith Polgar won against Garry Kasparov. Despite that pesky thing he once referred to as her 'imperfect feminine psyche.'"

I laugh. I laugh, and I don't stop for a good minute. "This is—this is *amazing*."

"I know." Defne laughs, too. Then her face grows serious, and she takes my hand. "Mallory, I grew up in this world, and I know how these assholes think. There has been a reckoning. The old farts at FIDE realize that they can't keep women out of chess, and they saw you as an opportunity. An outsider who made a big splash at high-profile events. Unlike with other women who've been around for years, they can justify their choice by saying that your score is only low because you're new—but that you're also promising enough to invite. They can use you to virtue-signal. But I *know* them. I know that they also think that you can't be *that* good. That your victories were probably a fluke, and that you won't win the Challengers."

Something tightens low in my gut. Isn't it the same thing I've been telling myself for weeks? That I cannot compete. That I'm unprepared. That I'm not as good. *I'm not going to win* has been the default status in my brain. Because . . . I'm inexperienced. Because I don't want it or deserve it. Because I'm a woman?

Do you know how incredible you are? Nolan asked me in Toronto. I told him yes, while still believing deep down that I wasn't anything special after all. Which one is it, then?

I look Defne in the eye. She has always encouraged me. Always been honest. No relentless, toxic positivity with her.

"Do you think I can win the Challengers?" I ask her, trembling a little at the prospect of the answer.

She takes my other hand, and I feel *held*. I feel *comforted*. I feel *stronger*. "Mallory. I think you can win the World Championship."

Chapter Seventeen

A sedan picks us up from the Las Vegas airport and brings us to the Westgate. In the elevator, a businesslike FIDE employee tells me about the press conference room, the VIP lounges, and a daily meal expense allowance that thoroughly humiliates the Greenleaf monthly grocery budget. There is a black embossed letter on my pillow: an invitation for an opening gala—Nevada governor in attendance. The US ambassador to Azerbaijan, too, since he's scheduled to make the ceremonial opening move.

That's how big of a deal the Challengers is. So big, I have to wonder if the current world champion is present. Then promptly slap myself for it.

Since thinking about Nolan has only been a source of problems.

"Are you *sure* there isn't a dress code?" I ask Defne across our neighboring balconies. I wish Darcy and Sabrina were here. Mom, too, would love making fun of the ridiculous extravagance. But they're back home, nursing the lie I've left them with ("visiting Easton in Boulder"). Mom's relieved that I get to hang out with her again. Sabrina hates me because I am "more self-centered than a dartboard." Darcy is googling me hard enough to make Silicon Valley stocks rise two hundred points.

And I'm here alone. Well—almost.

"No dress code," Defne says. "Though it'll probably be a blazer-over-button-down parade. Lots of grays."

"Should I buy a black pencil skirt?"

"If you want. But I'd miss seeing you onstage in your primary colors crop top."

I grin, feeling a sudden surge of affection. "Lucky for you, I packed it."

For the gala, I put on a sheath dress Easton bought me at Goodwill for seven dollars. Because my life is a shit McMuffin, and because I've given up on any attempt not to eat it, I'm not surprised when the first person I meet is Koch.

"Well, well, well," he says, like a poorly written Austin Powers villain. "Look what Sawyer's dick and FIDE's pity toward the less fortunate dragged in."

"Is it very expensive, Malte?" I ask, plucking a chocolate-covered strawberry from a tray.

"What?"

"The vintage sexism you wear all the time."

His eyes narrow and he steps closer. "You don't belong here, Greenleaf. You're the only player who didn't earn her place in the Challengers. You're *nobody*."

I want to push him away. I want to punch him. I want to stuff the strawberry in his nose. But the room is full of press. I spot PBS cameras, cable TV mics. ChessWorld.com is going to milk the shit out of this event, probably live stream the players plucking their eyebrows. There is no margin of error.

So I smile sweetly. "And yet, the last time you and this nobody played, this nobody won. Food for thought, huh?"

I whirl around and look for an alcohol-free drink, cherishing the image of Koch's eyebrow twitching. I can't find Defne, or anyone else I know, but I'll get acquainted with the other players soon enough: the tournament is round robin, one game per day. A lively piano song plays, and I drift to the table, eager to stuff my face, where someone hugs me from behind.

"Hiiiii!"

"Tanu!"

"This *dress*," she tells me, looking at the bright green embroidery. "Daddy likey."

"Tanu, we've been over this." Behind her, Emil shakes his head and leans in to hug me. "I cannot take her anywhere, Greenleaf. I don't know why I persevere."

"Guys, what are you doing here? Shouldn't you be at school?"

"School, shmool." Tanu waves her hand. "We live freely. We're not chained by the obligations of modern mundanity."

"Winter break," Emil explains.

"Ah."

"We're here to study. For when Nolan preps for the World Championship."

"Oh. Is Nolan here?"

"Mal, we'd love to help *you*, too," Tanu says. *Not* answering me.

"Help me?"

"Most players are here with a team of seconds. You only have Defne, right?"

Seconds are players' assistants who help them train and debrief, analyze old games, come up with new attack and defensive strategies. "Defne, yeah. And . . ." And Nolan. Nolan's texts. Which seem to answer my questions before I ask them. Not that I'll admit it. "Oz Nothomb said he'd be available to talk strategy."

"Then let us help. We could meet in the mornings. Go over your opponent's weaknesses and strengths. Some openings. Mal, you're so talented, and this stuff—it could make a difference."

"Did Nolan put you up to this?"

They exchange a short look. "Listen," Emil says, "Nolan might want you to win, but so do we." He pouts like a child. "Did that poutine we shared in Toronto mean nothing to you?"

And that's how I find myself walking into an IHOP with Defne at seven the following morning. Tanu and Emil are already sharing a custard-filled French toast, and if Defne needs an introduction . . . she doesn't. She hugs them tight and asks Tanu how Stanford is treating her, when she got bangs, and what about her cat? I'm considering demanding a drawn schematic of how everyone knows everyone else when Emil whips out a board and says, eyes NFL-coach sharp: "Thagard-Vork. Danish. Thirty-six. Excellent positional player, though well past his prime. He loves opening with d4 and c4."

"But sometimes he does some weird queen stuff, e4, c5, qh5. You *gotta* see this, Mal. It's nuts."

It *is* nuts. And three hours later, when he does some weird queen stuff and I know exactly how to answer, it's even more nuts.

My name, and the US flag next to it, are everywhere. Not taped pieces of paper, but embossed on the side of the table, the panels, the chair, like someone spent a whole lot of money at Kinko's. There are five tables on the stage and five hundred deadly silent people in the audience. Live-stream screens are everywhere, and ominous graphics run during idle moments.

10 players.

9 days.

45 matches.

1 winner.

Zum zum zuuuum.

The press crowds every corner, but in a respectful, distanced way, as though the players are not to be disturbed. I glance at the monitor while Thagard-Vork eyes my knight. All the players look the same, little soldiers in neutral colors frowning down at little boards in neutral colors. Except for the girl at the fourth table, who sticks out like a sore thumb with my white-blond hair and teal sweater.

I smile, close my eyes, and win without ever being in jeopardy. It takes me eighteen moves.

"She was a million miles ahead of me," Thagard-Vork says at the post-game analysis press conference. My first interview. I tried to skip, but one of the directors showed me his fancy badge and said, *"It's mandatory."* "When she sacrificed her knight . . ." He shakes his head, looking at the replay screen. I notice a weird cowlick on my forehead. "She was a million miles ahead," he repeats.

"It was a challenging game," I lie to the host.

I don't fully relax until I'm alone in the elevator, away from all the cameras.

Chess computers are so powerful these days, so quick to find the perfect move that electronic devices and even watches—hell, even *lip balm*—aren't allowed in the tournament to prevent cheating. Which means that my phone is charging at my bedside table, full of notifications. When I get back to my room, I open Darcy's first.

DARCYBUTT: How can the entirety of your hair be as straight as a limp noodle except for one single curl smack in the middle of your forehead?

I laugh.

Eight games to go.

I WIN THE FOLLOWING GAME (KAWAMURA; US; #8) THANKS TO a half-open file, and the one after (Davies; UK; #13), although it takes me five hours.

By the end of day three I'm number one in the tournament, tied with Koch and Sabir. All other players have either suffered a loss or settled for draws. That's when the press decides that respectful distance won't cut it, and starts circling around the lounge area, where I'm sitting with Defne eating pistachio Oreos.

They look thirsty. Sharky.

"Maybe you should give an interview. Before they corner you at the IHOP with Tanil," she muses.

"Tanil?"

"Tanu and Emil. It's their ship name. Anyway, the other players have been giving interviews. You should do the same."

"I already do the post-game analyses."

"You don't get it. They don't want to know about your chess. They want to know about *you*."

And that's how I find myself with a CNN mic hovering an inch from my mouth. It smells like burnt plastic and cologne. Or maybe it's the journalist.

"How is it, being the dark horse of the Challengers?"

What's a dark horse again? "It's . . . great."

"Is it odd, being the only woman?"

"It's odd that there are so few women in chess. But I don't feel odd."

"You're the daughter of a GM. What would he say if he were here?"

Breaking news: I officially hate giving interviews. "I don't know, because he's not here." Darcy better never see this.

"What about Nolan Sawyer? How would he feel if you ended up becoming the Challenger, given your relationship?"

There is no relationship. "Good question. You should ask him."

"A lot of people think that it might come down to you and Koch. What do you say about that?"

I'm not sure why I choose that moment to look at the camera. And I'm not sure why I lean a bit into the mic, which really does smell foul. "I'm not afraid of Koch," I say. "I've defeated him once, after all."

"We might have to work on your interviewing skills," Defne tells me the following morning at the IHOP with Tanil (it's growing on me). They have taken to bringing a list of openings and positions that they want to show me. The list has three different handwritings on it, but I pretend not to notice. Their analyses are sharp, on point, brilliant, brilliant past what I'd expect from two talented players who never quite got to the top. I pretend not to notice that, either.

My first draw is on the fourth day, against Petek (Hungary; #4). The game is a mess of Najdorf Sicilian, which I knew he'd play, long pockets of mind-numbing boredom, and me attempting to surprise him into a retreat Defne once taught me when we were looking into Paco Vallejo's games. I come this close to winning—*this* close—but after six hours, when he holds his hand to me and offers a draw, I take it.

"It's for the best," Defne tells me the following day. "Tomorrow you'd have been exhausted otherwise." But I draw on my fifth game, too, and then on my sixth and seventh, and I'm exhausted anyway, exhausted from worrying and second-guessing myself and hating the opportunities I'm missing. I'm not good, after all. I'm a mediocre player. Defne was wrong. Nolan was wrong. Dad was wrong. CNN is suddenly less interested in interviewing me. I leave the post-game analysis with my head down, and I can barely thank Eleni from the BBC when she smiles and tells me that she's rooting for me. Maybe if I pull a Lindsay Lohan and trash my room I'll feel better?

> **DARCYBUTT:** Koch has one more win, but he also has a loss against Sabir. You're not out of the running. At all.

> **DARCYBUTT:** Though it would help if you beat Sabir tomorrow.

> **MALLORY:** bb do you even know how to play chess?

> **DARCYBUTT:** I don't need to know how the little priest moves to understand a score system.

I've been starfishing in bed and woe-is-me-ing for one hour

when someone sends a bowl of noodle soup and three Snickers bars up to my room. I refuse to think about its origins as I devour all of it, and then, with my stomach full and my skin warm and the sweet taste of chocolate lingering in my mouth, I fall into a deep, dreamless sleep.

The following day I wake up rested and win against Sabir with the Trompowsky.

IT DOES COME DOWN TO KOCH AND ME.

Sabir trails a point behind, but with only one game left, he might as well be fracking on Jupiter. Some overworked intern from the IT department whips up new graphics: the monitors are now pictures of Koch and me from previous games. I bite down on my lip; Koch looks at the ceiling. He squeezes his eyes shut; I nibble on my thumbnail.

I didn't even know that I do that. But I've looked at myself on camera more in the past week than in the previous decade. Every time I see myself play with the tips of my hair, I want to shank myself and flip the monitor table. Instead I smile politely and tell the post-game analysis host, "There, I was considering knight e5. But then I went for d4. More pressure, I figured."

Good Morning America, Defne tells me, did a short piece on me. NPR requested an interview—Terry Gross. I've been asked for at least twenty autographs—which, I realize around the seventh, are the same signatures I use at the bank and put me at significant risk for identity theft. An Etsy store sells T-shirts, sweaters, onesies, with my stylized face on them. Eleni from the BBC wears one.

People must be unhinged. I can't really comprehend it. I might be dissociating, but focusing on Koch's old games makes it better. Mom calls at night, asking how I like the mountains, and I want to tell her, I want to tell her so bad that my guts are twisted and I feel like crying and tearing apart this entire hotel and people need to stop, stop, stop looking at me and asking me how my form is and I wish she was here, I wish Dad was here, I wish I didn't feel so alone.

Instead we talk about Sabrina's birthday next week, how the backpack I ordered for her should arrive any day and Mom should intercept the package.

"I'm afraid that I always forget to tell you," Mom says in the end, "but I love you. And I couldn't be prouder of you." I want to say it back, how much I love her and miss her, not only having her near, but . . . being someone's daughter, taken care of, protected. Having someone standing between me and the world. But it seems wrong to add that bit of truth to all the lies I've been saying, so I hang up and sit on the edge of the mattress, head in my palms like some tortured action hero from a nineties movie, thinking that I will have to tell her. About the chess. The second I get back home, I will. If she doesn't catch sight of me on *Good Morning Fucking America*.

I dry my eyes and shuffle downstairs to steal a sandwich from the lounge area. Some of the other challengers are sitting there, eating and drinking and laughing. They're all going to be playing tomorrow, but the stakes are low for them. Their tournament is over.

Davies, the British guy I beat on day two, notices me and beckons me closer. My previous informal interactions with other chess players have taught me to just . . . *not*, but I can't believably pretend I didn't see him. I go to him, clutching my caprese panini, fully expecting some version of *She doesn't even go here*. The group quiets. "Greenleaf, we need to ask you something."

I brace myself. "Yeah?"

"A favor. Not a question."

The bracing intensifies. "What's that?"

"Could you please massacre Koch tomorrow?"

Everyone laughs. *At* me? *With?* "Excuse me?"

"We'd be really grateful if you could humiliate the shit out of him," someone adds.

"Every time he loses, a dragon shits a goldbrick."

"Sex is good, but have you ever heard Koch's little whine when he's checkmated?"

"Basically," Davies cuts through the others, "we despise him as a human being and we'd revel in any unhappiness you could provide for him."

"Please, Greenleaf, don't doodle on the score sheet."

This time when everyone laughs, I join in. "Wow. And there I was, thinking I was alone in my revulsion."

"No way. He's been a total dickhead to every single one of us."

"And his stupid tricks. When he trash-talks during a game while you're trying to focus."

"Or when he starts walking in circles around the chessboard. I'm thinking about the next move and he's making me dizzy!"

"You've only been dealing with him for a few months—we had to put up with his cologne phase."

"Sauvage by Christian Dior. Jesus."

"He *bathed* in it."

"I'm pretty sure he drank it."

I shake my head, laughing. "I'd love to win. I just don't know if I can."

"You are an alchemist," Thagard-Vork says kindly. "You can do anything you want, Greenleaf." I feel myself flush.

"Hey, Greenleaf." Kawamura. "Are you on Discord?"

"Discord?"

"The messaging app. We have a server with most of the top-twenty players. We talk chess, gossip about FIDE, the usual. I'd love to send you an invite."

"Oh." I scratch my neck, looking around. These guys range from my age to late thirties. Would I even fit in? "I'm not in the top twenty."

They laugh. Someone says, "Yet," and they laugh harder.

"Koch isn't in it, by the way. Which is great, since we have a whole channel dedicated to him."

"And we'd rather crap glass twice a day than voluntarily interact with him."

"Our love language is anti-Koch memes." More laughter.

"Nolan's also not in it."

"But we did invite him. He declined."

"Yeah, we don't hate Sawyer. Though he did used to be a little shit," Petek says.

"He just used to be a teenager," Kawamura says. More laughter. The mix of accents and intonations is almost musical, and it makes me feel a little uncultured. I barely speak English. I don't really know the difference between *lay* and *lie*, and I keep forgetting when to stick an apostrophe in *your*.

"But Sawyer is not important, you see," Davies explains. "We can't beat him—no one can, except for you. So we like to pretend he doesn't exist."

Petek clears his throat and turns to me conspiratorially, voice pitched low. "Please don't tell Sawyer I said that he used to be a little shit. He's really fit, and I have a wife and two beautiful daughters back home who would really miss me. I'm teaching them to play chess, and they were rooting for you during our game. They wouldn't mind an autograph, actually."

"Why would I tell . . . Oh. *Oh.* No, Nolan and I . . . we're not really dating. We're barely friends. Don't believe the press."

"I usually don't. But I thought that might be true, since he showed up for the Challengers. He usually doesn't. My apologies. Would you like to see a photo of my family?"

Like it's becoming a habit of mine, I lean forward to see the picture, and pretend I didn't hear the rest.

Chapter Eighteen

The match between Koch and me is delayed, because the live-streaming demands are record high and something needs to be done to adjust FIDE's website's capacity. It takes about twenty minutes to fix it, which I spend in the lounge, eyes closed. I try to think about nothing, but flashes of critical positions pop up behind my eyelids, snatches of earworms I cannot purge.

Koch and I are alone on the stage. I'm wearing the long-sleeved white maxi dress that Darcy and Sabrina call "my *Corpse Bride* outfit," purely because it's Mom's favorite.

I think I need a hug.

But I also think I might be able to win this, if I manage not to go all Bob Ross over my score sheet.

I do what Tanil (God, it's catchy) recommended and open with the Ruy Lopez. It's the opening Koch has the worst track record with, and I'm happy to be playing White. He answers with the Berlin variation, and I reply with the anti-Berlin. A couple more moves, and Koch castles short.

That's when the problems start.

"Touch-move. Bishop," he says when I'm in the process to move my knight.

I look up. It is, I realize, the first time I've looked at him since the game started. My contempt for him is almost physical. "Excuse me?"

"Touch-move. If you touch a piece, you have to move it. I know you're not familiar with chess rules, but—"

"I barely brushed against the bishop with the back of my finger."

"That's touching, isn't it?"

The audience cannot hear us, but they can see us talk, and there are curious murmurs creeping up to the stage. Koch is well aware that this is a stupid moment to call touch-take, but I can see exactly what he wants me to do: turn to the tournament director and kick up a fuss. Since I'll be the one having to defend myself, he's hoping that whatever happens next will upset me enough to destabilize the rest of my game.

I'm not saying he's the worst human being in the world. I'm sure there are worse ones hanging out on 8chan or on the board of directors of British Petroleum. But Malte Koch is, quite frankly, the shittiest person I've ever met.

I exhale and look at my bishop. I didn't plan to move it, but . . . But.

Defne is a fan of attacking the king with the bishop pair. She just loves that stuff, to the point that I've studied a bunch of games with it. Which means that . . .

I press my lips together and advance my bishop.

"Here," I smile sweetly, activating his clock. His eyes widen in shock, and it feels good.

I gain the upper hand quickly. No chance to finalize the game, but minutes go by, then hours, and I'm the one showing the most initiative, dominating the center, building attacks on the sides. Koch is, and it hurts my brain and my heart to admit it, an excellent positional player, able to fend off the little locks I lay out, the threats I prepare, the combinations I orchestrate. He doesn't, however, think as far ahead as I do, and it's just a matter of time before I have him.

He might know it, too. He's starting to get nervous, judging by how much he stands to pace around. He's a fidgety player, but this is a lot, even for him.

I feel an optimistic, voracious sort of hope bloom inside me. I'm going to do this. I *can* do this. I am going to the World Championship. I'll play against . . .

Nolan.

It's *incandescent*, the blend of joy and excitement that seizes me. Something utterly new and reckless finally allowed through the floodgates. As impossible as it sounds, I haven't let myself think about it, or dream of it. I haven't admitted it to myself before now, how much I want to sit across from Nolan, a chessboard between us. How much I want to look him in the eye as he does the astounding, magical things only he is capable of. I want to be his adversary. I want to tear his strategy apart, I want to field his attacks and terrorize him with my own, I want to chip at every little tactical choice, till he looks at me and says again, "Do you know how incredible you are?" He will smell like he did on his couch, soap and leather and sleep and that unique scent of him. He will smile, small, lopsided, and I'll smile back at him, and neither of us will hold back, and it will be the perfect game to—

Koch sits back in his chair, moves his queen, starts my clock. I drop back into my brain from whatever *that* was.

I frown. I'd figured he'd go for my rook, or break a file. But he moved his queen to a position I did not expect, so I study the board. I could—no. He'd check me in two moves. But I still need to back my knight. If I don't . . . a mess. A disaster. No. I could counter with my other bishop—though he would easily block the diagonal. And there's the fact he'll be queening in three moves. It wasn't really a problem before, but now that his queen is *there*, it changes everything. I cannot really fight back there.

But I can elsewhere, I'm sure.

I start scanning the board again, deconstructing every position, every move, every combination, listing long-range threats, analyzing possibilities, scouring for the one choice that will end up saving my useless king, sure that it'll become apparent any moment now.

Any second.

When I come up for air, fifty-seven minutes have passed on the clock, and I have not found a way out of this pin.

Because there is none.

My mouth is dry. My throat stings. If I were to move a piece, my hand would shake.

Because if I were to move a piece, I'd be dooming myself to defeat.

I look up to Koch, and I see it in his eyes, in his knowing, cruel smile: he was just waiting for me to come to the realization that it's over. I was running in circles all along, and he was watching from the sideline. Triumphant. Entertained.

I turn to the overflowing audience. A sea of faces I'll never know, and my eyes stumble on Defne's familiar hair. She streaked it pink—so pretty. I wonder what she'll tell me when all of this is done. I'm sure she has the right words. I'm just sorry she'll have to use them.

I take a long, deep breath. Then I force myself to look back at Koch, and I force myself to say what I must.

"I resign."

Chapter Nineteen

I wonder if the waitress at the IHOP finds it weird that we're showing up twelve hours later than our usual time. She deposits our coffee mugs on the table, and doesn't bat an eye at how obviously shell-shocked we all are, or the tight way I'm sandwiched between Defne and Tanu in the booth. Then she disappears into the bowels of the kitchen, never to be seen again.

We should tip her a thousand percent.

"Impossible." Across from me, Emil shakes his head. His board is out, arranged on the final position of my match. *Very tactful, Emil. What a triumph of empathy you are. Consider a career in counseling,* Tanu told him when he started setting it up, but I shook my head and she fell silent. The image is scorched in my brain anyway.

"It was the perfect move." Emil's voice is half reverential, two-thirds horrified. "It tied up your pieces. It had staggering long-range implications. It pinned your active *and* inactive pieces. It's . . . I've never seen *anything* like this. Definitely not from Koch."

I hate his name. I hate how it reminds me of his soulless grin when I resigned, of his gloating during the endless mandatory press conference, of the disappointed expression on the faces of the other candidates, the women in the audience, even some of the reporters. *I knew you'd show your belly*, he whispered in my ear. *Tell Sawyer he's next.*

"You didn't do anything wrong," Defne tells me. "You didn't make any mistakes. Not until . . . You played beautifully, Mal."

"Does it matter, though?" I ask. Not bitter. Just curious.

She sighs. *Not really* is the clear answer. "The second-place prize is still fifty thousand. And it's *yours*."

I nod. Earning money for my family was always the goal. Financial security was the destination—chess, just the means to get there, like an old, beat-up car I wanted nothing to do with but had to ride on my yellow-bricked quest. In the last half an hour I've made enough to solve all our financial problems and then some. I should be celebrating, not sitting in an IHOP, trying not to burst into tears over my stupid hunk of junk croaking.

And yet.

I feel like I'm falling. Like I'll never meet the ground again.

"If it makes you feel better, the entire VIP lounge gasped when you resigned." Tanu sounds concerned. I should reassure her that I'm fine, but I can't tear my eyes from the black queen. "No one expected this from Koch. I swear, they all . . ." She trails off. A tall shade appears on the board, and someone slides into the booth, next to Emil.

I glance up and let out a shaky laugh. Nolan is wearing his usual jeans-and-shirt combo. His hair is starting to grow long, and like every time I see him after a while apart, I'm surprised by how much room he takes up—at the table and in my head.

"You asshole," I say without heat.

He lifts one eyebrow. "Uncalled-for."

"Finally revealing yourself."

"You knew I was here."

Until ten minutes ago I'd have denied it, but yes. And I liked the idea, though I'm not going to admit it to him or to myself. There's been enough soul-searching for today. Time to engage in some soul ditching.

"We didn't tell her," Tanu hurries to say.

"She knew anyway." Nolan doesn't look at her. He doesn't look at anyone but me, and I feel blood in my cheeks.

"I did. It was that fishy smell."

He laughs, low and deep, and after a second I'm laughing, too, and the others look at us like we're bananas. Which we might be.

"Thoughts on Koch?" Defne asks him when we're done. She, too, seems unsurprised by his presence.

"I hope he sits on his balls," he says. "Aside from that, none."

"Really? No thoughts about this man you flew cross-country to creep at?"

"*Not* why I came to Vegas." He shrugs. "Koch's the human equivalent of a dirty toilet brush, and hasn't changed in the ten years I've known him. Would you like more hot takes?"

Part of me is surprised to hear Nolan and Defne bicker like they've been acquainted their entire life. But it doesn't get to ask follow-up questions because of the *other* part of me, which is too busy wallowing.

"But what did you think of the game?" Defne insists, and something shifts in Nolan's eyes, something that might be disappointment, displeasure, disenchantment. The feeling of falling morphs into an uglier, colder one.

"That I'd like to talk about with Mallory alone. Could we have some privacy?"

Defne snorts. "I'm not leaving you alone with her."

"Why?"

"Because."

"Not an answer."

"She's my responsibility."

"She can speak for herself. And you realize we've been alone together before, right? On multiple occasions."

"Not like that," I hasten to say. "Not alone like *that*." Everyone is giving me weird looks, and I don't know why I'm blushing. Nolan should be the flustered one. That's *his* job.

Defne looks at me. "Do you want to talk to Nolan, Mal? Just the two of you?"

No. Yes. No. "Yes."

"I'll walk her back to the hotel," he says. "No need to stick around."

It takes some shuffling, but we end up alone at the booth— us, Emil's board, and six different flavors of waffle syrup. I look at the black queen again and wait for him to speak.

Maybe he'll say that he was wrong about me, that I was never *incredible*, that he won't be texting me advice anymore. I'm tempted to justify myself, to apologize, to say that I did my best, and if it's not enough, well. This might not be the first time that I'm not enough, but it hurts just like all the others.

But he says nothing. His hand travels across the table, and I think he'll cover the back of mine with his palm. Instead, he twines our fingers together.

A simple, loose touch. Barely a touch, really, but it warms me and grounds me, just enough to look up at him when he says, "Be my second."

"I . . . what?"

"Be my second."

"Nolan." I shake my head, confused. "You have a million seconds, you can't want me to—"

"I have five. And I want *you*."

My temples throb. "Why?"

"The World Championship is in February. I need to train to defeat Koch. I need *you*."

"No." Koch is not Nolan's rival, he's his enemy. I let down both of us by losing. "You don't need me. You probably don't even need to prep against Koch. I just *lost* to him, so I'm the last person you should—"

"I didn't see it, either."

My breath catches.

"The queen. I watched the game, and I was as defenseless as you, Mallory. I . . ." He swallows. "I didn't see it coming, and then I didn't see a way out of it. I would have resigned, too."

I exhale. "How is it possible? You beat him a few months ago."

"I don't know. It's not unheard-of for players to improve years into their training and make big jumps. But this . . . this was a chess-engine-level move. Perfectly designed to disrupt every single action, every single initiative you had going on—and you were playing some fucking great chess. It was something a computer would come up with." Nolan is distressed. I always thought of him as a hothead, but it's the first time since we met that he seems genuinely upset about something. Genuinely insecure. "Mallory, if that's the level he plays at, he's going to win the World Championship."

His fingers are still solid, still warm against mine.

"But I didn't make it, either."

"I know. But let's figure it out together." He leans forward, eyes burning into mine. "Be my second. Help me take that piece of shit down."

"I . . . if I become your second, won't I be training with you *all the time*? I'll know everything. I'll be so familiar with your style, you'll have a hard time taking me by surprise again. If I become your second, I'll *know* you."

There is a beautiful, indecipherable half smile on his lips. "You think I don't want you to know me?"

"Nolan . . ."

I overturn our hands and look down at his palm. It's so much larger than mine. The lines and grooves, so deep. So easy to trace with my fingertips, to follow to the source.

I . . . I just don't know. If it's a bad idea. If I'm good enough. What this is, this luminous, tethering thing that always seems to pull me closer to Nolan. I don't know if I can stand to be near him, and I don't know if I can stand *not* to be.

I don't know anything, but there's something I need to ask.

"Nolan?"

"Hmm?"

"Why did you come to Vegas?"

His fingers tighten around mine. My heart cartwheels.

"Mallory. I came because you did."

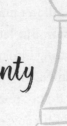

Chapter Twenty

"—if you go rook g5—"

"—then the bishop—"

"—but that pawn—"

"—in g7—"

"—no, if you want to keep your king safe—"

"—there's this thing called *castling* that—"

"Um . . . hey, guys?"

Nolan and I turn to Tanu with two aggressive, annoyed, simultaneous, "*What*?"

She leans in, hands on the doorframe, more skeptical than intimidated. Her hair is up in a messy bun, and an oversized koala onesie hangs from her tall frame. She's wearing glasses, which means she took out her contacts for the day, which means that . . .

"It's eleven forty. You've been in the same position since two and seem to be doing great, but in case you decide that the heroic feats of a midcentury Ukrainian Grandmaster are not nourishing enough, there's chicken potpie in the fridge."

Nolan scowls. "Why didn't you guys call us for dinner?"

"We did. Three times. Each time, you both just grunted. I

recorded it and mixed it with Dragostea for TikTok. Wanna see it?"

"Goodnight, Tanu," he says. She knows him well enough to scurry away when he stands. "Let's eat."

"Wait." I stop him with a tug of his shirt. "We need to finish this—"

"You need to *eat*. Come on."

When I told Darcy that I'd be spending part of December and January at Nolan's house in upstate New York (yes, he owns one; yes, I did mutter "Eat the rich" when he informed me), she gave me a skeptical look and asked, "Is it wise, to go to a cabin in the woods with the Kingkiller?" It's been weeks, and I'm still not sure what the answer is. I sit on the kitchen counter and observe Nolan as he eats standing up, businesslike, brisk, as though shoveling coal into a furnace, mind clearly still on the game we were analyzing.

It's awe inspiring, his discipline.

He wakes up earlier, falls asleep later, works harder than anyone I've ever seen. The rigors he puts himself through, the single-minded, indefatigable stubbornness as he stares at the engines, dissecting, retracing, combining, projecting. He's tireless, unshakable. Driven in an indomitable, near-obsessive way. This iron-hard tenacity of his is an oddly attractive quality.

Not that he needs more of those.

He has five other seconds: Tanu and Emil, who are staying at the house, and three other male GMs in their thirties, experts on openings and pawn structure, who come and go a few times a week. Nolan trains with all of us—problems to solve, Koch games to analyze, his own old games to run through software and mine for weaknesses—but his time with the others seems almost like an afterthought. Brief interludes in the sea of his days, which are spent with me.

It's because there are things they don't see. Combinations and tactics that elude them and seem to click only in my and Nolan's heads. "Let's just go watch *Doom Patrol* while the grown-ups work," Emil said one night, after it became clear that no one could keep up with us.

But there's something else, too. I pad barefoot across the hardwood floor first thing in the morning, knowing I'll find him in the breakfast nook, ready to tell him about whatever revelation I had during my sleep; his eyes scan every room he enters, quiet only when they settle on me, and sometimes I have the urge to lean forward to flatten the curls growing on the nape of his neck.

We still don't play against each other. We study, analyze, dissect, reenact other people's chess, but we never play a match that's ours. And yet . . . Something is happening, but I don't know what. This thing between us is layered, complicated, fractured unlike anything I've experienced before. It lacks the coziness of a friendship, the ease of a hookup, the distance of everything else.

Maybe Nolan should just be some guy: not a rival, not a friend, not more than a friend, just some guy who plays good chess. Some guy who's in my head and acts as though I live in his own.

"Can I borrow your car tomorrow?" I ask. We're about one hour from Paterson. I've been visiting home once a week or so. Christmas, New Year's. Whenever Mom needs me—which, with the new meds we've been able to afford, is not a lot. She thinks I'm making good money and sparing myself the commute by taking night shifts at the senior center, and . . . well. The money part, at least, is true. Nolan pays his seconds well.

"Sure. Where are you going?"

"Home for the day. Darcy's birthday."

He reaches for a dinner roll. "Can I come?"

"Don't you have to, like, analyze Capablanca's first-grade macaroni art?"

He shrugs. "It's my free day."

"And you want to spend it at a thirteen-year-old's birthday dinner."

"Will there be meat loaf?"

"I'm sure Mom can scrounge up some." I scan his face. His handsome, ever-so-familiar face. "Don't you want to spend your free day with Tanil?"

He looks pained. "Not you, too, with the ship name. Besides, my room is next to theirs. They won't miss me at all."

Emil and Tanu are on again—as all non-hearing-impaired individuals on the East Coast no doubt know by now. "They *are* loud."

"That, or they have sex to whale noises."

I laugh. "Still. You could . . . go skiing? Wear cuff links? Be positively *aghast*? Whatever it is that you rich people with vacation homes do."

He gives me a dirty look, but he does come over, and my sisters are as happy to see him as they'd be Jungkook. I think about the interview I saw of him years ago, how stern and guarded he seemed, and I can barely recognize the open-smiled boy who gives Darcy a PetSmart gift card, lets Sabrina show him two hours of roller derby videos, raises one eyebrow at the Mayochup on our table.

"How's Easton?" Mom asks while I clean the kitchen.

"Great," I lie. My heart curls into itself a little. Truth is, I have no idea. She spent the holidays in Delaware with her grandparents, and I haven't seen her or heard her voice in over four months. Based on my Instagram stalking, I suspect she's dating someone named Kim-ly. I could ask, but it feels like admitting how apart we've fallen, since once upon a better time she used to text me pictures of all her meals.

"He's good with them," she says, looking at Nolan fixing Sabrina's broken Polaroid in the living room. "Must be the caregiving experience at the senior center. I bet he's great at reading romance novels to the elderly, with that voice."

Of course, I chickened out of telling her the truth. I'm not going to the World Championship, which means that media interest in me has melted like sugar in hot water. I'm nobody. Nobodies don't need to hurt people with uncomfortable truths.

"Yeah. He really brings turgid manhoods to life."

Mom laughs softly. "You guys still not together?"

"Nope."

"You sure?"

I turn to face her. "Of course." I don't have committed relationship experience, but I do know that it's not a continuum. Either you're in one, or you're not. And if you are, you *know* you are. How could one—

"Excuse us." Warm hands close around my waist and shift me an inch to make room in the kitchen door. "Darcy is going to teach me how to make a cup cake."

"*Mug* cake," Darcy corrects him with a patient sigh. "Mom, do we have any sugar?"

Mom's eyes dip to Nolan's hand, still pressed against my lower back, then lift up to meet mine. She tells Darcy, "In the cupboard next to the fridge," her smile knowing and very, *very* annoying.

Sabrina doesn't talk to me once, but I manage to corner her in her room just before leaving. "Everything okay?" I ask. As early as weeks ago, the picture above her nightstand was of me giving her a piggyback ride in a pumpkin patch. Now it's a collage: her derby team, some school friends, even a Polaroid of Mom and Darcy making faces.

I've been deleted.

"I'm sorry I haven't been around. But I'm earning really good money with this overnight thing."

"Good for you," she says distractedly, rummaging in her drawer, looking for a derby T-shirt she promised Nolan since *it's too big on me anyway.*

"How has Mom been?"

"Fine."

"Right. And Darcy?"

"Good. She's actually almost bearable when you aren't around. You must be a bad influence."

I stifle an eye roll. "And you?"

"Fine."

I sigh. "Sabrina, can I have your attention for sixty seconds?"

She finally looks up. Annoyed. "Mom's fine. Darcy's fine. I'm fine. The entire damn world is fine."

"I'm serious. I rely on you to man the fort and tell me if I'm needed, so—"

"Oh, *now* you care?" Her blue eyes shine with tears. For a second, I see genuine hurt in them, and my heart lurches in my chest. But it's all gone in a blink, and her expression suddenly turns half uncaring, half hard. Maybe I imagined all the rest.

"Excuse me?" I ask.

She walks to me. I still have a couple of inches on her. Will she grow more? God, she's *fifteen*. "We're fine, Mal. We can function without you."

"Well, last time I left, you seemed pretty upset, so—"

"We're fine. You can put your power trip away. No one needs to 'man the fort.' Mom, Darcy, and I are *people* and can take care of ourselves. We're not pets you need to feed and walk." She steps past me, T-shirt in hand. A surge of irritation courses through me—seriously? *Seriously?* Do I *deserve* this?—and I slap the doorframe. It only gets me a splinter stuck in my palm.

When we leave, they wave at us from the porch. "Come back soon, Nolan," Darcy yells.

"And don't feel like you need to bring Mallory with you," Sabrina adds archly.

"What's up with that?" Nolan asks once we're on the road.

"You mean, with the way my sister would love to drown me in a barrel of mead?"

His mouth twitches. "I did sense some animosity."

"I'm not sure." I sigh. "I'm doing my best with her. I make sure she has everything she needs and nothing to worry about."

"Maybe that's the problem."

"What do you mean?"

"When you're with your sisters, you act like they're your responsibility. Like you're their parent, almost. It works with Darcy, but Sabrina might find it infantilizing." He shrugs. "Maybe she just wants you to be her sister."

"What do *you* even know about sisters?"

"Nothing. What do *you* know about defensiveness?"

I cannot help laughing, and then we fall quiet for a while. Nolan drives like he plays, steady and focused, and for once I don't feel antsy for not being at the wheel. I let my eyes wander over the halo of the streetlights, the snow weighing down the pine trees, his firm hand as he shifts gears, like he's moving a bishop across the board.

He's thinking about chess. He's thinking about the Koch game we analyzed this morning, the one with the Queen's Gambit that he lost to Davies three years ago. I know it. Not sure *how* I know what's in Nolan's head, or when it started, but here I am. Knowing.

"Knight e5 was a stupid move," I say.

He doesn't skip a beat. "Koch's attacks backfire a lot. Well." He shrugs. "Backfired. Before he ate spinach and got an upgrade."

"It might be a good strategy, luring him into becoming aggressive."

"Yeah."

I think wistfully about the tactics I'd use against Nolan if I were the challenger. He's such an unpredictable player, always thinking of long-term advantages, of seemingly silent moves to exploit later, unexpectedly. I've heard commentators say that our styles are similar, but I think we're oceans apart. I like to strangle my opponent, wear them down slowly, drain them of active play and attack possibilities one by one, until it's just us— me and their king.

But Nolan would know how to deal with me. What to be on the lookout for. To beat him, I'd have to learn to let go of minute positional advantages and take more overt risks, earlier on. I watch him stretch his neck, strong muscles tensing under his skin, and think that maybe it would work, seducing him into a blunder. Maybe it wouldn't, but it would keep him on his toes. He'd give me one of those long, knowing looks. Smile, even. He'd smile at me, and I'd get to smile back as I took his king.

It sounds like a dream. A thing imagined.

"Darcy pulled me into your room," he says, "and conspiratorially whispered that she's 'in the know.'"

"Unlike Mom and Sabrina, she googles. Probably hangs out on the dark web. Signs up Goliath for Piggie-Tinder."

"She asked me to teach her to play chess."

"Darcy?" I perk up. "For real?"

"She said it's . . . hot shit girl?"

I laugh. "Hot girl shit. You should really try to be online a little." Most of the other top-ten players have Twitch and YouTube channels. Nolan: Twitter and Instagram—both with *NOT DIRECTLY MANAGED BY NOLAN SAWYER* written in all caps in the bio. I bet his social media guy got sick of people DMing him nudes. "Why are you not online, anyway?"

"I'm online way too much."

"What do you mean?"

"There are pictures of seven-year-old me mining his nose for boogers while playing Nakamura. Throwing a tantrum like a whiny brat after a loss at fourteen."

"Oh."

"We all have embarrassing phases growing up, but mine were immortalized. Whoever's *online* looking for me already has plenty to find."

I remember Emil's words: *It's not easy, growing up as a prodigy in front of the cameras.* "Do you mind it? Your . . . troublemaker reputation."

"You mean, total piece of shit?" He laughs softly. "It's deserved. I was one. I can only try to be different in the future."

He's succeeding, too. I try to recall recent incidents and come up empty. "You still get mad at the people who beat you."

"Is that what you think?" He shakes his head. "I get furious at *myself*. For making mistakes. For not being the best I can be. And every time *you* blunder, you feel the same."

"Not true. I—"

He gives me a side look, and I fall quiet. Whatever.

"I showed Darcy how the pieces move," he says quietly.

"How?"

"She had a set under her bed. Pink and purple."

I close my eyes. A knot tightens in my belly. "I thought I'd gotten rid of that."

"You should teach her yourself."

"What does she need to learn for?"

"She wants to. She idolizes you."

I snort. "She calls me Mallopee and constantly makes me 'Lamest Greenleaf' graphics in Photoshop—which *I* illegally downloaded for her, by the way. Ingrate."

"She wants to be like you."

"I'll never teach her."

"Why?"

I turn away. The road is deserted, and the pines are becoming thicker. "Chess is a bad idea."

"Why?"

"Look where it got me."

"It got you here. To *me*."

Blood rushes to my cheeks, but his tone is matter-of-fact, not suggestive. He doesn't mean it like that. He means . . . I don't even know.

"It was you who saw him, wasn't it?" Nolan asks. I look back at him, puzzled.

"What?"

"Your father. Something happened between him and that woman—that arbiter at the Olympics. You found out. Your mom kicked him out. I'm assuming you were estranged for a few years. And later his accident happened."

I straighten. The seat belt tightens into my sweater. "How— how do you know? When did you—?"

"I didn't. But I remembered some rumors going around the tournament circuit at the time. About Archie Greenleaf. The rest . . . I just guessed."

"You *guessed*? How?"

"Little things. Your reaction at the Olympics. You obviously love chess but talk yourself into thinking that it's a loathsome thing. You feel responsible for your family, not just your sisters but your mother, too." His tone is even, idle, like he's reading a boring textbook to the rest of the class. "You constantly act like you're guilty of something awful. Like you deserve nothing but scraps for yourself."

Me. The boring textbook—it's *me*.

"Because I *am* guilty," I blurt out. Surprising myself. It's not something I've verbalized out loud to anyone before. But if I hadn't told Mom about Heather Turcotte, if Dad hadn't left home, if he hadn't had a reason to be driving drunk at 3:00 a.m. . . . If. If.

If.

"Did you know," he says conversationally, "that I was the reason my grandfather was institutionalized?"

"What does this . . . No. I didn't."

"He'd been acting weird for a while. He'd say and do really inappropriate stuff, sometimes in public. My parents had gotten wind of it, but I think they just chalked it up to my grandfather being old. And I was staying with him a lot at the time, so I covered for him when I could. I honestly thought he just needed to sleep more or some shit like that. But then . . . it was his birthday. I went to his apartment, the one you've been to. I walked upstairs—same doorman as now, he doesn't give a shit—and let myself in. I had a present for him, a chess set I'd made. Nine months of woodworking."

He signals right and takes the exit. We must be home. Nearly. "We'd met the day before. We met every single day, but this time he didn't recognize me. Or he did, but thought I had bad intentions. I'll never know, I figure. He wasn't a violent man, but he had a knife. I saw him take it out of the block and thought he wanted to . . . chop celery? I can't fucking remember. But instead he stared into my eyes, ran at me, and the cut was deep. I needed stitches, which meant going to the hospital, which meant filing a report, and that was it. My father had the ammo he needed to lock him up. Said it was for the best, and maybe it was, but that's not why he was doing it. He'd always hated his father for caring more about chess than he ever did about him."

His voice is clinical. Like he's turned this story in his mind so much, told it to himself so often, it's a memorized thing by now. He thinks about it every day. Every hour. I know this, because I'm in his head. "I'm the one who gave my father that power. And my grandfather died in that institution, medicated to his eyeballs. It's the last thing he wanted, and it's something I have to live with every second of every day. So when you talk about guilt—"

"What—no. No." I twist toward him. The seat belt digs into my breast. "It's *not* your fault. You did what you could, considering that you were— How old were you?"

"I was fourteen. How old were you, when you saw your father?"

I close my eyes. Because it's not the same. At all. But he makes it sound like it *might* be, and I do *not* deserve to be let off the hook and—

Suddenly I am furious. Explosively, incandescently furious.

He—he manipulated me. He pretended to self-disclose, and instead turned me into . . . whatever the hell this is. He sacrificed his queen to checkmate me, and how *dare* he? How dare he come into my home and analyze my family as though we were a *Morphy* game?

"Fuck you, Nolan."

His expression is indecipherable and unsurprised. "Did I say something untrue?"

"Fuck you. What do you even know about families?"

"Is that the problem? That what I said is true?"

"Stop trying to—to *trap* me. To *checkmate* me. You might want to play chess against me more than anything, but it doesn't give you the right to—"

"Not more than anything," he murmurs with a lingering glance. I ignore him, enraged.

"Is that what's happening? You want to win against me so bad that you'll score points however you can? Tic-tac-toe? Taking cheap shots at my family?"

"It's not—"

"Nobody got stabbed in my family. I could have kept my mouth shut, and things would have been fine. It could have been *my* secret to keep, *my* burden, and no one would have known or suffered for it. Mom would have had health insurance, and my sisters would have had the family they deserved, and Dad would be alive—" I stop. Take a deep, shuddering breath. "You don't *know* me, or my sisters, or my mom, and you most certainly did not know my dad. So don't try to pretend you and I are similar in any way, or like what *I* did is comparable to what happened to you."

"You're not being fair to either of us," he says calmly. Maybe he's right, but I'm past caring.

"You know what?" The seat belt cuts into my throat. I'm overflowing with anger now, anger at . . . at Nolan. Let's say Nolan. "Screw this shit. We're going to play. Tonight. We're going to play this stupid chess game, and you'll quit the armchair psychology."

"I—" He stops, registering what I said. His throat works. "You're not serious."

"If you're not interested—"

"I am." He sounds eager. Young. "I am." Then he's silent, as though he's afraid to spook me, that I'll change my mind. He barely looks at me until after the car is parked, the passenger door slammed closed, our coats tossed in a corner of the living room. We usually work across from each other, but he sets the board on the coffee table, and we sit side by side on the couch. Because this is *not* an analysis of someone else's game, and it needs to be clear.

It's midnight. The heat has been off for hours, but I don't feel cold. "Okay?" he asks, serious, making sure this game is consensual.

You know what wasn't *consensual? The stuff you said about my dad.*

"You can be White," I say, cutting, expecting—*wanting* him to be offended.

"Thank you," he replies with no trace of irony. "I'm going to need that."

It makes me hate him even more, and so does his stupid opening—pawn to e4. I answer with the Sicilian. I roll my eyes and put my knight in c6, just to derail him, some niche line I vaguely remember studying with Defne—Rossolimo Variation.

Lots of pressure, very fast, and he doesn't care, doesn't hesitate, doesn't even blink in the dim lights. His forehead is smooth. Hands steady. His knee brushes against mine, not every move, but sometimes. He doesn't seem to notice, and I hate him. I feel clumsy, a lumbering, unwieldy, broken beast next to him. I feel raw, see-through, broken open, like he can reach inside my skull and pluck sharp, painful shards of my past and make me bleed with them.

Then I lose a pawn, and I feel stupid, too.

"Fuck," I mutter.

"It's just a pawn," he murmurs without looking up.

"Shut up." I advance my knight with shaky fingers, and then it's not just a pawn. I left my bishop uncovered, screwed up my castling opportunities. I watch Nolan unhurriedly take my piece and immediately attack him from the side with my rook—I'm going to make him *hurt*. Except, I knock over two pieces and completely overlook the way his queen inches toward my king and fuck, fuck, *fuck*—

"Mallory." His hand covers mine, trapping it on my knee. I look up to his handsome, hateful face. "I'm sorry about what I said. I was out of line."

I don't want to hear it. "Let's finish."

"I don't know how things went with your father—"

"Let's. Finish."

He shakes his head.

I laugh, bitter. "You've supposedly been pining for this game for months—"

"That's not what I've been pining for, and you can stop lying to yourself about it. I don't want to play with you like this."

"So now you need perfect conditions to play? Should I rearrange the furniture? Sage the room? Let me know what your *esteemed requirements* are, what you want, and—"

"You know what I fucking want, Mallory?" He leans forward, suddenly furious. "I want you to not be here."

I gasp in outrage. "Screw you! *You* asked me to be your second—"

"I want you to be elsewhere. Training with your *own* seconds in preparation for *me*. So we can play a real match in Italy. The real thing." His eyes blaze. His hand is still flat on mine. Pressing. Warm. "Your presence in this house might be what gets me up in the morning, but we can stop pretending this situation is anything like what either of us wants or needs."

I close my eyes. He is right. This . . . It's wrong. All wrong.

"It was our only chance," I whisper. "And I fucked it up." Just like I fuck up everything. Friendships. Families.

"There will be other tournaments." Nolan takes a deep, calming breath. "In two years there'll be another World Championship—"

"I'm not going to be doing this past the summer."

He swallows. "Okay. Well . . . It is what it is." He glances away. Then turns back to me, his expression softer. "I *am* sorry. You're right—I don't know anything about families. Please, accept my apology so you can stop playing the worst game of your life. Let's just . . . let's go to sleep. We're tired."

I look down at the board. Black's position is an amateurish, reckless mess. "God, what's wrong with me?"

"Transient global amnesia, one can only imagine."

I let out a laugh, and my anger melts like snow in the sun. He laughs, too, and I can feel the warmth of his breath against my cheek. We're that close.

"I'm sorry. For this game."

There are little specks of gold in his eyes. He has freckles, light and scattered, just a handful, and they look . . . pretty. Yummy. "You *should* be sorry."

I chuckle. Clear my throat. "You might want to move away. Since there are other people in this house."

He seems confused. "And?"

"They could come in. Think we've been making out or something."

He smiles. "They're more likely to think we've been murdering each other over an en passant—"

My brain short-circuits. Maybe it's the late hour, or how I just dropped my knight less than ten moves into a mortifying game. Maybe it's Nolan's clean, familiar smell. All I know is that one moment I'm looking at him, and the next I'm not—because I've leaned forward and pressed my mouth against his in a . . .

A kiss.

There's no way around it. That's what it's called, this clumsy, juvenile peck. I'm kissing Nolan Sawyer, and—

I jerk back, appalled. "I'm sorry. I'm so sorry, I—" I shoot to my feet. My knee knocks over the board, scattering the pieces. I lift my fingers to my mouth, and—it feels weird.

Different. Changed.

"Mallory."

"I don't know why I did that. I'm just—I'm so so sorry." Nolan stares like I'm the center of gravity of the room, like nothing else ever existed but me in all of space and time. It makes my heart beat in my throat, it makes me want to kiss him again, it makes me want to run the hell away. "Sorry, I—"

"Touch-take rule," he murmurs. He stands, too. Every step back I take is one forward for him.

"I— What?"

"You touched me. Can't stop now. Touch-take rule."

"I . . . This is not chess." My back hits an obstacle. "I can always stop."

"Then just don't." His hands come up to cup my face. He towers over me, cages me against the wall, and I . . . I don't mind. Which scares me. "Please, Mallory."

"This is . . . We should finish the game. You said you wanted to play."

"I said there were things I wanted more."

I squeeze my eyes shut, but Nolan is so *here*—I can smell him, feel him in every pore of my being. "Weren't you the one who chose Kasparov over getting laid?" I say, petulant, whiny. When I open my eyes, his smile is faint.

"And you think it's because I want to play you less than I did Kasparov?"

"Of course. Why else— Oh." I close my eyes again. "Oh."

"Can I kiss you?"

"But our game—"

"I resign. You win. Can I kiss you?"

"No! I mean . . . why?"

"Because I want to." He's being patient. Why am *I* being a total wreck while *he* is being patient? "You don't?"

"I . . ."

I do? It's not a big deal. Nolan's easily the most attractive guy I've ever met, and I'm not one of those *kissing is too intimate, let's do it from behind* Tinder weirdos. I've done a lot of things, and regret none of it. So what's stopping me?

Maybe it's that I want it too much, I think. And then I hear myself say it aloud as my toes push up, and I'm doing that odd thing again—that light peck on his lips that makes me feel like I'm thirteen and sneaking behind the gym. But this time I don't have to slap myself for being a total weirdo, because Nolan kisses me back.

He's not good at it. Not immediately. Not bad, but there is an airy moment of hesitance, of suspended disconnect, when I think the kiss just won't work out. Not meant to be. Two ships passing in the night, going their separate ways, a narrow miss.

But then he does something. Tilts his head, maybe. Adjusts his grip. Presses more firmly against me, and it all changes. His ship crashes into mine and my back is flat against the wall, and *oh*, he wants it. He wants it very, very much. He wants it as much as I do. I can tell from his leg sliding between mine and pinning me to the wall, from the way his hand shifts to my hip, assertive like on a chessboard. From the guttural sound in the back of his throat.

He *is* good at it. Warm and forceful and *thorough*, and he tastes good and—

A door opens somewhere in the house. Laughter. Footsteps. The hallway light turns on. I push on Nolan's shoulders, and we break apart just in time.

"Oh, you guys are back." Emil. Standing in the entrance, quickly tying his robe closed. "What are you doing?"

I glance at Nolan, thinking that Emil's *his* friend. The burden of coming up with a plausible excuse should fall on him. Problem is, Nolan is staring at me, pupils wide, lips full and . . . kissed?

"Um, we were just . . ." I clear my throat. Smile tentatively at Emil. "Talking about that Koch game that—"

"Say no more, Greenleaf." He shuffles to the fridge. "I cannot get sidetracked or Tanu will murder me. She sent me to forage." He piles leftover pizza and three cupcakes in his arms, then disappears with a swish of his robe and a careless "Goodnight."

I'm alone with Nolan again.

Nolan, who hasn't stopped staring.

"It's getting late," I say, not meeting his eyes. I feel flustered. Because of a kiss. I *am* regressing to thirteen. "I'm tired. I . . ."

He nods and does something weird: holds his hand out to me. Calmly. Quietly. As though he expects me to take it. And it's exactly what I do: I slide my fingers in to his, and when he leads me down the hallway, stopping to turn off the light, I follow him meekly. We walk past Tanu's door without reacting to the muffled laughter from inside, past Emil's empty one, past all the others, too—including mine, until we're in his room, which smells like clean skin and mind-bendingly good chess and his couch back in the city.

He nonchalantly takes off his jeans, all long, muscled limbs.

"What are you doing?" I blurt out. He doesn't look at me, just smells his shirt, deciding that it belongs in a laundry hamper.

"Getting ready for bed."

"I . . ." What is happening? *Why did I follow you? What. Is. Happening?* "Why aren't you nervous?"

"About what?"

"About"—I gesture inchoately between us—"*all of this.*"

He glances at me. "I don't know. It feels right. Besides, I don't get nervous much."

Darcy once told me about a study they did, monitoring the heart rate of top chess players during important games. Nolan's was always the slowest. The steadiest. Is that why he's standing in front of me in boxer briefs and a Coimbra Chess 2019 T-shirt and I'm shaking like a leaf?

"Do you not want this?" he asks.

"No. I mean, yes. I mean, I don't *not* want this. But . . . we just kissed out of the blue, and you seem so okay with it, and . . ."

He shrugs. "It's not out of the blue for me."

"It isn't?"

"I came to terms with this months ago, Mallory. The first time we played, maybe."

I swallow. "I don't understand."

He comes closer. In two steps he's in front of me, and for some indecipherable reason I'm shaking. A small-scale earthquake's happening inside me, twenty kings are being tipped over, and Nolan just cups my face again.

"I've got you, Mallory. Nothing bad is going to happen. You can let yourself want this, because you already have it. You have me."

Oh God. Oh God, God, *God*. I'm shaking harder.

"I . . . Are we . . . Are we going to fuck?"

I'm purposely trying to rattle him. And it's not working.

"No. We're going to sleep."

We lie down, and somehow it's a smooth thing. I'm wearing leggings and a soft shirt and no jewelry, and that's why I'm so comfortable. Not because my head is pillowed on his chest and his legs are tangled with mine, and I feel his slow, steady heart like a warm clock under my ear.

"I haven't even washed my face," I tell him. I'm still trembling, albeit more quietly. I'm a mess.

"That's okay. Antonov won Coimbra 2019."

I laugh shakily. "I . . . don't think I can sleep."

"Want a bedtime story?" His hand combs gently through the hair at my nape. "It's called 'Polgar Versus Anand, 1999.' It starts with e4. c5."

I groan. But I'm smiling when I ask, "And then?"

"Knight f3. d6. d3."

"Mmm."

"Yup."

"And then?"

"Knight xd4. Knight f6. Knight c3 . . ."

I fall asleep mid-game—for the second time in my life held by someone, for the second time in my life held by Nolan Sawyer.

Chapter Twenty-One

By 3:00 p.m. on the following day, Nolan has spoken fewer than fifteen words to me.

Why knight a5?

Could sacrifice the queen.

And my personal favorite: *Getting a muffin—want one?*

Maybe I hallucinated the previous night. Maybe our kiss was a dream. Maybe the way I woke up in his empty room, a mug of hot coffee on the bedside table—maybe I need a checkup to—

"What do you think, Mal?" Tanu asks. From her tone, not for the first time.

"About what?"

"This position. What would you do?" I glance at the board. We're analyzing a Koch game from last year. Well, *they* are analyzing. I'm ruminating.

"It's weak. The left side could be exploited."

"Yeah, that's what Nolan said, too."

I look up at him, and instantly flush. Because that's apparently what I do now—stress over whether some dude I didn't even sleep with isn't interested in me anymore because I'm a

total mess, because I toss and turn at night, because my morning breath smells like the dumpster behind a fish restaurant.

This is uncharted territory. An entire new galaxy. I'm used to
caring about what Mom, Darcy, Sabrina, Easton think of me. I
have room for no one else, and—

"Would you agree, Greenleaf?" Emil asks.

Shit. "Sorry, with what?"

"With what Nolan said."

Nolan's eyes are unreadable. "He castled too late," he repeats.

I glance at the board. "Or he shouldn't have castled at all," I
say, pretending I'm not flustered.

"Koch's so uneven." Emil rubs his temples. "How can one go
from disastrous blunders to near-genius moves like the one
against Greenleaf? He's like two completely different players."

"And which one will he be in Italy?" Tanu asks.

No one answers. Nolan stares in the mid-distance, and I
stare at him like a twerp.

We analyze Koch's end games until late. By the time Nolan
and Emil stand to make dinner, the sun has been down for
hours. "You're staying till the end of January, right?" Tanu asks
me, voice low. The others are arguing over whether one should
throw the pasta into the water before it boils. (Nolan: "Who
cares? It'll be faster." Emil: "You are—and I cannot stress this
enough—a *tasteless peasant.*")

"That's the plan. You aren't?"

"Only until the semester starts."

"Oh." I think of Nolan and me alone in this house. "Oh."

"Defne will come up and help, of course," she continues.

I frown. Defne approved of me becoming Nolan's second be-

cause she said that it would be great training for me, but . . . "I
didn't think they were that close."

"Oh, they're *super* close. They both trained with Nolan's
grandfather before . . . well. But Nolan still needs *you*. He doesn't
show it, but Koch's unpredictability rattled him. He needs someone *he* cares about who also cares about *him*. Like you do, you
know?"

Oh God. "Tanu, Nolan and I . . ." I shake my head and shift
closer, perched on the edge of my chair. "I guess we *are* close in
some ways, but we're not . . . together."

"Oh, I know relationships are weird." Her smile is reassuring.
"I mean, Emil and I technically aren't together, either, because . . .
well. Not that he deserves me, but mostly, the distance sucks. But
Nolan is so into you."

"It's . . ." I shake my head. "It's complicated."

She laughs, a mix of confusion and amusement. "Well—I
don't know what's going on, but I've never seen him as calm and
happy as when you stick around, so—"

"Hey, do you guys want to play two versus two?" Emil interrupts me. "There're four of us, so two teams."

I quickly consider the possible permutations. I'd be either
against Nolan, or—

"I'll team with Mallory," he calls from the kitchen.

Tanu lifts her eyebrow at me, and I close my eyes. They're still
closed a few seconds later when Nolan returns from the kitchen
and, instead of taking a free seat, lifts one leg and slides between me and the back of my chair.

I nearly gasp. He takes up a lot of room, always, and this isn't
going to work. I'm going to fall over.

Or I'll be fine, here in his lap. The hand that's not busy adjusting the black pieces to the center of their squares casually rests against my abdomen, spanning its width. It's the same hand as last night—confident, soothing. This feels nice. Smells even better. Tanu's eyebrow lifts a millimeter higher, and Emil moves his pawn to d4, unbothered by me sitting between his closest friend's thighs.

"Want to go first?" Nolan murmurs, lips to the shell of my ear.

I shiver. Then I nod, and my hair brushes against his chin. My skin heats, and I'm too flustered to think, so I do the first thing that comes to mind.

Knight to f6.

I remember how much Nolan hates the Grünfeld only after he groans and sinks his teeth into my earlobe.

WE PLAY FIVE GAMES. NOLAN AND I WIN ALL EXCEPT FOR ONE, and that's my blunder's fault. The hanging queen.

"That was . . . a move," Tanu says, advancing her knight, and Nolan makes a choked noise in the back of his throat and hides his face in the curve of my neck, as though unable to witness the mess I made. I want to hiss that if he weren't tucking me into himself with a hand on my belly, maybe my brain wouldn't be a slushie. But his breath tickles my nape, and while everyone thinks hard about the next move and the room is silent, I can feel his heartbeat warm against my back.

It's the closest I've ever been to someone without sex.

The closest I've been to someone *with* sex.

And the most distracted I've ever felt in a chess game, in life, and the worst part is, I don't believe Nolan's toying with me. Sometimes his chin rests on my shoulder, boyish, artless, and I know that he's just doing what feels good. It just *happens* to distract me.

He's the first to say, "I'm going to bed," when Tanu offers to put on a movie. He loads the dishwasher, heads to his room with an absentminded wave, and I am left there, stuck between his absence and Emil's scathing takedown of Aronofsky's filmography. I'm a balloon, blown larger and tighter and fuller by the second, ready to explode.

So I bolt. I leave the Aronofsky convo behind and march down the hallway. I don't bother knocking—just open the door and let myself in Nolan's room. Not my best idea, since he just took off his shirt and is wearing only his jeans.

I lean back against the door. *Shit. What am I doing?*

"That hung queen," he says with a small smile, like me barging in is as natural as sundown. He's fit and well muscled. I wonder when he finds time to work out, to look like that. "Though I'm sure Tanu and Emil appreciated the win—"

"Can you please explain?"

"Explain?"

"Last night"—I gesture confusedly—"and then this morning, and then today, tonight, just *now*."

He tilts his head. "Yes. That *is* how time works."

"No, I—" I squeeze my eyes shut. "I hate this."

"Hate what?"

"That I'm here asking you . . . that you're in my head, and I—" I run a hand down my face. "No. Listen . . . I don't care. I'm not *supposed* to care about whether you . . . I'm not supposed to be thinking about you at all—I have a *family* to take care of. Shit to get done. But you *kiss* me, then ignore me like nothing happened—"

"Right." He crosses his arms. "That's *your* move, isn't it?"

"What?"

"You're the one who ignores people. Leave them behind before they leave you, right? Spare yourself the mortifying ordeal of being known."

"That's unfair." I push away from the door. Begin pacing inside the room. "It's different. I don't usually—I have *responsibilities*. I don't have time to *moon*, Nolan. I cannot be distracted by people who don't need me, but then you—*you*—"

My eyes catch on something on his desk, buried under a pile of chess books that's not unlike something Dad would set aside to make room for me on the couch.

It's the German Chess flier. From Toronto. From the night we . . .

"The tic-tac-toe sheet."

"What?" He comes to stand behind me. "Oh, yeah."

It's on his nightstand, preserved like a trophy. He brought it from Toronto, to Moscow, to his apartment in New York, to *here*. Warmth spreads in my stomach.

I resist it. Bite the inside of my cheek. Then give in, and ask. "Why did you keep it?"

"It made me think of you."

His arms close around my rib cage, right below my breasts, and I close my eyes. "Why would you keep something that makes you think of me?"

I feel him shrug. "Because I think of you anyway, Mallory."

I turn around. Break contact. This is unbearable. This closeness with him. These tugs toward him, deep in my stomach. It's what I've been avoiding—something that I know can only end in lies and betrayal. I've seen it happen before.

"What do you want from me, Nolan, and—will you please stop *smiling*."

"I'm not." He grins wider.

"I'm serious, if you don't quit smiling."

"That's not a threat. It's not even a grammatically correct sentence."

"What do you want from me? What are we . . ." I bury my face in my hands. This is too raw. Too untraveled. Too risky and confusing. "I don't understand why you're in my head."

"You're in mine, too. But I know why."

I groan and make myself look at him. He's not smiling anymore. "Just . . . what do you want from me?"

"I want everything." His tone is calm. Matter-of-fact. Naked, in a way that has nothing to do with his clothes. "I'm all in." He slowly lowers his forehead until it touches mine. His eyes merge together into one, right on his nose. All I can hear is the sound of our breathing, and something inside me clicks into place. "What about you, Mallory?"

I don't answer. Instead I do what I know: I push my chin up to kiss him, and it works just as well.

It's even better than yesterday. His arms cage me against the dresser, and mine loop around his neck. I'm wearing a T-shirt, and my hands make contact with the vast expanse of his back, smooth and sunshine-hot. I open my mouth, and he licks my lower lip before his tongue slides against mine, clumsy and hot and insistent and delicious. The helpless, eager, guttural noises we're both making are maybe embarrassing, but it's okay.

Even if I never catch my breath again.

"Slow down," I tell him. "Let's just . . ."

"I think about this every second of every day." His palm slides up my back, and my body is like a pawn in his hands. He turns us around and then we're on the unmade bed, the twisted sheets digging into my spine. "You'll be playing the most beautiful chess I've ever seen, and I dream about having you under me. It's fucking *confusing*."

We're both wearing too many clothes, and suddenly I'm impatient. I want bare. I want skin—*more* skin. I want him closer, in a seamless, sticky way. He's hard against my stomach, and the two of us feel both familiar and soul-baringly intimate, like nothing has been before.

"Do you . . ." My hand slides down his abs, meets the waistband of his jeans, and it's finally there, a hint of that hesitation, that wobbliness I expected from him. "No?" I ask.

His throat bobs as he swallows. His full lips tremble for the barest second. "Are you real?" The air between us swells, overflows. "Sometimes I'm scared that I imagined you. Sometimes I think you're only in my head."

"I'm here," I breathe out. I'm a pool of liquid heat.

"I have no idea what I'm doing," he says, biting softly the hollow under my ear.

I shiver. "I can help," I tell him, even if my neurons are boiling to mush.

"Yeah?"

"It's kind of like chess. I do one thing . . ." I undo the first button of his jeans, slowly. Feel, more than hear, the hitch of his breath. "And you do another."

He holds himself up on his arms and looks down at me, like he's inventorying, deciding where to start. His index finger hooks on the hem of my shirt and drags it upward, stopping right below my bra. He stares at my navel for what feels like minutes, then says, "I want odds. Since it's my first time."

"You want a handicap?"

"I want *two* moves."

I laugh. And then sober when he pins my hands above my head, in a way that suggests that he might not know what he's doing but he has plans, fantasies, strategies, a rich interior world that will be put to use, and . . .

"I hope," I say, serious, "that you're going to like this as much as chess."

"I think," he tells me with a small smile, "that I already do."

Chapter Twenty-Two

We wake up early in the morning. Do a bunch of slow, sleepy stuff with our hands that feels really good and also happens not to require a condom. I had only one, left in my backpack from who knows when; Nolan had none. Apparently we really had fooled ourselves into thinking that this wouldn't happen. I fall asleep on his chest, his arms looped around me, feeling his rapid breathing slow down to something calmer, then slide into sleep and pull me under.

The buzz of Nolan's phone on the nightstand wakes us up once the sun is high. He answers with a huge yawn. "Yeah?" His voice is too loud. Or maybe not. Maybe it's the way we're pretzeled together skin to skin, legs coiled, his free hand tangled in my hair and holding me into the curve of his shoulder. "That's because I *was* sleeping. Yup. Yeah. Sure." He sounds unimpressed. He sounds like the delicious, warm version of Nolan that kept ordering me to stop fidgeting at 3:00 a.m. This is not real life. "Uh-uh." I pull back to watch his slitted, tired eyes and his swollen lips. He smells fantastic. I want to sink under his skin. I want to move between his legs and dwell on the expanse of his chest. I—

"Sure. She's here. Let me ask her."

Nolan presses his phone against his shoulders. My eyes

widen. "What?" I whisper. "Don't tell them I'm here! They'll think that I . . ."

He gives me a confused look. "That you're here?"

I groan and hide back in his neck.

"There is a charity event. Someone wants us to play together, against . . ." He picks up his phone again. "Who would we be playing against?" I hear a brisk female voice on the other side. "Some tech industry person," he tells me, and then into the speaker again, "Is it Bill Gates again? Elle, he's *bad* at chess. I can't make the game last longer than one minute against . . . Yeah. I'll call you back." He tosses the phone to the side and pulls me closer, covering our heads with the blankets.

The outside world disappears.

"Who's Elle?" I ask.

"My manager." He pushes my hair behind my ear. "What should I tell her?"

"When is this happening?"

"Not until the spring."

"Why the tech industry?"

"It's full of people who have a hard-on for chess, apparently."

It makes a surprising amount of sense. "Why do you have a manager?"

"All pro players do. You'll need one, too."

I won't be a pro, Nolan. You know it. "Would you recommend Elle?"

"Hell no. Save yourself."

I laugh. "Can I . . . think about it? The charity thing."

"Sure."

We fall quiet, cocooned by the soft cotton of sheets, impossibly close. *Did last night really happen?* I wonder, feeling stuck in a dream. *Did it happen to you like it happened to me?*

Then he murmurs, "Good morning," while pressing a kiss on my forehead, and it all starts to seem warm, and precariously good, and true.

NOLAN HAS NO POKER FACE. NO ABILITY TO LIE, OR TRICK, OR hide. No intention to, either.

He tracks my movements with a small smile whenever I step away from the chessboard to grab a glass of water. He kisses me against the fridge while the three GMs are talking about the French Defense five feet from us. He takes my hand and pulls me out for a walk in the snow as the sun is about to set, like healthy habits are something he suddenly cares about.

I wish I could say I minded, but I love every second of it.

There's a curious, painfully honest confidence about him. Last night was good, *really* good, but it was also his first time, *our* first time: messy and imperfect, full of hushed questions and trials and errors. His hands on me were bold, but inexperienced and tentative. Other guys would be drowning in their fragile masculinity today, but Nolan just seems deeply, genuinely happy.

Then again, remembering the sounds I made, the gasps . . . I guess he got glowing feedback.

"Can't believe he used an Evans Gambit three years ago," he says about the Koch game we just analyzed. His footprints in the snow are almost twice as large as mine.

"Yeah, well. It was a bad choice, since Thagard-Vork destroyed him."

"Still. I haven't seen the Evans since the week I learned how to play."

I smile. "When was that, by the way?"

"What?" He gives me a curious look.

"When *did* you learn to play chess?"

"I don't remember. Pretty sure it's on Wikipedia."

"Yeah. But unlike my sister, I refuse to read it. Boundaries and stuff." I stop him with a tug on his coat. I'm wearing his gloves, because it's freezing and I forgot to bring mine. They dwarf my hands, and Nolan smiles at the sight. "But I still want to know."

"I was . . . five? But I didn't *really* understand. Not until I was well over six."

"Your grandfather taught you?"

"Kind of. He was training a lot of people at the time, and I just . . . I wanted to be in the midst of things. He was the coolest person I knew, and I wanted him to pay attention to me."

"And your parents didn't want you to?"

He shrugs. "My dad's an asshole. And even if he weren't, he just doesn't have the chess bone. When I was little, I would spend hours thinking about puzzles or Legos or toys, reasoning over them, analyzing, and he couldn't understand why. He thought there was something wrong with me. Put me in all sorts of sports. And I was good enough at them, because I was tall and quick, but they were never . . ."

"They weren't chess?"

He nods.

I think about Dad. About how he was the opposite, constantly pushing me toward chess. About how if he were still alive, we'd probably be just as estranged as Nolan and his father are. Vastly different paths, same results. "Do you hate your parents?"

He lets out a small laugh. "I don't think so. I don't think

about them much. Haven't for a while." He swallows. "Somehow, it hurts even worse."

I reach out, sinking my hand in the pocket of his coat. He exhales, a white chuff in the late afternoon air. "It didn't matter when my grandfather was around, because he got me. He'd been like me as a kid, or similar enough. When my parents divorced, they stopped feeling like they had to care about me. Mom remarried. Then Dad. Then his new wife got pregnant and it was almost a relief. I was an afterthought, and I could just stay with my grandfather for weeks at a time. It was just me and him. Playing, playing again. Playing some more."

"Did you ever win?"

"Oh, no. Not for a long time. Not until I was nine or ten. Then I did, and I was almost afraid. He hated losing as much as I do. I thought he'd be mad. But . . ." He shakes his head. "I think it was the happiest I'd ever seen him."

"So maybe he *didn't* hate losing as much as you do."

"I think . . ." He stops, and so do I. Holds my eyes. "He told me once that sometimes, with some people, it's not about winning or losing. That with some people, it's just about playing. Though for the longest time, I didn't really believe him."

"Yeah?" I look away, toward the setting sun. "I still think about losing to Koch. Every day. Every hour."

"I know."

"Stop reading my mind." I poke him in the stomach. He snatches my hand and pulls me closer to him. "How do *you* deal with losses?"

"I don't."

"So you just feel like shit? Every time?"

"You basically have to hate losing to be a top player. Pretty sure the genes are on the same chromosome."

"Is that why you're a terrible loser?"

"Yup. And why *you* are one."

I smile. "Not gonna lie, it's validating. Growing up, I couldn't figure out why Easton was so chill about losing all those matches. Meanwhile even draws sent me into a deep funk."

"Easton?"

"Oh. She's my best friend." I swallow. "Well. Former?"

His head cocks. "Did she take your queen?"

"No. She . . . left. For college. Colorado."

"Ah."

"Yeah. Haven't heard from her much ever since." I sigh. "How do you keep in touch with Tanu and Emil, again?"

"It's not the same. Emil's still in New York and hates the dorms, which means that he's always at my place. And you know how Tanu is. I'd have to work hard on ditching her."

"Yeah." I try not to sound too jealous. "Easton finds me boring and uninteresting now that I don't . . . I don't even know. Play beer pong with her?"

"She told you that?"

"No. But I know it."

"Could you be assuming?"

"No."

He nods, and I like that he's not trying to lie to me. To convince me that I'm imagining it all. "Have you considered confronting her?"

"No. I . . . I don't want her pity. I want her to be with me because she wants to."

"Ah, yes." He nods knowingly. His chin dips into the raised neck of his coat. "You do like being in charge."

"What do you mean?"

"You like having the upper hand. Feeling like you're doing something for others. Like you're in control."

"No." I frown. "That's not it at all."

"I think it's easier for you to be with people when you feel needed than when you need them. Less risky. Less messy, right?"

"But it's not true. I mean, according to Sabrina my family doesn't need me for anything but money anymore. And Easton's the one who went MIA. And you—*you* most certainly don't need me—"

"But I do."

I snort. "Come on. You have a million seconds, and legions of adoring fans, Tanu and Emil, Elle the scary manager, the press, the entire *world*—"

"Mallory." He stops me. His expression is solemn. "It's lonely, chess. You may have a team around you, but when it really comes down to it, you're on your own. You play on your own. You lose and win on your own. You go home, and you're on your own." He takes in the disappearing light, his eyes darker than ever. And then looks back to me, presses a pale strand of hair behind my ear, and asks something I didn't expect. "Will you come to Italy with me?"

"To Italy?"

He nods. "For the World Championship."

"I . . . Why?"

His throat works. "I had my grandfather with me for the first one, six years ago. But after that, I was always on my own."

"But Tanu and Emil are going to be there, and—"

"They are. But . . ." I can see the gears in his head, like he's trying to articulate a fuzzy, ungraspable feeling. "They'll be there *with* each other first."

Somehow, I know exactly what he means. *I feel it, too*, I want to say. *I feel the same. Like everyone around us is part of the same connective tissue, and you're just floating about. Unbound.*

My heart beats faster, because this feels like a threshold. A touch-take decision that I won't ever be able to undo. If I say yes, then Nolan and I will be something different. Something *together*. More than the sum of our parts.

Then, no. No should be the only possible answer. I have no business promising to be there for anyone. I have priorities. Duties. But.

"Do you want me to be there?" I ask.

He nods instantly.

I take his cold palm, lift it in both my hands, and press a soft kiss in the middle, where the fate line slashes between the head and the heart.

"I'll be there, then." I smile up at him, right as the last of the sunlight fades into the snow. "For you."

IT OCCURS TO ME THAT NIGHT, AFTER WE CHECK SOME OF Koch's recent Challengers games against engines and instead of staying up late to pore over the results we decide to go to bed at eight, that maybe the timing for this thing is a little off.

We should be training hard. We should focus on strategy, tactics, preparation.

We should *not* be staring at each other across the table.

We should *not* drift off during Tanu's passionate speech on why Velveeta is legally not cheese to exchange faint, un-prompted, unjustified smiles.

We should not needlessly brush knuckles as he hands me his plate for the dishwasher.

And most definitely, we should not fall on each other the second we're in his room, the wood of his door smooth under my back, his front pressed against mine as we kiss deeply. The mechanics of this are familiar, but the impatience simmering inside me is new. The feeling that one more minute apart will be too much. Seeing the same eagerness mirrored in Nolan.

"We still don't have a condom," I tell him, and he grunts against my throat. Then steps an inch back.

"I'm going to get one from Emil—"

"No. *No*."

"Why?"

"I'd rather they not know."

"Mallory." He presses a kiss on my cheekbone. My nose. "They know."

"Yeah, but they don't *know* know, and . . ." I'm the one to groan now. "Let's just go to CVS tomorrow."

"Tomorrow?" He pulls back and looks so horrifically, theatrically appalled, I have to laugh and kiss the expression off his face.

"We can do *other* things in the meantime."

His fingers slide down my spine, slowly massaging each knob. "Like what? Shovel snow? Color by the number?"

I laugh against his mouth. "So many options."

"Please, list them for me. I am *very* new at this." His hand slips inside the waist of my jeans, and I exhale sharply.

"Illegal move."

"Should we call in the arbiter?"

"Only if—" My phone rings, and he groans. I whimper, working my hand between us to retrieve it from my pocket.

"It's Defne," I say. I have a déjà vu—months ago, on Nolan's couch. She has *atrocious*, cockblocking timing.

"Ignore her," he orders, and I'm happy to. I toss it on Nolan's dresser, and we're back on each other, graceless, uncoordinated, voracious, until he kneels in front of me and starts unbuttoning my pants. "So." He speaks against my hip bone. "These *things* we are going to do. Could they involve me—"

My phone, again. No, Nolan's—it's *his* phone buzzing now. "Fuck," he grunts, pulling it out of his pocket and throwing it next to mine.

But my eyes fall on the caller ID, and I stiffen. "Wait. It's Defne."

She hasn't called once since we came here, just the occasional text. And now . . .

We halt.

Nolan's phone stops buzzing. A second later mine starts ringing again.

We exchange a long look, both out of breath. He lets out a deep, frustrated groan, and hides his face in my stomach. His hands close around my waist, trembling slightly. I take it as tacit permission to pick up.

"Hey, D—" He inches my shirt up and nibbles on my belly button. My breath hitches. I giggle, sigh, try to push him away. Then the cycle starts all over. "Hey, Defne," I finally manage. Nolan licks a stripe below my navel. "How are you—"

"Mallory, I'm on my way to pick you up. You need to return to New York immediately."

Chapter Twenty-Three

"What do you mean, Koch cheated? There were too many cameras for him to—"

"Someone has been combing the footage."

Defne's voice is grainy over the speakerphone, background noise ebbing and flowing as she drives up the interstate. Nolan and I sit on the bed, eyes locked, but his expression is indiscernible. His hair is still tousled from my fingers.

"Remember how he kept standing to pace? He'd hidden a smartwatch around his elbow. He'd leave the board, find a place without cameras, and use it to communicate with . . . well, we don't know. Presumably, someone who had access to a chess engine. But he miscalculated, because they have *two* instances of this on video. And one right before his final move against you."

"That piece of shit," Nolan mutters. His jaw is tight, one large hand fisting the sheets.

"What does that mean?" I ask Defne. "For the World Championship?"

"FIDE hasn't made a formal announcement yet. And Koch is still denying it and threatening lawsuits. But Mal, the evidence is *damning*. They will have to disqualify him."

"So, if Koch is disqualified . . ." I consider the implications. A knot of disappointment tightens in my chest. "It means that Nolan will win by default? And we should stop training?" The prospect is more devastating than it should be. I face it for a long, silent moment, in which Nolan gives me more of that inscrutable look, and Defne breathes audibly.

"Mal," she starts, "you—"

"That's not what it means," he interrupts her.

"What, then?" I frown at Nolan, confused. "They can't redo the Challengers."

"They don't need to," he says calmly.

The space between us charges, a sudden magnetic field, and then it occurs to me.

They don't need to, because they already have a runner-up.

Someone who was poised to win until she lost to Koch.

Me.

"But we . . . Nolan and I . . ." I shake my head, flustered. "Nolan and I have been training together."

"That's why I'm coming up to get you, Mal. I'll be there in a few—"

Nolan hangs up on her. The phone immediately starts buzzing again, but we ignore it. His eyes hold mine for a second, for ten years, and I have no idea how to feel. What to think.

"I'm sorry, I . . ." I get off the bed and stare at the books stacked on the dresser, mind racing.

If Defne is right, if FIDE *does* ask me to be the challenger . . . three million dollars. That's the mortgage paid off, Mom's meds, my sisters' college tuition. Hell, *my* college tuition. We'd be set for life.

But I'd have to come clean to Mom and Sabrina. They might

hate me. And there's the biggie: Nolan. Three minutes ago, I was trying to get inside his skin. For weeks, I've been his second. I've been studying his weaknesses, strategies, tactics. Challenging him now would be like robbing him with a house key he handed me for safekeeping. Utterly unethical.

Oh *God*.

I cannot imagine how devastated he must be feeling. How terrified. How betrayed by the idea of me exploiting what I've learned about his game.

I turn around and look up at him, meaning to reassure him that I won't, promise that I wouldn't, and find him . . .

Smiling?

"What . . . why do you look so happy?"

"Because it's perfect. Because it's you." He steps closer, grinning. So hard, I spot a rare dimple. "I'll get to do this. With you."

"I . . . no. We can't."

"I think we can." He reaches out for me, and I let him.

"I need to think."

"Sure. Think. Think out loud." His curved lips press against my throat. "Think while I kiss you. Everywhere." I laugh. Then his fingers drop again to the button of my jeans. My breath stops with how much I want this. With him. "Can I . . . I have this dream that you let me—"

"If I . . ." I pull back to look at his eager, happy face. Suddenly, I'm just as happy as he is. It's going to happen. The two of us. Me and him and a chessboard. "Would I need to leave?"

"No."

"But we can't train together for . . ."

"Then we won't. I'll train in this room. You take the rest of the house."

"But still—I know your strategies, Nolan. I know your prep. And . . ." I reach up to hold his handsome, stubborn, delighted face between my hands. Bite his lower lip because I cannot help myself. "This is a mess. Why are you so happy?"

His smile doesn't waver. "You don't know?"

My heart revs up to a million. Nearly beats out of my chest with everything that I'm feeling for him. I don't want to leave. I want to be with him. I want to sleep with him in this bed. I want to wake up to him pulling me into himself. I want to eat the overcooked pasta he makes and share his toothpaste and know his moods by heart.

"Nolan," I whisper against his lips.

"Mallory."

"Don't be alarmed," I say, mostly to myself. "But I think that I might be—"

The door slams open.

"Oh my God, oh my little baby Jesus, guys, did you see— Oh, sorry."

Nolan groans in frustration. It takes a minute for us to disentangle and turn to Tanu. Who just barged in without knocking.

"Koch?" Nolan asks. His voice is raspy. His hand reaches out to touch my waist, as though he cannot bear to be apart. I lean into him, because I can.

"He cheated! That birdbrained bitch! We should have known he was using engines!"

I grin. "We really should have."

"And that TikTok? Dick of dicks, much?"

Nolan blinks. "What TikTok?"

Ten seconds later, Koch (@bigKoch; I despise him) is talking in front of a wall that boasts an unironic oil portrait of himself. His German accent is thicker than usual.

"*I did not cheat. The images were doctored, and my lawyers have already gotten in touch with FIDE. I'll be going to Venice to hand Sawyer his ass.*"

Behind me, Nolan snorts softly.

"Oh, he just posted a new one," Tanu says. "Let's see how low he can go."

"*I wouldn't be surprised if Sawyer's team was behind this. He's very scared of facing me, because he knows he'll likely lose. He has been trying to prevent it from happening. For instance, he not only got his girlfriend a spot on the Challengers but also paid for Greenleaf's fellowship at Zugzwang. This is a clear attempt to manipulate who would be his opponent and to avoid me, the strongest player, in order to keep his World Championship title.*"

I scoff, indignant. "Can he just go out there and say things that are factually false? Legally, I mean?"

I glance at Tanu, who's pre-law, hoping for a "Hell no." But all I find is a wide-eyed, guilty look that makes every last trace of warmth freeze inside me.

"He *is* wrong," I say, half statement, half question. "It's not true. Nolan has nothing to do with my fellowship. He didn't get me into the Challengers. He . . ."

I turn around. Nolan is silent, dark eyes even darker than usual. I shake my head. "No." I swallow, and it's glass down my throat. "No."

"Mal. Nolan, I'm *so* sorry," Tanu blurts out.

"Will you leave for a minute?" Nolan asks her.

"I had no idea he was going to mention that— I didn't think he even knew—"

"Tanu," Nolan repeats, and in a heartbeat she's gone, and the door closes, and my brain careens. This is . . . no. Nope. Fuck this.

"Did Defne know?" I ask. "That you were paying? Because she vaguely mentioned multiple donors to me, that—"

"She knew," he says calmly.

I clench my teeth. "Right. Well, Tanu did, too, so I'm guessing Emil was in on it, too, and since it reached Koch—"

"I had to disclose my donation to Zugzwang to FIDE. I assume that's how he found out. But this has nothing to do with us, we—"

"This has *everything* to do with us." The last six months have been a party, and I'm the last to get here. Or maybe I was here all along, blindfolded and locked in a closet. "Was it fun, coming to our house, knowing you were keeping the lights on?"

Maybe I should be grateful, but all I feel is deceived. Manipulated. Like when Dad kissed a woman in the arbiter lounge of a Hoboken tournament and told me it was nothing.

You lied to me. How could you?

"You really believe I'd ever think about it in those terms, Mallory?" His fist clenches and releases. He runs a hand through his hair. "You played the most beautiful chess I'd ever seen. I wanted to give you the opportunity to—"

"How did you even know I was going to accept it?"

"I didn't. I just hoped. You worked in a shitty garage, and needed *out*."

"What do you even know about my shitty garage— Oh my God." I take a step back like he punched me in the solar plexus. "Did you somehow have Bob fire me?"

His arms widen in irritation. "Who the hell is Bob?"

I don't believe him. I *can't* believe him, not anymore. "Did you have anything to do with me losing my job back in the summer?"

"I didn't, but I fucking wish I *had*, Mallory." He huffs impatiently. "I wish I could take credit for shaking you out of the life you settled for."

I gasp. "I provide for my family, Nolan! I didn't *settle*, I needed stability for them." My tone is well past civility. He steps closer, nostrils flaring, face lowered an inch from mine.

"It's easier like that, isn't it? To hide behind them," he tells me. "Use your family as a nice little cushion between yourself and real life."

I lift my chin. "How *dare* you? My mom is sick and my sisters are—"

"Taken care of, as of right now. As of a while. And yet, you continue to use them as an excuse to do absolutely nothing with your life, with your talent, with this thing between us—"

"'This *thing* between us'? You mean, the fact that we've fucked? Because clearly that means nothing. Or the fact that you've been lying to me for months? The fact that you manipulated me to go back to chess, to do the Challengers, to be your opponent at the World Championship? Because I can't imagine what else you might be referring to—"

"I love you," he says plainly. Not a desperate plea, but a calmly stated fact. His eyes are so close, I can count the different shades of dark in them, and it makes me see red.

It's not the first time someone has professed to love me after an ocean of lies.

"No," I say sharply, "you don't. If you did, you'd have told me the truth. If you did, you'd understand that my family will always come first. If you did, you wouldn't have played with my life just to get to pick your next World Championship opponent—"

"Jesus, Mallory, I didn't—" He takes a deep breath, struggling to de-escalate. "Listen, I know you don't like this, and I respect it, but you're starting to sound nuts."

"And *you* would know crazy." I say it calmly. Coldly. And even when I see something fracture in his eyes, I power through. "You don't love anyone except for yourself. You're manipulative, selfish. You're alone, because your family hates you. And now *I* hate you, too."

The door opens abruptly, but I don't need to look to know who it is. I keep my gaze on Nolan's beautiful, hurt, deceitful expression, and make sure to scorch into my brain the pain I feel in this very moment. Here they are. The lies, the betrayal, the disappointment I was waiting for.

Never stray, Mallory. Never believe. Never trust anyone.

My heart trembles, and I grip it tight enough to choke it.

"Hi, Defne," I say, proud of the firmness of my voice. "Perfect timing. I'm ready to leave."

Chapter Twenty-Four

I push my frozen fingers into my pocket, take a deep breath, and fail at not sounding too impatient when I say, "I promise your hair looks perfect and the scrunchie matches your top. Can we leave now?"

Sabrina takes her sweet time to fluff her hair, fix her lipstick, and grab her backpack, and pauses in front of me on her way to the door. "Amazing, how you were gone for"—she checks a watch she doesn't wear—"*weeks*, and we managed to function perfectly and be late for school"—another pretend check—"a grand total of *zero* times." She taps her chin. "It's almost as though we don't need you to boss us around. Food for thought, hmm?"

She slides past me. I sigh and follow, stepping over crunchy snow on my way to the car.

It's almost like she's not happy with me.

Then again: *no one* is happy with me. Darcy spent the three nights since Defne dropped me off sleeping in Sabrina's room—apparently, her rage at me for deciding not to go to the World Championship healed the years-long rift between them. Mom's a mix of tired, worried, and suspicious of me for being back weeks before my "double-pay night shifts at the senior center" were supposed to be over. Even Mrs. Abebe glared at me, for shoveling our shared driveway too early and waking up her toddler.

But it's A-OK. It's actually pretty fitting, because I'm not happy with anybody, either. Screw Easton for leaving that Adam Driver Wall Punch meme I sent her on read, and rebuffing my attempts to reconnect. Screw Sabrina and Darcy for making me feel unwelcome in the home whose mortgage *I* pay. Screw Tanu, Emil, and Defne for being all in on the puppeteering of my life, and screw Nolan for . . .

He doesn't bear thinking about. It's just me now. And the people who hate me, the people whom I hate, and of course, the auto-mechanic certification tests I finally registered for. The one thing I promised myself I'd do during my fellowship—not learn the Stafford Gambit, not fancy myself half in love with some manipulative liar, but secure my family's future.

I'm back on track. Over chess. Free from distractions. In control.

My mornings are spent at the testing center, neck-deep in multiple choice options about heating and air-conditioning. Automatic transmission. Engine repair and performance. Brakes, suspension, and steering. Electronic systems.

Then I go get boba and smuggle it into the library. In a new low, I'm now lying to my family about going to my fake job, which means having to kill time till 5:00 p.m. At least I'm finally catching up on the García Márquez readathon. The rest of the online group moved on to Haruki Murakami in December, but I'm no quitter.

I don't think so, at least.

DARCY AND I HAVE BEEN WAITING IN THE CAR FOR TWENTY minutes when I decide that I've had enough.

Any other time, I'd be happy to let Sabrina hang out with her derby friends in fifteen-degree weather while Darcy and I shoot the shit and bellow KIIS FM songs, changing every instance of *love* into *fart*. But Darcy's either too angry at me for refusing to engage on the topic of chess with her (day four of silent treatment—she really *is* maturing) or too taken with reading *You Should See Me in a Crown* to pay attention to me. I could pass some time on the phone, but I've learned my lesson: when there is a surge of media interest in you, it's probably wise to stay off socials.

So I get out of the car and yell across the half-empty gym parking lot: "Sabrina. Time to go."

"Yeah." She's giggling and staring at her friend McKenzie's phone. "Give me a sec—"

"I gave you a second ten minutes ago. Get your ass in the car."

The eye roll, the shoulder-heaving sigh—those, I barely notice. But the way McKenzie leans forward to whisper something in her ear, Sabrina's murmured response, the fact that they both giggle while looking in my direction . . . that's hard to overlook. I feel a pit of something that could be anger deep-fill my stomach, and remind myself that she's fifteen. Her frontal lobe? Just a mass of cookie dough. And if she and Darcy spend the ride chatting about *Riverdale*, without including me in the conversation, it's okay.

I'm plenty busy white-knuckling the steering wheel.

"I need a ride to Totowa for a meet on Saturday," Sabrina says once we're home, while I dig in the freezer for leftover chicken.

"How about a *please*?" I mutter.

"I wasn't talking to you."

"Well, Mom is not up for—"

"I've been really good with the new meds, Mal." Mom smiles. At Sabrina. "I'll drive you."

"Awesome." She kisses Mom on the cheek, and they both disappear down the hallway. I'm left in the kitchen, cutting up veggies for the Crock-Pot, wondering if while I was gone, my family outgrew its need *and* its want for me.

Wondering what else chess has taken away from me.

Mom, Darcy, and Sabrina are chatting in the living room—a new post-school ritual, seemingly—when someone knocks. I wipe the scallions from my fingers and get the door, expecting Mrs. Abebe to ask me to move the car.

It's worse. So much worse, I slip out and slam the door shut behind me. I'm wearing only a T-shirt and it's freezing cold, but desperate times, hypothermic measures. "What are you doing here?"

Oz looks around my porch, hands stuffed in his Burberry pockets, upper lip curled in what looks a lot like disgust. "Is this where you live?"

"Yeah." I frown. "Where do *you* live? A high-rise in Hudson Yards?"

"Yes."

I don't know what I expected. "Okay, well . . . congrats. Is there a reason you're here, Oz?"

"I just stopped by to say hi. Chat a little." He shrugs, eyes fixed on the broken trampoline. "See if maybe you're ready to pull your head out of your ass."

I blink. "Excuse me?"

"Just checking in if you're done acting like a big whiny shit who's all alone against the world. Any updates?"

I blink again. "Listen, I know being mean is your whole shtick, but—"

"I think it's *yours*, actually."

"Excuse me?"

His green eyes harden. "Have you, at any point in the last week, considered that deciding to ostrich your way through the biggest scandal FIDE has seen in the past thirty years might affect people who *aren't* you?"

"What's happening has nothing to do with me. Koch cheated. Good on him." My breath paints the air white. "I'm done with chess."

"Ah, yes. You are. Because boo-hoo, your boyfriend paid for your salary without asking for anything in return and didn't tell you. Cry me the fucking Nile."

I stiffen. "You have no idea what—"

"And I don't care. You want to be mad at Sawyer for not disclosing? Go ahead. Chuck his PS5 out of the window, I don't give a shit." He steps closer. "I'm here to talk about Defne, and the fact that after *everything* she has done for you, you're ruining her life."

"I'm not ruining . . ." I hug myself. My goose bumps are fat little hills on my arms. "I'm not."

"She acts as your trainer and manager. Which means that FIDE has been hounding her for confirmation that you will attend."

"Well, I'm done with chess and everyone involved in it. She can tell them that I won't."

"Oh, yes, sure. She'll just tell them that. 'Sorry, guys, Mal had a domestic with her boytoy and is outta here.' It won't in any way impact her credibility or her standing in the chess community, the fact that the player she vouched for disappeared from the face of the earth. That the player she bent over backward to get into tournaments turned out to be the selfish, flaky—"

"Wait, what? She didn't. I only ever participated in open tournaments."

He scoffs. "*Open* doesn't mean walk-ins welcome. There's still a selection process, and people need to prove their credentials— of which you had *none*. Defne made sure you could play in Philly and Nashville. She paid for you to go there, and let you keep one hundred percent of your earnings. And now FIDE is considering unaccrediting Zugzwang, because Defne's star player is refusing to be in the World Championship, because . . ." He gives me a withering look. "Why?"

Anger bubbles up. "Defne *lied* to me."

"Ah, yes." He rolls his eyes. "How, precisely?"

"She didn't tell me Nolan gave her the money."

"Even though you asked. Despicable of her."

"I didn't ask, but—"

"Of course you didn't. You were told that the money came from donors, did not ask follow-up questions, and now you're high-horsing her into the ground."

I glare. "Oz—why are you even here? How do you know all this stuff? Why would Defne tell you . . ." He's looking at me like I'm the dimmest bulb in the cookie jar. And I am. "Wait. You and Defne aren't . . . ?"

He ignores me. "Do you think chess clubs are a lucrative enterprise? That Defne makes bank? Rethink that. She bought Zugzwang because she wanted to create an environment in which *everyone* felt welcome in chess. To prevent others from feeling the way she had. And she has to rely on donors. Sawyer has been one of those donors for years, and here's what happened: yes, he gave her the funds to track you down and offer you the job. But when you refused the fellowship, Defne started looking into *other* possible players to sponsor. Because Sawyer's donation was just that—a gift with no strings attached."

I swallow. "He was involved in me losing my job. I'm sure of it." Almost.

"Maybe." Oz shrugs. "I wouldn't put it past him. But Defne? She never wanted anything from you except to see you succeed. Which is the reason she's not here pointing out how much of a whiny little bitch you're being, or suing you for breach of contract. But I have no such qualms, Mal. I don't care if you come back to read *Love in the Time of Cholera* while you should be studying *Modern Chess Openings*. You *owe* it to Defne to see this year through. And to have a conversation with her about the World Championship. To help her deal with FIDE without losing face."

He takes a step back. His perennial belligerent air deflates a little, and for once he seems more open than irritated. "Listen. I try hard not to learn things about the people around me, but . . . I've heard about your father. I know you take care of your family. I know you're dealing with stuff like"—his chin points at my yard—"that rusty trampoline. But if you unzip your asshole and pry your head out of it, you might realize that there's more to life than feeling sorry for yourself." He nods once and then turns around, hopping gracefully down the slippery porch steps.

I watch him walk away, a confused mix of anger that feels a lot like guilt swirling through me. I didn't ask Defne to train me. I didn't *ask* Nolan to sponsor me. All I ever asked was for Dad to not cheat on Mom in front of me, for him not to die, for Mom not to get sick, for my life to be *normal*. How dare Oz, from his Alps of privilege, treat me like *I* am the spoiled little girl?

"You don't know me," I yell after him. A cliché—that's who I am.

"And I don't particularly care to." He opens the driver's door of his Mini. "Not if this is who you are."

When I slump against the inside of the door, the house feels impossibly hot. I take a deep breath and order myself to calm down.

It's irrelevant, what Oz thinks of me, because he and chess are out of my life. Maybe I'll call Defne at some point. Let her know that I'm out for good. But two nights ago I dreamed that every single person I met in the past six months was pointing at me and laughing: I'd been moving the rook across diagonals, thinking it was a bishop. No one corrected me, not even Defne. She was in the first row, sniggering with Nolan.

So, yeah. Not ready to reach out.

I press my palms into my eyes and go back into the kitchen to finish making dinner. I stop at the entrance, and no one notices me.

"—kind of gross," Darcy is saying, peeking at the Crock-Pot. "Like . . . ew?"

"Super unhealthy, with all that oil," Sabrina points out. "Maybe she needs a cooking class for her birthday, Mom."

"That's a lovely idea, Sabrina. She'll love that."

"I'm not getting her a present," Darcy grumbles.

"I see what she was trying to do. But it's not a recipe that calls for thigh, you know," Mom muses. "Maybe breast. Or pork."

"I don't wanna eat this," Sabrina mumbles, and that's the moment I feel it happen: like a tough little bubble, bloody and red, giving off the tiniest of pops inside my head.

"Then *don't*," I say. The three of them whip around at the same time, eyes wide. "As a matter of fact, why don't *you* make dinner?"

Sabrina hesitates. Then rolls her eyes. "Jesus. Chill, Mal."

"Yeah." I nod. "I *will* chill. I will stop doing the dishes. I will stop grocery shopping. I will stop earning money for food. Let's see how you like it."

"That's totally fine." Her hands come to her hips. "You were gone for *weeks* and we were doing *amazing*."

"Oh, really?" It's like a knife twisted in my rib cage. "You were doing *amazing*?"

"We were free of this weird dictatorship where we can't even comment on dinner," Sabrina says, and I see Mom's mouth opening to chastise her, but I'm quicker.

"You are such a *bitch*," I hear myself say.

It sounds horrendous in the silence of the kitchen. It shocks Mom into silence, and Darcy physically steps back. But Sabrina narrows her eyes and stands her ground. So I continue.

"You are an ungrateful bitch. Since all I do is chauffeur you around and make sure your fees are paid."

"I didn't ask for *any* of that!"

"Then don't *fucking take it*, Sabrina. Go out and do the thing *I* did. Don't go to school, quit your precious roller derby—let's see how much your little buddy McKenzie likes you when she's in college and you aren't! Completely give up on every little thing you love so that you can take care of your bratty, ungrateful little sister"—I point at Darcy—"who, by the way, is also a high-functioning bitch."

"*Mallory*," Mom interrupts sternly. "That's enough."

"Is it, though?" I look at her. My eyes are blurry, burning with the same heat that's in my stomach. "Not that you're much better, since you're currently *also* being a bitch—"

"*Enough*."

Mom's harsh voice is followed by a thick, terrible silence.

It's my undoing: suddenly, I'm in my body again. And with that, I can hear every vile thing I just said like a played-back tape, and it's unbearable. I'm too horrified, too angry, too stricken to stay one second longer.

"Oh my God. I-I . . ."

I shake my head and turn around. Stagger to my room, vision fuzzy.

I just called my mom, my thirteen- and fifteen-year-old sisters whose lives *I* ruined—I called them *bitches*. I threw in their face what I've done for them—despite the fact that it wouldn't have needed doing if it hadn't been for *me*.

I close the door behind me, fold onto my mattress, and hide my face in my hands, ashamed.

I never cry. I didn't cry when I told Mom about what Dad did. I didn't cry when he packed his bags and left. I didn't cry when we received that phone call from the highway patrol at five thirty in the morning. I didn't cry when I declined my scholarship offers, when Bob fired me, in Defne's car on my way back from Nolan's house. I never cried, even when I wanted to, because when I asked myself if I had the right to those tears, the answer was always no, and it was easy to stop myself.

But I'm sobbing now. I hide my face in my hands and wail loudly, messily, fat drops sliding down my face, pooling in my palms. At once, the last few years all feel so *real*. All my failures, my mistakes, my bad choices. All the losses, the minutes, and the hours spent going in the opposite direction of life, the fact that Dad is not *here* anymore . . . It's all stuck in my throat, dirty rags and broken glass, suffocating, gut wrenching, and all of a sudden I don't know how I'm going to bear the hurt of what being *me* has become for even half a second longer.

And then the mattress dips, right next to me.

A warm, thin hand settles on my shoulder. "Mallory," Mom says. Her voice is patient but firm. "I've tried to give you as much space as you needed. But I think it's time for us to talk about the World Championship."

Chapter Twenty-Five

I can think of several things to say to Mom.

Sadly, they're all swallowed by my hiccups.

Fortunately, Mom seems to be able to read my mind.

"Yes," she says calmly, pushing my wet hair back from my eyes. "I know."

"H-how?"

She smiles. "Darcy told me the moment she found out. But I knew something was up long before then." She shrugs. "Your hours didn't make any sense, your stories sounded like what someone who's never been in a senior center would make up from reading pamphlets. And . . . there is something about you when chess is on your mind. You feel like another person. A much *happier* person." Her smile turns rueful. "Mal. They talked about you on *Good Morning America*. Did you think I wouldn't have gotten phone calls from every distant cousin of mine about how you should really perm your hair?"

I groan. Between hiccups. Mom lets out a soft laugh and pulls me closer with an arm around my shoulders, like she doesn't hate me for calling 67 percent of the people she gave birth to bitches.

"I think I'm doing this wrong," she says gently. "Maybe before we talk about the World Championship, we should talk about your dad."

I instantly shake my head. "No, I—I'm sorry. I was *way* out of line. We don't have to—"

"But we do." Her lips press together, and her expression morphs into something sad. "It's been over a year, and I take responsibility for not doing it earlier. For a long time, I lied to myself that I was doing you a favor. That you were deeply hurt, and didn't need to be re-traumatized."

"I'm not." I wipe my eyes and let out a phlegmy laugh. "*I am not the one who's traumatized. You* are the one who got cheated on. *Sabrina and Darcy* are the ones who grew up without a father. *I* am the one who made it happen—I am the *bitch* here."

"No, no, no." Mom shakes her head, looking crestfallen. "See? That's why we should have discussed this. You are *not* responsible for any of that. You know who is?" A beat. Her eyes shine in the late afternoon light. "Your father. Your father made some terrible, cruel, careless choices. And part of why I don't talk to you girls about him as much as I should is that it's very difficult, even years later, for me to come to terms with the person he'd become toward the end. But I will *never* hold you responsible for *any* of it."

"You should. It was my fault. If I hadn't—"

"Mal, our histories are not made of *ifs* and *buts*. Although, if this is the game you want to play: *if* you hadn't told me about what you'd seen at that tournament, I would have found out anyway. Because it wasn't the first time he'd done that. And your father had a long history of dealing with problems with alcohol, and he'd had two DUIs before his accident, so even *if* he had still been living at home, there's a good chance that what happened would have happened anyway."

I take a shuddering breath, thinking about Dad. How much I miss him. How he could have done that to us. "Sabrina blames me for it. And she's right—"

"No, I don't."

I glance at the door. Sabrina is leaning against the doorframe, glaring at me.

"I *know* you do." I'm sobbing again. "And you have every right. I stole Dad from you, and—"

"I don't, you *bitch*. And I never did." She looks down at her feet. "However, I *am* familiar with your Red Cross nurse tendencies and with your habit of shouldering the universe, Atlasstyle." She swallows. "So I *may* have used the knowledge that you blame yourself for every damn thing to ever happen to my advantage. When you piss me off."

Mom sighs. "Sabrina."

"I apologize, okay?" she says defensively. "I didn't think you felt *this* bad about it—it's not like you show emotions, ever. But it also *is* your fault, a little bit. It used to be fun, hanging out with you. We'd do stuff without Mom and Dad and Darcy, and I'd feel like you and I were a thing. You treated me like a *person*. Now it's like you're ready to narc me out on anything I do. You give me orders and act all superior and like you're trying to be Mom. You treat me more like a child now than you did when I was a child—" Her voice breaks, and she quickly bends her neck to hide her tears. "Maybe I'm a bitch, but I'm *not* ungrateful. I'm *very* grateful, actually. I know how much you do, and if you didn't try to be so secretive about it, maybe I could actually show it. But if you want, I can send you a thank-you card, or—"

She stops between sniffles, and I want to stand, I want to go hug her, I want to tell her that it's okay and I don't want her stupid card, I just want my sister to stop crying. But Mom's hand closes around mine.

"When you stopped playing chess, Mal, I assumed that you did it because your father's actions made it too painful for you. I assumed you'd find your way back to it once you were healed. And when you decided not to go to college . . . well, you seemed genuinely hurt and offended whenever I tried to talk you out of it, so I told myself that you were an adult, and were making choices that were best for you and your well-being, and I had to respect that.

"But when Darcy told me about your fellowship, it occurred to me for the first time that maybe there were *other* reasons. That maybe your main goal was to protect *me* from something, and if that's the case . . . let me tell you something: when I think about chess, I don't think about Archie, or about the other women." She smiles through her tears. "When I think about chess, I think about my brilliant oldest daughter, doing what she loves, and kicking ass while she's at it." Her chin trembles. "I watched you at the Challengers, Mal. Hours and hours of you being so beautiful in your"—she lets out a wet laugh—"in your *Corpse Bride* dress. And even though I couldn't understand one single thing you were doing, I was so proud of you—"

I can't look at her anymore. I can't bear one more word, so I hug her. More forcefully than I should, given her joint issues. And she hugs me back, her arms around mine, like she used to when I was little and needed my mom. And when I hear a put-upon "Oh, fine," and Sabrina's arms close around us, I feel whole in a way I haven't in over four years.

"Way to make me feel excluded, *bitches*."

"Darcy," we all say at once, all in the same disapproving tone.

"What?" She shrugs from the door. "I thought we now just sprinkled the word generously in conversation. For seasoning."

"We most certainly do not," Mom tells her.

"God," Sabrina mutters, shuffling away from us. "There is no privacy in this house."

"Of course not," Darcy says. "It's minuscule and the walls are made of toilet paper and Tazo tea bags. Mallory, can you please win that stupid World Championship and move us elsewhere with your smart checkers money?"

I scowl at her. "Great job keeping secrets, by the way."

"Technically, I kept the fact that I *hadn't* kept the secret, secret from *you*."

I mull it over as I rub my cheeks clean. Then I nod, impressed despite myself.

"Well." Mom pats my knee. "Now we can move on to talking about that handsome 'senior center coworker' of yours."

"Right. Do you and Nolan fall asleep together to scalp massage ASMR like Twitter says?" Sabrina asks.

"What? No! We're not— I'm not—" I wipe my nose with my sleeve, which comes back full of something that looks suspiciously like snot. *We really need a parental control firewall*, I almost say. Then remember what Sabrina said about me trying to be her parent.

"Did you guys break up?" she asks. "What'd he do?"

"He . . . lied to me."

"Ah, yes. Lying. Something you'd never stoop to." Mom's tone is soft, but I wince anyway. "Let's hear about this lie."

I tell her about Defne, and the fellowship, and Koch's TikTok. After I'm done, Mom takes a deep breath and says, "Listen, I like Nolan. And when I saw the two of you together . . . I think he's been good for you. But this is not about him. It's about chess, and about you." She squeezes my hand. "You made good money from the tournaments you've been in. My new meds are working well, and I've been able to work regularly for weeks. Things are so much better than they were even just six months ago. I appreciate what you've done for us, but now it's time to focus on what *you* want.

"Guilt and responsibility are heavy burdens, Mallory. But they're also something we can hide behind, and now you can't do that anymore. You are free to do what you love. Which might be never thinking about chess against and moving to Boulder to be with Easton. It might be becoming an auto mechanic. It might be taking a year off to backpack around the world. It can be whatever you want—but it has to be *your* decision. Your choice, free of constraints. And to do that, you're going to have to look into yourself, and be honest about what you want. And yes, I know that's terrifying. But life is too long to be afraid."

I snort wetly. "Too short, you mean."

"No. Years spent carrying grudges, talking yourself out of things that might make you happy? They go slowly."

I turn to Darcy and Sabrina. They're looking at me with identical shades of blue eyes, identical serious expressions, identical wispy blond strands framing their pretty faces.

"And one more thing," Mom says. "If you need something, you *are* allowed to ask for it. God knows *we* have been. But I know you're not good at it, so I'm going to offer: whatever you decide to do, about chess, about your life . . . may we be there for you? May we be part of your life, from now on?"

I can't bring myself to say yes.

But maybe I'm making progress anyway, because at least I manage to nod.

PART THREE

End Game

Chapter Twenty-Six

Darcy spends the eight-hour plane ride to Italy quizzing Oz about the ins and outs of the World Championship.

"When does it start?" In five days.

"Why are we going so early, then?" For Mallory to get used to the time zone.

"How many games?" Twelve.

"How many hours per game?" No limit.

"So they can go to the following day?" We're in the computer era—games cannot be adjourned anymore, or players would just turn on an engine and evaluate their positions.

"Who wins?" Whoever wins the most games.

"What if they draw?" That's why there are twelve games.

"What if they draw *aaaaaall* the games?" They go to tie breaks, which are rounds of rapid chess, and . . .

Oz scowls. "This flight has complimentary Wi-Fi. Can't you Bing it or something?"

"Mom won't get me a smartphone till I'm fourteen."

"Mrs. Greenleaf," he tells Mom, who's sitting with me and Defne in the center row, "I will be purchasing a cellular phone for your youngest gremlin."

"Oh, there's no need."

"I insist," he says, lowering his sleep mask.

"Mom," Sabrina whines, "if Darcy gets a present from Oz, I want one, too!"

"As long as you shut the hell up." He aggressively stuffs plugs into his ears, just in time to block out my sisters' booming "Yay!"

Next to me, Defne is frowning. "I have to say, the tie breaks do worry me a little. In the last month we worked ten hours a day, seven days a week, and still barely had time to train you for regular chess. We haven't practiced rapid and blitz at all." She shrugs. "Oh, well. Let's just hope it won't come to that." The silver fig leaf earrings that I got her when she wouldn't let me apologize for being a dick dangle prettily from her ear. *A dicklet at most*, she told me before pulling me in for a hug, her lemon scent sour-sweet in my nostrils. *I should have told you where the fellowship came from. I want you to know, I'm on your team.*

I believe her. Because, as Oz so lovingly put it, I finally relaxed my sphincter enough to act like an emotionally mature person. I'm vaguely befuddled that following a hefty amount of groveling, he actually agreed to be my second. And just as befuddled that he and Defne *might* have a thing. I want to *know*, but I don't want to *ask. Till you work up the courage, it's Schrödinger's fucking*, Sabrina told me knowingly. I could only nod, proud of her grasp of theoretical physics.

At the Marco Polo airport duty-free shop, while I'm yawning and paying for an assortment of Kinder products Darcy selected, a girl in an *I Heart Rome* sweater stops me for a picture.

I don't bat an eye. It's been a little over a month since I formally accepted FIDE's invitation to be the challenger, and after a bunch of viral TikToks on my games, this has been happening a lot. In line at the grocery store. At the DMV, standing in line to get Sabrina's permit. While I attempt to jog, per Defne's workout schedule.

According to Oz, I need a media team. According to Darcy, I should go on *Celebrity Survivor* if they ever ask. According to me, I just smile and sign whatever I'm asked—a receipt; a carton of Arby's curly fries; on one memorable occasion, a dirty Nike sock. If my sisters are with me, they try to get in whatever selfie is happening. Everyone lets them because they're cute AF.

"Do you think you're going to win?" *I Heart Rome* asks me, vowels gliding happily. I don't have the heart to tell her that I seriously doubt it. That I'm scared shitless.

"Who's to say?"

"Well, I hope you do. I was first board on my middle school team. Had a Judith Polgar poster in my room. Never thought I'd live to see a woman in the World Championship with how terrible the men in the sport can be. And by the way, I know you and Nolan Sawyer have a thing, and it's gotta be a little sad to have to play against him, but don't go easy on him, okay?"

She leaves before I can think of an answer. The back of her sweater is an anthropomorphized Colosseum, winking at me.

"Is it?" Darcy asks.

I glance down at the piece of candy she's already eating, disturbingly shaped like a hippopotamus. "What?"

"Sad? To play against Nolan?"

I take a deep breath. For a few beats, my heart turns heavier in my chest, twists and contorts into something painful that resembles regret. I wrench it back into shape and wrap my arm around her shoulders.

"Come on. We gotta go through customs. Let's see if I screwed up our visas and we have to turn around."

THE WORLD CHAMPIONSHIP LOGO IS BAFFLINGLY, INEXPLICA-bly, alarmingly ugly.

We stare at it—a stylized dude's limbs knotted with another, equally stylized dude's; a stripey, Picasso'ed chessboard on their laps—and almost miss the all-caps *GREENLEAF* on the sign.

"I . . . guess that's our ride?" I say.

"Pretty sure that's position number thirty-five in the *Kama Sutra*," Sabrina mutters, which degenerates into Mom having to explain what creative intercourse is to Darcy.

I think I imagined Italy would be warm, but the February chill is nearly as sharp here as back home. The salt wind is cold, my hair tangles on the shuttle boat, and I let Darcy snuggle under my plaid coat while we point at the beautiful houses facing the canal. *Romantic*, I think. I've never been one to use the word, but the maze of calles and bridges spreading around the lagoon, the water lapping gently at the stone homes, it all seems so *pretty*, so ready to be explored. "Do you think Mrs. Abebe is feeding Goliath on schedule?" she asks.

The sun is on its way out. We chose a late-landing flight to minimize the wreck on our sleep cycle, but it almost feels meant to be: Mom, my sisters, Venice at sunset. Me.

I knew they needed me. But I never quite understood how much I needed *them* before this year. "I think Goliath would take her daughter hostage if she didn't," I tell her. "But I could text for updates, okay?"

The boat drops us off at a small dock in front of the hotel. The horrifying FIDE logo is everywhere, and I'm debating covering Darcy's eyes, Sabrina's, *Mom's*, sending an aggressively worded email, turning back and sailing away, but I'm paralyzed by the grandiosity.

"Is this a castle?" Darcy asks.

"No, it's . . ." I blink. "Maybe?"

"We're not paying for this out of pocket, right?" Mom asks.

"FIDE's on it. They shit money. Sorry, poop—they *poop* money." She hands her suitcase to a smiling porter with a stilted "Grazie," and I wonder how many months of mortgage a stolen ashtray would fetch.

I expect to share a room with Darcy, but Sabrina takes her in with a firm "We need you to rest and win and earn enough to sponsor my roller derby team."

"They will buy new uniforms," Darcy adds. "And I'll be their new mascot. In a guinea pig costume."

"Hmm." My heart squeezes, like it always does when they assume that I'll win. *It's not so simple*, I want to scream. *This is difficult*. But they're just trying to be supportive. "Sounds like you two have been talking this through."

"Oh, we have *plans* for your money."

The suite looks like something from the dry land half of *The Little Mermaid*, full of canopies, luscious rugs, antique furniture, and wall art that's older than my monkey ancestors. It's also empty, though, empty of something that I cannot pinpoint. I unpack three weeks' worth of not-warm-enough clothes, set the chessboard to the Korchnoi versus Karpov, 1978 game I was studying on the plane, snap pics of the canal view through the arched window—then realize that every single person I might send it to is currently treated to the same sight.

I slide into bed, toss and turn for a handful of hours, admit to myself that I'm too *something* to fall asleep, slide out.

There is a large pool downstairs that the fancy brochure informs me is fully heated, and I'm splashing in it less than five minutes later. The water is filtered from the ocean and smells like salt rather than chlorine. I let the complimentary Nashville Open T-shirt I tried to sleep in billow around me, and stargaze.

Remembering the last time I was in a pool would be rolling down a dangerous path, full of unbearable things I don't like to think about. So is the time before that: Easton and me, house-sitting for one of her neighbors. It was the summer before senior year, and that pool was full of bugs and stuff that I refused to believe was squirrel turds. Easton kept repeating, "Ew," but I managed to persuade her to dip her feet. I spent one hour floating about while she read her SAT prep questions out loud in a fake French accent.

I haven't heard from her in two months. Before August, our record was two days. I oscillate between being angry, begrudgingly wishing the best to her and the girl she's Instagram-official with, and being taken aback when I find myself still on the verge of sending her a *Dragon Age* TikTok despite our lack of recent history.

It's risky business, focusing on the past. The future, the utter humiliation that's to come in four days, even riskier. The now is where I am: ice-cold stars, mellow water, and Korchnoi's inexplicable rook to a1 drifting inside my head.

It's the deep of the night when I push out, shivering poolside in the cold air. All the hotel lights are off, except for a single window. I think I spot a tall silhouette through the curtains, but my eyes must be tricking me.

I blink once, and when I open them, there's nothing left to see.

Chapter Twenty-Seven

"Your next three days are wide open, so we'll just be running your games through engines and looking for weaknesses. The day before the match is when things start filling up. You'll have the morning for yourself, but there's a press conference in the afternoon. And the opening gala at night, but just an appearance is fine." Defne smiles from across the breakfast table. This morning she appeared out of a room that she may or may not be sharing with Oz. Sabrina mouthed "Schrödinger," and I nearly choked on my spit.

"Defne, why is this hotel so deserted?" Mom asks.

It's just us in the ocean-view dining room, and a small mountain of flaky, warm, gooey Nutella croissants. Darcy ate so many, she had to go back up for a nap before leaving for a glass factory sightseeing tour. We'll never be able to talk her back into oatmeal.

"Hotel Cipriani doesn't open till mid-March, so FIDE rented it out of season. They hold the championship here every few years—I've always wanted to come, but never got a chance before. I assume people will start trickling in, though. Organizers, commentators, FIDE higher-ups. The current champion and his team."

She doesn't meet my eyes. My heart tugs.

"Then there are the chess superfans who always show up, mostly Silicon Valley and tech people. Some press will be staying here, though most journalists will have cheaper accommodation and ferry in for the games." She shakes her head. "I still can't believe NBC is broadcasting the event this year. What are we, the NFL? The curling league?"

I wistfully wave at my family as they board the shuttle to Murano, and then turn to Defne, ready to be scolded for my inability to equalize tough positions in time trouble.

"Should we do it in my room or yours?" I ask. I'm wondering if I can use the situation to solve the Ozne mystery once and for all, but one of the concierges nose-blocks me.

"There are training spaces set aside for players," he says, Italian accent heavy through perfect English. "Shall I show you?"

He leads us through a set of gardens that are surprisingly beautiful and green. "Not at their best in this season, I'm sorry to say. We call them the Giardini Casanova."

"Like the manwhore?" Defne whispers at me.

I shrug just as the concierge nods. "Like the legendary lover, precisely. And that's where the match will take place next week." He points at a construction in the center of the gardens that looks a little like a hothouse. It's a simple square, but all four walls and the ceiling are made of glass. The inside is empty, with the exception of a wooden table, two chairs, and a simple chess set.

My heart kicks in my throat.

"It's fully heated, of course. And soundproof." His smile is reassuring. "This is the fifth championship we've hosted."

"That's a lot of camera tripods and lights all around." Defne pats me on the shoulder and grins. "No worries. I can help you with that cowlick."

Our training room is under a cloister, behind a wooden door. Inside there are chess sets, laptops we can use to connect to the engines, rows of opening and middle game books.

"This is incredible." Defne runs her fingers over a glass set. "I'm seriously jealous."

"Yeah. I'm not surprised they host lots of championships. They are *prepared*. I bet they . . ."

I notice the picture on the wall and forget what I was about to say. It's of two men, standing in the same glass house I just passed outside. One is nearly bald, the other has a full head of dark hair and a small smile. They're shaking hands on top of a developed board, and Black—the bald one—must have resigned, two moves from being checkmated, all his pieces disastrously pinned or mercilessly tied up. The other player's eyes are hooded and stern, familiar in an almost disorienting way, and for a second I feel an inexplicable, leaden weight in my chest.

Then I read the tag below: *Sawyer vs. Gurin, 1978. World Chess Championship.*

"He is . . ."

"Yup." Defne steps to my side.

"You knew him?"

"I trained with him."

Right. Yeah. "How was he?"

"Very positional. As Black he almost always played the Najdorf Sicilian—"

"I mean, what kind of person?"

"Oh. Let's see." She purses her lips, eyes on the photo. "Quiet. Kind. Dry, sharp sense of humor. Honest, almost to a fault. Stubborn. Troubled, sometimes." She takes a deep breath. "He's the reason I have Zugzwang."

"What do you mean?"

"He gave me the money to buy it. A loan, I thought, but once I could pay him back, he wouldn't take it."

Sounds like someone I know: generous, sarcastic, bad at lying.

Somber eyed.

I bet he didn't know how to take a no. I bet he was single-minded and mercurial and inscrutable. I bet he was charismatic but also arrogant and obstinate. Mulish, and difficult to understand, stupid, irritating, necessary, annoying, so, so addictive in that frightening, out-of-control way, so warm and gentle and genuinely funny, right, ruthless, impossible to get over—

"Mal?"

I startle away from the picture. "Yeah."

"Your training . . . What we have been doing, studying your play, it's good. Focusing on your weaknesses is good. But we should really take a look at some of his—"

"No," I interrupt her. We're not talking about Marcus Sawyer anymore, but it doesn't need to be spelled out.

"I don't understand why you refuse to—"

"No."

She huffs. "It's only fair. And expected. This is not a tournament, Mal, it's the World Championship—the match between the *two best players alive*. You should be honing your skills with your opponent in mind, not training on old games and overanalyzing your own style. He's probably studying *your* games, and I doubt that he'd expect you not to—"

"No," I say for the last time, and she knows it's final just as well as I do. "Let's continue as planned."

Defne frowns. But she nods nonetheless.

I'M BAD AT CONSOLIDATING.

I attack too early. Or too late.

I'm not decisive enough, except when I'm *so* decisive, I blow my advantage.

I cannot comfortably trade into end games.

I rely too much on my favorite openings—a cardinal sin, since players with preferences are players with weaknesses.

I should focus on the sides to take the center.

And:

"This game against Chuang," Oz is saying. "Your queen was completely open. Not saying go all ministry of defense, but—"

"Okay. Okay, I . . ." I rub my eyes. "You're right. Let's go back to the engines. I feel like I'm—"

"It's past midnight, Mal." Defne is shaking her head. "You should go to bed."

Shit. "Okay. Tomorrow morning—"

"We've been locked in here for two days, Mal."

We have. With brief food interruptions and sporadic visitors—Mom stopping by to kiss my forehead; Sabrina barging in on an analysis to show me an article from *The Cut* in which a journalist begged me to "step on her"; Darcy coming by to ask if her blue top was in my suitcase (it was) and to show me her pretty new pendant.

A murrina, it's called!

So beautiful. I stared at the colorful circles of flowers. *Where did you get it?*

N—Mom bought it for me!

"I think you should take a break," Defne says.

"What do you mean?"

"Tomorrow, take the morning off. Sleep in. Maybe go somewhere with your sisters? You have one day left before the match, and half of it is going to be full of press."

I frown between her and Oz. "You guys keep saying that my centers are so close, they look like checkers."

"Yes, but there's nothing we can do about it now."

"Okay. Yeah. You're probably right." I try not to pout as I amble to the door. My thighs ache from too much sitting.

"Hey."

I turn around. Oz is putting the sets back together and turning off the computers. I take in Marcus Sawyer's photo in the background, the sharp contrast to Defne's pixie hair. "Yeah?"

"I told you once before. But in case you forgot . . . I think you can win the World Championship. I think you can do whatever you put your mind to."

I smile faintly and walk away.

I'm not sure I believe her. I'm almost sure I don't.

The hotel has been filling up, to the point that it's become difficult to walk around avoiding impromptu interviews and pic requests and people wearing T-shirts with *my damn face* on them. It's probably why I've stopped emerging from the training room: this close to the start of the championship, and I'm feeling more and more like a fraud, like a kid at the adults' table, like I'm not worth the ink my name is printed with. I'm not good enough. I don't deserve this. I'm shit with the Night Attack against the Caro-Kann. I heard the words *First woman at the World Chess Championship* once, and have been trying to expel them from my head ever since. Does it mean that if I lose, it'll be a failure for all women? Does it mean that I'm suddenly more than just *myself*? I have no idea, and I can't deal with any of this. So I don't, and focus on the way I didn't know about the Raphael Variation until this very morning.

Sounds healthy, huh?

This late at night, at least, the place is as blessedly quiet as when we first got here. I walk past the reception counter, and one of the concierges waves at me.

"Your roommate is arrived," she informs me. "From United States."

I halt. "Excuse me?"

"Your friend arrived." She points at the elevator. There might be a bit of a language barrier here.

"I . . . What? Where?"

She smiles. "Your room."

My heart pounds as I sprint up the stairs. Is there really someone else in my room? Only one person could have arrived tonight from the United States.

But he's not

He wouldn't

We haven't even talked in

I said some things that I really regret, and he probably

I look down at my trembling hand, feeling like my DNA helices are unwinding. I grab the handle and open the door, just to get it over with before an aneurysm annihilates my brain.

There is someone sprawled on my freshly made bed.

My heart stops.

Then restarts, a mix of relief and something else.

Then derails again.

"Mal, this room is a vibe," a voice tells me from the bed. "You're really coming up in life, bitch. And all because I pushed you to embrace the important cause of gluten sensitivity."

I close my eyes. Take a deep breath. Open them again.

And whimper, more than ask:

"Easton?"

Chapter Twenty-Eight

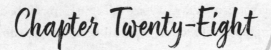

Her hair has grown a lot since August, well past her shoulders. It looks darker and glossier than back in the summer, after the sun bleached her tips and the seawater frizzed them. Perhaps it should surprise me, but it doesn't.

Thank you, Instagram stalking.

"Why . . . What are you doing here?"

She rolls on the bed, then props herself up on her elbows. "Sabrina texted me."

"Sabrina?"

She nods. "Yea tall? Blond? Pubescent? *Aggressively* sullen?"

"I know who Sabrina—" I shake my head. "She *texted* you?"

"I made the mistake of giving her my number before leaving New Jersey. During the week of all those rides? I blame you for it."

"You've been corresponding with my fifteen-year-old sister?"

"No. I've been leaving your fifteen-year-old sister on read when she sent TikToks of people dancing, about which I care nothing, or TikToks about roller derby, about which I care, astonishingly, even less. But a couple of weeks ago she texted me about you. So I replied."

I'm slowly recovering from the near stroke. Easton is here. On my side of the bed, without even taking off her shoes. We haven't talked in ages. Millennia.

It's possible that I'm annoyed.

I cross my arms over my chest. "Shouldn't you be in Colorado?"

"Shouldn't, shmouldn't."

My eyes narrow. Maybe *annoyed* is not the right word. "I'm surprised you were able to pry yourself away from college, since you love it so much." I sound so acid, I nearly wince.

Her head tilts. "I don't remember ever saying anything like that."

"You didn't need to say it."

"You read my mind?"

"I read your *Instagram*."

"Ah, yes." She nods sagely. "I do bare my heart and confess my deepest pains to Instagram."

I lower my eyes, feeling like an idiot of the pettiest kind.

"I mean," she adds with a shrug, "I do see where you're coming from. It's not like I didn't think the exact same."

"Really?" I lift my eyebrow back to sour. "I haven't updated my Instagram since I saw that giant leopard moth three years ago."

"You haven't. But one doesn't need social media to keep up on the whereabouts of the great Mallory Greenleaf. Not when *Jezebel* has an entire article about your wardrobe."

"No, they don't." I exhale. *Shit.* "Do they?"

"They have, like, four. Anyway." She rolls some more and sits on the edge of the mattress. "There's something exquisitely humbling about finding out that your best friend of *many* years is dating someone, for the first time, and didn't bother telling you—"

"I'm not dating—"

"—or that she neglected to mention that she won the Philly Open, that she was selected for the Challengers, that she is now buddies with the best player in the world, that she is going to be his opponent for the World Championship—should I go on?"

I don't answer. I just look at her as she stands and steps in front of me. A dozen little puzzle pieces are working overtime to click together inside my head.

"You know . . ." She scratches her temple. Her brown eyes are serious and beautiful. "When you started texting less and less, I thought you were over me. You had this super-cool fellowship, an objectively hot boyfriend, prize money, and you are—Jesus, Mal, you're *famous*, it's so *weird*. And I figured I was just being . . . phased out. I was being outgrown."

"I—"

"But then." She lifts her finger. "Then Sabrina texted me about how much of a miserable mope you've been, and I remembered something very important."

I swallow. "What is that?"

"That you are an idiot."

I flinch.

"Here's the deal," she continues. "You've always been like this, and I don't know how I could have forgotten. Even before your dad did what he did, you didn't want to be a burden. Didn't want to *impose*. You were always the *leave 'em before they leave you* kind of person. And normally I would have realized sooner what you were doing, but I was a bit in my head, too." She wets her lips. "College is . . . not easy. And not that fun, sometimes. And it's pretty lonely. And I gained six pounds. Now my bra chafes."

"Ouch."

"It's okay, I've ordered new ones. The point is, I was too busy to realize that you were just trying to anticipate my move with that chess brain of yours." She pauses. I watch her slip her shoes off with her toes. "I think that when I left, you were scared that I'd get over you. So you decided to get over me sooner."

"I didn't—"

"Maybe not consciously, but—"

"I mean, I didn't *decide* it," I say, voice thick. My last vestige of irritation is washed away by something dangerously close to tears. "I just thought that you . . ."

Easton sighs. Pats me on the shoulder, once. Then moves back to the bed, sprawling again on top of the covers. Still on my side, but at least this time she's barefoot. I have no idea what to do, so I opt for what's natural: take off my own shoes, step around the mattress, and settle on the free side. We both turn on our pillows, facing each other, and this could have been us during a sleepover eight, five, three, two years ago. Any number of times, in any number of places.

"So." I clear my throat. "You're going out with that really hot girl?"

"Kim-ly?"

"Yeah."

"Mal, I'm so *gone* for her. She's so cute. Out of my league."

I nod. "Yeah, a bit." She punches me on the arm, and we both laugh in what feels like not just amusement but also relief. And then I blurt out: "Will you stay for the championship?"

"Dude. You think I came to Italy for a heart-to-heart and now I'm turning around?"

"You have school."

"I'll be fine."

"I can't ask you to take off two weeks for me."

"That's fine. Since I'm offering."

I close my eyes, feeling my chest swell. "I love you. And I'm sorry. And I missed you." I'm tearing up again. It's like crying once tore down what used to be a very architectonically sound dam: in the past month I've sobbed while watching *My Girl*, after Darcy's teacher told me that my sister is gifted, when Sabrina won her derby meet. I'm a crier now. Maybe I always was.

"I missed you, too."

"Easton, I . . ." I sniffle. "I'm never going to win this stupid championship."

"Maybe not. But it doesn't matter. You're doing the thing you always wanted the most, surrounded by people you love, while sharing a room with yours truly—who, by the way, recently redeveloped sleep terrors. Lucky you." She twines her fingers with mine, like she used to when we were little. "Mal. You *already* won."

We fall asleep like that: my hand in hers, and our hair tangled together across the pillows.

I SPEND THE NEXT MORNING BEING A TOURIST WITH EASTON, and it feels like taking our friendship for a joyride.

It starts a little rocky: we ask the concierge directions for the Trevi Fountain and are met with a scandalized look and the revelation that it's actually in Rome, some five hundred kilometers south. But it moves up when we manage to make our way to Piazza San Marco, get pecked by a horde of pigeons, end up furiously scrubbing bird shit from our clothes.

After the second person asks me for an autograph, we buy two pairs of cheap, heart-shaped sunglasses and spend forty-five minutes browsing for a murrina for Kim-ly. We ask the shop owner, "What's most suited for someone whose favorite singer-songwriter is Taylor Swift and whose favorite director is Ari Aster?" and are left to our own devices when he pretends not to understand English. We eat three breakfasts. "Like the Hobbits," we keep saying, sinking our teeth into baci di dama and bignes and frittelle. It's not really that funny of a joke, but just being together again is intoxicating, and we giggle over it for two whole bridges.

Look at us.

Who would have thought.

Not me.

We're attempting a selfie on the Ponte di Rialto when Kim-ly texts a simple Hey, how's Italy? 💚

The bridge is packed with tourists trying to get a good view, but we spend twenty minutes taking space on the banister, formulating the perfect response.

"Don't send *that*—add that you miss her," I insist, trying to steal Easton's phone.

"Too clingy."

"She sent you a *heart*."

"A *green* heart, which means *nothing*."

"Oh my God." I laugh. "You're an idiot. I love it."

"Shut up." Her cheeks are rosy, not just from the cold. "By the way, when are we talking about Sawyer?"

"Never." I glance away, taking in once again the pretty houses packed together and the stunning view of the Gran Canal.

"Ha."

"There's nothing to talk about."

"I doubt it." Her elbow pushes against mine. "Where are you guys?"

"Nowhere." She's looking at me expectantly. And I'm trying to be more open and forthcoming about my needs and feelings, so I say, "We haven't spoken since the Koch thing. I found out that he'd been paying for my fellowship. We had a huge fight over it, and that was it."

"And he's okay? With it being it?"

"Nolan is . . ." I stop.

This is the first time. The first time I've said his name out loud since our argument. The first time I've allowed myself to acknowledge him and the novel, oddly shaped hole he's left in my chest. It's like picking at a scab. Digging a wound open, finally admitting that it was never patched up.

"I think we both said some things that we regretted." I swallow. "Things that we knew would hurt." I swallow again. "Mostly me."

"That's what happens when you fight with someone who gets you."

I close my eyes. The reminder of how much Nolan gets me is like a punch in the stomach. "I accused him of orchestrating Bob firing me."

Easton snorts. "What?"

"It just seemed like suspicious timing."

She bursts into laughter. And laughter. And more laughter. A group of French tourists gives her suspicious looks, but she sobers up when she notices my glare. "Dude, I was there when it all went down. I'm pretty sure that's not what happened. Bob had been *gagging* to fire you ever since your uncle left. You were cramping his upselling lifestyle and were utterly replaceable."

 I glance away, irritated. And then I admit something for the first time—out loud and to myself. "I know."

"You know?"

"I do. But I still have the right to be mad that he didn't tell me about the fellowship."

"Okay, but it's not the same at all. I mean, getting you fired from your job is taking something away from you. The fellowship is giving you something. The two are not even comparable, and—"

"I *know*," I repeat through gritted teeth. I did not miss *this* about Easton. The way she reads my mind. I'm just thankful she and Nolan don't know each other and never will. "The worst of it is . . . when I accused him, he didn't even bother denying it. He just said . . ." I swallow.

"What did he say?"

"That he *wished* he had." I sigh. "That I needed to be shaken out of my life."

She nods. The horn of a ferry punches the lingering quiet between us. "Well, you know how I feel about agreeing with white guys with trust funds, but . . . I might have to give him a brownie point here."

"God." I groan and lower my head between my forearms. "The things I *said* to him. About him. About his family. I just . . . I was so *mad*, Easton."

"Who were you mad at, Mal? Nolan? Your dad? Life? Yourself? All of the above?"

I don't want to face the answer to that. So I just lay my head on her shoulder, let her pet my hair, and for the first time in weeks I remember how much I liked him, even when I didn't. The way I laughed and felt unsettlingly, tantalizingly seen. The thrill of watching him play, and my trembling heart as I watched him sleep. The odd relief in acknowledging that *with* him was exactly where I cared to be. And then the anger I felt for allowing myself to do that.

For the first time in weeks I can admit it:

I wish I had the prospect of exchanging more than gambits with him. I have no idea how to sit across from him for twelve games.

I will have to shake his hand tomorrow, before the first game even starts, and my fingers itch from wanting it so desperately. He must be close, on this island, and I feel it in my bones, his presence. I feel him in my stomach.

"Easton. I think I messed up," I say.

"Yeah." She nods. "But I think that, maybe because of what happened with your dad, you tend to believe that when people mess up, that's it. They don't get a second chance. And sometimes that's true, but other times . . ." She shrugs. "I'm here. Your family is here. Nolan . . ." She doesn't continue.

So I sigh. And she sighs, too. And for a long time we just listen to the seagulls, watch the boats paint white stripes in the canal, and pretend there's nowhere we need to be in about one hour.

Chapter Twenty-Nine

I enter the press conference a little like Meghan Markle would: flanked by two FIDE people whose names I didn't catch, followed by a burly man who, I suspect, has something to do with security. The camera flashes explode the second I step into the room, but in a subdued way that's more *middling politician announcing long-shot presidential run* than *BTS land at LAX*.

I know, then and there, that I'll never, ever, *ever* get used to this. And that I probably shouldn't have worn my green Chucks with the hole in the left pinkie.

A couple of journalists in the first row greet me. I've never met them before, and yet they smile at me like I'm the distant cousin they see only at weddings and baptisms but nevertheless like. This is . . . weird. Much weirder than casual chess fans asking for autographs.

Never, ever, *ever*.

"Hi, guys." I wave awkwardly and glance around. There's no one I know here: press passes were required, and Defne didn't get one. I'm crowdedly alone in a fancy Italian room full of antique velvet curtains, and the worst is yet to—

In the last row, someone is grinning and waving at me. Eleni from the BBC, half submerged by the small mountain of equipment she's carrying. Clearly, still an intern. I smile back at her and feel marginally better.

The table on the podium is long and narrow, with three sets of mics and plaques. The middle one is already taken by the moderator, a middle-aged man who happens to be one of FIDE's many VPs and whom I vaguely remember from the Challengers. The one on the right bears my name, and that's where I sit.

The remaining one, at the moderator's left, is empty when I arrive.

And stays empty for one minute.

Two.

Two and a half.

Three, and I was already a bit late, because the ferry system is not exactly straightforward, and Easton and I needed a fourth breakfast. We're now almost ten minutes past schedule, which is why the journalists, and there are *dozens* of them, whisper like this is a scandalously juicy Victorian ball.

I look at the moderator in panic.

"Don't worry," he whispers conspiratorially, hiding our conversation with a sheet of white paper. "He won't dare no-show. We've learned our lessons with him."

"What do you mean?"

"He hates press events and always tries to skip them. But"—he points behind us, to the panels decorated with sponsors and brands—"FIDE makes lots of money from them, especially this year. So we write steep fines into his contracts that make it impossible for him to avoid them." He gives me a cunning, if warm, smile, and lowers the paper before clearing his throat and turning on his mic. "Well, everyone. It seems like there are some delays. Why don't Ms. Greenleaf and I entertain you all with a game of chess. I'll take White."

The murmurs get louder. I glance around, find no set, then realize what his plan is when he says into the mic, "d4."

"Oh." I scratch my nose. "Um, d5?"

"c4." His eyes shine and he turns toward the journalists. "Will she accept my gambit?"

I usually don't. I usually decline the Queen's Gambit with e6 and then build up a solid position, but he looks so hopeful, and people do love an accepted challenge, so I grin and say, "c4, take pawn."

People cheer. My grin widens. The tension in the room melts a little as the moderator laughs and nods, pleased. "e3," he says, and I'm considering moving my knight to f6 just for the fun of it when—

A door opens.

Not the door I came in from, but one on the side that I hadn't even noticed. The cameras start again. A red-haired woman whom I recognize from Philly Open—Nolan's manager, who must be better than Defne at obtaining press passes—walks briskly into the room, looking less than happy, and right behind her . . .

I thought I had successfully fortified my defenses. Because I spent those three minutes with Easton in the bathroom, following her instructions on how to brace myself. I squared my shoulders, took a deep breath, and repeated at her insistence: *I'm a big girl, and I can handle a reunion with my ex in front of a dozen countries' major TV outlets—okay, Easton, no. This is counterproductive.*

Still, I did think I'd be fine. But when Nolan enters wearing his usual combo of dark shirt and dark jeans, eyes guarded, hair shorter than the last time I ran my fingers through it, I'm *not* fine.

I'm not okay at all.

He doesn't glance in my direction, not once. He calmly steps onto the podium, and when a woman from the fourth row says, "You're late, Nolan. Everything okay?" he just answers, "Yeah." He speaks into the microphone, effortlessly confident. He's done this before. He might hate it, but he has a decade of experience on me. "My car broke down," he adds, and everyone laughs.

I fist my hands in my lap until I'm sure they're not shaking. By the time the moderator goes through a few introductory words and picks the first question, I've recovered. At least a little bit.

"Karl Becker, DPA. Nolan, you haven't made a statement about Malte Koch's cheating scandal. Is the three-year suspension he received fair? And what do you think about him?"

"I try not to think about him at all." People chuckle. "And it's up to FIDE to decide what's fair."

"Lucia Montresor, *Ansa*. Nolan, how is your playing shape compared with the Pasternak?"

He half huffs, half winces. "Can't possibly be worse, can it?"

More laughter. Nolan hasn't changed much since that talk show interview several years ago, the one that makes me think of Mrs. Agarwal and baking soda. He's still charismatic, almost despite himself. He still doesn't want to be here, doesn't mind admitting to it, and yet manages to navigate the questions in a relaxed, charming, uncomplicated way.

I look at him *not* looking at me, and my heart squeezes.

"And a question for Mallory: This was your breakout year. How does it feel, being here?"

"It's . . ." Everyone turns to me. Except for Nolan, who keeps looking straight ahead into the crowd.

He hates me. For what I said. For leaving. I screwed up, and he hates me, and he's right.

"It's an honor." I attempt a smile. "I am happy and grateful."

"AFP, Etienne Leroy—question for both. You two have close family members who used to play chess at high levels but are not here anymore. Does that make your championship more meaningful?"

I stiffen. I can't talk about Dad. Or: the last month has shown me that I can talk about Dad, but I don't *want* to talk about Dad in front of dozens of people who—

"Nope," Nolan says flatly, saving us both. The moderator picks another journalist, and I'm flooded with relief.

"Reuters—Chasten. Nolan, there is a rumor that Ms. Greenleaf was part of your team of assistants before the cheating scandal came to light and she became the challenger. Care to confirm or deny?"

"Not particularly, no."

Laughter.

"Either way, some say that having been your second will give Ms. Greenleaf an unfair advantage."

Nolan shrugs. "If *some* think that she needs an unfair advantage, then they need to pay better attention when she plays."

The room drops into murmured quiet. My heart beats into my ears.

"Mallory, Fox News. You are the *first woman* to make it to the World Championship. What do you attribute it to?"

"I just . . ." I bit into my lip. "Only to the fact that I had a nontraditional path to chess. And didn't have to suffer through the sexism of this environment as much as most female players do. Didn't have a chance to get discouraged."

"So you don't think you're better than all the women who came before you?"

"No, not at all. I—"

"Then, since you have never even been part of a super-tournament, what makes you qualified to be *here* today? Why *you* and not someone else?"

I swallow. "I just . . ."

Nothing. I got lucky. It's a mistake. I'm not good enough and—

"Man"—Nolan snorts into the mic—"she *literally* won the qualifying tournament to be here. Keep up, will you?"

Fox News lowers his eyes, chastised. I glance at Nolan, who really works the crowd like a stand-up comedian. People laugh, and a couple even clap, because they find him amusing and like him even when he's not likable. I want to scream at them, *I know. I've been there.*

I still am.

"Mallory? AFP again. Does your past romantic relationship with Nolan make this championship more complicated for you? Will it in any way affect your play?"

Well.

Probably stupid of me, but I really didn't think they would go there. And I'm positive the moderator didn't, either, because I feel him tense next to me.

I almost turn to Nolan. Because, let's be honest: every other hard, difficult question that might have made me stumble, he took, blocked, deflected. This one, though . . . he simply can't. And even though I could probably deny that our relationship was ever romantic, or straight-up refuse to answer, or even tell the truth, I'm not prepared for any of this. So I take the easy way out, and hear myself say:

"No."

It echoes in the murmuring room like a slap, and I immediately want to take it back. I want to look at Nolan and say . . .

I don't know what. But it's okay, because I don't get the chance. "Very well," the moderator interrupts. "We seem to be pressed for time. I think we'll call it for today, but—"

"One last question—Trent Moles, the *New York Times*. In the name of good sportsmanship, could you both say what you admire the most about your opponent's play?"

The moderator hesitates, like he knows this question is a bad idea. But then he looks to his left. "Of course. Would you like to take it?"

Nolan wouldn't. At least, that's what I assume when he stays sprawled back in his seat, like we're back in New York and he's watching Emil fail at making sourdough, like the entire world and dozens of Instagram accounts dedicated to his hands and dimples and gambits aren't watching like hawks.

But then he shifts. I watch him lean forward, just an inch, then another, and inhale minutely before speaking into the mic. "Every last thing," he says. Simple. Decisive.

Heart shattering.

It's followed by a moment of silence. For the first time, no one laughs. No one speaks. No one scribbles notes on their pad. No one raises their hand for another question.

My heart presses desperately against the borders of my chest.

The moderator clears his throat and turns to me.

"Mallory," he asks. "What do you admire the most about Nolan's play?"

"I . . ."

What do I admire the most? What?

He is so dynamic.

He fights to the last point, using every piece, every moment, every resource, bleeding the chessboard dry.

He is deadly and meticulous.

He is fun and interesting and unpredictable.

He is an *adventure*.

And that frown on his forehead, when he's thinking about how to make the next move as nuclear and chaotic as possible. It makes me want to reach out and pull his visor-hands away. It makes me want to smooth it. It makes me want to play my own best chess and—

"Mallory?"

I look up from my Fiji water bottle. There are a million eyes on me. I swallow.

"Right. I . . ."

I am lost for words. I am overwhelmed, swept away, disoriented. And the moderator nods, then smiles kindly.

"Well, I guess *her* answer is nothing." A few forced chuckles. Then more journalists raise their hands, clamoring for one last question that isn't to be. "Thank you for coming, everyone. Of course, we'll have longer press conferences after each game, so I'm excited to . . ."

A FIDE employee asks me to stand. She takes my elbow to guide me off the podium. I follow her past Nolan's chair, and when my hand brushes against his shoulder blade, I'm not sure whether it's an accident or desperation.

I step out of the room knowing that he hasn't looked at me a single time.

I STAY AT THE GALA FOR LESS THAN TEN MINUTES. I'M chewing on my fifth bruschetta and craning my neck, on the lookout for broad shoulders and cropped dark curls, when Defne whisks me away with a hand on my wrist. "Okay, you made your appearance. Now we leave." Her bright red lips stick to a polite smile as she crisscrosses me through the crowd.

"But I only just got there. And the bruschetta is *amazing*."

"And you gotta be in bed by nine, since tomorrow's the most important game of your career."

"Is it? Because as far as I know, I have twelve coming up."

"The first one sets the tone, Mal."

"I . . . Won't it be rude to leave?"

"Maybe." She pulls me up the stairs. "But your opponent didn't even bother showing up. As long as his rudeness eclipses yours, you're golden."

That's how I end up wearing my jammies at 8:53, tucked in, pillow punched underneath my head. Easton slides in on her side of the bed, Darcy curls right between us, and Sabrina settles at the foot of the mattress.

A veritable slumber party.

"According to my trainer, I should be asleep in five minutes," I point out.

"Ah, yes." Sabrina doesn't look up from her phone. "Is Defne going to come burp you, too?"

"Come on, Sabrina," Easton scolds her. "You know she first needs a diaper change."

We argue for the longest time over what to watch on the 8K TV. Then we give up on finding a movie that won't be vetoed by at least one other person, and settle for pulling up random You-Tube videos. After nine centuries of surprisingly violent roller derby footage that have me worried for the state of Sabrina's brain, Easton blesses me with a *Dragon Age* playthrough. For a minute it feels like it used to be—the two of us, and Solas being an asshole on screen. When I turn to grin at her, I find that she's already grinning at me. Then I remember something, and my smile slips.

"What?" she asks.

"Nothing. Just . . ." I shrug. "I watched one with Nolan once."

"A playthrough? Is that gem of a boy into *DA*?"

"Not really."

"Ah. I've seen your press conference, by the way. Nice job making it look like you totally despise him even when he said nothing but super-nice things about you."

"I *didn't*."

"Yes, you did," Darcy and Sabrina say in chorus, without tearing their eyes from the TV.

"Whatever." I roll my eyes. Because they're right. "He hasn't really . . . Maybe he said *mediumly* nice things, but don't be fooled. He hasn't acknowledged my presence."

"Mmm." Easton nods. "Have you considered acknowledging his first? Maybe be like, 'Hey, whadup, I didn't really mean the many horrible things I said about you.'"

"Right." I clear my throat. Look away. "No."

"Did you call *him* a bitch, too?" Darcy asks.

I tilt my chin up and groan. "I refuse to engage on this topic with anyone who's *under* eighteen, or with anyone who's *over* eighteen but needs a twenty-five-minute pep talk to add a heart emoji to a text," I declare. But ten minutes later, while a Texan lady nurses an injured bat back to health (Darcy's selection), I start composing a text. The most recent blue bubbles are dated January 9, middle of the night: the response to my Either Emil's really good at sex or he's gutting Tanu, was You mean, it's not a foghorn that woke me up? I half smile and write:

can we talk?

Then I delete it. And type again:

you're right about some things. maybe not all of them. but I overreac

Delete.

did you know in your 2016 game against Lal you missed a check-mate. nice queening, though.

Delete, delete, delete.

im sorry about

Delete.

hi.

I don't hit Send. But I leave it there, in the typing box. And when I set my phone against my chest and go back to watching TV, it feels several pounds heavier than ever before.

Chapter Thirty

After a match—usually during one of those press conferences that I always assume will have twelve viewers but instead are streamed by hundreds of thousands of nerds like me—people will ask me how, in a specific moment, at a specific turn of the game, I decided what to do. *How did you know to sacrifice the pawn? Why that trade? Rook e6 was perfect—what made you think of that?*

People ask me. And all I can say is: I just knew.

Instinct, maybe. Something innate within myself that helps chess come together like a fully formed shape. A rudimentary, gut understanding of how things *could* be if I let myself follow a path.

The pieces tell me a story. They draw pictures and ask me to color them in. Each one, with its hundreds of possible moves, billions of possible combinations, is like a beautiful skein of yarn. I can unspool it if I like, then weave it together with others to create a beautiful tapestry. A new tapestry.

Ideally, a winning tapestry.

If it hadn't been for Dad, that instinct would have stayed

coarse, unspun within me. If it hadn't been for years of hard work, of practicing, studying, analyzing, thinking, reliving, obsessing, playing, playing, *playing*, my instinct would be worth very little. If it hadn't been for Defne, after falling asleep for four years, it would have stayed dormant.

But I would *still* have it. If things had been different, my instinct would *still* be a raw ball of unknowns knotted inside me: waking me up at 3:05 a.m. on the most important day of my life, thrumming within me, pulling me out of bed.

I don't even remember falling asleep. The TV is still on, Netflix pointedly asking if we're still watching *Riverdale*, and I have no idea why my sisters decided to infiltrate my room instead of returning to their overpriced suite. Climbing out of bed takes Cirque du Soleil–grade coordination and a nearly sprained ankle. Once I've peed and drunk what's left in my water bottle, I'm just not motivated enough to dive back in.

I try to keep quiet as I put on Easton's *CU Boulder* hoodie. It stops just below my shorts, and I should probably grab a coat and some thick sweats, but I don't bother turning on the light for something warmer, and instead let myself out of the room.

The hallways are silent and gelid. The sea, quiet. There are no ferries, no boats, no seagulls, because all of Venice is fast asleep. I make my way down the stairs, the shiny pinks and whites of the marble floors pure ice under my bare feet, hair bouncing over my shoulders.

I don't know where I'm going, but I know in my stomach that it feels right. It's good, this: being alone with the night sea breeze, exploring the deserted gardens, inhaling the smell of grass and salt. I spot some lights in the distance, from the little glass house where I'll spend the next two weeks, immersed in chess and heartache. I follow the stone path, shivering, tracing the steps for the first of thirteen times. Wondering if come morning, the precious calm I feel right now will tangle into a pile of exposed nerves.

I stop in my tracks when I see him, but I'm not startled. Maybe I should be surprised to see him there—the time, the place, the coincidence don't exactly make sense—but my gut tells me that this is fine.

This is why I'm here: for Nolan.

He gives me his back, standing tall in front of a familiar frame. Marcus Sawyer's picture has been moved into the glass house, flanked by three others—all the world champions who have been crowned here in Venice. Tomorrow, when the first game starts, they will surround the players. Place them right within history.

I watch the relaxed line of Nolan's shoulders and think about my next move.

Think about turning around.

Think about my cold limbs and the pile of sisters back in my room.

Think about his messy hair and a box of Froot Loops and his wide eyes as he said, *Kasparov was there.*

Think about him nuzzling my belly button, and his penchant for the Scotch Game, and the way I liked being with him so much, maybe I got a bit scared.

A lot scared.

My next move, then, is to keep on walking. Horizontally,

through an unoccupied path. Like a rook would. And Nolan . . . he must hear me open the glass door and enter, but he doesn't turn. Nor does he acknowledge my presence. He continues to study his grandfather's picture, dark eyes to dark eyes, stubborn jaw to stubborn brow. When I come to stand right next to him, close enough to feel his heat, and say, "I've been studying his games," his answer is simply:

"Have you?"

I missed his voice. Or: I missed the way his voice sounds when it's the two of us and no one else. Rich. Lower than usual. Stripped of its coats and edges. I missed letting it flow through me.

"Because I couldn't bear to study yours."

"That boring, huh."

I exhale a shaky laugh. "No, it's just . . . Come on. You know."

He nods, still facing the picture. The soft lights play beautifully across his skin. "I do know."

"Yeah. Anyway." I push my hair behind my ear. I'd love to meet his eyes, but it's not going to happen. Not if we continue this way. Not if he won't look at me. "My favorite was the one he played against Honcharuk at some point in the early eighties. Tata Steel, I think, back when it was called . . ."

"Hoogovens?"

"Yeah."

"That game when he offered a draw even though he had the losing position?"

"Yes." I chuckle. "It must be such a mindfuck, having Marcus Sawyer do that. You have to assume he's seeing something you're not."

"Right. I still can't believe Honcharuk accepted instead of slapping him." He shakes his head fondly. "God. What an asshole move."

"Clearly runs in the family," I say. He laughs a little, silent, wistful, and I immediately want to kick myself and take it back.

I'm sorry

I didn't mean

I lied when

"Clearly."

"No. No, I . . ." I cover my eyes with my hands. I'm a mess. I'm making a mess. "I didn't mean to . . . For what it's worth, I don't think you're an asshole. Or manipulative. Or selfish. Or . . ." *Unloved.* "Or most of the other things I called you in New York, really. Or maybe you are, a bit, but no more than any other chess player in the entire universe. No more than me." I try to take a deep breath, and the air almost chokes past the ache in my lungs. "I *really* didn't think any of the things I said. And when I called you 'crazy' . . . I'm *really* ashamed of that. I was . . ."

I don't know what I was. But Nolan does. "Angry. Tired. Hurting, and wanting to make me hurt just as much. Scared out of your mind."

I close my eyes. "*Absolutely* fucking terrified."

He nods. Still not looking at me. "I never wanted to manipulate you, but . . . you can pay me back for the fellowship, if it'll make you feel better. That way you won't owe me anything, and you'll be free of me."

My stomach sinks. "Would *you* like me to pay you back?"

He lets out a small, self-effacing laugh, and finally turns to me. The night air is sucked out of my chest. "How are you, Mallory?"

"I . . . Good." As it turns out, *I'm* the one who can't stand to meet his eyes. I'm the one studying Marcus Sawyer's impeccable suit now. "I don't know if I'm good. But I'm . . . *better* than I was," I add, because I think he wants a real answer. "It's . . . You were right. About the way I acted, especially with my family. But things have been better. Well." I scratch my neck. "*I* have tried to be better. Less of a control freak on a path to martyrdom and more of a . . . person?"

He studies me for a second. Then I feel him shift forward and I tense—caught, immobile, strung out. Awaiting. He could take my hand. He could tug me to himself. He could wrap his hand around my neck and kiss me as hard as he once did.

He just pulls a loose strand of hair from where it stuck to my lips, straightens back, and says, "Darcy and Sabrina seem good, too."

I'm . . . dizzy. Disappointed. "You've met them?"

"We went for a walk the other day. And I took them for gelato this morning."

"They didn't tell me." I'm scowling.

"It was very hush-hush. Since you are, I've been told, known for throwing hissy fits."

I scowl harder. "Is that why you were late for the press conference?"

He nods. "Darcy needed to try every single flavor before settling on an order. A problem, since samples are not a thing in Italy."

"Did you have to fisticuff a brawny ice cream man with a gold necklace?"

"Depends. Would that make me more or less cool than bribing him with fifty euros?"

I laugh into the back of my hand. And after that I look at him, and he's serious once again.

"Nolan—"

"I'm sorry, too. About what I said. I had no right to imply that what you've been doing for your family is not the right thing. And I know I can't imagine what you've been through with your dad."

"Actually, I think you can."

He studies me for longer than is comfortable. Galaxies pass through his black eyes, and I wonder whether this second could last a century. Whether the universe could be just me and him, understanding each other on a forever loop. "Yeah. Maybe I can."

I clear my throat. Okay. Here goes.

"In the spirit of acknowledging that I've been hiding behind . . . a bunch of stuff—mostly Mom, and my sisters, and Dad—and that I've been using what needed to be done as a shield, I've been trying to practice verbalizing what *I* want. So that I can, you know, live my life for myself."

"Good."

"Yeah. For instance, I know now that I want to keep on playing chess. Professionally. I want it to be my job."

Nolan's mouth twitches. His eyes widen with that boyish gleam that I've come to love from him. "Yeah?"

"Yeah. So I'll do that. Or at least I'll try. And . . . My friend Easton is here, which is nice. And we made up. But once we leave, I'll still want to talk with her every day. So I'll just . . . call her myself. I'll make it happen. If we're not up in each other's business till the day we die, it won't be for my lack of trying."

He nods. "Fair."

"And also, I've been talking about Dad at home. Slowly. But more and more. I've been looking at some of his games. I've been showing them to Darcy as I teach her how to play. Because even if I can't forget the bad, I want us to still remember the good."

He knows exactly what I mean. I can tell from the rueful twist of his smile. "You should."

"And also . . ." I swallow past the lump in my throat, near-frozen toes curled into the floor. "Also, I've been considering things like fate, and coincidences, and the past. Sappy, I know. And you probably never thought of it, but when I was a kid, and you were a barely older kid, we both played chess, both in the same geographical area. And for some reason we never met, but I have to wonder if maybe we were at the same tournament or at the same club, just in different divisions. I have to wonder if maybe we played on the same chess sets, one after the other. I have to wonder if we were meant to be, and only missed each other narrowly. Because when I stopped playing, I was done. *Done*. Years passed, and it should have been it for you and me, we should have been that narrow miss and nothing more. But Defne's tournament happened, and it was . . . a second chance." I take a deep, shuddering breath. "I don't think I believe in destiny. I believe in solid openings, and middle games that show initiative, and swift transitions to end games. But I can't stop wondering if maybe the universe was trying to tell us something, and—"

"I can't believe you prefaced all of this with 'you probably never thought of it.'" Nolan's tone is dry and amused, and I can't keep the words inside me anymore.

"I want to be with you," I push out. Shaky. And then, when nothing explodes at the revelation, I repeat it more firmly. "I want to be with you. As much as I can. As much as you'll have me."

I've said it. It's out there. I've set it free, and I watch Nolan hawkishly, on the lookout for an answer, for any kind of emotional reaction. But his dark eyes are as inscrutable as ever.

"I'm glad you said that," he tells me. Like he's complimenting a good chess move. Like this is not the biggest leap I've ever taken.

"Why?"

He's staring at me with a small smile. It's barely noticeable, but somehow manages to make the entire earth tip over. "Because now I can say it back."

I close my eyes, feeling like my every atom is in the middle of a seismic event. But Venice is still witching-hours calm, and Nolan's heat is so close, it centers me, grounds me more than I thought I could ever be. "The last time we talked, I said a lot of things that weren't true. And I forgot to say one thing that was. Which is that I was happy with you. The days we had in New York were . . ."

He seems vaguely amused at my inability to articulate my emotions. "Good?"

"Yeah. Very. And I'd like to have more. A lot more. Starting . . . now, if possible. Even though . . ." I look around and let out a choked laugh. "This is really poor timing on my part."

He smiles. "I don't know if I agree."

"Why?"

He gestures to the board with his head. "We *are* about to spend a lot of time together."

"Right. There is that." I scratch the back of my neck to stop myself from reaching out for him. I want to. But maybe I shouldn't. But I *want* to. "By the way . . . since you're not a newbie like me, do you have any advice?"

He tilts his head, pensive. "Make sure you have breakfast."

"Right. Breakfast."

"Something with protein, if possible."

"Okay." I wait for him to continue. Frown when he doesn't. "Really, that's it? Are you hoarding advice?"

He shrugs. "That's all I have."

"Come on, Nolan. You've done three of these."

"Yeah. But this one is unlike any other championship."

"Why is that?"

I look at him looking at me, and overflow with something I cannot put a name to. "Because when I'm with you, Mallory, everything is different. When I'm with you, I want to play more than I want to win."

My eyes begin to tear up, but I'm not sad. For the first time in a long, long while, I'm a million things, and sad is not any of them.

"You know," I say, taking a step closer. Then another. Then one into him, and it's like stepping into a new world. A new era of my life. "I've been reading a lot of chess theory. Big, tedious books. And they all say that when chess is solved, when the perfect game is played—they say that it will be boring. Because it will inevitably end in a draw."

I feel his smile in the beat of his heart. "They do?"

I nod.

"Well, then." His arms close around me. His lips speak into my hair. His chest rises and falls against my ear, and I know it in my gut, like I know chess, that this is where I'm meant to be. "It will be fun when we prove them wrong."

Chapter Thirty-One

Six and a half hours later, the mayor of Venice, a tall man with a thick black beard and a hard-to-pronounce last name, sets my queen's pawn on d4 in the ceremonial first move of the World Chess Championship.

The cameras click.

The spectators clap.

The waves push patiently into the lagoon.

Then the mayor leaves, closing the glass door behind him, and the garden lulls into a peaceful quiet.

I (Mallory Greenleaf; US; World ranking: #1,843) glance at my opponent (Nolan Sawyer; US; World ranking: #1).

I find him already looking at me, a warm smile in his dark eyes.

Epilogue

Two years later

THE NEXT WORLD CHESS CHAMPIONSHIP AND THE FACT THAT EVERYONE IS TALKING ABOUT IT—EXPLAINED

By Eleni Gataki, Senior Chess Correspondent, BBC

The upcoming World Chess Championship, which will start on March 15, is going to be the most viewed in history. By a lot. This is a biannual event that, in evolving formats, has been occurring since before any of us has been alive (the first championship took place in New York City in 1886). And yet, it is safe to bet that most people haven't heard about the World Chess Championship until this year. So, what changed, and what are the five factors suddenly making a chess match discussed almost as much as the Super Bowl? Well, let's start from the obvious:

NOLAN SAWYER, THE CURRENT NO. 1 CHESS PLAYER IN THE WORLD

Chances are, if you've heard of only one chess player in your life, it's Fischer, Kasparov, or Sawyer. The grandson of former world champion Marcus Sawyer, Nolan Sawyer (22) has been a phenomenon since his childhood. You've probably seen pictures of him looking adorable and vanquishing opponents four times his age at 8 years old, or you might have heard of his terrible temper and that story about him beating (not only at chess) disgraced player Malte Koch (although this is just an unsubstantiated rumor), or you might be familiar with him from the year he made *Time*'s 100 Most Influential People list at the age of 15. The fact remains, you're likely to have heard of him. And his notoriety has only been increased by . . .

MALLORY GREENLEAF, WHO . . . EXISTS.

Soon to turn 21, Mallory Greenleaf is currently ranked No. 5 in the world . . . and yet she is the world champion. It might seem counterintuitive, but whereas the world champion is determined by a specific tournament, the ranking is a combination of all the games a player undertakes.

But don't let Greenleaf's "lowly" No. 5 fool you: the only reason she's not ranked higher is that her path to chess was very unusual. A high school graduate from New Jersey with a GM father, Greenleaf played in unrated tournaments from ages 5 to 14, then returned to chess at 18, just in time to triumph in the last World Chess Championship, which took place two years ago in Venice, Italy. Greenleaf defeated Sawyer on the twelfth match, after eleven draws. As the first woman to not only qualify for but also win a chess championship, she made headlines. For her chess abilities, sure, but also because . . .

NOLAN SAWYER AND MALLORY GREENLEAF . . . WELL. IT'S UNCLEAR.

Rumors regarding a possible relationship between the two players abound, but they have not been confirmed, as both Sawyer and Greenleaf have refused to answer questions about their private lives. That said, they are regularly photographed together holding hands. According to her Instagram post, when Greenleaf dropped off her sister at Brown University last fall, Sawyer was present. Sources close to the two have revealed that they live together in the same Tribeca apartment that was once Marcus Sawyer's. And then, of course, there was the long hug between them that happened in front of the cameras after Greenleaf defeated Sawyer in the World Championship (noteworthy, in a sport whose players usually limit themselves to a handshake). There is also the fact that three months ago Sawyer appeared to lean in and playfully bite Greenleaf's ear while walking away from the final game at the Linares International Chess Tournament, in which he defeated her. Plenty of clues have given rise to speculations, but whether Sawyer and Greenleaf are soon to be the first family of chess, or are just good friends, is still unknown. And yet . . .

NOLAN SAWYER AND MALLORY GREENLEAF WILL BE PLAYING AGAINST EACH OTHER.

When Nolan Sawyer dominated this year's Challengers tournament, therefore adjudicating a spot as Greenleaf's opponent in Montreal, the possibility that the next World Championship might be a romantic affair became titillating. Could the two be just good friends? Yes, undoubtedly. But what if they aren't? What if in addition to being adversaries, they also brush teeth side by side in the morning and know the other's go-to take-out orders? What if they can read each other's minds over the chessboard, or they have inside jokes about the other's weaknesses?

The idea is simply fascinating. And it's probably the reason so many people have shown interest in chess in the last two years: first they were drawn by the brilliance of these two talented players, then they decided to learn to play chess themselves, and then they realized that . . .

CHESS IS COOL, ACTUALLY.

The sale of anything chess related—sets, timers, accessories, tutorials, online classes, apps—has soared following the most recent World Championship, and the wave is here to stay. What's most notable is that interest in chess is, for the first time in decades, higher among women than men. Furthermore, there are currently more women and nonbinary people in the FIDE Top 500 than ever before. "It's because we feel that the environment is less and less hostile to us," GM Defne Bubikoğlu, Greenleaf's main trainer and owner of chess club Zugzwang, told us. Her club has been thriving, officially surpassing Marshall, New York City's historic chess club, in membership.

IN CONCLUSION . . .

We don't know how the World Championship will play out. But we do know that because of the circumstances surrounding it, more people will be tuning in than ever before, and for the first time in decades, chess players are becoming household names. And whether the more juicy, romantic aspects of this championship are true or simply rumors, the fact remains that they make for compelling narratives.

And if you "ship them hard" and "want to believe," you might enjoy this little clue: three weeks ago, at a charity event, Nolan Sawyer—who is a notoriously bad loser—did not stop to take questions from journalists. But eyewitnesses reported that when asked how he felt about the possibility of Mallory Greenleaf accruing enough points to take the No. 1 spot from him, he simply smiled before walking away.

Author's Note

The study on gender stereotypes and chess performance that Defne mentions in the book is real. It was published by Maass et al. in 2008 in the *European Journal of Social Psychology*, and then replicated by several other research groups in the following decade. Fun fact: it's the study that first sparked my interest in chess.

In 2008 I was trying to decide what to focus on for my undergraduate thesis, and in one of my classes I came across the concept of stereotype threat: when people find themselves in situations in which their social group is stereotyped to be inferior, they are more likely to perform poorly (I highly recommend you check out Claude Steele's original study on the topic, and anything by Nalini Ambady's group, but if you run into paywalls the Wikipedia entry will do). I was immediately interested in the idea, and delighted to find out that there was a research group on stereotype threat in my uni. I started reading their studies, hoping to convince one of the profs to take me on as an advisee, came across the chess study, and the rest is history. Okay maybe *not* history, but: I'd learned how to play the game as a child (very poorly), but I'd never thought about the *players* much. I hadn't known about the gender gap, but once I found out I began looking forward to seeing it bridged. The idea of a story set in the world of chess percolated through my head for years—until 2021. I was anxiously waiting for my adult debut to come out, and it was finally time for me to write "my chess book." Full disclosure: when it comes to the chess, I took lots (AND LOTS) of poetic licenses to move the story along (plot before realism?) and if you noticed them . . . I'm so sorry. I hope you were still able to enjoy Mallory and Nolan's journey.

(Also, in case you're interested: the prof did end up taking me on!)

Acknowledgments

This is book five or maybe six (omg!!), and I'm sort of running out of ways to write acknowledgments organically, so here's a bulleted list for your pleasure:

- Thao Le, my amazing agent, who encouraged me and said it was finally time to write my chess book. Not to be Academy Award–y, but she truly is my rock in the harsh landscape of publishing, and it's very safe to say that without her I would perish, like a naked mole rat exposed to the cruel elements.

- Sarah Blumenstock, my section-break-hating editor, who agreed to take a chance on my YA even though she's an adult editor (almost as if she knew about my debilitating anxiety and fear of change).

- Liz Sellers. She's the one who came up with the rook-ie pun, btw. Make this woman the CEO of PRH *right now*, please!

- Polo Orozco, who gave Sarah and me invaluable advice that helped get the book to be in its best shape, for its best audience.

- My marketing and publicity team at Berkley: Bridget O'Toole, Kim-Salina I, Tara O'Connor, Kristina Cipolla. I am grateful for them and everything they do, even if I still don't fully understand the difference between marketing and publicity.

- Christine Legon and Natalie Vielkind, my managing editors, as well as Jennifer Myers, my production editor, and Laurel Robinson, my copyeditor.

- Lilith, who illustrated the perfect cover once again because she's capable of nothing but greatness, as well as Vikki Chu and Rita Frangie, who designed the cover.

- Cindy Hwang (my grandeditor) and Erin Galloway (my grandpublicist). They're the best.

- Everyone else at Berkley and Putnam Young Readers.

- Everyone at SDLA, in particular Andrea Cavallaro, Jennifer Kim, and Jess Watterson.

- My delightful film agents, Jasmine Lake and Mirabel Michelson.

- My friends. They know who they are and by now are probably tired of reading their names in my acknowledgments anyway.

- Taylor Swift. You know what you did, Taylor.

Photo © Justin Murphy / Out of the Attic Photography 2022

Ali Hazelwood is the *New York Times* bestselling author of *The Love Hypothesis*, as well as a writer of peer-reviewed articles about brain science, in which no one makes out and the ever after is not always happy. Originally from Italy, she lived in Germany and Japan before moving to the US to pursue a PhD in neuroscience. When Ali is not at work, she can be found running, eating cake pops, or watching sci-fi movies with her two feline overlords (and her slightly-less-feline husband).

CONNECT ONLINE

AliHazelwood.com
🐦 EverSoAli
📷 AliHazelwood
♪ AliHazelwood

Ready to find
your next great read?

Let us help.

Visit prh.com/nextread